### Bearing Secrets

"A lean, mean novel with a sense of style that is urgent and gripping . . . smooth and lyrical."
—Michael Connelly, author of *Blood Work*

"A richly textured novel brimming with complex and all-too-human characters. Barre's writing is lean and muscular and thoughtful. And the story bristles with a kind of ever-expanding suspense that kept me turning the pages. Richard Barre and Wil Hardesty are an E-ticket ride."
—Robert Crais, author of the bestselling Elvis Cole novels

"A sensitive introspective private eye . . . A crime of vast complexity, firmly rooted in the past . . . [Barre is] a new writer of . . . obvious skill and sensitivity."
—*Los Angeles Times Book Review*

"This tangled tale smolders like slow fuse dynamite . . . Barre skewers each sorry player with a master's deadly accuracy."
—*Kirkus Reviews*

"One of the best thrillers of the year . . . A literary work of striking originality, with some of the best hard-boiled writing to come along in some time."
—Ken Hughes, *Critics' Choice*

"An intense, can't put-it-down read."
—Janet Evanovich, author of *Two for the Dough*

## *The Innocents*
### *Winner of the Shamus Award*

"A truly powerful and moving novel...an intriguing world of mystery, deceit, and murder. Richard Barre is a skilled writer and *The Innocents* is a gripping story."
— Michael Connelly, author of *Trunk Music*

"The book's strength comes from the chances it takes... Add some fresh characters, a couple of clever plot twists and you have an auspicious debut."  — *Chicago Tribune*

"Barre delivers...An engrossing mystery that moves quickly in prose that is as sleek and muscular as its protagonist. This first outing easily handles, then transcends, the genre requisites for a lively, intense read. Reserve a long evening for this one...It delivers the tension and pace that mystery readers demand, but Barre goes beyond that. Hardesty is no cardboard cutout. He and several others pop into 3-D and transcend the posture of their own drama."
— *Santa Barbara News-Press*

"A powerful novel...a violent novel of action and suspense that is, in the end, a voyage of self-discovery."
— Michael Collins, author of *Crimes and Misdemeanors*

"There's much to admire in this first Hardesty novel: crisp, street-smart dialogue; a likeable protagonist; and very nasty villains. A solid debut."  — *Booklist*

## Blackheart Highway

"Whitney [is] a complex, sympathetic character, the most believable fictional musician in recent memory, and Barre has filled his book with many other equally interesting people—including a thorny former cop and Whitney's loyal first wife."  —*Chicago Tribune*

"Make[s] you wish the book had been packaged with a soundtrack CD."  —*Los Angeles Times*

"Hang on tight pulling out onto *Blackheart Highway* . . . Richard Barre keeps the pedal to the metal all the way. This one's a winner. Save yourself a second trip to the bookstore and pick up the other books in the excellent Wil Hardesty series now."  —Jan Burke, author of *Liar*

"Haunting, compelling, and beautifully written . . . Richard Barre touches the soul. He is simply one of the best."  —Harlan Coben, author of *One False Move*

"Barre's plot is complexly woven . . . The tensions and layered plot . . . will keep you reading and guessing."  —*Santa Barbara News*

"An absorbing, amusing thrill ride."  —*Santa Barbara Independent*

"A rising series."  —*Booklist*

"Reading like a country song, *Blackheart Highway* is a story of tragedy and redemption . . . An insightful, moving read."  —*Romantic Times*

*continued . . .*

# BLACKHEART HIGHWAY

## RICHARD BARRE

BERKLEY PRIME CRIME, NEW YORK

This is a work of fiction. Names, characters, places, and incidents are either the product of the author's imagination or are used fictitiously, and any resemblance to actual persons, living or dead, business establishments, events, or locales is entirely coincidental.

**BLACKHEART HIGHWAY**

A Berkley Prime Crime Book / published by arrangement with the author

PRINTING HISTORY
Berkley Prime Crime hardcover edition / June 1999
Berkley Prime Crime mass-market edition / May 2000

All rights reserved.
Copyright © 1999 by Richard Barre.
This book may not be reproduced in whole or in part, by mimeograph or any other means, without permission. For information address: The Berkley Publishing Group, a division of Penguin Putnam Inc., 375 Hudson Street, New York, New York 10014.

The Penguin Putnam Inc. World Wide Web site address is http://www.penguinputnam.com

ISBN: 0-425-17467-0

Berkley Prime Crime Books are published by the Berkley Publishing Group, a division of Penguin Putnam Inc., 375 Hudson Street, New York, New York 10014. The name BERKLEY PRIME CRIME and the BERKLEY PRIME CRIME design are trademarks belonging to Penguin Putnam Inc.

PRINTED IN THE UNITED STATES OF AMERICA

10  9  8  7  6  5  4  3  2  1

*At last, for Susan . . .*
*With love and thanks*

Thanks to Commander Richard McCathron and Sergeant Glenn Johnson of the Kern County Sheriff's Department and to former Kern County District Attorney Al Leddy.

Major thanks also to Bill Rintoul for his visionary grasp of things oil-related, his invaluable books, and his 50-year-young column in the *Bakersfield Californian*; Gerald Haslam for his magnificent writings, especially *The Great Central Valley, California's Heartland*, with Stephen Johnson and Robert Dawson's hauntingly evocative photographs; Greg and Deborah Iger for their insights and typically Bakersfield hospitality; Inez Savage for the inside look at B-town's music scene; Marge Hopkins at the unique and wonderful Kern County Museum and its equally fine bookstore, treasures both; Marion Collins and Judy Salamacha, Mesa Marin Raceway, for their overview; Ron Arnold, California Department of Conservation, Division of Oil, Gas & Geothermal Resources; Shelly Lowenkopf for his counsel; Raymond Pulverman for his legal and business acumen; Jim Rochester for his always-keen eye; Chris Jensen, Jensen Guitar & Music, for keeping me in tune; and my friend, Jackie Belluomini, Bakersfield CVB, for opening the door.

Thanks to Glenn Chantler and Jonas Marquez for putting up; Ruth, Mary, and June for their usual inspiration; Gail Fortune and Philip Spitzer for their faith; Beale Memorial Library (and all libraries) for being there; and the friends, relatives, readers, and bookstore folk who gave unstintingly their encouragement and balm.

And to those who write it, play it, sing it, pulse it . . . don't ever stop.

*Blackheart Highway, looks like the right track*
*But you go down that road, you ain't never comin' back*

—*Doc Whitney*

# BLACKHEART
# HIGHWAY

*Bakersfield, California, August 27, 1978*

*Bob Tate broke off from the low-rider '63 with the sparkle paint job and the expired plates; shooting the smirking occupants a next-time thumb and forefinger, he gunned the big Dodge west onto Stockdale Highway. Great, just great—heading into the blowtorch was all he needed now—counting today, nineteen consecutive days of over a hundred degrees, the insulation on his and everybody else's nerves burned down to bare wire ready to arc and spit at any time. From breakfast beefs that turned nasty with fists and kitchen utensils right up to closing time at the eastside bars—pool cues, blades, and Saturday-night specials the day's legacy there. Residual heat. No end in sight, either, still a hundred and eight outside the black-and-white, the road ahead pulsing with mirage, sun lancing through the Polara's front windshield and off the glazed-glass commercial buildings receding in the rearview.*

*Hell, if anything it seemed hotter now than at midday.*

*J. J. Quillan, filling in until his regular partner recovered from a rafting accident, squinted as he fiddled with the air conditioner.*

*"Sounds like asshole's at it again," he said in the drawly voice Tate already had tired of after one shift. "Doing whatever he damn pleases."*

Tate lifted the radio mike off the dash, pressed the button and wilco'd the disturbance report: firearm—likely shotgun—discharged at a too-familiar address. He thumbed his sunglasses back from where they'd slid down in the heat—square-frame styles he'd kept after being mustered out of Castle AFB for a position with the Kern County Sheriff's. Little matter of upward mobility then, the county lifting a post–Vietnam War freeze on hiring, keeping him close to where Abbie figured they'd settle down near her folks.

"Two-six-two, what is your ETA?"

"Two-six-two, Mona—ETA about seven-fifteen. Lucky us. Any more on the ten-five-seven?"

"Same old same old," she came back. "Neighbor said it sounded like that from the booms and splashes. Said she was ready to sign a complaint this time. I won't use her exact words."

A double flatbed blew past, Tate feeling its rumble and draft in the unit's steering. "Can't really blame her," he said.

"You went to high school with him, didn't you?" Mona voiced out of the static.

"No copy on that, dispatch. We'll roger when we get there." He replaced the mike—no way he was going to get into all of it with her, the "what's he really like" stuff. Questions he'd been asked for what seemed like forever, moony neighbor girls right through housewives twisting their rings as they hung on his words, a fevered flush rising up behind their stuck smiles.

Quillan gave the a/c a final thump; he sat back and resettled his drop-styles, ran a hand over his buzz cut. "Enough to piss you off, you think about it."

"Might as well forget that thing when it's this hot, Jay. Concentrate on something else."

"Come on, Sarge, you know what I mean. Think if you was Doc Whitney, all he's got, you'd come up with *better to do'n fuck up your life on a regular basis."*

Tate exhaled heat and fatigue. *"I suppose."*

They passed a billboard heralding the coming Kern County Fair. Part of a beer ad, the bottle beaded with condensation, peeked out from under a sun-peeled corner.

*"So did you? Go to high school with the guy?"*

*"Not you, too."*

Quillan cocked an eye at him. *"He anything like this back then?"*

Tate regarded a group of Mexican day laborers standing around talking and laughing, waiting for their ride into town, their ability to take the heat in stride making him suddenly envious.

*"He was wild then. Who wasn't?"*

*"You, I bet."*

*"Right."* Youngsters assuming they had the damn monopoly on it, Tate thought. *"I'd have to say no, he wasn't—not like this. Sure was hell on the ladies, though. Regular heartbreak hotel."*

*"Big surprise. What's this, wife number four?"*

The smug drawl again. Tate hedged. *"Maybe it's tougher than you got figured."*

*"And that's supposed to let him off the hook?"*

*"Arlene and the girls are the best things ever happened to Don Lee Whitney. Nothing he hasn't said in print."*

*"So what's the deal, then?"*

Tate adjusted his visor, tried to see under the glare. It was getting brutal now, like some last reminder it wanted to leave you with. Off to the left, a dust devil spun itself out over empty ground while a tractor lumbered like a giant beetle toward the highway.

*"People handle pressure differently,"* he said, choosing the words carefully. *"I don't know—booze helps him write or sing with authenticity or something. All that*

*pain, he told me once. Like it was this big lake and he was baptizing in it."*

"That'll be the goddamn day. Terry saw him comin' out of the River Grill a while ago, couple of his boys helpin' him stand up. Real local hero."

"You ever been to one of his concerts?"

"I'll grant you he's givin' ol' Buck and Merle a run for their money, but so what? I ain't impressed. Not much into country anyhow."

"Why did I think that?"

"What?"

He sighed. "Picture nobody moving for two hours, not even to go to the john."

"He work the shotgun in, too?"

*Tate threw him a look J. J. didn't pick up on, just kept riding it: "All I'm sayin' is, let's see what's left in a few years, the rate he's burnin' up his candle."*

*They thumped across railroad tracks ahead of a slow-moving engine trailing half a dozen cars. Tate whooped the siren once in response to the engine's air-horn greeting before getting back into it with Quillan.*

"And I'm saying there's more to him than this other bullshit. That's what I'm saying, okay?" *He was starting to get PO'd, being forced to defend Doc Whitney this way, not much firm ground from which to do it. Big as he'd gotten lately, Doc still would have to see they were serious and knock it off before he hurt somebody. Pay serious money in fines for a change, then somebody to wean him off the sauce. That or go down the drain like so many of them.*

"All of us should have this guy's problems," *Quillan persisted.*

"Save it, Jay—you can sneer at him in person in a few minutes. Make his day."

"Don't tempt me."

"Better yet, jump in his pool."

*They'd come up on fields of cotton, belt-high and blue green, the pods just beginning to split and reveal puffs of white. Farther on, orchards showed and uncultivated tracts with vegetation shriveled into dirt-gray clumps by the blowtorch, scatterings of tumbleweed awaiting the winds of November. Then the sun was flaring out behind the Temblor Range and they were pulling up outside a walled property with a house that reminded Tate of Southfork on the TV series—surrounded on three sides by cotton, one other house across the access road and slightly west of it. Couple more just going up beyond the eastern expanse.*

*Tate could see the neighbor woman sitting on her porch. He waved to her as J. J. radioed their arrival, pulled at his damp undershirt as he got out of the car. After the relative cool of the Dodge, the air felt as if he'd opened the door to an old-time furnace. He watched J. J. go over and depress the button on the squawk box, letting the occupants of the house know it was the sheriff, to release the electronic gate.*

*Nothing happened. No response, no gate swinging back.*

*Tate walked over and spoke into the wire mesh. "Arlene, Doc? Bob Tate. Need to come in and talk a minute."*

*Still nothing. Earth-heavy air, the sound of a dog barking.*

*"They're in there," the neighbor shouted thinly from her porch. "Haven't seen anybody come out since I called you people."*

*"Excuse me, Sarge, but this guy goes back with you? This is bullshit."*

*Tate hit the intercom again, waited, then pressed a three-digit code on the number pad and watched the gate swing slowly open. Quillan looked at him, started to say something, thought better of it.*

"We go easy here, Deputy," Tate said. "This is not a roust. You got that?"

J. J. met his eyes, looked away.

"Glad that's understood."

They traversed the yard, still showing sprinkler lines and new plantings, pebbled concrete slabs, slate walkway leading to the front of the house. Doc's black Eldorado convertible pulled up to the entrance, one tire sunk in a flower bed.

Tate caught a turquoise glimmer of pool out back. Nobody answered his knock. He tried to crowd out the sense of unease.

"Try the rear, Jay."

He heard barking escalate into wild yelps, then: "Easy boy, that's it—good dog. Sliding door's unlocked, Sarge. TV's on in there somewhere. I can hear it."

Hand on his holster, Tate double-timed it around the corner of the house: flagstone patio with table and chairs, shade arbor, lounge furniture, scattered toys, spent shotgun casings on the deck. Shredded inflatable rafts at the bottom of the pool.

Through the chain-link separating the backyard from the cotton fields, he saw glints of broken glass, intact beer bottles—Doc Whitney's private skeet range, drunken barbecues often ending up here, country musicians and entourage members heaving the bottles up for Doc to blast out of the sky.

Or so he'd heard.

At the sight of him, Quillan lifted his service revolver from his holster, held it down by his leg. Tate drew his own gun, heard the sound of a central air conditioner humming somewhere, zany music and cartoon voices a silly-ass contrast to his apprehension.

"We goin' in, Sarge?"

Tate rapped the sliding glass with his pistol butt. "Doc, Arlene . . . Sara . . . Meg? Anybody?"

*Nothing.*

*"Open it, Jay, standard search procedure. Let's go."*

*They went: spacious kitchen all clear, dining and living areas looking as if the furniture hadn't even been sat on yet, the whole house smelling faintly of Sheetrock and fresh paint, that new-house smell before the day-to-day aromas overwhelmed it. He head-gestured Quillan toward the louvered doors to the family room. As Quillan took up a position to the left of the frame, Tate listened, called again and waited, popped the doors back with his foot.*

*The curtains had been drawn against the sun, and in the gloom and fading outside light, the first thing that caught his eye was the TV: Elmer Fudd chasing after Bugs Bunny, zigzagging ahead of the harmless boom-bangs, the picture slightly out of focus, washed by something that looked like runny cranberry sauce.*

*Couldn't be . . . just couldn't.*

*Like somebody'd taken a bucket of the stuff and heaved it toward the screen, red drips running down onto the braided throw rug and spotting the TV control panel, the coffee table and couch, the framed album cover shot of Doc holding a guitar by the neck and trying to look badass beside the Eldo, long hair brushing a black leather vest with conchas sewn in. Tate saw the feet then: two little pairs of sneakers, a woman's sandaled soles sticking out from behind an overstuffed chair. A grotesque still life. More of the spent red casings on the hardwood surrounding the rug. The smell of gun discharge and blood thick enough to chisel.*

*"Jesus dog," Quillan said in a voice that sounded like he'd swallowed a rock. "Sumbitch smoked his whole family."*

*Tate said nothing. Fighting his own panic, he kneeled over Arlene, the tacking puddle and matted blond hair, her flowered shirt and white shorts awash in it. Dreading what he had to look at next.*

Lord God, Donnie. Why?

*"Over here, Sarge. Fucker must have done himself, too. Still got a finger inside the trigger guard." Pause. "You BASTARD."*

*Tate caught a flash of khaki pant leg, black shoe, the thud of a powerful kick hitting home.*

*"Jay, goddammit," he said, getting to his feet. "You touch anything else and I swear you're finished with me and anybody who'll listen. Now go outside and call it in. NOW!"*

*Quillan was turning to go when Tate heard the moan, then Quillan's voice again, almost normal, the edge coming back as he rechecked the body on the floor.*

*"Well, damn if he didn't leave us something to do after all."*

# ONE

*Golden West Truck Stop, April 1998*

The waitress is young and blond and pretty. Despite the predawn hour, her smile is unflagging as she moves about the sparsely peopled restaurant—here to drop off steak and eggs, there a side of browns and a check for a guy running late, biscuits and gravy for another who has joined a table of two already eating. All of them keeping their voices low if they speak at all, bleary or unconsciously respectful, as though in church or a library.

Grabbing a breath she spots an arrival, heads that way to coffee the man in the black Levi's jacket and jeans, the pulled-down trucker's cap reading *Kenworth Diesel* above the bill—dark hair struggling against it, scar above the right eyebrow and another losing itself in a sideburn. Stubble defining his chin, wary eyes framed by deep deltas; dried-up rivers, she thinks, wondering why.

Probably because he is handsome in a worn sort of way. And from the security of her position behind the uniform and coffeepot, intriguing even: hands notched with more scars, no ring on the third finger left as he positions the cup so she can fill it, which she proceeds to do with a little flourish.

The man is a relatively recent addition to her

graveyard-shift universe: big-rigs in angled formations under the outside lights, drivers resting or getting blown in their sleeper cabs by the night divas. Others fueling and departing in huffs of engine rev following their pit stops and foam cups. Maybe a video game or shower, a deadline-to-meet breakfast of jerky, powdered dough-nuts, and Snickers bars as the sun glows to life in the Tehachapis. Nose-to-tail up the Ridge Route then—or north into valley-flat Fresno, Modesto, Stockton, Sac-ramento. Mist rising off the canals and fields to become haze later on.

The man nods, orders without reference to a menu, the established routine. Chat is a waste of breath, her words and smile seldom returned, check back in five for a refill—morning ritual as set for most of her customers as any act of grooming. This one mainly staring at his hands or out the window until she sets down eggs done hard, whole-wheat toast punched down twice, thing of strawberry preserves he's finished every morning so far.

To each his own, she thinks, scribbling it down . . . fine by her. His tips are always generous, meaning he appreciates her reading him, even though he says noth-ing to acknowledge her. Anyone else for that matter—just sort of *materializing* in his spot by the window. Sometimes he doesn't even wait for the check, money and an empty plate the only sign he's been there.

Her number lights up and she goes for the order, catching a couple of guys she hasn't seen before watch-ing her leave the man's table from their booth across the room. Before she can get there with a pot, one moves toward the pay phone; by the time she does get there, he's taking his seat again, shifting his gaze toward the man's back.

As she takes their order, the tall one with the salt-and-pepper buzz cut flashes some kind of badge and presses a finger to his lips. Gestures her closer.

"Guy by the window there, you know him?"

She follows his nod, pretending not to know which guy he's talking about—safer, she's learned. She shakes her head and smiles.

"But he's a regular here," he says, fishing.

"I wouldn't know."

The man withdraws a twenty from his wallet, lays it on the table. "He ever talk about where he lives, what he does, that kind of thing?"

"Just his breakfast order. He's real quiet."

"So he is a regular."

"Sorry, you'll have to excuse me. I've got food up."

The squarish wide-shouldered one gestures toward the opening to the bar, nobody there at this hour, the lighting subdued except for the neon in the jukebox. "That thing in there play country?"

"At a truck stop in Bakersfield? Is the pope—"

"Get us some quarters with this?" Buzzcut puts his hand on the bill, shoves it toward her.

Glad to leave, she takes the bill to the register, gets the change, brings it back, and sets it down, the men taking no notice of her now, their eyes on the man by the window. As she leaves, the squarish one strides to the juke, pores over the list, nods back at the tall one. He's dropping quarters into it when she eases over to the man in the black jacket. Refills his cup.

"Might not want to look now, but the guys in the booth asked if I knew you. The one had a phony-looking badge."

His face rises to hers and his eyes emerge from the squint, their gold-flecked green startling contrast to the dark hair and pale complexion unlike most truckers.

"What'd you tell 'em?"

The voice is direct and hard, yet laced with a resonance that takes the edge off somewhat. Still, it's not a voice she'd like to have directed at her in anger. Shaking her head, she takes a swipe with the rag she's brought along.

"Nothing. But they were asking about—"

*Flat-out haulin' down a cold dark road*
*Thirty-two years and twice that old*

The song is "Truck Stop Angel," one of about six old Don Lee Whitneys the drivers favor when it turns raucous. Songs that bleed over from the bar and into casual memory, even though she listens mostly to Alanis, Toad, Pearl Jam, like that. Something in the guy's delivery, though—an edge like John Lennon had—keeps them from becoming repetitive.

*Wife and three kids back in Tennessee*
*How big a damn fool can one man be*

The bass rises to meet the guitar-backed voice and the tremor through *him* is a tangible thing.

*White lines flyin' by under my load*
*Game I'm playin' is takin' its toll*

Hurriedly he pulls a paper napkin from the container, the Bic from her order pad. Shadow filling an indentation in his cheekbone she's not noticed before, he jots down a phone number and hands it to her.

*Bettin' man's countin' on ten-to-one*
*Hundred bills down on me comin' undone*

"Ten minutes, then you have one of the cooks check the yard. If something's gone down, call that number. No cops, though—is that clear?" He wads up a bill from his pocket, shoves it into hers.

"Say it back," he says to her protest.

"No cops." Reluctantly, but no match for his intensity.

"That a promise?"

She nods.

*Truck Stop Angel, can't stop to cry*

He checks her name tag. "Danielle. I owe you one."

*Tell me how I'm ever gonna say good-bye*

He is up then, moving quickly for the side exit. Through it into predawn, his breath leaving a trail before her eyes shift to the two men hurrying after him, each taking a different route. Like the herd dogs at the ranch she grew up on.

Feeling foolish, she crosses her fingers for him before getting back to work, half there at best. Despite the orders from new arrivals, refills, special requests, her eyes sweep the clock. At eight minutes she goes into the kitchen, knowing instinctively that the cook, a gaunt man with an apron that looks more like a topographic map, will be no help. His relief is late, and a string of muttered curses about that prima donna college-boy son of a bitch showing up whenever he feels like it is her answer.

It's up to her.

Ignoring his look, she exits into chill air, scans the pump area: two rigs fueling, engine cowlings hinged forward for service; wash station—dark and empty now; scales—lumber truck on one of the pads, the other vacant; motel—no activity, window glimpse of the night guy bent over a magazine.

She's running now, heading for the angle-parked squadrons, sounds of the idling diesels reminding her vaguely of snoring. Looking under and between the rigs, seeing nothing unusual, more relieved with each grouping she passes. One left to check at the outer edge of the lot bordering the freeway—the units there dark and silent.

It's there she sees him. Doubled over on his knees between a couple of road-crusted trailers; face down on one arm, clutching his middle with the other. Moaning as she bends to ask how bad it is, heart in her throat until he nods slightly, his breathing rasped and shallow.

No sign of the men from the café.

He puts out a hand and tries to use her for leverage, but the pain is such that he slumps back down. In that moment she catches sight of his face, however, and to her vast relief it is unbloodied.

*"No cops,"* he is able to reiterate, and napkin in hand, she rushes to keep her promise at the pay phone beside the racks of faded singles tabloids and yesterday's news.

# TWO

With the second roll-around of the morning they were late leaving La Conchita, so now Kari Thayer was horsing the Jetta hard, citrus groves on both sides of 126 blooming fragrantly and laden with oranges, lines of healthy-looking eucalyptus, poplar, and avocado trees serving as windbreaks. Even the hills steepening toward the Ventura County backcountry looked verdant, wild mustard still yellowing some slopes.

As it did on the slide that nearly ate La Conchita, Wil Hardesty thought. Three years ago? Seemed like yesterday.

He eyed the speedometer as she took the inner lane around an Econoline full of brown-faced kids peering back at him. Still trying to figure out how a relatively new water pump could let go like that—one second fine, the next spewing steam and radiator fluid all over the Coffee Grinder's parking lot. At any rate, it dictated they take her Jetta; no way around *that*. Minimum of a week to get in a replacement pump for a '66 Bonneville, his usual wrecking-yard sources no help this time. As she regained the fast lane, he swung around to check behind them.

Just the van, as if standing still.

"I can hear it now: 'Always nice to see you again,

Ms. Thayer. No idea a VW could go so fast with all that aboard, Ms. Thayer.' "

Take it all, decide later: Kari's idea of packing for a weekend.

Eyes not leaving the road, she said, "I'll just tell them what made me late. Then we'll see."

"See what? There I am in the shower, minding my own business—"

"Cops look at evidence, bub. Shit-eating grins, for instance."

"Another would-be Philip Marlowe."

She mooned a smile at him. "You see would-be here?"

"What I see is eighty-five miles an hour."

Shrug. "One way to look at it."

"Think you might want to slow it down a tad?"

"Racing the clock to save the world from empty journalism is another. Boss loves that kind of stuff."

"Beurlein . . ." Wil looked out the window at the citrus groves flashing by.

"Beurlein, right. And you'll thank me in the end, you know." Flashing him a little grin.

"Not sure I like the way you say that."

She overtook a sedan before the lanes merged, orange cones and a flashing arrow forcing her to slow down, look at her watch. "Damn," she said. "I'll have to make it up on the Ridge Route."

"TV people never say anything meaningful on Saturday morning. Think they're going to start today?"

She ran up behind a moving van, began drumming the steering wheel. "I hate being late."

"Indoors in some convention hall?" he needled. "When the Kern's running high?"

"Thanks a lot."

"You ever driven up the canyon? Deep gorge, rapids

right beside the highway? Big rafting river, the Kern—
*big*. Scared the heck out of me once."

"No. But I like hearing you get jazzed about something for a change."

He glanced over at her, that one stopping him—like
holding up a mirror and seeing you'd forgotten to shave.
Making him wonder had he really been that bad lately,
the chances probably better than good. He made a mental note: try filing the past where it belonged instead of
running it back and forth like some tape you could edit
to spec. Guaranteed to make you crazy.

"You forgetting about this morning?" he asked.

"*Au contraire.*"

He laid his hand on her knee, the tight denim feeling
like a second skin. Making his smile deepen as she throt-
tled back and took a breath, loosened a hand from the
wheel, and rested it easily on his.

"And what big media personality is ever on time?"
she inquired. "Can you think of any?"

"Nope. Just isn't done." He levered his own seat back
a notch, used the opportunity to take in her profile, the
smooth of her neck, light touch of Jessica McClintock
wafting out from behind her ear.

A very appetizing ear.

"What?" she asked, picking up on it. Running her
hand self-consciously through sun-streaked, toffee-
colored hair he could still feel from this morning.

"Just taking inventory," he said. He reached for the
thermos. "Want some java?"

"No, thanks—rest-stop city guaranteed." That smile
again. "You offering anything else?"

He flashed one back as she turned her attention to the
slow-moving line. She was something, this one—despite
a twelve-year age difference, as taken with him as he
was with her, Wil still in need of a stabilizer after the
disaster that had been Trina Van Zant. And before that,

the twenty-plus years with Lisa, thoughts about her divorce action still blindsiding him when he least expected it.

But those incidents were becoming fewer now, and generally when he was alone and in deep shadow.

Something Kari'd had a lot to do with.

Running into her on the Van Zant thing had been instrumental in helping him over a number of hurdles. Like coming up empty when he'd gone to find his friend, the Ensenada hospital staff tight-lipped when asked about the gringo with the blond hair and the bullet wound. Denny Van Zant: nobody knowing *nada*—not one single person, hospital or otherwise, in the long week of trying to pick up a trace. Denny's doing, likely, cold feet despite being the one to break silence. Or perhaps Trina's fine hand—American dollars like obscuring leaves across her brother's trail, Wil left with the hope that one day Denny might change his mind and just show up.

And that was the best-case scenario.

The worst? Denny's old pals eager to finish a job they'd started and had thought finished. Finding him, somehow.

At any rate, he and Kari had pulled out finally, leaving behind a flurry of his business cards and the promise of a modest reward. But Wil knew better—his kind of money had little chance against what had put the veil in place. Wrenching when you had your hopes up, the truth as ugly as any he'd worked to uncover.

So he'd leaned on her—easy at first and then harder. Too hard perhaps in light of the attendant complications with her son, Brian, fifteen-year-old resentful of Wil's entry into the picture, a threat to long-nurtured hopes of a family reunion.

Talks, singly and together, had only deepened the rift, evincing at the same time a fall in school performance and a big rise in attitude. Ergo parking Brian with his dad—who ran a tire outlet in La Habra—and getting away for a weekend. The occasion: an Association of Television Production Professionals convention in Bakersfield that the station she worked for asked her to attend in place of her boss.

A respite, all things considered.

Being on his own in a town he hadn't been through in years was the only drawback. But he'd find something to do. And not worrying about being unbusy, normal MO in light of his monthly nut and his fluctuating income, had its appeal right now.

"Ah—freeway," Kari said, spotting the interstate ahead. Leaning on the Jetta through the on-ramp. Surging toward the fast lane in a whine of pre-overdrive. "It's about time."

Appealing, he thought. Provided they made it there alive.

An hour later they were descending—along with an omnipresent line of northbound trucks—through dry-growth mountains, scrub, and the occasional stand of trembly lime-green cottonwoods. As the air warmed and the land at the base of the grade fanned toward a valley horizon already obscured by haze and dotted with high clouds, both he and Kari fell silent, taking it in.

California's Central Valley, though familiar to him, always seemed like a foreign country, so different was it from the coast. Unrelievedly hot in summer; fog-shrouded and bone-chilling in winter; patterned by precisely laid out farms and orchards; meandered across by rivers, aqueducts, and canals. Not to mention as big as some countries—four hundred miles by the fifty odd running east-west. Sierra Nevada mountains rising to unseen snow on their right, coast range more gradually on their left.

Yet it was the flatland that called him. The trips along its length with his father—impressions planted at an early age like seeds that rose from dormancy each time he returned. Impressions of vastness and abundance. Of roadside places in the shape of giant oranges, sweet-cold juice that made your face ache and your vision dance if you drank it too fast. Of first-light breakfasts sitting up to Formica counters: corned-beef hash with biscuits and gravy; steaming mugs of half milk and sugar, half coffee. Brought by a waitress who winked at you while the truckers talked of places that always seemed diminished when viewed later as an adult.

Back then, they'd traveled to avoid the heat. Through endless-seeming warm and humid nights—air-conditioning a luxury then—the windshield on the old Buick piling up with bugs, side windows rolled down to admit every order of new thing. Hay and green manure, cattle pens and plowed earth, the ferment of abandoned melons. Moonlit rivers flowing under WPA-built bridges. Planetarium-sharp stars, close enough to reach out and touch. Forlorn train whistles. Cricket hum sounding like buzzy power lines.

On cooler-month trips or when they had no choice but to travel by day, they'd seek respite at the fruit stands hyped for miles in either direction by hand-painted signs. Sucking on Sno-Kones, they'd wander among the displays of fruits and nuts, honey and vegetables, cider and apple butter, the aromas heady and irresistible.

Always they'd buy too much—things that wound up overripe, wilted, or moldy, tossed out later by his mother. All except for the artgumlike apple or apricot candies dusted with powdered sugar that invariably wound up on his pants and all over the car upholstery. They never seemed to buy enough of that, not to suit him anyway. And late at night when they'd stop to take a leak he-man-style in the weeds, headlights killed and the engine off, frogs croaking in a nearby irrigation ditch, the vastness would rise in his throat like a fist, making it hard to swallow. Scary, except for having your dad there.

Later he'd know the Valley through writers like John Steinbeck, William Saroyan, and Gerald Haslam, their takes on it. But the memories that lingered for him were those that he and Terrance Hardesty sowed and reaped on old Highway 99 back in the fifties—when all of life seemed an open road and their constant companion was the reedy, schmaltzy country music his father rarely tuned in anywhere but on their treks. And if he did linger on one of the few stations playing it when they were out for errands with his mother, it was always: "Terrance, isn't there *anything* else on?"

Or words to that effect.

"You're quiet," Kari said.

In answer, Wil hit the radio's scan button until it found a station playing pedal steel guitar under a singer who'd heard a rumor that somebody he loved, loved him back.

"Country?" Kari asked after it was obvious.

"When in Bakersfield," he said.

"Did I miss something?"

"Well, I guess so, if you don't know the hotbed. When I was young, my dad and I used to drive the Valley to visit his relatives up north. Always tuned in the Bakersfield stations—Tommy Collins, Bob Wills and His Texas Playboys, Buck Owens later . . . God, he used to love that stuff. Irish-American poetry, he called it. He grew up in Belfast."

They listened while a song about an emotional girl segued into one in which the singer had his fingers crossed that his relationship would work out. Practicing hard at it. As they passed fields under cultivation, a line of palms marking a road paralleling 99, now split off

from Interstate 5 heading up the west side, another song
laid out why a girl had to do what a girl had to do.

"It's different from the stuff I remember," Kari said
finally. "A lot more polished."

"Hooks you in, all right."

"But what?"

"But nothing . . ."

"Nice try." She glanced at him. "I'm getting to know
that tone."

Wil shrugged. "Not exactly 'Cold, Cold Heart' or 'I
Walk the Line.' 'Silver Threads and Golden Needles.' "

"You care to amplify or shall I just nod my head
wisely?"

"As if the songs were put together from the outside
in. What's at the core is just the hook or a play on words.
Less blood and muscle than you'd like."

She cocked her head at him.

"What—you never wrote a song?" Recalling his own
youthful and usually lovelorn attempts: the sore fingers,
bruised from hours on the guitar; words surfacing with
all the ease of impacted wisdom teeth; the piles of
crushed-up notepaper. The results . . .

"Mr. Music," she said.

"That would have been news to my groupies."

"Kidding me . . . you were in a band?"

He smiled at the recollection: Buzz, Trey, Del, and
Wil; their high-school-yearbook earnestness and bitter-
sweet parting; one reunion about twelve years ago minus
Del, who hadn't come back from Chu Lai. Everybody
just as glad to be too busy since the one time.

"If you consider four guys banging away at folk rock
and Beatles a band," he said. "Birthdays and parties.
Lots of garages."

"And what did *you* play?"

"Guitar. A little harp. Neither well, but I could move
around without falling down. That was big with us."

Kari thought about it. "I took piano lessons but hated playing for people. Too shy, believe it or not."

"We made up for that by being loud. The Roadmasters, after my dad's old Buick. Four Flats would have been about right."

She laughed. Wanting to keep it rolling, Wil said, "Ever hear the joke about what you get when you play a country song backward?"

"What?" Raising an eyebrow at him.

"Man gets his wife, his dog, and his pickup truck back."

"That's it?" Deadpan.

"You know . . . loses them in the song, gets them back when it's reversed?"

"I see. Well . . ."

"Sounds like the people we used to audition for."

Down the center of the old highway, a line of been-there-forever oleanders hid the oncoming lanes, Kari taking a moment to admire the pinks, reds, and whites, the dark green foliage. As the next singer described walking around like a lovesick fool at work, she asked, "So where're the pickup trucks and the dogs?"

"Times change," he said. "Look at daytime TV."

"You look at it. What about the music?"

"This? Pull the steel and it's pop with an accent. Likable enough, but . . ."

"What?"

"I don't know . . . In tune, but off its moorings."

She was quiet while the song ended and another came up, this one about a guy on the verge of being in love. Tapping it out on the steering wheel along with him.

"Take it with a grain," Wil said. "Wouldn't be the first time I was out of step."

"Speaking of that, you listened to rock lately? Brian plays it. Talk about sad."

"Country used to bleed sad."

"You know what I mean."

"Yeah." He eased a flip of hair over her ear so he could admire her neck again.

She eased the flip back down, smoothed it. "Am I wrong, or is Merle Haggard from around here?"

"Used to be," he said. "Not anymore."

"So who is?"

"Buck Owens, I think. Not sure about Doc Whitney."

"Who?"

"Don Lee Whitney. Singer-songwriter—big deal in country about twenty years back. Had some trouble, as I remember. You ready for a break from this?" He reached to try the scanner again, find some talk or jazz or—

"Hold it there, Hoss," she drawled. "Either it's what went on this morning, or I'm kinda gettin' hooked here."

Wil glanced in the side mirror, saw red lights flashing, the black-and-white Caprice closing in fast. "Don't say I didn't warn you," he said.

The conference center was just up from some prominent and visually arresting civic buildings on Truxtun, a wide avenue with a divider of trimmed grass and deodar cedars. It also happened to abut the Holiday Inn where Kari's station had taken advantage of the conference rates. Neither fact seeming to impress her.

Just beating the red through an intersection.

*"Since when is keeping pace with the traffic breaking the law?"*

"When it exceeds the speed limit by a dozen?"

"Right, side with them."

"Told you I'd split it with you," Wil said. "It's not worth ruining—"

"Easy for you to say. Your insurance rates aren't going through the roof." Pulling up in front of the roundish facade, the "WELCOME BROADCAST PRODUCERS" sign.

Scrambling in the backseat for her conference materials, tossing things aside until she found them. Checking her watch again. *"Shit!"*

"Deep breath," Wil said, getting out. "I'll park the car and check us in, be back in the room by five. You get hung up, no problem, I'll get a book. Just have a good—"

For a second it looked as though she were going to run right through him, but instead she stopped just short and bent her face up for a smack before hustling for the entrance, Wil admiring this view of her as well. Still feeling the morning in his thighs.

He found a space and parked the car, managed to get their stuff inside the atriumed lobby in two trips, the bellman putting it on a cart as Wil handled the check-in. Upstairs, racking Kari's hangers while the bellman readied the room, Wil inquired where he could find the nearest bookstore, about places to eat, museums, library, things to do if he felt ambitious. Rewarding the man with a nice-sized tip after jotting them down. Scanning Bakersfield from the window now.

Already it felt more substantial than he'd anticipated—kept-up neighborhoods and a downtown that reminded him of a smaller Sacramento, that same quiescent solidity. Hands on the helm and money in the bank. Much as he'd seen, anyway.

Drawing the curtains and changing into trunks, he went down to the outdoor pool, did unambitious laps while a couple of kids watched him, finally giving up to crash in one of the lounges, the sun warm on his back. Dozing off to thoughts that Beurlein or whatever his name was, Kari's boss, was pretty much okay by him.

# THREE

After a sandwich and a shower to wake up, Wil dressed in jeans, khaki shirt, and loafers, checked out the big library adjacent to the hotel, then set out for the bookstore recommended by the bellman. It was only a few blocks, the day invitingly mild, so he kept going for a scan of the stores and shops on Chester—which seemed, the farther north he got from the civic buildings, to have seen better days, the usual attempts at revitalization evident in some blocks, less so in others. At least the area was holding its own, passersby not at the malls unafraid to take his measure and nod back.

Try that in L.A., he thought.

Only two guys qualified as street types, and they were deep in conference against an alley wall behind a restaurant. The air felt fat and still, nicely presummery, temp lazing toward seventy-eight according to a bank sign.

He saw a used-book store and sprang for a pre-Robicheaux Burke in guarded condition—a warm-up purchase before heading back toward the original store—thinking here we go again. Like the joke he'd seen in *The New Yorker*: two roundish older women looking in the window of a bakery, one saying to the other, "Let's just go in and see what happens." In his case, usually two or three titles per visit, an equal number rotated out of his jammed shelves to the library donation bin, the worthiness of the cause quieting his book-junkie conscience somewhat. Still, the stacks of read-me's were almost touching the clothes in his closet.

Could be worse, he figured, entering the store. Hard shots and beer backs came to mind, twelve-step programs and talking to yourself. Making no sense even then.

The woman behind the counter smiled a welcome, went back to what she was doing as he cased the place. It was pleasant enough—adequate if not very deep in what interested him—and empty for a Saturday afternoon. Classical music played softly in the background; air whispered in the vents. He was browsing new releases, wondering where the time had gone and trying to decide among a Harry Bosch, an Elvis Cole, and a Leo Waterman—knowing the inevitable—when he became aware of the voices. Little explosions in the store's atmosphere of calm.

Setting down his selections, he stole a look, saw the two guys he'd seen in the alley fronting the woman behind the counter, her look wide-eyed. No one else was in the store, the wall clock showing nearly four, the door sign turned around. Not that anyone was trying to get in or question the early closure. Not even traffic moved on the cross street outside.

Of the two, the heavyset guy in the tank top and jeans was doing the menacing, holding a scaled-up hunter's bowie to the clerk's face, her stare pinned on its dark-stained drop blade and upswept point. A transfixed mouse looking into the eyes of a rattlesnake. The other man was slightly built, perhaps with Indian blood in him—standing there in plaid pants and a too-small yellow tee. Looking wired as he covered heavyset's back.

Neither, evidently, had noticed Wil.

They reminded him of the loaded-up losers encountered during port security work on his second tour. Human flotsam, adrift on cheap Vietnamese smack or the hundred-plus black-market firewaters you could virtually hear turning whole sections of brain into head cheese.

Still, a blade that big . . .

Heavyset held up a fistful of bills. "Shit money—think I don't know that? You got till I count three." Drawing the point across the clerk's chest.

"Sir, we don't *have* a safe."

"Those things bleed, take my word. That what you want?"

The clerk went even whiter. Covering her mouth, she shook her head, looked ready to implode. Heavyset sliced one of her shirt buttons onto the countertop, where it made a thin plastic sound.

"They must pay you a lot to be so brave," he said. "We're gonna find the money anyhow."

*"I told you. We don't have a safe."*

The slight one pushed black hair off his eyes. "Ain't no safe, Billy. Take the cash and let's get out of here."

Heavyset shook his head; he looked at Slight. "Swell—now she knows my name. You happy, *asshole*? Just watch the damn window."

"Told you not to call me that."

"Fucking crazyhorse, call you anything I like." He shifted the bowie toward Slight. "Got a problem with it?"

Slight stood there, feet anchored but swaying, as if the horizon were playing tricks.

"Gonna have a serious heart-to-heart talk after this," Billy said. "Yes, we are."

"What about now?"

"Whatever I do, glueboy, it's your fault. Now shut up and watch the front." His eyes swung back to the woman. "Think it's time you and me went to the ladies' room, don't you?"

*"Oh God . . . no."*

"EXCUSE ME," Wil said, emerging with a stack of books—squinting as he approached. "I'VE LOST MY GLASSES."

"Son of a bitch," he heard Billy say. "Checked it out, huh?"

"I—"

"Ought to cut your damn head off."

"SET THEM DOWN TO PUT A BATTERY IN MY HEARING AID AND NOW THAT'S GONE, TOO." Still squinting and bent from the weight, but closer to the knife, Billy already dismissing him if the look on his puffed face meant anything.

"Fuck that shit," he said to Wil. "Kind of cash you got on you?"

"SPEAK UP, PLEASE."

"I SAID—LONG AS YOU'RE HERE, TURN THEM POCKETS OUT 'FORE I CUT YOU A NEW ONE." The blade coming up from where he'd lowered it.

Wil moved toward him. "WHAT KIND OF STORE CHARGES FOR SOMETHING LIKE THAT?" Still straining as if to hear. "WELL, DON'T JUST STAND THERE. TAKE THESE SO I CAN FIND MY WAL-LET—"

Close enough to smell the booze on him, Wil stumbled so the man's reaction was instinctive, catching the stack before he realized his mistake. Which allowed Wil to tighten his grip on the world atlas he'd had on the bottom, thwock the big hardcover off the man's head, sending him ass-over into a display of genre paperbacks.

Dazed, Billy tried to get up, and Wil stepped forward and hit him again, harder if anything. He raised back for another, but Billy was done—flat on his back and moaning softly.

He cast about for the knife.

"This what you're lookin' for?" The nicked-up handle lay balanced in Slight's open palm, forearm muscles twitching as though pulsed with a current. His eyes held an empty sheen, the pupils resembling oiled black marbles.

Wil held his hand out. "Don't make it worse, friend. We're okay so far."

"Ain't your friend," Slight said, shifting his grip on the bowie, an easy familiar movement. "And drop that thing."

"It doesn't have to go this way." Up close he could see shine on the man's pants, sweat stains under his arms, bad teeth as he drew and exhaled through his mouth. The hone he'd put on the blade.

"Knife cuts paper. Or do you want to see?"

Wil set down the atlas, caught movement: two uniformed cops taking positions on either side of the front window, three black-and-whites just pulling up. Glancing at the clerk, he got a nod back, figuring she'd pressed some kind of silent alarm or phone code before it got dicey. With luck . . .

But the slight man had seen the arrivals, too, and he moved the blade to the clerk's throat. "Ain't going to jail," he said. "No fucking way."

Through a piano sonata, Wil made out the sound of pump guns jacking—chamber music of a different kind—the absurd notion that he might die in a bookstore slipping in along with the rounds.

"What's your name?" he asked, trying to look beyond the panic in the clerk's face.

"You heard Billy. No names."

"That was earlier. I think it's okay now. My name's Wil."

He blinked, obviously struggling with it. "Might be Cedrick, might not."

Wil could smell the man's odor and rank breath. He met the clerk's eyes, asked her name, heard *"Shirli."*

"Don't make me cut her, man."

"Cedrick, what do you say we let Shirli get back to it—get us something to eat?"

"What? . . ."

"Get you some food. Get Billy some help." He could almost hear the focus mechanism whirring, see the lens locking down. To his relief, Cedrick lowered the knife; for a moment he regarded Billy at his feet. Then he bent down and plunged the bowie into him, bringing it out and up with amazing speed.

Shirli screamed, looked away.

Billy spasmed, groaned, coughed, rolled over and lay there, his breathing ragged, blood beginning to darken his tank top, ooze out under the armhole.

"Drunk bastard—keep quiet or I'll do it again," Cedrick said. He looked at Wil. "He'da stuck me later on, don't think he wouldn't. Just uses people and takes their shit." Stepping over Billy, he pointed the blade again at Shirli. Who nearly jumped out of her skin as the phone rang.

Wil nodded to her, though it rang twice more before she could shake the sight of Billy bleeding on the floor to answer it. Hearing who it was, she flashed *What-do-I-do?*

"Not going back," Cedrick said.

"Tell them Billy needs a doctor and Cedrick can't go to jail," Wil said. "That's the deal."

As she relayed it, Wil saw several of the cops go into an animated discussion. "You heard her, Cedrick. All right?"

Cedrick shoved his other hand deep in a pants pocket.

"At least let them take him to the hospital."

"Fucking doctors ... said they'd fix me up after I come home. You think I'm fixed?"

*Follow the thread.* "Where were you?"

There was a long moment. "Kay-San."

Wil thought of some of the Khe Sanh survivors he'd met, their looks when recalling the siege. "I came back hurt, too, Cedrick. I know you don't want to hurt us. For Billy to die."

But Cedrick's black eyes were twin drains. He began to chant—oddly in time to a piece from *Carmen*—while outside, a TV reporter came into view, then another, scrambling to set up for live coverage behind the line of cops. Gawkers beginning to fill in around them.

Wil inched toward him. "Isn't that right?"

Cedrick stopped chanting. Suddenly his hand left his pocket with a fistful of black caps he jammed into his mouth, dry-swallowing them before Wil got to him, got a hand on his wrist, and wrestled for the knife—just as the cops crashed in through the glass door and took Cedrick down in a swarm of blue uniforms and thrashing plaid.

Wil heard the sound of gagging and then, oddly, Kari's voice shouting closeby.

*"Where's that EMT? His hand's bleeding bad."*

It wasn't, actually, just needed a few stitches and some ointment.

Burning until the local kicked in and took the edge off.

The media had followed the EMS van to Mercy Hospital. Evidently Shirli had talked to them first, about his part in it, because their questions all related to why ... what it felt like, how he knew what to do, who he was. Hardly knowing *what* he answered until Kari dragged him into a waiting taxi, stares and scattered applause from the onlookers who'd bothered to follow it up.

Later, after he'd slept, she told him how word had spread among the conferees, fanned by the scannerheads among them. How they'd near sprinted the few blocks to the bookstore to watch it develop—especially the media side—and still were discussing it. How she'd gone down and caught the first report in the bar; that of the two, Cedrick had the better chance of making it. The only positive thing about Billy—two pints transfused and still in surgery—was that somehow the blade had missed his heart.

Unreal how fast things could turn. Which led to thoughts of what he'd have done differently—aside from packing his .45, brought along and cleverly left in the room. But beyond live and learn, no neon-lit answers came. Just demons you steered clear of or got eaten by— at the least, had your gears stripped.

Right now he was just glad to be alive.

Kari leaned to kiss him and he rolled her up, buried his face in her hair—taking in the fainter-now Jessica, the warmer composite of *her*, not being able to get enough. And if his feelings about the rest were not completely sorted out, that was as it was; they'd change nothing anyway. You did what you did, took the heat if there was some, and went on. Or you didn't.

Reveling in NOW, he rolled them back and forth on the spread.

"Hey, cowboy," she said, "you trying to bust your stitches?"

"All three of them . . ."

She broke away and sat up, brought serious eyes to bear. "You had me scared shitless, you know."

"I know. I'm sorry." Not liking the weenie way it sounded, but not unsympathetic either.

"What were you thinking?"

He sat up, swung his legs over the edge of the bed, steadied a moment, and walked to the window—southeast facing, with a view of the mountains, pink light beginning to soften them now.

"I'm not sure a lot of thought was involved."

"Any chance the creeps were just trying to prove to themselves Shirli wasn't holding out? That they might have been on their way in another minute?"

Wil could hear the bubble in her voice; similar scenes with Lisa flashed. Accusations and denials until his gut wound tight as a tennis racquet—knowing she'd been right, just as Kari was now. And yet, *not*. No way he could have walked away from it.

Without turning from the window, he said, "That was not my assessment of the situation, no."

"I see."

He walked to her, conscious of the shine in her eyes and his thoughts about Lisa, the way that one had gone: tears that had started as a trickle and became a torrent, eroding too many years together. Not even a foundation left to stand on.

"What can I tell you? I'd do it again."

She stepped forward, put her arms on his shoulders— lovely arms frosted with tiny blond hairs—the color rising in her face like a blush. And then he realized it wasn't tears that were causing the glisten.

"Hearing what you do *excites* me," she said. "If you hadn't told me, I'd have asked. If you still didn't . . . I don't know what I'd do." Softly intent now. "Do you get that?"

"Not really."

"If you tried hard?"

"Shouldn't be a problem right now."

"Good. May I propose we consider this the beginning of an exhaustive probe?"

She pulled back from him, began to slowly undo her

denim shirt, followed by the black jeans, hints of warm skin and white lace throwing his mind into another gear entirely, complete with grinding teeth, smoking clutch, and vibrating linkage.

# FOUR

It had to be late. Well after the invitations from other attendees heading out to the Basque restaurants and steak places, to Buck Owens's Crystal Palace or the honky-tonk clubs—wanting her to come along and bring *him*. Well after the bistro had delivered up the pizzas and salads they'd eaten in the room. Watching the sky go from pink to slate to moonless charcoal, the Sierra bulking up black and ragged, lights coming on down below and across the city, feathering out toward the Tehachapis and the Ridge Route thirty miles to the south. Night air wafting up jasmine and the dusty fragrance of privet.

Determined to stay up for the late news, they'd made the mistake of muting the volume and trying to read, Wil actually falling asleep trying to remember the last time he'd made love three times in the same day. Fighting a buzzing in his head now.

Second buzz.

Jerking awake, he glanced over at Kari oblivious, the TV running a wee-hours talk show. Hard to tell whose from the guest, some animal person talking to a white cockatoo that reminded him of Edward, now with Lisa and Brandon—Lisa's "client" of the live-in variety. Reminding him to check and see that softballhead wasn't mistreating Ed. Let alone Lisa. Not a bad description for the way things stood between them.

The phone.

"*Yeah*." Nearly knocking a glass off the nightstand.

"Hardesty?"

"He's asleep right now."

"The bookstore Hardesty . . ."

Damn media people; it was fortunate Kari was in production and not a reporter or news anchor. "You are aware of the time?"

"Am I drunk, you mean."

"Maybe you didn't—"

"My name is DeVillbis, Luther DeVillbis. Which may or may not compute since you're not from around here. Bottom line is, we need to talk."

Wil rubbed his face, forced polite. "How about if I check my day tomorrow? I'm sure—"

"No. I mean tonight."

*No problem.* "That's really not possible, Mister . . ."

"DeVillbis."

"Good night, Mr. DeVillbis."

"Five hundred dollars to hear me out—an hour of your time. Then you're back in bed, five bills richer and sleeping like a baby. Fair enough?"

Middle of the night, somebody offering him ten times his hourly rate? Happened all the time. At least he *sounded* sober.

"But then, perhaps I've made a mistake . . ."

Setting the hook, DeVillbis figuring that would do it; probably a 99 percent success rate, important to keep up the average—Wil could hear it in his tone. "Why me?" he asked.

"You can't be that asleep."

"Take my word for it."

"I saw the news—what you did. And I've been thinking about it. You stood up and said no. You didn't bullshit, you didn't negotiate, you didn't turn your back. That's the kind of man I'm looking for. Somebody who can make a tough choice and live with it."

"What I did almost—"

"You must be pretty flush to forgo five hundred bucks just to hear me out."

Not much he could think of to say to that.

"Well? Yes or no?"

Wil pinched at a spot in his neck where he'd slept wrong. "Are you always like this?"

"Till I get what I want, anyway. Ten minutes—down in the bar."

The voice became dial tone.

He was wondering what he was doing—the bar all but deserted at two A.M., one other couple with their heads together over a crusted margarita glass—when a man of slightly less then medium height and build rose from a corner table. Sports-car-style cap over a fringe of gray hair, nearly white beard trimmed to a point, black rayon jacket with *Winston Cup Racing* on it. Sun-browned hand outstretched.

The real one anyway.

Wil shook it—consciously keeping his eyes above the realistic but obvious prosthetic device that was his other hand.

"Mr. DeVillbis?" Feeling the man's blue eyes taking him in: ten minutes out of bed and not yet up to speed. Needing a compound low to gear out of the swamp.

"Call me Lute, everyone does. Feels like I already know you after that TV story. Hell of a deal." His voice had a nasal quality, up in register and without depth.

As they sat, he removed the cap with his artificial hand. "No need for subtlety with me," he said, wiggling it to show it worked. "Lost it in an oil-field accident. Cable pinched it off. Funny thing is, I still feel it—or think I do." He looked at Wil's hand. "That from to-day?"

Wil nodded, reminded it still throbbed. "Could have been worse."

DeVillbis gestured at two double whiskey neats with water backs, a mug of coffee. "The bar was closing, so I took the liberty. If you want something else, we can always—"

"Just the coffee, thanks."

Wil poured milk in and sipped bottom sludge, about what he expected. He watched the man take an inch off the Scotch, its fumes heralding something breathtaking. Outside, the hotel swimming pool shimmered with re-fracted light.

"So, you're in oil?"

The man reached into a pocket, came out with a card.

*MARSTON, DEVILLBIS, TRUAX & HILL—ATTORNEYS-AT-LAW*
*Bakersfield, Fresno, Modesto, Stockton,*
*Sacramento*

"Lot easier than wildcatting, though oil's still a big interest of mine. Come by tomorrow and I'll cut you your check."

No address on the card. "Come by where?"

"Walking distance." DeVillbis pulled out a gold-plated pen, turned the card over, and drew a little dia-gram, handed it back. "How's eleven sound? Nice and quiet. Chance to talk some more."

Kari's Sunday session started at nine, he remembered. "It's a possibility."

DeVillbis ran his real hand over his beard. "My daddy peddled burial plots during the Depression. Always be-lieved in laying out his business and letting the custom-ers get back to theirs—yay or nay. That work for you?"

Wil nodded, thinking Texas, Oklahoma, Arkansas, somewhere in there—the accent ground down close to bedrock but not quite gone.

"Good." Second tug at the Scotch, sharp little exhale afterward, no move yet toward the water. He glanced over at the couple getting up to leave, then leaned forward. "Mr. Hardesty, I have reason to believe someone's trying to do me harm. My son Cole, as well." He paused to let that sink in.

Wil massaged his neck.

"And I know who it is."

"How's that?"

"Go with me on this, okay?" Eyes flicking to the departing couple, nobody but the two of them in there now. "Don't you want to know who it is?"

Wil said, "I'd be more interested in how you know."

"That's fair. Couple of things: one, Cole's seen the guy sneaking around his clubs—these two night spots he owns. Also seen him out at the track."

"The track . . ."

"Racetrack. Cole drives the firm's Winston Cup entry." He bloused out his jacket below the racing logo.

"Marston DeVillbis owns a race car?"

"Bet your ass—best advertising we do. Helps us stay up on the competition." He saw Wil's look. "Hot-and-cold-running celebrity speakers?"

"I don't—"

"Never mind. Point is, Cole's spooked."

"And why is that?"

"Five hundred horsepower—a hundred and forty going into the turns? About two hundred things that could go wrong if somebody wanted them to?" He emptied the Scotch, started on the other. "Takes you a while to wake up, doesn't it?"

Wil raised the mug, smelled the contents, thought better of it. He slid his chair back. "Thanks for the coffee,

Mr. DeVillbis. I sincerely hope you get to the bottom of—"

"Jesus Peesus, don't be like that. Thing has me strung out like a hound on a high wire." Sincere along the lines of a thwarted adolescent. *"Please,"* he added—a pinched tape distorting across a cassette head.

Wil said, "Look, it's late. Why don't we reevaluate in the morning. Maybe it's the police you need."

"Cops do squat till somebody's standing over you with a smoking gun. You must know that."

"Stalker laws. Court injunctions."

"Yeah—tell it to the orphans. Mama with her head blown off, the old man in jail for murder. Sorry, but my way isn't to wait and hope he misses."

A step from calling it a night, Wil stopped, curious despite himself. "He . . . ?"

A little smile crept in around a lighter hit of the whiskey; DeVillbis set down the glass. "Don Lee Whitney," he said. "Black heart of the country himself. Fresh out of Folsom Prison because of some miserable, do-gooder, sit-down-to-whiz, parole-board fuckups." He saw Wil's look, let a beat go by.

"Well now. Do I finally have your ear?"

Four A.M. Looking up at the ceiling, then over at the new moon, the silent-movie screen of window; beside him, Kari's measured breathing. She'd awakened when he'd come back to bed, settling in against him as he began to replay the dialogue in his mind.

DeVillbis: "Well now. Do I finally have your ear?"

Wil: *"The* Don Lee Whitney. *Doc* Whitney."

"I prefer the self-indulgent son of a bitch who shotgunned his whole family, then said he couldn't remember any of it. Ring a bell?"

"Not much of one."

"Right next door, the library's full of it. Biggest thing

around here before or since. And they turn this guy loose? In Oklahoma, he'd have been toast inside of six months."

A slur had crept in, the water backs still untouched, Wil thinking easy enough to hear DeVillbis out among the roughnecks and roustabouts. Men who chased their shifts with shots and beers.

"Two little girls and his wife. Well, he's gonna find us a lot tougher. I guarantee you that."

*Us.* Wil asked about the connection.

DeVillbis took a breath, drummed the table with his good hand. "Why not?" he said. "We've come this far. Early sixties till he took off, I was partners with Gib Whitney—Doc's daddy. Born salesman, but an operator. You know the type. Glad-hander—bit of a womanizer?"

Wil nodded.

DeVillbis reached into his jacket, came out with a silver flask, twisted off the top. "Thing is, Gib was nothing like *his* old man. Old Clell Whitney, one of the original Dust Bowlers come out here in the thirties. Real *Grapes of Wrath*. Stillwater I think Clell was from, young Gib picking cotton right along with him and hating every second." He laughed quietly. "Bakersfield was full of Okies then. Read the daily obits, you'll see what I mean. Still some dying off."

"Gib *was*—that what you said?"

"You listen. I like that." DeVillbis tilted the flask, exhaled at the whiskey's bite. "Gib and the old man parted company sometime after high school. Real bitter parting. Gib and I met when we were supplementing our GI loans with work in the oil fields." He squinted at Wil. "You do know about *them*?"

"Vaguely." Still wondering about Doc Whitney's connection to Lute DeVillbis, thinking he'd give it another minute or so.

"Picture three billion-barrel fields within sight of here

on a clear day. Still pumping, coming up on a hundred years each. You have any idea how much oil that is?"

"No," Wil said.

"You ever seen Oildale? Midway-Sunset around Taft? Elk Hills?"

"Nope."

"Not but three states produce as much as this one little county does—Texas, Alaska, Louisiana. You with me?" Beginning to sound like an evangelist. "Now, Kern River Crude is—"

"What about Doc Whitney?"

"I'm gettin' there. Point I'm trying to make is, Gib left without so much as a good-bye. Stuck it to all sorts of people. Damn near everybody he knew except me."

"And Doc?"

"Kid was barely in his teens when Gib disappeared, but it spun Donnie off like he had no brakes. School, juvie, sheriffs, cops—you name it, he had trouble with it. Not to mention the four marriages, the booze and whatnot. Stuff finally killed his mom."

"What about his music?"

"Screw his music, I'm trying to tell you something here," DeVillbis said. "About the way Gib's leaving affected him."

"How's that get back to you?"

DeVillbis looked around as though seeing faces in the shadows and not liking it much. "Some years ago, when Donnie was still in prison, Gib turns up."

Wil said nothing.

"Politicians—anything oil and they're all over it, right? So the state gets snookered into cleaning out this old sump hole northeast of town. Even though nobody ever sees the thing but the coyotes. Anyway . . ."

"Gib?"

He nodded. "Bullet hole in his skull. Guess he'd been in there about as long as he'd been missing." DeVillbis took another swig. "Make a long story short, Donnie either knew about it when they found him or he does by now. Bet your butt on that."

"So what? He suspects you?"

"I wouldn't put it past him."

Wil just stared.

"Hey, hey—don't go gettin' ideas. I loved his old man." He drained the flask, clattered it on the table. "Plus he knew not to screw around with me. That I damn well *would've* killed him if he had."

A desk clerk strolled over, peered in at the source of the noise, then withdrew.

Wil said, "But now you think Doc Whitney's back—same town where he was convicted of killing his family—and that he's after you and/or your son. Is that it?"

DeVillbis eyed him, a little fuck-you squint forming around the blue eyes. "What I think, after a question like that, is that you need to meet my son. Hear some things from him. That is, if I still have the right man in mind."

Fade.

As Wil lay there now—red glow coming from the clock radio and the moon edging offscreen—replaying Lute DeVillbis pulling on his cap and walking away, he tried to recall any photographs he might have seen of Doc Whitney, pre- or post-1978 press he might have ingested, songs—even just titles—and came up with nothing. But then the screen and all the rest of it, Billy and Cedrick and the bloody knife included, broke up into MTV-like scenes that funneled down to points of light and disappeared.

# FIVE

The canal stretched away into darkness with a primal certainty that was the province of all rivers—even concrete-channeled and diverted ones. Southward toward the massive pumping station that would, nothing short of miraculously, boot it two thousand feet over the Tehachapis toward the long slide into Los Angeles. Seemingly resigned about it, not much more than a whisper as it flowed.

"You ever think about that?" the squarish man in the Members Only windbreaker said to the tall one in the *Semper Fi* sweatshirt. "One minute you're a snowflake falling on this beautiful pine tree in the mountains, the next you're going down the drain with a fat load of shit." He creaked upright in his folding chair, spit a stream of tobacco juice into the dust near the Coleman lantern. "Kind of reminds you of the human race, doesn't it?"

The tall man drained the rest of his beer, crushed the can, and arched it into the canal where it silvered and sank. "To answer your first question, Farley, no. And speaking of shit, you always this full of it at four in the goddamn morning?"

"No bugs, no people; best time to fish, best time to think. Might try it sometime—Buster Crabbe."

Tall's line jerked slightly. He grabbed his pole, swore

when he realized nothing was there, began to reel in. "What the fuck you think I'm doin'?"

"The thinking part, Jay. Where you use your head for something besides head butts."

Jay finished reeling; reaching for the hook, he replaced the nibbled piece of chicken guts with a fresh one from the plastic bag. "Very funny. Like you should talk—right?" He cast out again.

"Hey, I'm just sayin'."

"Save the jokes, Farley, I ain't in the mood." Halfway across, ripples spread out from the splash.

"No kidding," Farley said.

Behind him, a field pump stood out against Bakersfield's far-off glow; power lines caught the last of the moon in ghostly sweeps. Against the pump's hum and the low hiss of lantern, crickets sounded.

"Long as we're on the topic, how *is* the head?"

Jay just looked at him.

"Well . . . ?"

"What do you think? Sumbitch lucks out and lands one before I get the brass on him. Bodywork, my ass. Figure I owe that sucker one between the eyes." He put his hand on the fishing line as if to give it a tug, changed his mind. "Didn't even recognize him at first, how much he'd changed."

"Question is, did he recognize you?"

"And I told you already, no way in hell."

"You think."

"Relax," Jay said.

"You're one to talk."

"What's that supposed to mean?"

"Nothing." Dampness rose off the surface of the canal, behind them the heavy scent of turned earth and fertilizer. Farley kept his eyes on his line. "You take your Motrin like I suggested? *No* . . . Buster Crabbe's too smart for that."

"You gonna give that Buster Crabbe shit a rest, or do I use you for bait?"

"Sure—take it out on me, your only friend if you had one. Here I thought getting out would do you some good. *Nooooo*, you still got this personal thing going with the dude." Farley reached down into the bucket, pulled out a catfish, began gutting it. "That's it for *this* night."

"Jesus," Jay said. "You're some piece of work."

"Just forget it."

"Don't worry, I will."

"Why do I even bother? Tell me that."

Jay was seriously considering picking Farley up and throwing him into the canal, right beside the "STAY OUT, STAY ALIVE" sign, when he paused at headlights turning onto the dirt road that ran along the levee. Half mile or so downstream from Farley's Plymouth Duster.

"You expecting company?"

Farley looked up, catfish slime and gore dripping off his fingers. "At four in the morning? Get outta here. Some bracero hitting it early is all."

Jay said nothing, just watched the lights approach.

"I got a .357 in the tackle box," Farley added. "Ease up already."

"Who knew we'd be here?"

"There's this rule, see? Tacos get up early and change pipe. Agriculture is our friend. You want to give me a hand?"

"I don't like it."

"Fuck, then don't give me a hand."

"I meant the pickup, dumb-ass." Pulling to a stop just above them, cloud of dust drifting by in the headlights. The door opening then and a man getting out, silhouetted in the lights—somebody in a billed hat. Looking at them a moment, as if to be sure, then bringing a pump shotgun out from behind his thigh.

*Shit.*

The first blast caught Farley going for the tackle box and deposited him, twitching spastically, where the dirt met the sloping concrete bank. Somehow he'd held on to the fish knife and was carving little notches with it in the air. The second blew him clear down the bank and into the water. No twitches this time.

As Farley began to drift in the current, Jay was conscious of the truck's motor running, of Travis Tritt coming from the cab—crazy how the mind worked. Then the shotgun swinging his way.

*"The fuck are you?"* he yelled.

No response.

*"Say something. What do you want?"* Jay thinking he might have a chance after all. "Look, if it's money, I just got paid." He held his hands out, slowly reached into his back pocket, and came out with his wallet. Flashed it open. "Seven hundred bucks. What do you say?"

Still nothing.

Jay breathed a little. Judiciously, he underhanded the wallet up the bank. "Whoever you are, welcome to it." A dark thought rose—enough to give voice to it, hedge his bets. Even though he might look stupid if this wasn't the guy. "That was just a job the other night, that's all it was, I swear to God. Nothing personal."

The silhouette was like a statue. In fact, Jay was struck by the absurdity of talking—pleading—with a statue.

One pointing a shotgun at him.

"It wasn't me kicked you in the face back then. Tate, that's who it was. Goddamned Bob Tate."

Nothing. Dust lifting and the sound of his own sweat. Dwight Yoakam floating now from the cab—"Long White Cadillac."

"Look, you're messing with the wrong man. I'm not just—"

Two loads of double-aught buck painted the rest all over the "STAY OUT, STAY ALIVE" sign.

Kari's blow-dryer finally woke him at eight-fifteen, sun angling in the window and room service been and gone.

"Didn't know what you wanted, so I ordered you what I got—coffee and oatmeal," she said. "Running late, as usual."

Wil rubbed his eyes, accepted her flyby kiss; from the bathroom she said, "Thought I'd lost you there last night. You get a better offer or something?"

"Five hundred bucks. Picking it up today."

She came out drying her hands. "Well, damn. Should I ask what you had to do for it?"

Pouring himself a coffee, he explained DeVillbis etc. to her, thinking just over three hours' sleep should make for an interesting day. He used the bathroom then, working carefully around her stuff, emerging as she was finishing up.

"DeVillbis wants to meet," he said. "At eleven. Figure I might as well."

"Any idea what he wants?"

"Something to do with Doc Whitney. Guy was all over the place last night."

"And you think it might be a good idea to brush up on old Doc before you go."

He shrugged.

"Explains that look, anyway," she said.

"The library's closed Sunday—I checked."

"But you didn't know if I'd brought the laptop . . ."

"If not, you brought everything else in those bags."

She checked her watch and sighed.

"Perhaps we could arrange a suitable trade," he said.

"Ah—the magic word."

She walked into the bedroom, where he heard her rummaging, came out with her laptop and modem. Hooked the modem to the phone jack, the other end to the computer. Booted up.

"Try the *Californian*," he said.

"I doubt it, a paper their size—they'll have a Web page, but nothing going back that far. What you want is a database."

"*L.A. Times?*"

"My thought, too. At least the station's a subscriber to their base."

He nuzzled her hair, leaned over her shoulder as she keyed in, paying close attention so he could work it himself after she left. More remotely than intimately familiar with that end, as she was through her work.

"I love it when they hit," she said, finally. "This what you're after?"

"I'm in awe."

"Credit the rag," she said. "Size counts for something, right?" Winking at him as she got up from the chair.

Wil watched her grab her stuff and fly out—air kiss at the door, her warmth on the seat, cross-filing it for future reference. Scrolling down through the find as he downed his oatmeal and took notes. Among the highlights:

8/28/78: WHITNEY SHOOTING ROCKS COUNTY
Bakersfield: Country-western music star Don Lee "Doc" Whitney was arrested on-scene and jailed in the brutal shotgun murders of his wife, Arlene, and their two daughters, Sara, five, and Megan, three. Whitney, heavily under the influence at the time of arrest, denied any knowledge of the incident. In addition to alcohol, traces of an unnamed drug were found in his system. Arresting

officers, both of the Kern County Sheriff's Department, were stunned at the savagery—as were those who knew the family and the entire community. Swift justice was pledged by the county prosecutor. Etc., etc. . . .

And photos—almost a spread's worth—Whitney in happier days, Arlene with him at what looked to be a stock-car race, the kids heartbreakingly perfect, blond towheads with dancing eyes. Whitney at a farm benefit concert. Shots of him receiving the first of his awards for Number-one Country Hit Record, "Home Is Where We Say Good-bye."

Wil remembered it crossing over briefly onto the pop charts. Scanning the several publicity stills included, he saw in the earliest one—Doc at twenty-two, according to its caption—an intent, handsome face with eager eyes and a hellraiser's grin, hunger dripping from the stance: jean jacket with the collar up, hand tightly gripping a Gibson Hummingbird. As though anticipating its sudden flight.

Later ones showed dark hair grown longer, tight T-shirts and motorcycle leathers, one of him on a Harley-Davidson not unlike Wil's busted-up one, the shot bringing with it a little rush of nostalgia before he moved on to others. Wayfarers now were an ongoing part of the package, standard props in the evolution to star. And previous wives: Jenelle first, then Darla and Marlette—with the exception of Jenelle, whose face was angled away from the camera, each could have modeled, Whitney's taste for blond women obvious post-Jenelle, whose photo revealed hair the color of his.

A more recent shot showcased the singer-songwriter rampant: long hair swept across a look of pure juice, cigarette dangling as he ran out a lead riff on a Telecaster electric. Finally, Doc in a black leather vest beside an Eldorado convertible, hand on what looked to be a Dreadnought acoustic this time, his eyes completely hidden. No glimpse of what lurked there.

### 9/30/78: DEATH PENALTY POSSIBLE IN WHITNEY CASE

Sacramento: "Special circumstances" cited by County District Attorney James Lazaretto could lead to the death penalty for Don Lee Whitney in the murder of his wife and young daughters. Defense attorney Paul Gandorf, at whose motion the trial was moved from Bakersfield, will argue for leniency based on impairment, despite what is perceived as public backlash against a rash of such pleas. Whitney's story of not recalling the incident will be attacked by prosecuting attorney Elizabeth Wilde. Etc., etc. . . .

### 10/28/78: WHITNEY ATTEMPTS SUICIDE IN CELL

Sacramento: Don Lee Whitney, awaiting trial in the murder of his wife and daughters, attempted suicide by using strips of bedding to hang himself from the bars of his cell. He is currently scheduled to undergo psychological evaluation, although prosecutor Elizabeth Wilde called the attempt "a halfhearted and transparent means of diverting attention from the victims," vowing it would not succeed.

### 11/17/78: ELEVENTH-HOUR DEAL SPARES DOC

Sacramento: In a turnaround based on what observers believe are potential jury problems, the district attorney's office has reduced first-degree murder charges against Don Lee "Doc" Whitney to three counts of manslaughter. Despite apparent advice to the contrary, the country-western singer has instructed his attorney, Paul Gandorf, to plead to the lesser charge. Etc., etc. . . . Sentencing is scheduled for December 31.

Nothing, then, until a small notation dated six weeks ago.

### 2/26/98: WHITNEY ELIGIBLE

Folsom: Parole officials have declared Don Lee "Doc" Whitney eligible for early release after serving nineteen years of a thirty-year sentence in the 1978 shotgun slayings of his wife and two daughters. Good behavior and assurances from prison psychiatrists that Whitney is "poised for reentry" are factors in the decision. Release is expected sometime within the next two weeks. No etc.'s . . .

Wil was thinking of taking a shot at the Internet, key word *Doc Whitney*, when he caught the time and figured he had about enough for a thirty-second shower if he was going to make his meeting with DeVillbis.

Twenty minutes later, his hair still damp, he approached a seven-story structure with its own parking lot. Bands of reflective windows alternated with a staggered white facade, the overall effect not unlike the county complex near his hotel. Certainly it stood out relative to its neighbors—blue-collar structures that looked more like candidates for DMV offices.

Lute DeVillbis was waiting in the lobby. Dressed in green golf slacks, white polo shirt, and the cap from last night, he came forward to unlock the glass doors.

"Get plenty of sleep?" he asked.

"You mean it doesn't show?"

DeVillbis smiled as Wil took in marbled lobby, sconced lighting, enormous floral arrangement in front of an ornate mirror. He turned a key next to the elevator, pressed the number for seven as Wil entered the car behind him—mahogany paneling, muted lights, plush carpeting. Then the number dinged and they stepped out: same carpet, a reception area with more flowers, empty receptionist desk, wide hallway he ushered Wil down to a corner office with views of the city and the mountains. Tiled bathroom and shower evident through a half-open door.

"Home sweet home," he said. "Like it?"

"Impressive. All this from oil law?" Closer up and in the harder light Wil made out bloodshot eyes, tiny starburst capillaries, a waft of Listerine.

"Naw, that's just my bailiwick, that and water. Juniors handle the rest." He winked. "Now tell me you're not just a wee bit surprised."

"Guilty."

DeVillbis looked pleased. "There you go—some old Okie-boy coming on like gangbusters at two in the morning. Think I owe you an apology somewhere in there." He handed Wil a check with the amount and signature filled in. "Heat of the moment, know what I mean?"

"Yeah." Wil folded it up, put it in his shirt pocket. Waited as DeVillbis opened a drawer and came out with a ring of keys held together by an enameled Mercedes logo.

"More where that came from, son, a whole lot more. How'd you like to take a little ride?"

DeVillbis guided the silver Mercedes out of the lot and north on Chester—beyond where Wil had turned around yesterday, through a traffic rotary, by an elaborate-looking clock tower out front of what looked to be a school.

"Kern County Museum," DeVillbis said in passing. "Took historic structures from all over, set 'em up back there like a town where people could get a sense of the past. Now, do they promote it to speak of? Hell no. You figure it out."

Wil made a mental note to come back to it if he had the time.

"Got minor-league baseball over there, honky-tonks coming up. What more—right?" Up and over a four-lane bridge, water flowing underneath it, fairly broad at this part. No trace of rapids.

"That the Kern?"

A nod. "Call it that, though, everybody'll know you're from out of town. Around here it's 'the river.' Line between Bakersfield and Oildale—our own private jungle when I was growing up. Used to flood like there was no tomorrow before the dam went in." He paused to pass a backhoe, started in again as they reentered the commercial district. "Club you see over there—Redtail's? That's Cole's. Owns another called Cheri's back the other way on Edison. You fond of country music at all?"

Wil explained he was, how he came to it.

"Town used to be lousy with country-western. Lucky Spot, High-Pockets, Cimmaron Club, The Blackboard— those places and more goin' full tilt. Just Cole's and a couple others these days."

"What happened?"

"Cole can tell you. Think I'm bad, he'll talk your ear off on the subject. That particular one anyway."

He swung the Mercedes left into a modest neighborhood; several turns later he pointed to a boxy yellow house with a flat roof and a struggling lawn. "My old digs," he said, easing past. "Whitney's is just up the street. Right . . . there." He gestured to a green one with peeling trim, distressed eaves, vine roses on a split-rail fence.

"Gib was born in that house. Doc, too. No idea what holds it up after all that."

Before Wil could dwell on it, DeVillbis was back on North Chester, turning right onto China Grade—which became Round Mountain Road, the change nothing short of interplanetary: barren hills rolling east toward the Sierra, the odd tree or bush resembling lost outposts. And pumping units, skeletal horses with iron heads—thousands of them, some still, some painted and well maintained, others rusting and inactive. Chain-link fences lined the two-lane, here and there logos of major oil companies, the occasional unfamiliar name denoting an independent.

Phone cables and power lines ran aboveground, pipes along it, crisscrossing and looping on themselves, some in formations of six or more, others larger and running solitaire. Toward the river, waste gas flared from an incinerator vent. Occasional trucks moved down feeder roads, but by and large the field looked to be on autopilot: rigs rising and dipping—some eerily in unison, others to their own rhythm.

The smell of oil hung in the air.

DeVillbis inhaled audibly. "Something else, huh?"

"Hard to improve on that." Like old panoramics he'd seen of the Oklahoma and Southern California oil booms, the same numbing density and scope. Trying to imagine how an environmentalist might describe it.

"Remember me mentioning Kern River crude? Well, you're drivin' on it. Gib used to call this stretch Blackheart Highway for all the blood and tears getting at it." Exhaling audibly. "Ain't that the truth."

He slowed at a bend in the road, pointed off to the right. "Discovery Well—that's where all this started. Father and son bettin' on the come."

Wil regarded a nondescript plaque and some pipes.

"Think the industry'd find a way to pay it more mind, wouldn't you? Only got around to *that* a few years ago."

They drove farther through the field; then DeVillbis looped back, recrossed the Kern to track the south bank along the bluffs. They passed a park and farther on a lake with a lone hydro doing sprints.

"Stick around, you'll see 'em out there in force," DeVillbis said. "Cole had one for a while. Way it seems to work with us is I find the oil and he burns it. Regular field day for a shrink."

They started up through a section of undeveloped hills: low grasses bleaching out, chalky soil showing— weathered tableland with lumps. Overhead, a hard blue sky washed with milk-white streaks.

Wil lowered his window to chase the oil smell—real or imagined at this point. He commented on the day feeling warmer than yesterday.

DeVillbis snorted. "Come back in August, early September. Nothing like a hundred and twelve to clear the sinuses." He lifted his cap and resettled it.

Wil let a mile go by. "Mr. DeVillbis, if you're looking for a bodyguard, I don't do that. But I can recommend somebody."

"Who said anything about a bodyguard?"

"Nobody. It's just that—"

"I want you to find Doc. Tell him I didn't put his daddy in that sump hole. Get him to listen."

"That's it?"

"Get him to hear it from me."

"And if he won't?"

"All I want is a chance to talk with him, tell him how it was between Gib and me. Hell, Doc was just a kid then—kid's got no idea how the world works. I should know."

They came to a broader highway, DeVillbis pointing

toward the mountains. "Before we see Cole, Merle Haggard used to have a place down there where the river leaves the canyon. You want to drive by and see it?"

"Some other time, maybe. But it brings up a point. Wouldn't somebody local be better for what you have in mind?"

"Already went that route. How about double your day rate plus expenses? Counting today, of course."

# SIX

The raceway parking lot was coming up on their right—
the oval, pit area, and stands showing beyond and below
the embankment into which they were set. Some facility,
from what Wil could see of it.

DeVillbis pulled into the near-empty expanse, headed
for the entrance, where some pickup trucks were parked.

"So. What's it going to be?"

"Conditional. I talk to who I think will help, follow
it wherever. I check in with you. If you want something
disclosed to Cole or anyone else, that's up to you." He
let a beat go by. "Nothing personal, but I've seen the
way it can go."

"Anything else?"

"Yeah, no hard feelings if you don't see it that way."

"Done. Prime rib tonight at my club."

"Sorry—got a heart set on Basque back at the hotel,"
Wil said as they shook on it. "Some of her cohorts were
talking it up."

"The gutbuster special. Don't say I didn't warn you."

He smiled. "I won't."

They walked past the closed ticket stiles, up concrete
steps to the rim of the grandstand, where the offices and
observation deck began, through to a sweeping view of
blue seats and three-lane oval, the pit and service areas

below. In the center of the track, numeraled stock cars lounged in varying stages of repair, dual-wheel and extended-cab pickups, vans, a trailer or two, a low building with "WINSTON RACING SERIES" on the roof. Ads for other products and services, most automotive-related, lined the retaining walls. Behind them on both sides, light standards rose on metal stalks.

As Wil watched and DeVillbis's eyes searched the infield, an orange race car left the pit to begin a sprint around the oval, engine noise banging off the walls and the empty stands. Following it into the curve, Wil let his eyes take in surrounding tablelands yellowing in the sun, foothills and mountains to the east, highway they'd come in on heading for the notch that denoted Kern Canyon. Bakersfield about twelve miles off to the west.

"Follow me," DeVillbis said.

They descended to an opening in the chain fence bordering the track, a platform with steps leading to it. By then the orange race car was in the pits, so they crossed the lanes and a grass apron, entered the infield through a break in the inner wall.

Engines throbbed and revved; people working on them or just standing around nodded to DeVillbis, glanced at Wil. DeVillbis waved back, tipped his cap to some women, headed toward a bright red late-model Camaro with yellow trim and the number 19 in white numerals—spoilers and air dams all around, racing affiliate decals thick on the car's flanks. A man in red overalls, *DeVillbis Racing* on the back, tire- and oil-company patches sewn on, was leaning over the engine compartment. Another man was bent over watching something he was doing.

DeVillbis touched the bent-over one's arm, and he eased out and straightened up, Wil making out the name Cole where the logo went on polo shirts. He wore his collar up, black jeans and cowboy boots, red baseball hat, *DeVillbis Racing* in the same script as the overalls. Bushy mustache à la Richard Petty, that same dark hair and squinty eyes, the same rawboned good looks.

The senior DeVillbis said something over the gurgle of engine and Cole came forward—slightly taller than Wil's six-two and towering over his father. He lost the cigarette he had going, crushed it with an ostrich-hide boot.

"Cole DeVillbis," he said, extending a hand. Gold Rolex, pair of Serengeti Drivers hooked into the polo shirt's front.

Mid to late forties, Wil guessed as they shook hands.

"Wil Hardesty."

There was an awkward pause. Cole turned to the mechanic: "That's Tommy Arroyo."

Tommy nodded; Wil returned it.

"Switch her off, Tom," Cole said. "Take five."

Tommy nodded again, killed the engine. Without further interest, he reached into the open window of the black Dooley parked beside the race car, then moved away peeling the wrap off a pack of cigarettes.

"Nice car," Wil said to be saying something.

"You know racing at all?"

"Enough to have a healthy respect for people who race."

Cole smiled slightly. "Then I imagine we'll get along."

"Had you reason to doubt?"

"That's another story," he said, looking at his father. "I was telling Mr. Hardesty about our problem. He's agreed to track it down."

Wil looked at him, then back at Cole. "Way I understand it, Doc Whitney's been here and at your clubs. That you view him as a threat as well."

Cole's eyes went skyward before settling on his watch. "Let's get one thing straight. I know people who'll take this guy out if I say the word. The only reason that I—"

"*Cole . . .* "

"Then you're not exactly spooked," Wil said.

"By some broken-down ex-con? Is that what you've been led to believe? That I'm scared?"

"Where was he when you saw him?"

Cole took a breath. "There—about a third the way up." Pointing to the grandstand, right side, directly across. "Last Wednesday," he added.

"And you're sure it was him."

"I don't know what you've been told about our dealings with the Whitneys, but I'd know the man. Bank on it."

Wil glanced at the senior DeVillbis, back at the son. "What did he look like?"

"For the record? Black jacket and ball cap, face like a map of Desolation Valley—left as soon as I spotted him. One of the guys outside said they thought he got into an old pickup."

"And at the clubs?"

"So far, it's just Redtail's—last Wednesday night. FYI, that's—"

"He saw it," DeVillbis said. "I took him by there earlier."

"Lost him in the crowd before I could get to him. Tell you this much, if we catch the sumbitch there again—"

"You'll do nothing, not a goddamned thing," DeVillbis interjected. "The man's dangerous. Or maybe you've forgotten."

Cole fished a cigarette out of a pack in his jeans, fired it up with a chrome lighter. Focused on the stands.

"*Cole?*"

He let the smoke blow in the direction of his father. "Whatever you say, Daddy. Besides, your man here's got it all under control." He lifted the hat, smiled at Wil. "Right?"

"I never apologize," DeVillbis said. "But if I did, I would for my son back there."

They were driving back toward town, completing what appeared to be a giant circle, Wil homing in on the highway numbers as well: 184 to 58 west, 58 to 99 north, off at Brundage, west on same.

"No need," he said. "I'll live."

"Cole's more afraid than he lets on."

"Not afraid to say his mind, I'll give him that."

"Sins of the father," the older man said. "My wife's been dead a long time, and with my business interests, Cole got what I had left over."

"Maybe you're underestimating him."

"My son is my life. But toys do not make the man."

"Not the least of which are two clubs and a race car," Wil said.

"It's not that he's not capable."

"But . . . ?"

"Too goddamn much like me, I suppose."

Commercial blocks slid by: shopping centers, individual stores, strip malls, the avenue wide here for ease of access. "What dealings with the Whitneys was he talking about?" Wil asked.

DeVillbis thought, shrugged, goosed it through a yellow. "Probably that he and Donnie went to the same schools, did the same stuff. Always had kind of a sibling thing going on. Friendly rivals."

Wil said nothing.

"You ever have a brother? Somebody you'd spark off, but defend in a heartbeat?"

*Denny Van Zant . . . ripping up surf breaks from Santa Cruz to Todos Santos.* "Not that I was related to."

"But you know what I'm talking about. You knew his

moves, he knew yours. People like that you don't soon forget."

Wil looked at him. "Didn't sound much like—"

"Friends, rivals, enemies—what's the difference? I doubt if Cole could tell you."

Letting it go, Wil noticed from the street signs that Brundage had become Stockdale Highway. Familiar sounding. Then a hit from the database articles: Doc Whitney's old address, no number given, just the Stockdale part—so far, no hint from DeVillbis. He began to pay closer attention, decided to push it.

"We going somewhere here?"

"Follow along. You'll see in a minute."

The commercial section behind them now, they passed newish condos and apartments, developments walled with pinkish cinder block, isolated pumping units that, like spores, seemed to have blown in from Blackheart Highway and taken root. West past the Cal State Bakersfield campus to increasingly agricultural lands, the road narrowing now and orchards springing up. Power lines off in the distance.

"Any of Doc's ex-wives left in town?"

DeVillbis thought. "Somebody who knew her said Marlette died of cancer. Darla left town with a musician. Jenelle'd be the one—used to live not far from the Whitneys, or at least her folks did. She and Donnie got married right out of high school." He chuckled. "Tore up most of the girls Cole dated, that's for sure."

Wil made some notes in his notebook, reconnected with the road. Suddenly DeVillbis pulled off the two-lane and shifted out of gear, cut the engine.

"Over there," he said.

The house was well back from the road, big and behind a crumbling wall: crudely painted-over graffiti, rusting entrance bars, the name of a security company above a "No Trespass" sign. Middle distance, a Caterpillar ran arrow-straight rows with a surface plow. Closer in, Wil saw a chrome hubcap poking up out of a furrow—a beer can on the surface of the moon.

From the gate, they regarded the house's once-white paint—cracked now and streaked by stains—worn brick facade and sagging porch, split gutters and scaling shingle roof. Blackly vacant windows, despite the brightness outside.

Wind popped and sighed, sending the Cat's dust toward the power lines and the hills farther west. The warmth with it as well, Wil noted, although a buildup of clouds in that direction was likely contributing.

"You get what you're looking at?" DeVillbis asked. Birds twittered in the unpruned and dying bushes inside the gate.

"I have an idea."

"Believe it or not, Arlene's relatives still have it tied up in court, fighting to see who gets it."

"Sounds like nobody does." His eyes left the house, took in the fields around it. "What grows out there?"

"Cotton. They gin it not far from here."

"Wasn't there another house, a neighbor or somebody?"

DeVillbis nodded. "Woman who called it in died a year or so later. Place got so vandalized, the bank finally knocked it down. Only reason it didn't happen here is because the relatives hired security guards."

Wil thought about it, what happened here—even more isolated then. "Seems a curious place for a star to live."

"Donnie had a thing for his grandfather—honest sweat and toil, working the land, noble farmer. All that bullshit. Saw his old man as a traitor to that, this small-time oil hustler and ne'er-do-well. Least that's what Gib told me one time. Whiskey talk."

"And what did you think?"

"That everything's black and white to a kid. Grampa

Clell was about as cold a sumbitch as I've met." He drew a three-by-five photo print from a pocket billfold, handed it to Wil.

It was a good print—Doc with shorter hair, the eyes free of the Wayfarers and focused on something out of frame. Vulnerable, but still handsomely intense; compromised by fatigue and some swelling that looked like shadow around his left eye.

"Best I could come up with," DeVillbis added. "Friend of mine used to shoot for the paper." The wind made faint whistling sounds now, moans as it coursed through the empty interior.

"Why'd you bring me here? Not just to see it, I assume."

"No."

He waited.

"Guess I wanted you to feel it," DeVillbis said. "Feel what Don Lee Whitney did out here. What he's capable of." Looking over at Wil. "And I wanted it to mean something that we haven't heard yet from Kroft."

"Kroft . . ."

"Sorry—the last guy we sent out."

# SEVEN

The waitress set down one of the plates she was carrying—lamb chops in garlic butter—down the line until she'd served the entire table, forty feet of casually dressed diners. Eyes among the first-timers widened, but those used to the Basque portions simply dug in: soup, salad, bread and salsa, beans, pickled tongue, vegetables, rice, french fries, meatballs in sauce. And now the lamb . . .

Kari blew out her cheeks, rolled her eyes. "*My Lord . . .*"

"Getting enough there?" Wil asked.

"I saw you loosening your belt after the green beans." Still glowing from her presentation, all she'd talked about on the way over, how well it went, Wil basking in it, happy for her. After the Whitney ruin, happy something was going right for somebody.

"One of the few remaining guy perks," he said, winking at the boy across from him, a slim kid about twelve seated between a plump mother and a wiry father with gnarled hands. "More fries with those?"

"Anybody ever die doing this?"

"No, but the chef takes it personally if you don't finish. Made stew last week out of this one lady who didn't."

The boy looked up from his plate.

"How'd the chef know?" she asked, playing to the kid's interest.

"Waitresses. I don't want to be the one to say it, but the one who left the lamb's been eyeballing you."

"I'm too tough to make stew out of."

"Long simmering's the secret," Wil said. "Plenty of mushrooms." The kid pretending not to hear but smiling into his food as the waitress returned with slabs of blue cheese and began collecting the empties.

"Be sure and leave room for dessert," Wil asided.

Kari tilted her plate toward the boy. "Help. Save me from a terrible fate here?"

The boy did a quick left-right to see who was watching, then shrugged and forked a chop she hadn't touched off her plate onto his. Looked at her hopefully. "This mean you're not gonna eat your ice cream when it comes?"

Later, after the kid had polished off both their ice creams plus his own, Wil showed Kari a view of the oil fields, now a jittering lay of orangy lights spreading north. Breeze off the river carried earthy scents and something like honeysuckle as they walked the bluff, through the park that had been created to take advantage of the panorama.

"Pretty," she said, her arm around his waist.

"Sure is by night." And in a bit, "You up for some country music?"

"After the dinner from Noah's Ark . . ."

"Speaking of which, you check to see your fingers were all there when the kid got through?"

They'd stopped now; no stars showing, just the lights. Kari's eyes filled with them.

"Reminded me of Brian," she said. "Whose dad, incidentally, is dropping him off early tomorrow."

"Sounds fraught with implication."

"Like maybe we'd better hit it if I'm going to run you back."

Wil nodded, used the opportunity to explain De-Villbis's hiring him to find Doc Whitney and talk to him—that he'd be sticking around Bakersfield. News he was glad he'd waited to share.

"While I turn back into a pumpkin . . ." Her disappointment apparent.

"Pumpkins rule at Halloween. Not to mention pie time."

"God—how can you even think of food?" She was quiet a moment. "Promise you won't have any fun while I'm gone?"

"I promise."

"How will you get home?"

"Come back when I'm finished, bring Brian along. How's that sound?"

"*Comme si, comme ça*, the way he's been lately. We'll see."

"Want to steam up the car windows awhile?"

She did, but they didn't, agreeing it was probably better to get her on the road before it got any later, stopping back at the hotel first to bring down her things and load the car.

"Don't forget," she said as he leaned in the window to kiss her, tell her take it easy on the drive. "I want a full report."

"Not sure I can survive another full report."

"But what a way to go." She levered it into gear, winked at him. "So long, sweetcheeks. Take care of Dick Tracy for me."

Watching her taillights lose themselves down Truxtun, he decided on a couple of blocks to walk off the little ache in his throat, not to mention dinner. Sunday night, there was little traffic and almost no pedestrians about, the air smelling of mown grass. Mist rose from timered sprinkler systems. Rings marked a moon hidden by clouds.

The walk decided it: second-winded, he called Redtail's from the hotel, heard *Oh yeah* when he asked if it was an entertainment night. Twenty minutes later he was in a cab, asking the middle-aged driver, Jorge, what he'd neglected to ask Cole—about the club scene in town.

"Only a few left," Jorge said. "Not like before."

Reinforcement; Wil asked why and got a shrug.

"Oil was in the dumper, but it's up now, doin' good. Beyond that, *Yo no se.* Still working up to taking the old lady out to The Palace. Heard it's nice, no brawls and such, but we don't get around like we used to."

"I know the feeling."

They crossed the river, then Jorge flipped a U to let him off outside a longish building with no windows and a brick facade, illuminated sign showing a splay of hawk feathers. Red background paint coming through the outlined tips.

"You need a lift back, you call and ask for Jorge, no problem," he said after Wil paid him. Hitting it then, leaving a trail of blue smoke and four bucks' worth of tires on the pavement.

Who else? Wil thought, entering to a good-sized and busy poolroom left, dim longbar and table seating behind a low partition right, jukebox entertaining a modest crowd, the musicians currently on break. Ceiling spots bathed the smallish bandstand in red—drums, guitars leaning against their stands, high-low mike setup for voice-acoustic numbers. Around the bandstand, the dance floor fanned out to meet the tables.

Wil approached a blond cocktail waitress in white shirt and black hotpants who told him to sit anywhere, she'd find him with whatever. *Bridgit* on her name tag.

"Club soda with lime," he said.

"Big night out, huh?" Grinning at him appraisingly as her gold hoop earrings caught the light.

"Something like that."

"Sorry, but I'll have to charge you regular drink price, two-drink minimum. House policy."

He nodded, gave her some bills left over from Jorge, scoped out tables around the room. "Who's on tonight?"

"Some kid named Pruett. Never heard him personally, but Renee says he's a comer. Sunday's amateur night."

"Renee . . ."

"Bringing beers to that table."

"Ah . . . Cole on hand?"

"Not too likely after a practice day. Probably tucking in his race car about now."

"Some son of a gun, that Cole."

"Hon, you don't know the half." Tight smile as she wiped off a tabletop, emptied the ashtray into another on her drink tray.

"Who would? You?"

"Just a figure of speech."

"I'm a good listener."

"Not nearly good enough to consider talking about Cole. We clear on that?"

"Clear."

"Why you want to know anyway?" Her eyes narrowing. "You a cop?"

"Nope. Just a fan."

"That'd be page-one material. Look, the kid's due back—I better get your drinks."

Wil picked a table by the partition, checked out the crowd: young guys in cowboy and bill hats, boots and jeans with big buckles; dates, if they had them, wearing jeans and fringed shirts. Older types sat in groups, longnecks crowding the tables. Against the wall at the edge of the lights, a few singles in booths leaned over their cocktail tubs or pinched draft glasses.

Bridgit set down his club sodas. After which, Renee killed the juke, people drifted over from the bar, and a mid-twenties-looking kid with longish hair picked up one of the guitars—a wired-up Guild cutaway—and began tuning it. Two other men then sauntered out of the men's room, their faces flushed and grinning. The older one, his blondish hair pulled back in a ponytail, took his place behind the drums while the other picked up a bass electric and began backing the guitarist, who'd started in on an opening riff. Then the drummer laid on and they really got into it.

Though the juke had been loud, the live sound made conversation impossible. Heads left other heads and turned to face the band, full tilt now into a boogie number about roughnecks, references to the oil fields that brought whoops and hollers, the dance floor suddenly alive with hats, boots, and denim.

Finished with "Roughneck Stumble," the band kept it moving with one called "Oil and Water" the kid announced he'd written. Same tempo as "Roughneck," followed by "Six Days on the Road," that set everybody off.

Ronnie Pruett's voice was raw but earnest, backups pretty much on the money except for when the bass player was late coming off a bridge. Rockabilly numbers brought sweaty ovations before the group launched into a hoot called "Back Door Johnny" that had the small floor shaking when the dancers got in sync.

Forty minutes in, the band shut down with "Kern River Girl," another Pruett, then broke and headed for a room just off the bar. Almost before the door had shut, the blond waitress was back at Wil's elbow, asking tongue-in-cheek if he could handle a refill.

"Sure, why not?" Knowing he'd never get to them, but wanting more time with her.

"So what'd you think? We're supposed to ask."

"Good. What about the guys with him?"

"What about them?" The juke was back on now, and she had to raise her voice over "Together Again."

"Not exactly rookies, are they?"

"Cole does that to cover his bases. Guy on the drums, Crash Alvarez, he's been around forever. Bass guy— Ray Somebody—he's not far behind. Cole likes 'em 'cause they work cheap." She set his empties on her tray, swiped a bar towel across the condensation rings. "I should talk. You liked 'em?"

"I did. You?"

"I don't get a vote, but I'll pass it on. Back in a flash."

Eyes moving with her, he almost missed one of the booth solitaires emerging from the dim. Cinching the raised collar of his black denim jacket; settling the trucker's hat over his eyes as he headed for the door.

Not quite believing it, yet knowing, Wil came out of his chair. He was barely to his feet when shouts went up in the poolroom and a player in jeans and a rolled-up T-shirt came flying over the partition in a clatter of cues and pool balls. Then another, this one trying to kick and stomp the first player, two guys who obviously were bouncers attempting to grab and muscle the kicker toward the door. The same door that now had shut behind the man in black.

As Steve Earle came up loud—*Hey, pretty baby, are you ready for me . . .* —Wil did a fast scan, glimpsed a side exit through the poolroom, knifed his way through the soft part of the crowd, the shocked or goading looky-loos, and out into cool dense air.

No sign of him.

Around the front then, no one there but the guy who'd been ejected by the bouncers, peeing a yellow stream into the side of the building and mumbling to himself. Adrenaline-charged drunken eyes seeing Wil round the corner.

*"The fuck you lookin' at? You want some, too?"*

"No, thanks," Wil answered. No fast-retreating vehicles or Levi-jacketed figures hurrying into the night. Realizing now it had started to rain, the fat drops plopping on the sidewalk and the street—heavy smell of ozone, damp asphalt, and old exhaust. "Just me, I guess."

# EIGHT

Next morning felt freshly washed, the rain shower having stopped sometime after Jorge dropped him and he got to sleep—post two A.M., Wil figured. Wisps of vapor rose off the drying pavement and the lawns, the clouds looking like tufts of cotton against a hard-fired sky. Already the day seeming like warm weather.

After breakfast, he called DeVillbis and caught the lawyer going into a meeting. Briefly he explained the night before.

"Big as life, huh? Damn good thing Cole wasn't there, who knows what might've happened. You see what I mean?"

"Have you contacted his parole officer?"

"Yeah. It's like trying to determine who let a fart in a theater, all the privacy laws they got. Forget it."

Wil watched a train barrier come down not far from the hotel, the red light start flashing; through the window, he could hear the faint warning dings. "You told them the circumstances?"

"Hey, they're the ones who released him in the first place. You think they're gonna admit they might have been wrong?"

"I suppose not."

"So. Anything else you need from me?"

"Jenelle—she still go by the name Whitney?"

"Lord, no. After Doc and some other loser, she went back to her maiden name."

An engine pulling flatbedded containers slowly made its way across the intersection and out of sight down the track.

"Jenelle, Jenelle, Jenelle . . . *Shit*."

"Come again?"

"Never mind, I'll think of it."

The barrier went up; the cars resumed their flow. Wil said, "Library's open in a few minutes. I'll check back in the articles for it. This guy Kroft—did you hire him?"

"Indirectly through Rye Rossert. Fella I do business with sometimes, owns about half the town. Kroft was somebody he'd used before."

There was a muffled sound, then DeVillbis back on. "*Lockhart*," he said, "Jenelle Lockhart. Knew it'd come to me." In the background, a woman's voice saying, "*Thanks a lot.*"

Wil wrote it down. "What about Rossert?"

"Ryland Rossert, Rossert Investment Partners. Should be in the book. I'd check my Rolodex except I gotta go sue somebody's ass off."

After he'd rung off, Wil checked, found no listing for Ryland Rossert but did find one for the Partners and noted it. He scanned the book for Jenelle Lockhart and came across that, too: Oildale. Finally, he looked up car-rental companies and found one that rented pickups, fig-uring he might as well blend in. By ten-thirty, he was driving up North Chester in a newish Chevy S-10, swinging left on a cross street and pulling up in front of Redtail's.

Playing a hunch.

But the drummer wasn't there, nobody from the group was, Wil at least getting his name from the bored-looking bartender: Alvarez—Chris aka Crash. Subbing with a group called the Gnash Ramblers tonight at Cheri's, the bartender recalled. Either that or Tuesday.

Wil thanked him, heard a voice: "Can't stay away, huh?"

He turned, saw the blond waitress coming out of the door the band had gone into last night; same outfit, as though it *were* still last night. Today's smile chipper enough, though.

"I could say the same of you," he said.

"Ain't that the truth."

"So what happened after the fight?"

"Which one?"

"Like that, huh?"

She smiled. "Last night was crazier than most. But some of those people *come* for the fights."

"Any idea where Chris Alvarez hangs out?"

"You a big fan of his, too?"

Wil said, "Couple of questions is all. Wanted to ask him if he ever played with Doc Whitney."

The shutdown was immediate, her eyes flicking away to a table setting she began fiddling with. "Mister, what I'm going to say is on the house—no charge. When a man does what Doc Whitney did in a place like Bakersfield, it's like he doesn't exist anymore. No more radio play, no more fan club, no more saying his name even. Not unless you're *looking* for trouble. That plain enough?"

"Pretty much."

"This is a caring town, but most people I know wouldn't spit on him if he was on fire."

"So you probably wouldn't know where he was if I wanted to talk to him."

The pepper shaker clattered over; she righted it with hands that shook, banged it down in place. "My mother was Arlene Strickland's aunt—the Arlene that he mur-

dered? Which means we were related. If it was up to me
he'd have been strung up by his nuts."

Obviously it had been a while since Jenelle Lockhart,
formerly Whitney, lived in the old neighborhood. Cruising now, looking for the street address he'd written
down, mulberry-shaded older homes with swamp cool-
ers reminding him of sweltering summers past, Wil finally pulled over and rechecked the map. Locating at
least the street, he headed north through apartments and
condo clusters, mobile-home parks, strip malls with gas
stations, car washes, fast-food outlets. Nothing much
over one story.

Her unit—14A—was part of a gated grouping painted
blue gray and facing China Grade Loop. Undulating
green belts, landscaped pool area and clubhouse, good-
size pines probably as new to the area as the residents,
Wil guessing oil-company middle managers with families in from Houston and Tulsa.

Footsteps after he rang the bell paused to check him
out through the glass eye, and then she stood there. Had
to be, even before saying anything: dark hair short compared to the photo, face that had been turned away reminding him now of Emmylou, perhaps a younger Baez
or Cher, that striking natural quality. Mid to late forties,
he thought, although the years seemed more like a well-
matched accessory—the silver squash blossom around
her neck. Getting past it after a moment to stonewashed
jeans, leather sandals, rolled-up chambray loose over an
indigo tee.

"Yes?" Neither welcoming nor veiled.

Friendly smile: "Jenelle Lockhart?"

She blinked, glanced past him, then back. "Are you
aware we have a policy on soliciting in the complex?"
Surprisingly youthful sounding despite an edge now—
probably reacting to his knowing her name.

Wil handed her one of his business cards. "I was hoping you could help me."

"I see. And how would I manage that?"

"I'm trying to locate Doc Whitney."

She stared at him, saying nothing, revealing nothing. Harder to pull off than it appeared.

"It's important I talk to him."

"Doc is the past," she said finally. "I choose to live in the present. I assume you can find your way out." She began to close the door.

"People may get hurt unless I do."

"Is that what happened to your hand?"

He realized he'd been scratching his stitches through the bandage. "No, not really. Just an accident."

"Then you're talking about whomever you're working for."

"Assuming the worst, yes."

"And you'll share that person's name with me?"

"I'm sorry."

"No, I didn't think so." A hand went to the squash blossom, began tracing its curve. "Yet you expect me to be an open book, correct? What would make you think I'd do that? Especially when it concerns someone who—" She took a breath, smiled: back in control. "But all that is very old news."

"You know he's out of prison, don't you? That he's been seen in town?" Keeping his eyes off the necklace with some effort.

"It's a small town."

"Then you have seen him?"

"Please. Don't put words in my mouth."

"No, of course not. And I'm sorry to have troubled you, Ms. Lockhart." He moved to step off the porch.

She glanced again at his card. "Mr. Hardesty, I don't mean to be rude. But so we understand each other, my life is very simple now. It wasn't always. I'm about to graduate from college, there's a teaching job waiting, and I'm all in one piece. That's as good as it's been for a while. Can you understand that?"

"Sure. You think talking to me threatens it somehow."

"Let's just say 'think' is not the word I would choose."

"English," Wil said.

"I beg your pardon?"

"English major—you're graduating in English. Am I right?"

She smiled at that. "English lit. Good luck with your assignment, Mr. Hardesty. And take care of that hand."

Bottom step; he started to turn away, stopped. "If you change your mind, I'll be at the Holiday Inn a few more days. Until I find him."

"You're very sure of yourself."

"Not the way you make it sound. I nearly caught up with him last night."

She touched the necklace again. "You saw him?"

"At Redtail's." He waited, but nothing came of it; just hazel eyes taking his measure. Eyes you could fall into. "It's why I get the big bucks. Can't you tell?"

He grinned at the reaction, pleased he'd gotten another smile from her before saying good-bye. At least she didn't slam the door as he was walking toward the truck.

After lunch at a pretty fair taco stand, remembering how good a beer or twelve used to taste on a warm afternoon, he debated the wisdom of going to Cheri's: a) as the near occasion of sin, b) this early in the day. Not having backslid in three years, plus memories of upchucking floor sawdust along with the witches' brews he used to try and drown his guilt over Devin in—Dev of the *"Watch me, Dad"* and surfer-boy hair flip, the ever-present grin—helped settle the issue.

But insanity was always as close as the nearest pull tab or twist-off, aptly named for recoverers like him whose body chemistry resembled memory yarn, ready to snap back at a moment of distress or temptation, a whiff of the demon loose in a glass. One too many and a hundred not enough.

Driving toward the other side of town, he distracted himself with thoughts of Jenelle, what she'd been through with Doc Whitney, obviously no stranger to that kind of weakness. Married right out of high school, DeVillbis had said; kids still dancing to their own rock-around-the-clock. At least age was supposed to impart a built-in governor, a body of experience to even out the ride.

A willingness to *let* things ride.

Except in aberrations like stardom, where moderation had about as much meaning as virtue and flameout awaited those who flew too close to the sun. The immolation, of course, was rarely confined to self, consuming any and all foolhardy enough to venture along. Which so far meant Jenelle, Marlette, Darla, Arlene, Sara, Megan: Don Lee Whitney still running a tab, if DeVillbis was right.

> *Never let it get so big it can eat you.*
> *Never turn your back on the ocean.*

Cheri's was a dumpier version of Redtail's, probably its predecessor. Situated across from the railroad tracks that paralleled Edison Highway, it sat between a seedy-looking market and a used-appliance store, a mattress outlet down from that. But once inside, adjusting to the air-conditioned dimness, Wil found the dance-and-entertainment area of Redtail's equal if not larger, the difference being Cheri's had no poolroom. The bar also seemed bigger, stools about half-full of afternooners in jeans, plaid cotton shirts, a few straw hats.

With the opening of the door, the drinkers' heads turned toward him, then back as it dawned he was nobody they knew. The bartender, a Billy Ray Cyrus/bouncer type, waited expectantly.

"Coke and lime," Wil said to him.

"No rum?"

"No thanks." And after the bartender nozzled it into a glass, "There music here tonight?"

"Group called the Gnash Ramblers." He spelled G-n-a-s-h to make sure Wil got the play on words. "Buck-fifty for the Coke."

Wil paid him with two bills. "Any of them shown up yet?"

"You see anybody playing?"

"Figured they might be in early to practice or something. Crash in particular. Guess I was wrong."

"And you would be?"

He sipped the Coke. "Friend of a friend who wanted a word."

"Cop?"

"No. Any idea where he hangs out between gigs?"

The bartender searched his face a moment, told him to take a seat, which he did. Wil watched the man take a phone out from under the counter and dial a number. Talk for a bit, flash a glance at him, then hang up.

"See the door there? First trailer on the left out back. Tree sap and birdshit all over it."

"Thanks," Wil said.

"Just don't make me regret it."

An aging slabside, the trailer was one of six angled toward a center aisle like the stripes in a chevron, gravel alley showing beyond a low Cyclone fence, dented red Valiant pulled up alongside. The sap and birdshit were from a distressed ash whose foliage nearly engulfed the trailer's once cream-brown siding.

Wil stepped around some aluminum chairs with frayed webbing and knocked, heard *It's open*. Twisted the small knob and poked his head in, saw a fat boxer with a graying muzzle and rheumy eyes, lip curled slightly to reveal the left canine. No growl, however.

"Hey there." Wil put a hand out to the old dog until he realized it was stuffed. Extraordinarily lifelike. Eyes that followed him as he entered.

"Sid Vicious," a voice said. "My head of security. Looks like you're cool."

"Hell of a job," Wil said, touching the fur, letting his eyes adjust to the light. Across flattened carpeting he made out Crash Alvarez sitting in briefs on the edge of an unmade fold-down. Dim light from the shaded window picking out the strands of gray in his long hair, the silver-bead chain around his neck.

"Yeah, well . . . he was a good old boy and the alternative more or less stank. You want a beer?"

"No—thanks."

He had a guitar across his lap Wil thought might be the Guild cutaway from last night, the same inlay design on the neck, so he asked about it.

"Kid hasn't worked up to a good ax yet, so I loan him mine. You were there, huh? What'd you think?"

"Good. Tight."

"Not yet, but we're working on it."

"So. Drums *and* guitar?"

"Regular one-man band."

"Plus another group tonight."

"Helps buy groceries and get me fucked up occasionally. You gonna tell me who you are?"

Wil gave him a card, mentioned that somebody'd said he'd been around country music awhile. That it had put an off-the-wall thought in his head.

Alvarez set the guitar aside, pulled on a once-navy tee imprinted with *Stay Back 300 Feet*. He barefooted to the fridge, opened it, drew out a green bottle. "Had time to fail at nearly everything, you mean. Sure you don't want a beer?" He cracked it and chugged some, then some more, Wil wishing he'd brought along the Coke and lime. Mentally kicking himself as Alvarez scratched at day-old stubble, snapped on the gooseneck beside the bed, which creaked as he sat back down.

"So what's the thought?"

"Kind of out there," Wil said. "Wondering if you'd ever played with Don Lee Whitney."

The musician found a cigarette. Lighting it with a plastic lighter, he took a deep inhale, then shook his hair out, gathered it into a pony, and tied it off, Wil noticing the scars on the underside of his forearms. Thinking *toll road*.

"Guess I'd have to know for what reason."

He explained, or attempted to; but Alvarez's dark eyes seemed to be drifting to things that weren't there.

"You ever hear the man's music?"

"Not much, if any."

"Kind of hard when they won't play it anymore. I know a place still has his cassettes. Do yourself a favor."

"So you did work with him."

"Check the liner notes."

Wil nodded. "You have any idea where he might be?"

Alvarez snapped the light off, then on again. "Covers a lot of ground."

"So I can assume you've seen him?"

Off-on, each snap highlighting the fissures in his face. "This is like a game to you, isn't it? Twenty Fucking Questions."

"Twenty what? . . ."

Finally it dawned.

"Sorry," Wil said. "Just trying to keep it loose."

"Yeah . . ."

"And it's anything but a game."

Alvarez took a deep drag and blew smoke across the trailer. "All right . . . he called me after a gig. We met later for coffee."

"How did he look?"

Shrug. "Like he'd just gotten out from doing hard time and a lot of it. How do you think?"

"He appear dangerous to you? Bent on doing something he might regret?"

"Fuck . . . biggest danger to Doc Whitney is the man himself." He stepped to a closet, rummaged through it, clothes and things hitting the floor before finding the cassette and tossing it to Wil. "You familiar with country at all?" Before Wil could respond, he added, "And I don't mean this hunk-in-a-hat, playlist hit-shit the marketing nerds slide up your hole. Stone country—the kind that makes you feel something."

"Right . . ." Wil glanced over to confirm Sid's eyes on him. Glowing almost.

"Special reflective glass," Alvarez said as though anticipating the question. For a moment he regarded his smoke twisting in the light. "You have any idea what I'm talking about here?"

"The music? Yeah, I think so." Wil scanned the tape—*Alias Doc Whitney*—and recognized the photo from one in the database, the Eldorado/Dreadnought Doc.

"Genuine hundred proof, the real deal. All the good ones owe him. Which tends to scare people—especially record execs. Something he's paid for in spades."

"I don't—"

"Listen to it. That's number three. And if you can't get that this is a man who could never in a million years shotgun his family—two little girls, for God's sake—then go take a flying leap."

Wil dropped it in his pocket and stood. "Thanks. I'll see you get it back."

But it was as though Alvarez hadn't heard him.

"Best work *I* ever did, that's for sure. Nominated for album of the year." And as Wil was easing out, the screen door protesting, he capped it with, "Nice digs, huh? You have any idea what it's like to peak at twenty-six?"

Wil called the hotel to check for messages. After playing back one from Kari saying she missed him and was thinking of carving Brian into small pieces, he drove west on California until it followed a similar bend in the river a couple of blocks north, the street wide and treed and lined with industrial-park office buildings occupied mostly by national oil companies, investment firms, and financial institutions.

Light-years from Crash Alvarez's trailer.

Rossert Investment Partners was in one of the buildings off California—*34 East*—in a cul-de-sac with an oil well on the lawn. The well was surrounded by a hedge showing new growth and a nicely dug flower bed, the horse's head making its measured dips as butterflies dipped into marigold and lobelia. The structure was similar in design to Marston DeVillbis, that white-interspersed-with-reflective-glass look. But then most of the buildings around were; this one at least boasted curved surfaces. Also evergreen pear trees in bloom and a breeze to stir the blossoms. Not unwelcome—eighty-six the radio had announced on the way over.

Four forty-five: not too late, Wil hoped, checking the building directory. Double doors led him to a spacious suite with a reception area, a receptionist with auburn hair and too much makeup, but a nice smile. Nice view of the oil well.

"Ryland Rossert, please."

"He's, um—let me check." Picking up the phone, she punched a button, reached for the card Wil held out.

"Mr. Rossert, there's a Mr. Hardesty here." She flashed him a glance, the smile. Losing it as a voice Wil could make out from where he stood responded.

"Yes, Mr. Rossert," she said, hanging up.

"Am I in luck?"

"Depends. Go out that door, take the elevator to the top floor and the hall all the way to the rear of the building. He's working out with Mr. Garza."

"Who would be . . ."

"Mr. Rossert's associate," she said. "Another unique individual."

"Aren't they all." Thanking her and heading for the door, hearing *Not like that* before it closed.

Following her directions, he arrived at a frosted-glass door, behind it the sound of someone working a body bag, crisp punches with something behind them. He tried the handle; finding it locked, he rapped the glass.

The man who opened it was a fortyish Hispanic about an inch shy of Wil's height and sweating profusely. Short black hair, well-defined upper body, nipped-in waist, the muscled legs of a fighter. Left upper biceps circled by a sharp-linked tattoo, double teardrop on his neck below the right ear. He wore gray shorts, black Everlast tank top, and leather speed gloves.

He moved aside to let Wil in.

Wil entered to one other man in the private facility, older and catching his breath against the body bag suspended from the ceiling. He, too, was perspiring heavily despite the room's air-conditioning. Behind him, a speed bag dangled from a swivel mount. Free weights lined the walls, adjustable benches facing them, refrigerator in the corner. No TV.

"Wil Hardesty looking for Mr. Rossert?"

The older man shoved off from the bag. Faded red sweatpants, V-neck tee showing wet gray chest hair, regular boxing gloves. He stood about six feet, with salt-

and-pepper hair that looked touched up. Flushed face, thin scar above his right lip. Left earlobe showing a tiny diamond, as though someone had talked him into it and this was the compromise.

"Lute DeVillbis said you'd be by. Man working me into a grease spot there's Raul Garza."

Raul Garza went to the speed bag and began to move it with seemingly little effort; flicking a glance at the mirrored wall, his dark eyes bored into Wil's as if probing to see what was there.

Wil nodded at the reflection, held contact a moment longer than necessary, then shifted back to Rossert, whose face held a voyeur's bright light.

"You box? Nothing like it to keep in shape."

"Ages ago," Wil said.

"You must do something. You look pretty trim."

"Run a little. Surf when I can."

"Yeah, Lute said you weren't from around here. Thought you might be an improvement on Farley."

"Farley . . ."

Rossert smiled thinly. "Sorry—Farley Kroft, my mistake. Old no-show."

"The man who hasn't reported in yet on Doc Whitney?"

"The one and only."

"How long has it been?"

Using his teeth, Rossert loosened his gloves, popped them off. "Going on two weeks," he said. "But to be honest, Farley's been known to harbor a fondness for Nevada, some of the ranches up there, if you follow. Nothing I didn't know going in—just made the mistake of paying him in advance. Do a guy a favor and that's how he treats you. Right, *compa*?"

But Raul Garza was in the zone now, the speed bag sounding like an assault weapon under his fists. Sweat poured off him, the tank top stuck to his chest like black plastic.

"Impressive," Wil said after watching a moment.

Rossert smiled.

"You report Farley to the authorities?" Wil asked.

"For all the good it'll do. He'll come waltzing in sooner or later, crying for another chance. Too bad."

Raul Garza paused, nailed the speed bag a concluding left-right, then broke off, his breathing hard but controlled. He went to the watercooler, poured a paper cupful over his head, shook it off as a dog might.

"You through with the heavy bag, *patrón*?"

Rossert held up gloveless hands. "All yours." Then to Wil, "Why don't we go outside. Roof garden's just across the breezeway."

He draped a white towel over his neck, pulled bottled teas from the fridge. Handing one to Wil, he led the way to the roof garden, the nonrefrigerated air summerlike by comparison. Still, it offered the breeze and a look at the river, serpentining out beyond other buildings and the late-afternoon traffic on West Truxtun.

"Nice view from here," Wil said.

"Lute's clients across the river would tend to think so."

Wil couldn't tell if he was kidding or not, the refineries and tanks standing out in marked contrast when you focused on them. He twisted off the cap and drank some of the tea.

Rossert did the same.

"So. How does one become a Rossert Investment Partner?"

Rossert leaned against a concrete container with a birch tree growing in it. "Couldn't be simpler. All you need is money and an expansive attitude."

"What types of investments?"

"Oh—land and structures, the occasional ranch or golf

course. Like that. Some more flexible things as they become available."

"Flexible things . . ."

Rossert tilted the bottle, gasped coming out. "As they become available."

"Such as oil?"

"We've been known to dabble. Why—you interested?"

"More curious as to how things work. Always has fascinated me."

Rossert wiped his face on the towel. "Just so we're clear, Mister . . ."

"Hardesty."

"Right. No offense, but I can think of better ways for Lute DeVillbis to spend his money, even though he's not hurting for it."

"Funny, he said the same of you."

"Is that so—what else did he say?"

Wil savored his tea: lemon flavor. "Not much. Are you aware that Doc Whitney has been seen around DeVillbis interests?"

"Big fucking deal, the guy used to live in town. Good description of Cole, incidentally."

"Lute seems to be taking it seriously."

"In short, Lute isn't the bravest lawyer around. Man's a ninny and a worrier. He also drinks and he's let himself go to hell. And I can say what I want because I've known him off and on for forty years."

"May I ask in what capacity?"

Rossert smiled. "Long as you don't mind me not saying."

"Your business," Wil said.

"Put it this way—we're both the same age, sixty-four. As I assume you can see by looking at us, there the similarity ends." He rolled the tea bottle across his forehead. "Warm out here."

"Bottom line, then, you don't see Doc Whitney as a threat."

"What's to see? One more loser from a family of losers."

"So why Farley Kroft?"

"A favor to Lute, that's all. Kind of a subcontract."

"Nothing personal, then."

Rossert twisted the top back on his tea. "Since you don't know me, I'll let that slide. I'll also let you in on something else. I grew up in a converted railroad car in East Bakersfield trading punches with guys like Raul Garza. Four, five on one sometimes. No quarter asked and none given. Now they take orders from me and like it."

"And I take it you'd have no idea where I could find Doc Whitney?"

"None. Is that plain enough?"

Wil handed him a card. "You mind letting me know if something comes to mind?"

Rossert slipped it in his pocket without glancing at it. "I'll be sure and put it on my list."

"Thanks for your time, Mr. Rossert."

As he stood to go, Raul Garza came down the breezeway toward them. Blocking Wil's path momentarily, he gave him a rapid-fire combination of air punches and grinned as Wil edged around him.

# NINE

*He called me after a gig.*

*We met later for coffee.*

Crash Alvarez talking—someplace open that late, obviously. Or that early. Wil flipped through the phone listings: twenty-four-hour coffee places. Half an hour later, between the Yellow Pages and some help from the bellman, he'd made a list—calling to make sure they were still in business, thinning it thereby—and planned out a sequence for later.

He got back to Kari then, briefing her on what little he'd accomplished and hearing similar things from her: Work was back to being the pits, parenting an adolescent was the scam of the century.

She caught herself. "Wil, I'm sorry, I didn't mean . . . Devin. About parenting, I mean—"

"It's all right," he lied. "Just look at it this way—one day Brian will be thirty and none of it'll matter."

"If I don't kill him first. Oh damn, there I go—"

"Relax, Kari, I'm fine."

"You sure?"

"A day at a time," he said. "Pretty soon you have a whole bunch of them." *Book and verse.*

"Thanks—I think."

"Just don't ask if I take my own advice."

After the call, Wil refocused on things at hand—tried to, anyway. Not feeling like dining alone with people around, he'd ordered up a sandwich and sat eating it now, channel surfing: CNN about thirty seconds, ESPN, a country-music video channel—Chris Alvarez's words still echoing. Hard to *not* see the images through that acerbic filter. Worse than himself.

He tuned it out, thought about Rye Rossert.

Trying to scare him off? From what—something concrete or just as a matter of course? Finding a possible answer in Rossert's story about growing up in East Bakersfield: the idea that if you spent your whole life battling, you saw everyone and everything as a potential opponent. Standard Operating Procedure. Good business. That's for nothing, now start something.

And speaking of business . . . *Some more flexible things,* Rossert had said. *As they become available.*

*Not too* many possibilities there.

Bottom line on the Farley Kroft thing: Lute enlists Rossert's help, Rossert—who knows somebody— agrees. Only natural he might resent somebody Lute hires on the spur of the moment when his own guy doesn't deliver. File under tempest in a teapot.

At eight-thirty, he snapped off the light and lay there in the dark, beat and letting it all float: raw throb of the band last night; Don Lee Whitney moving ghostlike toward the door and disappearing outside; the cocktail waitress, grim-lipped and accusatory. Jenelle Lockhart's hand moving to the worn silver squash blossom.

Shattered now into starburst.

"Mr. Hardesty?"

"Lemme think." Still fumbling with the phone.

"Did I wake you? Of course I did. I'm sorry, I knew I shouldn't have called this late."

Nine-forty by the clock radio.

"Jenelle Lockhart," she added. "And it's nothing that can't wait."

He raised up, felt something kick in, a thermostat. "Hi. You think of something else?"

"I just—wanted to apologize."

"Apologize for what?"

"For today. For being abrupt and dismissive. It bothered me after you left, and I wanted you to know."

"And that's why you called?" Rubbing his face.

"You were only doing your job."

"Believe me, Ms. Lockhart—"

"Jenelle, please."

"I've been dismissed by experts—you're not even among the top hundred." He waited. "But thanks."

"Did you find him?"

"Frankly, I'm having a hard time finding two people who agree on who Doc Whitney *is*, let alone where. You want to tell me your version, I'd be inclined to give it more weight."

"So you could find him more readily."

"Maybe I'm more curious about him than I let on." He paused to let that sink in.

"You want some advice?" she finally asked.

"If it's from you."

"Put them all together—everything they told you—and shake the bag. Whatever you pull out is what he is at any given moment. Does that make sense?"

"As much as anything right now."

"Because that's the only way I can explain it."

With that, she said good night and hung up the phone.

The radio came on at one-thirty, his insurance wake-up call ten minutes later while he was in the bathroom. Having to dash out to grab it. Blearily he showered, dressed in jeans and denim work shirt, desert boots, light windbreaker over his shoulder rig. At two-fifteen, he was easing the rental out onto empty Truxtun, the list he'd made on the seat beside him. Overhead, the shell of a moon haloed by a layer of thin clouds, planets, and some brighter stars competing with the city's glow.

The air smelled of damp grass and late spring and had a nip to it. He was glad he had the jacket.

The first stop was an all-night café pouring a black substance that tasted the way mimeographs used to smell, even with cream and sugar added. Better than nothing, but only just—the nothing being what came of showing staffers the photo of Doc Whitney.

One down.

The next four were twenty-four-hour spots along and below Highway 99, still pulsing with amber-lit trucks, speedboats in a dark, raised canal. His questions brought varying responses, but the same result: shakes of the head, handing back of the photo. So far no one even recognizing the image, though in fairness, if the waitresses topped twenty-five, he'd have been surprised. At least the various interpretations of the word "coffee" was an education.

He hit a couple of truck stops next, one pink-clad waitress with big hair and a pleasant if weary smile hesitating—backing off when nobody else bought in. More nothing at two others followed, older places with what must have been the original vinyl, his watch coming up on three-fifteen. Accelerating the pace as the caffeine went to work, he angled away from the freeway and crossed off two real joints in which he nearly had to wake people to show them the picture, ask his questions before heading out.

The glamorous life of a PI.

Bound to get Kari's libido twanging. Which brought a smile—still getting used to that kind of reaction, but hardly complaining.

Cruising the deserted streets, he hit Edison again, and

Cheri's—shuttered and dark now, Wil wondering if Crash Alvarez and the Gnash Ramblers had had a big night. From the needle tracks, how many big nights Crash had left in him. He followed the street's southeast run through increasingly sparse and dismal to his next stop—taking a moment to size it up before pulling in, this big lit-up oasis. Restaurant and motel, acres of parked and idling big-rigs, their collective throb like the purr from a pride of mechanized lions. New arrivals took on fuel; others awaited service or a scale. For every truck leaving the lot, there seemed to be another pulling in.

After a trip to the restaurant's washroom, he eased into a booth, looked around: tans and greens with non-fluorescent lighting. Comfortable. Which probably explained the number of patrons at this hour, at least compared to his other stops. Center section offering privacy, tables, and a few more booths with window seating; bar and jukebox visible through an arched entryway.

"Decaf," he said to the waitress approaching with two pots and *Vicky* on her tag; waiting until she'd poured to show her the photo, ask his standard questions.

She shook her head. "Maybe Dani knows. I'm kind of new."

"Danny. Which one would he be?"

"*Danielle*," the girl corrected. "Soon as she gets a minute, I'll tell her. You want something to eat?"

Why not? he thought, surprisingly hungry—scrambled eggs and bacon, a stack of buckwheats, surprised at how quickly the kitchen turned them out. He was about halfway through the stack when she came over to the table. She was about twenty-three, blond hair and nose freckles, dusting of them on her hands and arms. *Danielle* reminding him of another girl named Holly Pfeiffer. Someone he'd always have feelings for— maybe someday even understand their meaning.

"Vicky said you wanted me to look at a photograph?"

Wil handed her the snapshot. As she took it, he said, "I'm hoping you might have seen this man in here. Alone or with someone else. Guy about the same age, long hair in a ponytail?"

"No," she said far too quickly, her eyes avoiding his.

He gave her his card. "Does that mean *no* you haven't seen him or *no* you won't help me?"

"Just . . . no. No I haven't seen him. Now, if you'll excuse me—"

"Dani, I'm not a cop, and I'm not out to hurt anyone. I'm just trying to find him. Talk to him."

"I still can't help you." Not meeting his eyes even now.

"Might save him some grief."

She looked at him now, a coldness there—or was it anger? "Is there anything else? Because I really have to go."

"No, that's it." Adding that he'd make a point of asking whenever he was in. That he really liked it there. In her section. "Find something you like, you stick with it—right?"

"Why are you doing this?"

"Because I think he's worth it, Dani." Tapping the photo before putting it back in his pocket.

And still she made no eye contact.

He thanked her, laid down a twenty—more than enough to cover the food. Walking through the restaurant and out into diesel throb, false dawn beginning to lighten the eastern horizon, he could see her through the windows. At least she was looking at his card.

*That's it—think about it.*

He stopped in the grocery store, flashed the picture to a couple of bored clerks, truckers ringing up candy bars and pepper sticks, getting the same blank looks from all of them. Drawing it out, he bought raisin cookies and trail mix, a thing of Tic-Tacs he opened. He was almost to the S-10 when he heard her voice behind him.

"Excuse me . . . Mr. Hardesty?"

He turned, offered her one.

"No, thank you." Then, "The long-haired man you were talking about. I . . . might have seen him."

"When, Dani?"

Obviously she'd thought about it, because there was no hesitation. "Ten days ago."

"I see. They were together, weren't they?"

This time there was hesitation, a look like *What am I doing?*

"How do I know you aren't with *them*?"

"Sorry, you just lost me."

"Them. The guys who beat him up."

"Who beat him up—when?"

She sighed. *I gotta tell somebody* there now.

"How about if we talk in the truck?" Wil said.

Her eyes went to it, back to him.

"Leave the door open, if you like." He unlocked the S-10, opened her door, went around to his side, and sat there, hands on the wheel. He watched her follow and sit gingerly, one foot in, one outside.

"Only a few minutes left on my break," she said.

"Thanks for talking to me at all."

She went through it then: how a short man and a taller one had come in and asked about the guy in the picture, this guy nice—quiet and polite—always ordering the same thing; good to her tipwise. Short and tall running him down in the lots, hurting him so he could hardly stand. About her promising him no cops, phoning the number he'd written down on a napkin. Helping him to the spot where she'd seen the long-haired man pick him up and drive away.

"Short and tall—can you describe them?"

"The short one had really wide shoulders. The tall one had a buzz cut. He's the one who showed me the badge."

"Badge—you remember what authority?"

"I didn't get much of a look. But no cop would do what he did. At least the kind who come in here."

*Dani one, thugs zero.* "Has either one been back in?"

She shook her head. "He's that singer, isn't he—the one they beat up?"

"Makes you say that?"

"Before they went after him, the short guy played a song on the box: "Truck Stop Angel," one of my favorites. It's why he left. Afterward, I heard the cook talking about the guy who wrote it—what he did."

Which meant they knew who Doc was.

"Is that why they wanted to hurt him?"

"I don't know, Dani."

"I have to go." She got out of the truck, leaned back in, one arm on the roof for support. "He couldn't have done those things—not him. Working with people, you get a sense." She was looking directly at him now. "You don't believe he did, do you?"

Wil parked the pickup under an elm tree just down from a used-equipment yard. Ten in the morning, a block up Edison Highway, he could see the Cheri's sign, the front entrance and narrow drive that led back into the trailer park. Before leaving, he'd called the club and left a message with the bartender for Chris Alvarez:

*Don't try to contact. Just get here, D.*

Hoping for a number of things to break right—or just not wrong. Mostly that Alvarez would simply take the message at face value.

He scanned the street again. Noise seemed as much part of the day as sun and haze: big-rigs, service vehicles, the daily pulse of cars, vans, SUVs, pickups—everywhere pickups. Occasionally, as if to justify the splay of railroad tracks across the highway, graffiti'd freight cars rumbled and creaked toward the yards.

Despite the vehicles, not many drivers wound up as foot traffic: a few Mexican women with strollers and serious-eyed kids in tow, leather-skinned day laborers loading up on water and pop at a gang-tagged grocery store, some patrons of the equipment yard down from there.

Wil resettled the roll-brim hat he'd purchased at the store—an exhausted shift worker grabbing a few winks behind the wheel, a husband in the doghouse sleeping off a few too many. Comfort zone to anyone watching: the idea, at least.

Eleven came and went, then noon—the urge to close his eyes nearly overpowering, the day already feeling like ninety. Shifting positions helped, and sparing use of the radio. But not much.

He pulled the Doc Whitney cassette out of the glove box: high-contrast black-and-white, long dark hair, and leather vest. The Wayfarers, of course. *Alias Doc Whitney.*

Removing the cellophane wrap from the cassette, he snuck a peek at the liner notes, the tiny type defying him on the lyrics, readable enough to make out Alvarez among the credits: *guitar, drums, and harmonica.* Nearly missing Crash himself pulling out of the driveway in the dented Valiant—peering intently ahead as he passed by the S-10.

Wil started the engine, flipped a U north onto Edison. Giving the red car a wide berth, he held to the slow lane, followed Alvarez into two right turns, the last an artery heading toward the foothills. For a moment Wil thought raceway, but the Valiant tooled past it, kept going east on 178.

Kern River Canyon.

By now the grasses had lost their soft green, the canyon entrance standing out in high relief against the yellow. Suddenly whitewater was right next to him on one side, blocky fractured granite rising from the road on the other. Hundreds of feet up, hawks circled below the crest. Shadows made it feel almost like morning.

The road itself was now in a narrow twisting dance with the river. Petite wildflowers graced the hillsides and turnouts; trees showing bright green hugged the bends, some actually standing in the spring runoff. Austere-looking campgrounds came and went. Sequoia National Forest signs, oaks and pale-blooming elderberry, glossy bay leaves bent with sunlight.

Keeping the Valiant in view, Wil slipped the *Alias* cassette into the slot, adjusted the base and treble around the opening riff—followed by a voice that reminded him alternately of Dwight Yoakam and Bruce Springsteen. In rare form.

He listened.

Gray-green pines began appearing. The road left the river, never long out of sight—here a rush of silver, there dark and subdued as though emerging from sleep. Rivulets tracked rock walls to merge with the stream; massive boulders created roiling pools and spillways, smaller ones riffles where a few fishermen stood. Not far from a sign indicating the Kern had claimed 191 lives since 1968.

Pretty soon 178 began to climb and snake, taking care of one problem while creating another. Though Wil saw no roads, there was always the chance of a quick turnoff ending the tail. He tightened the distance, crossed his fingers. But there was the Valiant emerging into a straighter stretch, and he let the gap lengthen again.

And listened.

They crossed the river. Fire had traversed a section, and the blackened trunks of burned trees lifted off the char as though still trying to escape the heat. The highway recrossed then, and signs began appearing—Bodfish and Lake Isabella, the old county seat of Havilah.

Another announcing they were leaving the national forest.

Thirty-five minutes after entering.

Minutes before the Valiant slowed and made a hard right.

Wil approached the paved road with caution, saw it turned to gravel a short way in, white dust still twisting in the shafts of sunlight. He followed—around the graveled curve, into half a dozen more, Alvarez obviously unaware that anyone was behind him.

The tape ended. The pines grew denser and thicker-trunked, the road dropping into a densely treed valley before climbing out of sight on the other side. Dust, no-dust: Wil took the dust fork into the valley and up the southside rise, where he reconnoitered from a ridge thick with manzanita.

Below, in front of a two-story cabin lifted from a 1938 Camp Curry postcard—log siding, green tin roof, mustard porch with lodgepole supports—was the red Valiant, dust still hovering around it. And Chris Alvarez lifting out a grocery bag and a lever-action rifle, heading up the steps. Knocking, hesitating briefly before going in.

Wil eased the S-10 down the slope in neutral, left it angled across the road with the emergency brake on. He approached the cabin, listened for sounds inside, then stepped up on the porch and knocked.

"Chris? Wil Hardesty."

No answer: buzz of insects, rustle of cottonwood beside the porch, the squawk of jays out back. Warm air smelling of pines and a creek that traversed the road beyond the truck. Wil backed off the steps, glanced inside the Valiant, then up at the second-floor windows, draped with heavy green material—like the ones downstairs.

*"Hello? . . ."*

Slight billow at a lower window, sound of the latch, the door opened a crack: Chris Alvarez—frayed cutoffs, black-and-orange Giants jersey, worn high-tops with the laces undone—standing there looking at him.

"What's the fucking idea?" Alvarez said.

"That was me who left the message with the bartender."

"I don't know what you're talking about."

Wil shrugged. "Not hard to check it out."

"The bartender's a friend of mine—forget it."

"Look, one way or another, I have to talk to Whitney."

"So find him and talk to him."

He rested a foot on the bottom step. "You always in the habit of knocking on your own front door?"

"Have a nice trip back."

"Long way," Wil said. "Mind some water for the road?"

Alvarez stepped out onto the porch. "Yes, goddammit, I mind. Find a gas station. Better yet, stick your head in the river."

The cottonwood rustled again; a crested jay landed in it and began to complain.

"Everyone's a critic. You ever notice that?"

"Are you going to leave or do I call the sheriff?"

"That's a hell of a tape," Wil said. "I played it on the way up."

"Good for you."

"How you feel about conspiracy—aiding and abetting?"

"*Aiding and abetting what?*"

"Whatever Doc decides he's going to do to some people without factoring in what might happen to you."

"You're out of your mind."

"Am I?"

The jay tried the peak of the house, then gave up and

flew off. Alvarez resembled a man listening to inner voices. "All right," he said finally. "I'll get your damn water." He backed inside, the door easing shut behind him.

Wil let a second pass, then was up and through the door, into comparative darkness—out on a limb, tactically speaking. Eyes fighting the gloom, he could only sense the presence behind him. Grabbing a fistful of hair, yanking his head back so as to lay the tip of a blade alongside his jugular.

*"Don't hear too well, do you?"*

Harsher, perhaps, but recognizable—as if Doc Whitney had come back into the studio after a long cigarette break. Despite the pain in his scalp, the watering of his eyes, weird-feeling after hearing the voice on the tape.

"If you say so . . ."

The hand bent him back until he was on his knees.

"You also got a mouth problem."

"Look at the bright side," Wil managed. "You're the one with the shank."

"Who are you?"

Wil told him, felt the blade stay put, Alvarez's hands discover the .45, unsnap and pull it out of its holster.

"Easy with that."

"No threat, huh?"

"It's the guy I was telling you about, Doc."

Wil heard Alvarez lever a round into the rifle, felt a gradual release of the pressure until Doc Whitney pushed off, his other hand gripping a box knife with a taped grip.

"One time and one time only," he said. "I am through being fucked with." Suddenly he drove a boot into Wil's back, pitching him forward onto his face, Wil balling up to protect himself from further damage.

But none came.

*"You hear me?"*

Wil nodded, used the moment, and saw him: leaning on a high-back chair, his face drained of color. Little resemblance to the jacket photo. This Doc Whitney seemed less tall, more muscular under black jeans and fitted tee, the square-toed boots. He reminded Wil of what James Dean might have matured into. Dark hair showing some gray. A face you might call handsome without the hard miles, the obvious pain. Flecked green eyes seeming to look through Wil and into territory he'd seen before on patients sitting in front of military-hospital windows.

"All right if I get up now?"

"Long as you do it slow."

Wil complied, eyes taking in the bulge under the T-shirt. "Broke some, did they?"

Doc glanced at him, then out the kitchen window, where thin curtains admitted what light there was to a main room smelling of old furniture and cigarette smoke. "Bruised, busted, what's the difference? The hell you know about it?"

"The waitress," Alvarez volunteered. "I knew she'd blow it."

"She didn't blow anything," Wil said. "And point that thing somewhere else." Waiting until Alvarez set the rifle down before shifting back to Doc. "She's concerned about you."

"Yeah, well. It'll take more than that."

"You know who the two guys were?"

The green eyes flashed. "You just jump right in, don't you?"

"I'm not the enemy here, Doc. Why don't you give the prison tough-guy act a rest."

"Fuck this," Alvarez huffed. "We don't have to talk to him. He's nothing."

"Don't confuse loyalty with sound advice." Wil

looked at Alvarez. "And I'm afraid 'we' doesn't apply here."

"Just my house you busted into."

"I wonder why . . ."

Doc Whitney turned to Alvarez. "Don't get me wrong, but aren't you due back for a gig anyway?"

Alvarez pulled the band off his hair, reponied it with a flip. "Hey, it's your party. Play it how you want. I just don't like getting screwed by a guy who—"

"I know, Crash. You want me to leave, you call it. No hard feelings."

"Ah, balls. Just take care of yourself, that's all I'm saying."

He walked out and banged the door. Wil could hear the Valiant start up and throw dirt around before the engine screamed over the rise, grew fainter, and disappeared altogether. Out back the jays started up again.

"Mind if I get that water?"

"Whatever moves it down the road."

"*Alias Doc Whitney*," Wil said from the kitchen. "Some piece of work."

"Ancient history."

He came back holding a faded and scorched plastic mug; took another gulp. "Reminded me of *Hotel California*—that kind of impact. My loss that I only just heard it."

"You gonna say what you came here to say?"

" 'Truck Stop Angel' is one of Dani's favorites."

"Yeah? Next time you see her, tell her it's about cocaine. That I wrote it and the rest stoned out of my mind or drunk as hell."

"Bullcrap."

"You're not careful, you're going to run out of luck here."

Wil drained the mug. "Okay. Your way for now. Lute

DeVillbis hired me to tell you you're barking up the wrong tree."

"*Lute DeVillbis . . .*"

"Over what happened to your father. Says he had nothing to do with him being in that oil sump."

"I don't believe this shit."

"He's afraid you're going to do something to him or Cole before he can clear things up. He wants to tell you in person."

Doc just looked at him as he went on.

"My take is he's more worried about Cole. You've been seen at the raceway and his clubs. I saw you myself at Redtail's. If something happens, it won't exactly be a mystery as to who did it."

Derisive snort. "I'm sure he'd rather I live in Wyoming. I'm sure they all would."

Wil put the mug back in the kitchen. "Mind a question? Why did you come back?"

"None of your damn business."

"True. Can I tell DeVillbis you'll talk to him?"

"Just say I wish him and his son all they have coming to them. On second thought, make it 'everything they deserve.' "

"Why not just defuse a situation before it gets out of control?"

Doc thought a moment. "You ever been to prison?"

"A few times to visit."

"It's an education—picture hyenas having total control over your life. Now try it when one of 'em's the voice in your own head." His eyes seemed to defocus. "Lot like dying without the death."

Bookstore Cedrick came to mind, his hand clutching the big knife: *Not going back.* "Then why risk it? You got a beef, let the law handle it."

"Swell idea. You even say it like you mean it." He bent slightly and blew out a breath, looked pale.

"Revenge is no light in the forest."

"I don't recall using that word."

"All I can do is relay it to my client."

Doc's smile was more grimace than grin. "*Client*—there's a nice word for ol' Lute. Nice and clean. Think I'd make sure the check clears before I left town, though."

"You want to expand on that?"

"No, thanks. I'm going to take one of Crash's little pills and lie down. Don't say it hasn't been real."

"The guys who worked you over. Was one of them named Farley?"

"I have no idea." He glanced at Wil. "Why?"

"Because Farley was hired by a guy named Rossert."

"Rye Rossert?"

"That's my understanding. He has a heavy named Raul Garza working for him, too."

"Garza I don't know. But if you're in with Rye Rossert and Lute DeVillbis, you might as well give it up and go back where you came from."

"I'm not in with anybody," Wil said. "I told you what I agreed to do."

"Yeah, so you did." Doc rose gingerly, unlatched the door, and pulled it back. He stepped aside to let Wil pass. "You may mean well. You may even be good at what you do. But trust me—you don't know shit here."

Wil didn't answer. He resnugged the .45 and was almost to the open door when he caught a flash of something up on the ridge, and then the first shot blew a good-sized piece out of the door frame and Doc Whitney back into the room.

# TEN

"You hit?"

He was trying to shut the door from prone, two more shots having splintered holes in the log siding now, Doc Whitney somewhere behind him—on the floor beside the couch, Wil thought.

*"Son of a bitch, you set me up."*

Wil managed to kick the door closed, look back into the room, illuminated now by three dust-laden shafts of light.

"Are you hit?"

"No, but *you're* dead."

"Let's hope not. I'm going to see if I can outflank him."

Not waiting for a reply, he crawled to the kitchen, unlatched the back door, swung it open. Jerked back and waited: thirty seconds, sixty . . . Down concrete steps onto dirt, around the corner of the house in a crouch, to the cottonwood tree without drawing fire yet. None since the three.

*So far, so good.*

He scanned the ridge for movement, saw nothing at first . . . in a moment, a flash of glass or metal. Too distant for the .45. He drew the gun and let off some rounds anyway, trying to throw a scare—at least cover his charge. He was up and running—boulder at the base of the slope—when he heard an engine roar to life, the gruff burr of tires on hardpack. Then silence.

Wil eased out from behind the rock and over to the S-10, got it going up the hill. This side of the turnout, he approached on foot and scanned for signs of the shooter, seeing only lingering dust, a peel-out mark with a slight berm in it. No footprints. And among the blooming manzanita bushes where he figured whoever it was had locked down on them: nothing . . . nothing . . . nothing . . . Small birds and insects cruising the bell-like clusters, shed snakeskin and some chipmunk burrows, couple of squirrels darting up a tree.

Nothing . . . nothing . . . glint of metal.

A brass rifle casing.

Wrapping it in his handkerchief, he put it in his pocket, thinking amateur—sloppy pro at the outside. That nobody very good would leave one like that. Somebody in a hurry to make a point or without a plan. Both perhaps.

He got back in the truck, descended the hill, and stepped up on the porch where Doc Whitney waited— door open behind him, foot-long piece of the frame missing. Splinters still in his hair.

"Looks like it was just the one—"

The punch caught him high on the shoulder—just as he saw it coming and flinched to defend himself. Still, it had enough behind it and he was enough off balance to send him off the porch. Feeling the nerves jump as Doc stood there above him, fists clenched and bent at the waist, his breath coming in short gasps.

"*Get out of here before I kick your damn teeth in.*"

Wil brushed dirt off as he stood. "With what—your telegraphic left and ribs like that?"

"You're about to find out."

"Don't be a fish, Doc. If this guy knows you're here,

how long before he's back with the other one? What do you do then?"

"Deal with it."

"I know, kick ass and take names." He flexed the shoulder. "Last call—get your stuff and throw it in the truck."

"Wouldn't you like that."

"Maybe you favor your chances here at the Alamo, but I don't." He walked to the S-10, turned the key through the open window. "You've got three minutes."

Doc Whitney glared—a wolf at bay—then appeared to sag. He turned and went inside. Three minutes later he emerged with a weathered canvas duffel he tossed into the truck bed. After locking the front door, he got in and snugged down a *Kenworth Diesel* hat as Wil levered the pickup into gear and bounced it up the rise.

They hit the main road without speaking—passed the sign about the Kern claiming 191 lives, the fishermen, down to almost river level, late-afternoon sun flaring off the riffles and bathing the boulders in light and shadow. Hawks still riding the updrafts a thousand feet up.

"Nice cabin," Wil finally said. "Hard to guess Crash would own it from where he lives in town."

"Came to him in a trust when his folks died. Otherwise forget it. And Cole used to run whores in that trailer."

Wil reached into his pocket. "Whoever shot at us left this," he said.

Doc picked it out of his hand. "What about fingerprints?"

"Moot point. Wouldn't mean anything away from the scene."

"Figured I wouldn't be making a complaint, huh?"

"Something like that," Wil said. "Got a take on the caliber?"

Doc scrutinized it more carefully. "Thirty-aught. Mushroom tips from the holes in the siding."

"What I was thinking, too." Wil kneaded his shoulder.

A minute passed, then: "Stupid to swing at you back there.

"If that's an apology, you're lucky I liked your album."

Doc Whitney was silent, his eyes on the river.

Wil said, "You interested in making music again?"

"No. Maybe. I don't know."

"The way I feel about half the time."

"One thing's sure. Thinking about doing it sober scares the piss out of me."

Wil nodded. "I know that one, too."

Nothing.

"Be a loss if you didn't," he added.

"Right. Talk to me about loss."

*Dev on his birthday board, ripping toward the pickets: "Waaatch mee, Daad." A slow-motion horror film without end.*

He took a turn too high and fast, causing the tires to squeal, duffel to thunk against the side of the bed, Doc against the door.

"Damn—trying to put us in the river?"

He eased up. "Sorry."

"You remind me of this shrink up at Folsom, a guy named Byrd. Relentless. Always trying to draw me out or climb inside."

"My mistake, obviously."

A couple of miles later, Doc thumbed the visor back on his forehead. "Look, I'd be lying if I said I didn't think about it." Then, "What am I talking about? Bad enough trying to write what they play these days."

"So don't. Turn it around."

"Easy for you to say."

"Always is—so what?"

He didn't answer. Wil slowed for a turn. "There's a song on the album: 'Way Beyond Me.' "

"What about it?"

"Thought it might be about your father."

Doc started to say something, hesitated, thought better of it. "Might be about a lot of things. I don't recall."

"Just blow it off, huh?"

"What do you know about my father?"

"Not much. He left without saying good-bye, was into a lot of people when he did."

"DeVillbis tell you that, or did Rossert?"

Wil glanced over at him. "Rossert knew him?"

"You ever think of giving it a rest? What do you care, anyway?"

"Maybe I just hate seeing you shine a gift I'd give my right arm to have. That's all. Like it was less than nothing."

"You're something, you know that?"

They passed the pumping station at the mouth of the canyon: river channel widening, valley spreading out in a roll of bent yellow mesas. Incongruous orange groves at the base of a slope, haze permitting no sense of the expanse beyond it.

"So where *are* you from?"

"No place you've heard of."

Doc grinned. "Don't like the shoe on the other foot, huh?"

Wil let out a breath. "La Conchita—little beach community between Ventura and Santa Barbara. Near the Rincon."

"Come to think of it, you look like a surfer."

Wil said nothing.

"You're right," Doc went on. "I never heard of it. But I know the area. Played the County Bowl once."

"Nice spot."

"Not bad acoustics, either. How'd you get mixed up with DeVillbis?"

Wil passed a slower-moving RV, decided *why not?*, and started into it. Mostly the places he'd been trying to find him; some of the people he'd talked to as well.

"I can only guess what they had to say." Doc smiling grimly.

"Tell me again. You have no idea about who the two guys were?"

"That's what I said."

"And they never let on why they were doing it?"

"No."

Wil looked straight ahead.

Doc's knee began to bounce; he tossed the hat on the seat.

"Shit. One had brass knucks, the other had a baton in his belt. Make a long story short, they beat the crap out of me. Or maybe you hadn't noticed."

"But they never hit you in the face or head."

"Small favors."

"You don't find that curious?"

"Maybe you should ask my body that question— check out the bruises."

Wil looked at him, then straight ahead. "You're right. What for?"

"What the hell do you want from me?" Doc said with heat. "Like I'm your new mission in life? I'm not the one working for Lute DeVillbis. I'm not the one kissing Rye Rossert's ass."

"So you said. Without explanation."

"Fuck it. Water under the dam."

"So I can tell DeVillbis that? He doesn't have to circle the wagons?"

"I say let crooks worry about what they worry about. If the man's got a guilty conscience, I'd be the last to keep him from it."

Passing the raceway now, some minor activity going on in the pits. "What about Cole?"

"Blood's thicker than water. You figure it out."

"That's first rate, Doc, real jailhouse con. Ought to take you a long way." Houses were appearing, and an increase in traffic, Wil feeling the kind of day they'd had down there. He reached over and flipped on the air conditioner.

"Speaking of which, where do you want me to drop you? Sad as I am at the prospect."

Doc's smile was membrane thin, ice brittle. "No use for me anymore, huh? Greyhound Bus depot—18th and F." A beat went by, white oleanders and trucks going the other way as 178 became freeway. "So you won't have to lie about where I've gone."

Wil pulled up to a long building with plate-glass windows and flat awnings, stab of late sun angling in despite them. Doc got out, resettled the hat, pulled it low against the glare.

"Thanks for the lift."

"Don't mention it."

He seemed to hesitate about something. "That song you asked about? I wrote it for my daughter. Most beautiful thing I'd ever seen till the second one was born. Now be smart and get the fuck out of here."

Doc Whitney muscled the duffel bag out of the truck bed and, like a character out of Steinbeck, headed upstream with it over his shoulder into a group of lost-looking arrivals in blue jeans, straw hats, and checkered shirts.

Lute DeVillbis was not happy.

"Lemme get this straight," he said. "You just let him go?"

They were sitting in his corner office. Polished wood gleamed softly in the track lighting, as did his capless head, the black stone on his bolo tie. An oil-derrick belt buckle cinched poplin suit pants to a white shirt.

A secretary poked her head in, announced that she was leaving. He'd be the last one on the floor.

"I'll lock up. You worry about that contract." He waited until she'd left then started in again.

"I can't believe you just *let* him go." Even the sun freckles on his bald spot looked agitated.

"Kidnapping is not highly regarded in some circles."

"Neither is a violent man stalking with the intent to injure—or worse. Couldn't you have called me? Had Cole and I meet you somewhere?"

Wil crossed a desert boot over his knee. "To what end?"

DeVillbis looked at him. "You ask me that?"

"Not the way you say it, no."

"I'm determined to end this threat. I thought you understood that."

Wil nodded. "Meaning I should have brought him to you draped over the hood of my truck."

"Don't think it hadn't occurred to me," he said, loosening the bolo and his top shirt button. "Frankly, I'm surprised it didn't occur to you, considering what's at stake and the way you handled those two jokers. Guess I was wrong about you, after all."

Wil said, "Have you considered that he actually might have left town? Because for all I know, that's what he did."

"I obviously failed to impress you with Doc Whitney's true nature."

"But you *are* clear on his response to your message?" Wil was getting tired of this. His shoulder ached where Doc had hit him, he was hungry, and the lack of sleep was catching up.

DeVillbis opened a drawer, pulled out the silver flask; not bothering to offer any, he poured three fingers into a water glass and tossed it off. "I'm clear. The mystery is why you aren't."

"I get it now. His head on a pike."

"You know, I really don't like your tone."

"Drawn and quartered? Dragged behind a chariot?"

DeVillbis did not smile. "Mr. Hardesty, whatever the circumstances behind this failure, your services are no longer required. I suggest you send me a statement while I'm still feeling charitable."

"Done," Wil said, getting to his feet. Across the street and a floor down, a bank of reflective windows shagged the sun's declining rays and fired them off a wall mirror.

"Before I go, have you seen Cole this afternoon?"

"Why the question?"

"Just curious. Do you know if he likes to hunt?"

"I fail to see the relevance."

"What about Farley? Anybody heard from him yet?"

"No. And I understand you talked to Rye Rossert about more than just Farley. Considerably more, in fact."

"Guy's a regular Chatty Cathy," Wil said. "And Raul Garza would not shut up. I think they've got a real problem there."

DeVillbis emptied the flask into the glass. "I suggest it's your attitude that's the problem, Mr. Hardesty, and beyond that, your nerve. Also that asking me for a recommendation would be a waste of time." He tossed the flask into the drawer and banged it shut. "Is *that* understood?"

Before Wil went back to the hotel, he drove out to the raceway, asked one of the pit people if Cole DeVillbis had been around. Earlier in the day, a man said, not remembering quite when. Avoiding his eyes at the name, Wil noted. Or maybe it was just him.

He found a phone up near the concessions and tried Cheri's first, heard Cole would likely be at Redtail's tonight, and drove there, finding a place just up from the parking lot around back. Among the few cars and pickups under a split-fixture floodlight above the door was the Dooley he'd seen at the raceway, the plate confirming it: COLE 1.

He knelt at the right rear flank, the black paint fresh out of a polish ad, the outer chrome wheel shiny enough to cast his image. But when he ran his fingers inside the rear bumper, they came back muddy, gritty, wet. And the dual wheel setup could have made the peel-out mark he'd seen up on the ridge.

Nothing an evidence tech would swear to in court.

He looked inside, little visible through the tinted glass except for shapes. Like the tip of something flat poking out from behind the rear seat. The flashing red alarm diode on the dash gave him an idea. He flipped the locked door handle a couple of times.

Immediately the alarm sounded.

Wil retreated to the rental, watched as Cole came out and deactivated it. Giving it ten minutes after he'd gone back inside, Wil did the same thing. And the same thing happened with Cole, though this time he looked around the lot before heading inside.

After the fourth time, Wil saw him swear, yank open the driver's side, reach under the dash to fiddle with something before slamming the door shut. And this time when Wil returned, the diode no longer flashed.

He approached the rear door to the club, cracked it and looked inside, saw Cole spelling the bartender. Talking with a couple of guys in hats—about racing from the way he was gesturing with his hands. Empty tables and stage, TV belting a video anthem about Independence Day in which Wil had found hope the night before, players lining up shots in the poolroom. And in a corner with Raul Garza, it looked like—not easy from his angle and the dim interior—Tommy What's-His-

Name, Cole's mechanic from the track. No one else appearing ready to leave.

Letting the door ease shut, Wil dipped into his pocket, uncapped the felt-tip-pen casing, and withdrew a pick he sometimes had luck with, began probing the Dooley's passenger-side lock. A minute went by . . . two . . . *Damn!*

He was about to try the driver's side, considerably riskier as it faced the exit, when the lock gave and he was inside—pulling out a tooled-leather gun case from behind the seat. Hustling it back to the Chevy.

It was a Winchester Model 70 with a Tasco Riflescope—about $1,500 worth of gun if he had it figured right—and from the smell, fired recently. Two rounds left in a magazine that normally held five. More important, however, were the spent casings that fell out into his hand when he shook the case.

He put on his readers, compared the casings to the one in his pocket. Even the strike marks looked identical.

He thought about it: Cole hearing from the Cheri's bartender about the note Wil had left for Alvarez, knowing about the cabin because he knew Crash well, putting two and two together. Seeable—bettable, in fact. Enough to think about what to do about it.

Molotov the truck? Torch the cars on either side of the Dooley? Not too sociable, he agreed with himself. Jump Cole and beat on him? Get jumped by the bouncers and wind up getting thrashed? Not too bright—dumb *and* unhealthy.

He wiped down the gun and scope, zipped them back inside the leather case, replaced it in the Dooley. Then he took the spent cartridges, rubbed any prints off he might have added, and left them on the driver's seat where Cole couldn't miss them. Two bottle-shaped shiners with a space in between for the third—his.

Lock and load that one, asshole.

He was back at the hotel, wishing he could be there when Cole found them—sweat beginning to bead up, looking around to see who was watching—when Kari called to tell him that Brian had been arrested for getting drunk with some pals and stealing a car.

"I think I'm going crazy. Thank God nobody was hurt. Thank God *he* wasn't hurt."

They were seated at her chrome-and-vinyl dinette set, blowing on coffees he'd stopped for a couple of blocks from her house in Brea. Nine in the morning, Wil having left Bakersfield just after six—through L.A.'s normally congested lower tract like pork through a goose for some reason. Wanting to come down that night, but Kari saying no, figuring it might become an issue later with Brian or his father or somebody. You never knew these days.

Not that there was anything he could do.

So he'd ordered up room service and waited . . . cleared up his tab and waited . . . went to bed and waited. Listening now as she went through it again: Brian was being released from detention today and was being picked up by his father at the boy's request.

Assuming everything went according to plan.

"So what do you do in the meantime?"

She looked up from her coffee. "Station's giving me family emergency, but that won't last. There's too much to do, and I need the work."

"I'm sorry, Kari."

"Telling me."

"Does he just not want to come home?"

She nodded, put a hand to her eyes, Wil covering her other hand with his.

"He's how old—*fourteen*?"

"Fifteen next week." Red still rimmed her eyes, and

she dabbed at them with the tissue. "He's due back in court in three months. Meantime they're assigning a pre-trial supervisor. But the juvenile system is such a mess—we did a series on it. Regular factory for little criminals."

"This his first brush?"

She shook her head. "We've had some truancy problems. Never anything like this."

"He have a lawyer?"

"His father got him one. That's why Brian's going to live with them. Theoretically."

"But you know better."

"Scott never disciplines, and Brian knows it. Mr. Best Friend."

She glanced at the photo plastic-fruited to the refrigerator: a blond surfer kid with intelligent eyes. Kari's cheekbones evident in the mix.

"Has to hurt." Wil sipped coffee.

"He won't see me, won't talk to me on the phone. I feel myself losing him."

"He's embarrassed. With his father, there's a whole different standard."

She nodded again. "Wait'll he sees juvenile court."

Wil let a moment pass. "Seeing as how all you have to do today is worry, how'd you like to do it at the beach?"

"I don't think so. What if he calls or something?"

"You can check the machine. No law against returning them from there."

"Seems like I should be here."

"Have you back in forty minutes if you really can't stand it."

She looked at the photograph.

"Take it with you," he said. "We'll buy it a corn dog."

On the way to Balboa, he played her the *Alias* tape, brought her up to speed on Doc Whitney, how all that had turned out. One more day in the life. Another happy customer.

Hearing the music helped. It also gave Wil a deeper cut at the lyrics—things he'd missed, subtleties and shadings, how strong they really were. Then they were breaking out of inland smog into breeze and blue sky, bluer ocean with whitecaps, Kari taking it all in.

"Is that what you meant about the music you and your dad listened to?"

"Yeah. Except it's better."

"Something to restore the balance a little."

"Assuming something could do that."

"Yes—assuming that."

He smiled at her. "Think you might be onto something there?"

She smiled back, squeezed his hand.

They walked the piers, took the ferry across to the island, and strolled about looking at houses and sailboats. They had lunch at the Crab Cooker, bought Brian a T-shirt at one of the surf shops. Watching the action at The Wedge, Wil told her how he'd nearly drowned there when he was Brian's age. Stepping across the breakwater, they watched the big cabin cruisers heading in from Catalina and made up stories about them.

Five times she called for messages, infrequently as the day wore on. At dusk, they watched the lights come on from a small park facing the harbor. He took her to a little place he knew where the shrimp was seared with tomatoes and peppers and garlic and the tortillas were handmade by the mother of the owner.

When they got back, there was a brief message from Scott that Brian was with him, talk to her about it tomorrow. After—but not right after—they agreed not to make love; instead she made him a thermos of coffee.

Then there was nothing left but the road. Heading up the freeway to another freeway and yet another freeway, and finally at midnight, eyes feeling the way they used to after a day at The Wedge, he was home.

# ELEVEN

Next morning was foggy and overcast, harbinger of the coming summer weather pattern: early-morning low clouds, sun by afternoon. Or sometimes not—usually when it was hot over in the Central Valley, the relationship predictably inverse.

By two, it was clear the sun wasn't going to make it.

By two-thirty, Wil had opened his pile of accrued mail, done his pile of laundry, checked in with Lisa: Brandon was being a pain, her accounting business was holding its own after last year's scare, her parents had had mostly a pleasant time seeing relatives in Japan but were happy to be back planted in their orchid greenhouses.

Thinking about it as she talked and he listened, it struck him. The concept of ex: how something he'd never predicted for himself had become part of the lexicon—as though something once amorphous and undefined had hardened into another something.

Gelatin exposed to cold. Same flavor, different context.

Now, for instance: the unspoken agreement—steer clear. All it ever did was remind each other why they'd busted up. Like bringing up something from a great depth and having it turn rank when exposed to light and air. So he listened, agreed when the opportunity called for it, moved around doing whatever little things he could accomplish with a portable phone to his ear. Fighting a sense of melancholy that being friendly with your ex was possible. Friends, no.

Later he called about the Bonneville, heard the water pump was fixed, thought about who might follow him over to Bakersfield to return the rental and avoid the drop charge. Left a message. With the remainder of the afternoon, he drafted his bill to DeVillbis; at four-fifteen, he drove it into Carpinteria and posted it, picked up some Arabian blend at the Coffee Grinder. On impulse, he made a run to a music store he favored partly for the selection, mostly because it wasn't staffed by body-pierced, slack-faced mumblers just putting in their time at this shit job until something better came along.

And there they were—in the country-western section— just as he'd hoped: lone CDs of each of the two previous Whitney albums.

Bargain-priced.

He bought them both, took them home to play on his pre-amp/power-amp setup. The first, *Tumbleweed*, was a compilation of energetic tributes to drifters, truckers, migrants, seekers—people who blew from place to place in search of things they seldom found. Little anthems like "Stillwater Moon" reminiscent of Springsteen's earlier work.

The second, *Downstream*, had a more plaintive edge and dealt primarily with matters of the heart: love lost and found, the meaning of it all. Vital in a different sense: more complex melodies and arrangements, lyrics that hit home emotionally. A little darker and more restless.

But it was *Tumbleweed*, plus his growing familiarity with *Alias*—songs like "Black Label Blues"—that led him to break out his old D40 Guild. Thinking of Buzz,

Trey, and Del, he blew the dust off, tightened the strings into something resembling a tune, began picking out chords and riffs. Enough to more fully appreciate Crash Alvarez's backup work, his edgy bottleneck runs on "BLB."

Forty minutes later, his right hand nearly arthritic, left-hand fingers painfully tender and indented, Wil was *ready* to pick up the phone when it rang instead of letting the machine screen it—Hardesty MO of late. Fully expecting it to be Kari with some word about Brian.

"Mr. Hardesty? . . . Jenelle Lockhart."

"Wil," he thought to say.

"The hotel said you'd checked out, so I tried the number on your card."

"And take my word, not a moment too soon."

"That music . . ."

"Yeah." Realizing he hadn't turned it down. Still a little high from it, he held the receiver out to the speakers. "Sound familiar?"

"I'm afraid it does."

He remoted it off. "Sorry. That was presumptuous."

"You found him, didn't you?"

"Yeah. How'd you know?"

Pause, as if she hadn't heard him. "I didn't know who else to call." Sounds of smoking—inhale, pause, long exhale. "This may not be a good idea."

"Why not let me decide?"

"All right," she said. "I have some money saved—not much, but something. It might be enough to . . ."

"Ms. Lockhart—Jenelle? I'm alert this time, but not that alert."

She coughed away from the phone. "God, where is my mind? You're right, of course. For some reason I thought you'd heard . . ."

Wil felt a tremor of anticipation, the clang of water-tight doors. "Heard what?"

"About Donnie—Doc. They arrested him. For murder. Someone named Kroft and another man."

Twin torpedo hits.

"I don't know what to say except he spoke highly of you, and he doesn't about many people." Punchline time: "Do you think you might be able to help?"

Men yelling and lifeboats lowering.

"That's why I'm calling. The truth is, there isn't anyone else."

Grapevine . . . ten the next morning. Temperature rising a good five degrees for every thousand feet Wil dropped, it seemed, Ridge Route leveling off into Central Valley checkerboard.

Already it felt like ninety—summer in April—THE topic on the weather updates. Snapping one off now to recall Jenelle Lockhart's words. More accurately, the lack thereof—Jenelle not exactly into the minutiae last night. Even if she did know much beyond the basics.

Which led again to the feeling of unease.

Something lurking.

The real reason he was going back.

Assuming law enforcement's attitude toward private cops ran true to form in Bakersfield, assuming the waitress at Redtail's had correctly pegged local reaction to Doc Whitney—aside from that. Well aside. Surely it was how he felt about underdogs—justice over expediency. Surely it had to do with his respect for Doc's talent, if not his judgment—the grit and flint of the man. Surely Jenelle Lockhart had little to do with it.

Trust. That's what he was responding to—her trust in him. Not even asking last night about his qualifications. Unaware, for all he knew, of the bookstore incident; for that matter, anything about him. *Keep it in mind,* he thought, giving up on open windows to put on the truck's air conditioner, blouse out the short-sleeved shirt he was wearing. White to go with the khakis. Cooler than jeans—better to make an impression.

*Justice. Respect. Trust.*

Better certainly at hiding the gun he had strapped to his ankle—in this weather, a jacket dead giveaway that something was under it. The gun itself was a Colt Mustang .380 backup he'd finally given in and purchased—about half the weight of the customized military model he favored and had packed away in the suitcase alongside him. Besides, the Mustang looked and felt like his .45. Regular member of the family.

There's a nice sick analogy, he thought. Time to ease up on the suspense novels. Use it to practice ankle draws.

He was maybe ten minutes out, signs indicating the agricultural communities of Arvin and Lamont off in the heat haze, the whole thing with DeVillbis and Rossert mental front burner again via Farley Kroft—when he noticed the Highway Patrol cruiser. Not crowding him exactly, just kind of hanging in there.

Little adrenaline rush, foot off the gas, a glance at his speed—the usual. But he was going the limit, Kari would be disappointed to know, and the CHiP, after staying with him a couple of miles, broke off and exited. Wil could see him in the rearview, talking on his handheld as the black-and-white disappeared down the off-ramp.

Out of the woods. That is until five minutes later, when the Kern County Sheriff's unit replaced it, keeping pace as he went through the flurry of Bakersfield mergings and exits, clots in the traffic before crossing the river and easing off 99 for Oildale. County turf, he realized. Particularly when the red light went on and the white Crown Victoria pulled him over.

He was waiting for the occupant to approach, ask for his license, when he heard: *In the pickup—place both hands on top of the steering wheel. Do it now.*

As Wil complied, several pedestrians stopped to look.

*Slowly exit the vehicle and place your driver's license on the roof beside you. Do it now.*

Three teenagers on BMXs swooped over from across the street to watch him.

*Step back and place your hands on the front fender. Spread your feet and keep your eyes straight ahead. Do it now.*

People appeared at the doors of businesses; motorists slowed to gawk. Wil caught a peripheral glimpse of a tall thin deputy emerging from the Crown Vic and coming forward, hand on the butt of his service pistol. The deputy picked up Wil's license, scrutinized it, then him.

"You are Sean Wilson Hardesty?"

"That's correct." Marveling at how much younger they kept getting. This one looking about seventeen, his hair trimmed as short as it was, basically scalp on the sides. "Is there a problem?"

"Your current address?"

"One-four-three San Nicolas, La Conchita."

It seemed to satisfy him. "Please remain where you are," he said.

"There's an automatic pistol strapped to my left ankle. The permit for it's in my wallet. I'm a private investigator."

The deputy stiffened. He drew his weapon, ordered Wil to put his face on the fender, hands behind him. When he had, the deputy strode forward and cuffed him, relieved him of both gun and wallet. Began going through the wallet.

"Think you might be overreacting a little here?"

"Walk to the patrol car, please."

"Mind telling me why?"

The deputy closed the wallet. "Sir, are you resisting?"

"No. But if I'm leaving the truck, I'd appreciate your

locking it. There's another pistol in the suitcase, which I'd just as soon not see stolen."

"Get in the unit. I won't ask you again."

Awkwardly, Wil got in the backseat.

The deputy shut the door on him, got the suitcase out of the S-10, put it in the trunk, slammed the lid down. As he whipped the patrol car around the pickup and down Airport Drive, Wil could see the crowd following him with their eyes and nodding, the boys peeling around on their bikes.

Five minutes later he was assisted out of the unit, into a flat-roofed modular building with palms at the entrance. Through glass doors and into a modest room with table and chairs.

"You mind taking off the—"

The door shut and he was left alone.

When the door opened again, it was by a well-built man in a beige shirt and paisley tie over dark pants. Athlete's nose and graying crew cut making him look like an ex-player of something. Without speaking, he placed Wil's wallet and driver's license on the table, then undid the cuffs and tossed them in the corner. He took a seat, began thumbing through a folder as Wil fought an urge to rub feeling back into his wrists.

"Don't mind me," he said.

The man did not look up.

"Am I under arrest for something?"

"Trust me, you'd know." A clipped, no-nonsense delivery.

"That's a relief." No point in antagonizing anyone yet, Wil thought. Outer calm—more flies with honey than vinegar. Or some such shit.

The man regarded him. "Considering the arsenal you brought along, I'd think it would be."

"Which I voluntarily divulged, and which I'm licensed to carry."

"Criminal what the law allows these days. Don't you agree?"

"Absolutely."

"Mr. Hardesty, I'm Xavier Acosta—Detective Lieutenant Acosta. In charge of the Whitney murder investigation. You're here because I need to know the extent of your involvement."

"Involvement . . ."

"Something about the word you don't comprehend?"

"Just wondering if I'm the suspect or the victim."

Acosta folded his hands, looked at them, half smiled. "I should tell you that serious and sincere works best with me. My wife thinks it's because of my work. She can tell right away when I'm not happy. Which brings me back to you. Especially since I keep hearing your name, no matter who we seem to run into." He reached into his shirt pocket, came out with one of Wil's cards, stained and dog-eared. "A truck-stop waitress named Danielle Moss, for example."

"How'd you know I was coming back?"

"Superbly coordinated police work. Now, preparatory to making a written statement, I'd like you to relate to me personally how and where you found Mr. Whitney. With some emphasis on the dates and times."

*Do it now.*

Wil did. Slowly and carefully—opening DeVillbis through closing DeVillbis.

The detective checked his notes. "Did you at any time see a shotgun in the proximity or possession of the suspect?"

"No."

"A weapon of any kind?"

"Not unless you count a box knife."

Acosta ran a nail along a chin already beginning to shadow. "And the last place you saw him?"

*So you won't have to lie . . .*

"Greyhound Bus. 18th and F."

"I see. And you are back in town why?"

"Bore you with what you already know?"

This time, Acosta's smile was about 20 percent non-existent, 80 percent somewhere else. "Humor me," he said.

Thinking *quid pro quo*, wishful or not, no real advantage to holding back, Wil told him, minus his introspection on the subject. As Acosta finished writing something, he asked about Doc Whitney's arraignment.

"Monday, nine o'clock—Truxtun and Chester."

"Where he is now?"

"Presently Mr. Whitney is incarcerated at our detention facility north of here. But I'd hate for you to think I was encouraging you in any way. *Comprende?*"

"*Comprendo.*"

"Good." Acosta removed a ballpoint pen from his pocket. Clicked it in and out. Put it on the tablet he'd brought in with the files. "Before you get to this, another matter involving you has come to my attention. Did you ask DeVillbis if his son Cole hunted?"

"I do recall something like that."

"For what purpose?"

Wil met his eyes. "Confirm an observation about him. It's how I make my living."

"I see—which means I don't. One more time?"

"Might help if I knew why the question?"

He took a breath, bit it off. "Cole reported about two thousand dollars' worth of hunting rifle and scope stolen from his truck."

"And?"

"We believe a pro was responsible. DeVillbis Senior indicated you left his office pretty upset. Want to pick it up from there?"

"He's projecting," Wil said. "DeVillbis and I concluded our business, and I left."

"What time was this?"

"Six forty-five. In there."

"You account for your whereabouts after that?"

"Sure. Raceway for a little while, then room 523, Holiday Inn."

"Include it in your statement," Acosta said. "Why'd DeVillbis fire you?"

"I disappointed him."

"How's that?"

"He was hoping I'd bring Whitney back in a body bag. But I'm sure he told you all that."

Acosta picked up the pen, tapped it on the table as if the rhythm were pacing his concentration. "Mr. Hardesty, let me take this opportunity to explain something. I was out there at that house. I remember what Doc Whitney did. I still see it. Now there's two more to lay at his feet thanks to the parole people, but that's another bitch entirely. Mine right now has to do with you staying the hell out of our way. Anything you don't grasp about that?"

"Don't think so."

"Fine—next topic: Media fawning aside, what you did at that store was bullshit."

*Here it comes.*

"You were lucky, and I hate luck. The more you rely on it the more it tends to run out on you and the more you rely on it."

"Anything else?" Wil could feel the heat rising in his face.

"Guess you didn't hear, being so busy and all," Acosta said. "Neither guy made it."

Like ice water on a fire, the cold spreading out inside him.

"Maybe they'd be alive if you'd left it to the real cops. You catch what I'm saying? Angle and bank and screw with the eight ball for a living, you end up like Jay Quillan."

Wil rubbed his right temple where a trip-hammer was starting to metronome. "I don't—"

"Pick up your things at the desk when you finish." Acosta paused at the door. "After that, watch yourself. You don't want my wife looking you up."

# TWELVE

Jenelle Lockhart's complex was only a couple of miles from the sheriff's and looked the same as Wil's last visit, except for the rainbirds now snicking water over the grounds. Keeping them green in the heat wave; close to a hundred, if his internal thermometer was working.

Making him wonder about August.

He parked the truck in what shade he could find and walked to her unit. She must have seen him coming, because she opened the door as he was starting up the steps.

"I was beginning to worry . . ."

Faded jeans and a T-shirt-style top. Periwinkle blue. Which did nothing to detract from the pearl-size silver beads and matching earrings she had on. Silver lapis ring on the hand she offered him.

Comparing this time to last, he took it—a firm brief grip—told her of being intercepted by Xavier Acosta as she held back the screen to let him pass.

"Do you know Acosta?"

"No."

"The name Jay Quillan mean anything?"

Inside now, looking at living room, fireplace, kitchen separated from a small dining area. Levels raised and lowered, high ceiling, white-painted walls: everything designed to make a small space look bigger—something he knew about from his own nine hundred square feet.

There the similarity ended, however. Where he went in for simple adornments like photographs, her interest was obviously Native American: rugs and weavings in Southwest colors and designs, baskets of varying sizes and materials, glazed and unglazed pots.

"Very nice," he said.

"Thank you."

"Not at all what I expected." Massaging his right eye where the ache had spread.

"Which was what?" Her skin looked almost bronze in this light, the hazel eyes leaning toward umber.

"I don't know. More English-lit-major?"

White teeth did nothing to detract either. "Out there, English lit; in here, part Cherokee. And to answer your question, one of the murdered men was named Quillan. Is that who you mean?"

He nodded. "Probably."

"They ran a story in the paper. I'll get it."

She went to a twig basket next to the fireplace, lifted the paper out, handed it to him.

### WHITNEY ARRESTED IN NEW MURDERS
Bakersfield. Don Lee Whitney, released from prison only weeks ago in the 1978 murder of his wife and two daughters, today is back in custody pending charges in the brutal slayings of . . .

"The light's better at the kitchen table," she said, heading that way. "Would you like coffee or tea?"

"Tea, if you're having some."

He spread the paper out as she opened a cupboard, turned the gas on under a kettle.

. . . private detectives Farley Kroft and J. J. Quillan. Kroft and Quillan, both victims of shot-

gun blasts—as were Arlene, Sara, and Megan
Whitney nineteen years ago—were found wedged
in a canal grate downstream from where investigators believe they were murdered. Fishing gear
and Kroft's abandoned vehicle were indicative
of . . .

"Not shy about relating it to seventy-eight, are they?"
Wil said, finishing the article. Bodies in the water for
several days, Doc Whitney recognized and arrested without incident by an off-duty sheriff's deputy shopping for
groceries, news conference planned for later today.
Much more on the prior conviction and early release.

"Can't blame them, I guess," she said.

An orange cat stirred in a window box pushed out
from the sink. Beyond the glass, small birds flitted in
the oleanders.

Wil put a thumb to his temple.

"Any idea why Acosta would link Quillan to me?"

She came over with a glass of water and three aspirin
tablets, turned back to the tea, Wil realizing as he
thanked her and downed them that he'd said nothing
about a headache.

"I interrupted," she said. "You were talking about
Acosta?"

"Bringing up Quillan."

"In regard to you specifically?" She set a mug down
in front of him, eased into a chair opposite.

"Uh-huh."

"Small town again, same business as you," she said.
"Maybe he knew Quillan."

"And you didn't?"

"Not that I recall."

Wil tried the tea and told her he liked it. Blackberry.
"You heard the arraignment was scheduled for Monday?"

A nod. "I was hoping we could go together."

"If you don't mind a mob scene."

"All the more reason."

He glanced again at the headline, the front-page photos of the grate and canal, thinking *What a damned mess.*

"Your hand is better," she said.

"Yes it is." Glancing down at the fading line of stitch marks, then at her. "I heal quickly. Helps in the work."

"I should have given you some aloe for it before. I wasn't thinking."

"It's okay."

"Would you like some now?"

"No—thanks." He turned the mug in his hands. "Can I ask you a question I'd like you not to take the wrong way?"

"That's why you're here, isn't it?"

*So much for patronizing.* "I know Doc very little," he said. "Is it possible he could have done this?"

Her face went tense, and she stared at him.

"Jenelle . . ."

"You know him from his music. How can you ask that?"

"It's not the same."

"But it is—he *is* the music. It's all he's ever been."

"People do what they do," Wil said. "Everybody has compartments."

"Then, no—any way you want me to say it. N-O. It makes no sense. Why would he?"

Sitting there nearly giving off sparks, she reminded him of Joan of Arc, that same kind of faith . . . sight. He wondered how Doc Whitney could have been so blind. But the more he considered it, the odder this belief in Doc seemed. Given the circumstances.

"Look—Jenelle—nobody appreciates loyalty more than I do. Just seems like a lot of years without seeing whether he still deserves it." Only half expecting what came next.

Deep breath, her eyes fixed on the window box: "I haven't been completely forthright. But I was afraid if I did, you might not come."

"Go on . . ."

"When he was arrested at that store, Doc was out getting some things we needed. You see, he's been here from the beginning."

Wil was conscious of refrigerator sounds, the rainbirds outside. Despite the air conditioner's being on, it felt warm in the room. Or maybe it was the tea—and the way her eyes had come up and were watching for his reaction.

*Son of a bitch.*

"I'll understand if you're angry, Mr. Hardesty."

"Wil . . ."

"Even wanting to leave."

"Hey, it's no problem," he said after a bit. "I was just thinking how helpful it would be if you'd start telling me what I need to know. That is, if I'm going to be of any goddamn use at all."

The Silver Mercedes topped the rise, eased down it to minimize dust on the wax job, applied that morning thanks to a friend of Cole's who owed him money.

Lot of them around, it seemed.

In spite of his concern for the car's finish, Lute DeVillbis gave it a bit more gas when he saw the black Suburban half a mile down the dirt road, off to the right under a big oak—only shade around for miles. He pulled up next to it, cringing as the dust washed past and over his windshield. Short grasses, yellowed from the recent heat wave, trembled in a breath of air.

And then the game began.

Smoked glass hid the occupants of the tricked-out

3500, idling to keep the air conditioner going. Empty for all Lute DeVillbis could tell. Giving it thirty seconds perhaps—salvaging at least some semblance of his pride—he slid out of the car and approached the Suburban's passenger side, the rear door opening outward as he reached for it.

"Hurry up," Rye Rossert said from inside. "You're letting all the cold out."

Lute put a foot on the running board and stepped into what felt like a supermarket meat case. "Nice way to develop pneumonia," he said.

"Not if you'd build up a little resistance," Rossert said as Lute sat down next to him. "You want some peach kefir to celebrate?"

*Peach kefir—shit.* What having a twenty-something mistress did for you, made you daffy. Although looking at him now, the hard lean body under tennis clothes, as if he'd just come off the court, it was difficult thinking of Rye Rossert in those terms. Besides, maybe he was just jealous.

"You got any Scotch?"

"No Lute. No Scotch."

"Think I'll stick to business then, thanks."

Rossert drank some kefir from the carton, looked at Lute's prosthetic hand. "Tell me something," he said. "That thing gonna stiffen up in here?"

In the front seat, Raul Garza snorted back a laugh.

Lute said, "I didn't hear anybody talking to you."

"Just wondering," Rossert added. "You're welcome to hang it out the window if you want. Keep it nice and pliable."

"That won't be necessary."

Rossert smirked. "Ever try jerking off with it?"

This time Raul Garza couldn't hold it in.

"And the horse you rode in on, Garza."

"*Sí, patrón,*" Garza said with the phony accent that

passed for insolence, Lute thinking if the guy lasted five seconds in *his* employ it'd be a fucking miracle.

He said, "Are we going to get on with this?" Already feeling a tightness in his sinuses and chest. "It's not as if I don't have enough to do."

"You know, Lute, it's hard to believe somebody who's been through as much as you have could still be so anal. You got to loosen up—smell the petroleum distillates."

*Petroleum distillates.* Rossert thinking himself the Johnny Carson of the oil business. Except Johnny Carson wasn't on anymore.

"You see the news last night and today?" Rossert was saying now.

"Of course I saw it. What do you think?"

"Just wanted to be sure. I never know with you."

"You never know with *me*?"

"Which brings me to the point," Rossert said. "Didn't I explain before that we had nothing to worry about? That I'd handle it."

"All I can say is it took you long enough."

"Hey—make it too easy and they get suspicious. Isn't that right, *compa*?"

There was a grunt from the front seat.

"See? Raul knows. Few days in the water and everybody's happy."

"Whose idea was Quillan?"

Rossert's voice turned cold. "Whose do you think? No, forget that—don't think. Last time you thought, you got a wild hair and pulled in this guy what's-his-name from out of town. The hero."

*That did it.* "How the hell did I know what you were up to? It wasn't as though you let anybody in."

"Told you I had it covered, didn't I? Remember Need-to-Know?" That pissy air-quote gesture as he said it.

"Right—throw that in my face."

"I'm not the one couldn't leave well enough alone."

Lute drew and released a breath, shifted uncomfortably on the seat. "You want me to say I made a mistake? All right, I made a mistake. You-know-who was smack in the middle of our lives and I felt I had to do something. So sue me."

Rossert had another slug of the kefir, sealed the carton as though milking the moment. "It's not quite that simple, Lute. I know you. You drink too much. Then you get all excited and put your damned foot in it. Good way to lose *it,* too."

Nothing much to say to that.

"I keep telling you, things bother you that shouldn't anymore. Might be easier dealing with Cole."

"Cole—are you crazy?" Thin ice, here, Lute knew—his tongue taking him places his feet wouldn't dream of.

Rossert smiled. "Something to think about, isn't it? Especially for somebody with as short a memory as you seem to possess." He slipped through the gap between the buckets, pulled the shotgun seat belt across his lap, snapped it into place.

"I don't like weak links—we'll leave it at that for now," he said. "Raul, show the man to his car."

Lute got out and slammed the door; after the cold interior the heat was like stepping into a foundry. Thinking over what Rossert had said as he walked toward the Mercedes, he didn't see Raul Garza's sudden pivot, the punch out of nowhere. Next thing he knew, however, the wind had been driven from his gut, and he figured he was going to die right there on the ground, the Suburban leaving a cloud of dust that already had begun to settle on him like a shroud.

"It's not what you think," Jenelle Lockhart was saying.

Birds having flitted off, the cat had left the window box for a bowl of dried food on the floor. Wil's tea had gone lukewarm, though he still sipped from it.

"I'm not thinking," he said, "I'm listening."

She leaned on her elbows. "Doc had no place to go. We'd been close once. I felt sorry for him."

"Yet he didn't come back here after he'd been beaten."

"He was afraid those men would find him again—that I might be hurt. He was thinking of me."

"Who knew he was here?"

"Beyond his parole officer, nobody. He didn't want anyone knowing. He went out at night because he had trouble sleeping after being in prison."

"Any idea where he went?" he asked.

"Not specifically."

"Best guess?"

"He liked truck stops, bus terminals, airports. Places he could sense things, get ideas for songs. Back roads and canals. Feeling the people who used to work the land."

"Like his grandfather."

Her eyes widened slightly. "You know about Clell?"

"DeVillbis mentioned him. Oklahoma during the Depression, trekked out here to save his people. Big step up from his old man in the kid's mind."

"Doc told me it was Lute DeVillbis who hired you to find him. You were wise not to tell me."

"Good money for not much work."

She looked at her hands. "That's something we need to discuss."

"We can talk about it—"

"Now," she interjected. "You see, I co-wrote some of the early songs. Doc's listed in the credits because that's the way we wanted him known." She moved the mug as if a pattern only she could discern lay under it. "He always saw to it I got my share. What better use for it now? . . . Mr. Hardesty? . . ."

"Sorry. I was just wondering what it was like. Creating music like that."

It drew a smile, talk of how it was in the beginning: two kids full of things to say, her look saying it all. "Fortunately it's what we remember about each other. He pulled things out of me I never dreamed possible."

"And vice versa, obviously."

"Some. But the truth is, he just kept getting better, more polished. Pretty soon he didn't . . ."

Wil waited as the cloud formed, lingered, passed.

"Yesterday's soap opera," she settled on. "Can you help him?"

"I don't know yet. It depends."

"On what exactly?"

"On him, on you," he said. "Whether or not you're expecting rainbows, for one thing."

"You're saying it doesn't look good."

"I'm open to opposing viewpoints."

She said nothing.

"Jenelle—look—I'll understand if all you wanted was someone to talk to in this. No harm done. I had to come back to return the truck anyway."

She shook her head. Finished eating, the cat sidled over and jumped up on her lap, began kneading her with its paws. "He didn't do it. Now or then."

Sip of cold tea. "Tell me about then."

"It was a nightmare," she said, after a moment. "For all of them. Do you have any idea what it must have been like sitting there in jail. Not being able to remember, but knowing either way, you'd had a hand in it?" She spilled her tea, ignored it. "He tried to end—"

"I know, I read about it. Also that he pled guilty to manslaughter."

"What was he supposed to do?"

Wil said nothing.

"If they put him away again, he'll die in there."

"He seemed pretty resilient to me."

"I know his heart."

"You *knew* his heart," he said. "There's a difference. And not just after nineteen years in prison. After nineteen years period."

"He saw something in you," she said heatedly. "You must have seen something in him."

"Yeah—about what I'd expect, considering. It's also my impression that something hasn't been right about this from the beginning."

She stiffened. Sensing it, the cat jumped down off her lap.

"An ex-con," he went on, "probably the most controversial in recent memory—read hated—coming back without any prospects. Hanging around truck stops like some ghost. Except to menace Lute and Cole DeVillbis over something that happened to his father, whom he loathed." He hesitated, seeing it coming. "I could understand it if he came back to you, but—"

The tears *were* coming now. Seeing a box of tissues on the countertop, he went and got it for her.

"My big mouth."

"No. It's all right."

"Do you see what I mean?"

Brief nod, a dab at her eyes, swipe at the tea spill. "We were married so young—another lifetime. But we have this *thing* between us, a dependence or something. Lord knows, we've been leaning on each other since . . ."

Wil waited.

"I'm just upset at what he might do."

"Since what, Jenelle?"

As if it might come out at a worse time unless she faced it: "Since we divorced. Since I lost my second husband nine years later. Since Doc went to prison for something he didn't do, *couldn't* have done—even if he didn't know how to fight it then."

He was about to say something, but she wasn't finished. It was spoken so softly he could hardly hear it.

"Since our son was born."

# THIRTEEN

Wil used the bathroom, Indian art there as well—Hopi, if memory served, strongly graphic. When he returned to the kitchen, the cat was back on her lap, and she was stroking its ears.

"Get you anything while I'm up?"

She shook her head.

Wil poured the water she'd left on warm over another tea bag, brought the mug to the table, sat down across from her.

"Helps explain why Doc came back here, at least."

"I suppose."

"Doesn't explain his interest in Cole DeVillbis."

"Not in Cole," she said. "In his clubs."

"I don't . . ."

"Redtail's." And when she saw his look, "Joe Pruett was my second husband."

And there it was: Ronnie Pruett, the kid performing that night with Alvarez and the other guy; Wil could have kicked himself for not having seen it. Music in the blood.

She said, "Joe wasn't the smartest move I ever made. He was a salesman. After Doc, anybody stable looked good." Massaging her neck with a hand. "Joe's idea of stability was to break my arm in three places. Just after we split up, he died. On 99 up near Delano in a fog. He never knew Ronnie wasn't his."

"Jenelle, you don't have to go into all this."

"Depends on me, remember?" She dug out a pack of Marlboros, lit one, set the ashtray down on the table. "Do you mind?"

"No."

"Ten years since I gave it up. Pretty stupid, huh?"

"One thing at a time."

She took a drag, angled the smoke away from him. "Doc was under a lot of strain that winter. Among other things, his grandfather died, which really affected his writing. He asked me to help." The cat nuzzled her hand, and she resumed stroking it. "I don't know if you're aware, but a lot of emotion comes up—has to—for the song to be any good. We were into this one, 'Home Is Where We Say Good-bye' . . ."

"The crossover."

"Later on it did."

"And this was?"

"February, seventy-eight. Ronnie was born in November."

*Click*: the database—Doc changing his plea in November. Wil made a mental note to confirm it, but it followed. Also, that Ronnie Pruett, coming up on twenty, was younger than he looked.

"Doc knew he was the father?"

Another drag, her look faraway now.

"But Joe didn't?"

"No."

"What about Ronnie?"

"Joe's his father," she said. "End of story."

"Doc goes along with it?"

"He knows how I feel. He only wanted to see him, he told me."

*Maybe.*

Wil said, "You mentioned Doc was under a lot of strain. What else besides his grandfather?"

"Money. As though he had a personal vendetta: The more he made, the more he spent."

"What about Arlene—that relationship?"

She hesitated. "Doc and Arlene were working some things out. What specifically, I didn't know and didn't ask. Figured I'd done enough. I do know he was getting pressure from his label. Larry Fordyce told me."

"Larry Fordyce . . ."

"Doc's manager at the time."

Wil jotted down the name. "Do you know what kind of pressure Fordyce was talking about?"

She thought a moment. "They wanted him to play along, shape up. He was wearing out his welcome."

"Not too hard to guess why."

She hit the Marlboro again, tapped ash into the tray. "He used to tell me it was like a train he couldn't get off, just go faster on. Even wrote a song about it, 'Blaze of Glory.' *Lookin' down the road at when/All I see is where I've been.*"

Wil remembered it from *Alias*. Words that conjured a fever-dream existence, beat like a racing pulse. "Did you see him during that time?"

"From a distance. It was like watching one of those additive commercials, waiting for the engine to burn up—this sweet ex-choirboy who used to pick peaches in the summer and bring us ice cream he'd made with them. After a while he couldn't work at all." She took a last drag, looked at the cigarette with distaste, crushed it out. "Have you ever seen anyone go through that?"

*Try the mirror.* "I have, yes."

"Then you know what it's like . . . then you'll help him."

"If helping you means helping him."

She thought about that. Took a breath and let it go. Smiled.

*Damn.* "You think Doc will figure he's worth it?"

"Who knows?" She tossed the butt, put the ashtray in the sink, and ran water over it. "Why don't I make us a sandwich before we find out."

They were in Jenelle's older but larger Ford 150—farm suppliers, concrete silos, and railroad cars sliding past on 99 north—when they heard it on the radio. Confirmation that J. J. Quillan and Farley Kroft had been positively identified as the men who'd assaulted Don Lee Whitney outside the restaurant.

"I could have done without that," she said between bites.

Wil edged the pickup toward the exit ramp, thinking Danielle Moss. "Old news. They had to have arrested him on some basis."

"So we're no worse off, you think?"

"That's one way to look at it." He bore to the right, headed east along a canal.

"Your sandwich okay?"

"More than okay." He realized he hadn't been eating and started on the other half. "Where does Ronnie live now?"

"Ron shares an apartment not too far from the college. He's in music studies."

"See him much?"

She crumpled her sandwich wrapping, tossed it in the bag she'd packed them in. "He's a young man. It's his time."

Wil smiled. "At least say it with conviction."

They passed vineyards in leaf, sprinklers irrigating a beanfield, power lines, a vast open area. In the distance through haze, the foothills.

"Changing the subject, do you know where I might find Larry Fordyce?"

"Lord," she said. "Why would you want to?"

"That bad, huh?" He passed a water truck. "I don't know yet. Happens a lot in this kind of work."

"Nashville comes to mind. I remember a Christmas card from there once."

"Not recently, I take it."

"Larry knew who buttered his bread—not to mention every dealer in the western hemisphere. If he's alive, I'd be surprised." She pointed. "That's it over there."

He looked left, took in a sprawl of cement-colored buildings rising fortresslike from the flat. Windows reminiscent of gun ports, endless coils of perimeter wire stacked to about twelve feet, sign indicating detention facility of the Kern County Sheriff. If there was a guard tower, it was well concealed.

Wil drove into the lot marked PRETRIAL and parked. Avoiding a knot of bored-looking reporters awaiting updates, they strode up a chain-link portico to the entrance. Inside, he got a gun locker for the Colt and the paperwork following up Jenelle's call. Then a deputy led them through a series of locks controlled by figures behind smoked glass, down cinderblock corridors muted by thick layers of off-white paint, to a glass-walled visiting room with a glass partition to separate inmates and visitors. At this hour the room was empty—families not due till six according to the sheet.

After the deputy left, Wil told her he was going to need some room to maneuver, not to take things too literally.

"Okay if I say some things first?"

"Of course."

Doc was admitted, then, and Jenelle gave a little gasp at a face hollow with fatigue and unshaven. He wore a dark brown pullover and pants, and he carried a phone receiver with a jack on the other end. For a moment they regarded each other through the partition. Then Jenelle sat, picked up the receiver on her side, pointed to it.

Doc didn't move.

Finally she mouthed the word *Please*, and he plugged in the jack.

They began talking: how Doc was being treated, how he was holding up, what the hell *he* was doing there—things Wil could make out even though he'd backed off to give them a degree of privacy. The issue of hiring a lawyer came up, Jenelle insisting that's what money put aside for a rainy day was for, Doc equally adamant, "*Had it with those bloodsuckers,*" Jenelle reluctantly agreeing.

"For now," Wil heard her say.

She called Wil over, and he sat facing the hewn features—dead prison light making the indentation in his cheek more prominent than he'd remembered. Still wondering how to play it, he took the receiver from her and spoke into it.

"Missed your bus, I see."

Doc shook his head. "Obviously you'll take money from anybody. Must be real proud of yourself."

"DeVillbis didn't pan out—you called it. And you can't insult me, so quit trying."

"Sweet Jesus . . ."

"Yeah."

Doc shifted on the metal stool. "Can you get me out of here?"

"Hard to see how if you're as open and trusting as before."

"My world is full of open, trusting types. Or hadn't you noticed?"

"Give me something to work with, Doc. A name, a place, a—"

"This thing with the two guys, it wasn't me. I don't care how it looks."

Wil glanced at Jenelle. "One person believes you."

"That's all you got to offer?" Doc said.

"If you can't convince me, how do you think you're going to do out there? They're not exactly fans—at least not the ones I talked to."

"What else is new?"

"Look, I'm working here. You want to waste my time, it's up to you. But you might give a thought to who bought the clock."

Jenelle leaned forward. "Doc, please."

For a moment there was nothing, no change. Then a fault inside him seemed to shift, cracks in the facade revealing a molten core.

"*Got to get out,*" he said.

"Yeah. And . . ."

"*One way or another . . .*" Shooting a glance at the smoked glass.

"Bad thought, Doc. Try this one: Where were you the night Farley and Quillan bought it?"

"Out driving," he said finally. "What I'd do every night."

"Driving how?"

"In the Ford," Jenelle said.

Wil held her eyes.

"What? . . . I loaned it to him."

"I understand, but they'll want to examine the truck for evidence. Better to contact Acosta than wait till he shows up—which he will."

"Jen, you stay away from—"

"Anybody ever go out with you, Doc?"

He tried to glare, but it stalled on him. "Crash went along a couple of times, but that was it."

"On that particular night?"

"No."

"What about a shotgun?"

"Right. Like I'm going to risk violating my parole by hanging around guns."

"Who's your PO?"

"Name's Gemello. He has an office in town."

Wil took it down. "Okay. Can you think of anybody who might have hit these guys?"

"No," Doc said. "You want to go for why?"

"What about a frame?"

"Who'd want to? I'm no threat to anybody. Sure as hell have nothing left to steal."

"Doc—I told him about Ronnie," Jenelle said quietly. "I had to."

Doc threw his head back, the cords in his neck lanyard taut. "God*dammit!*" He looked at Wil. "You tell anyone and I will kill you—you hear me? I don't care how long it takes."

"And if it means getting you out?"

"Find another way."

"And that's it?"

Doc didn't answer; Wil turned to Jenelle. "I need a minute. Meet you outside?"

She nodded. As she buzzed for the guard and left with him, Doc said, "The hell you think you're doing?"

"Nobody goes back into the lion's den without a reason," Wil said when they were alone.

"What are you talking about?"

"Why you really came back. The Ronnie thing sounds good, but you weren't even going to let him know. There has to be more to it."

"Like what?"

"Last chance, Doc. I can't get blood out of a rock. Tell me now or go it alone."

Doc Whitney was silent; then it was like someone else's voice coming out of him. "It's not about wanting—like some toy. Can you get that?"

"I think so."

"You know the dream where something's coming for you but you can't move? Couple of times last week I broke into that fucking pile of a house and just sat there, staring into the dark. Feeling it again. Trying to see it coming. Anything." He reached up, fingered the scar along his temple. "First year in Folsom—brother with a shank who just *knew* I'd done it." The one through his right eyebrow now. "Three guys in the yard while the rest of them made a circle and the guards looked the other way. You reading me here?"

"Where were you going to start?"

"Bob Tate, I figured. Just . . . hadn't gotten to it yet. Couldn't."

"Who's Bob Tate?"

"A guy I knew. Haven't exactly kept in touch." He let out a breath. "Bob was with the Sheriffs then. That day . . . August twenty-seventh . . ."

Wil waited, but it was as if the curtain had just risen on a scene the man had to get closer to. Or away from.

"Stay with it, Doc. Talk to me."

No dice. Doc Whitney had already pulled out the phone jack and was up and buzzing for the guard.


"There anything you want to add?"

They were almost to her condo, Jenelle having uttered all of about two words on the way home. Just staring out at the sun sliding down behind the layer of haze, this red dot above the western horizon, the light oddly flat and without shadow.

"Yes," she said, as if she'd been thinking about it. "I hope you know what you're doing."

"Be nice, wouldn't it," Wil said.

"I thought he looked awful."

"He has to know what happened—if he did it, if he didn't. Has to be in there somewhere."

"It's done with. Can't he see that."

"Not for him, it isn't."

She swung away from the window. "God, don't we have enough to worry about? What about now?"

"He knows he had nothing to do with that. There's a big difference."

"Lot of help it's going to be if he's convicted. The DA already said there'd be no plea bargains this time."

"They still have to prove it, Jenelle."

He swung the Ford into her spot and walked her to the door, about to take the S-10 and check back into his hotel. But it seemed so incomplete that he asked if she wanted to get pizza or something, and she surprised him by saying yes. While she fed the cat and freshened up, he dialed the hotel. He was on hold, the desk clerk not too optimistic about a room—Friday night and all—when she appeared on the landing.

"If you don't mind Doc's things in there, you're welcome to the guest bed. I haven't had a chance to get at it yet."

"Thanks," he said. "I'd better pass."

"Be a lot cheaper."

"It's not that. Acosta doesn't like me much to begin with."

"He'll want to go through that, too?"

Wil nodded. "You have a lawyer?"

"No. Should I?"

"Something to keep in mind."

The desk clerk came back on to say they were booked and to give him the name of another hotel, Bakersfield full of Jehovah's Witnesses in town for a conference. Which reminded him to call Kari.

She sounded tired, distracted: Things were still tense with Brian, but at least she'd talked to him, not much said before Scott took over and told her the boy needed his father now, he'd keep her apprised. Basically, butt out. Ready to make an issue of it, she'd nonetheless swallowed her pride and let it go.

"You believe that? He's my son, for God's sake."

To distract her, he filled her in on where he was and what had come up, but it was as if she was having trouble with the connection, asking questions about things he'd just covered. Finally apologizing and hanging up.

"Sounds like things are tough all over," Jenelle said.

She was dressed in white Levi's and a tucked-in blue blouse, a necklace made of silver coins, a bracelet set with turquoise chips around a central stone. As they went out the door, he explained a little about Kari's problems.

"Ronnie went through a phase like that—testing me all the time. I should call her."

"I'm sure she'd appreciate it."

"You have any yourself?"

No point in making her feel bad, so he didn't; just shook his head.

Her eyes scanned his face. "I said something wrong, didn't I?"

"Why do you think that?"

"I can feel it. Please tell me I'm wrong."

It was tempting—having somebody to talk to about losing a son when you were the one who put him in danger, watching it happen from safe up on the beach. But at least he'd known. Doc Whitney hadn't had even that much.

"You're wrong," he said, unlocking the rental for her. "How far's this place? I'm hungry enough to start on the upholstery."

Over pizza, Wil listened to her expand on what it had been like for her: the shock and disbelief, especially when Doc changed his plea; the guilty little suspicions she'd finally quelled; her writing to him in prison. Getting nothing back until the day he'd shown up on her doorstep, nearly causing her to faint.

"He mentioned someone named Bob Tate. Do you know him?"

She nodded, sipped red wine. "From school—he was a friend of Donnie's. As I recall, Bob either was first or among the first of the sheriff's people on scene. Very dedicated. I can see why it finished them as pals."

"Any idea if he's still around?"

"No. There was some trouble—quite a while ago. I'm not sure what happened after that."

"Trouble . . ."

She rubbed her eyes, yawned. "Sorry, it's been a long day . . ."

He waved for the check, got a nod back from the waiter.

". . . and I haven't been keeping track," Jenelle finished.

But she was trying to recall. "Seems to me Bob was wounded—around the time Joe died. I felt bad for not following up, but I had my hands full then."

Wil handed the waiter his credit card, excused himself to check the pay-phone directory. Coming back, he said, "No luck. If Tate's in the area, he's unlisted."

"I'll make some calls, someone will know. This is Bakersfield, remember? At least we have that going for us."

# FOURTEEN

The man in the wheelchair wore squarish wire sunglasses—under his baseball cap, red-and-white jersey reading *Braves*,—jeans over obviously withered legs. As Wil approached, he was deep in conversation with a kid about nine whose eyes were fixed on the ground.

"Keep your eye on it, let it come to you. Then swing like I showed you—through the ball. Okay?"

Wil saw the kid nod, the flip of a ponytail, and realized it was a girl as she went running back to the dugout.

"Help you with something?" The green glasses were fixed on him now, an altogether different challenge, the man's angular features showing no expression.

Authority face, Wil thought: coach to cop in microseconds.

"Still the same game, I hope."

"Little hard to tell sometimes, but yeah. You come to see it or me?" Cop direct.

Another kid strode to the plate as a pitcher of like uniform and sex waited for the ball and a team in blue huddled around their coach.

"Name's Wil Hardesty. Your wife said you might be able to spare a minute between innings." He handed Tate his card, watched him scrutinize it.

"You talked to my *wife*?" Cop paranoid.

"Jenelle Lockhart called her about me. You'd left already. I'm helping her—"

"If it's about who I think it is, don't bother."

"Maybe you'd just hear me out," Wil said.

"Maybe not."

"She told me you and Doc Whitney had been friends. Perhaps I misheard."

Tate said, "You ever hear of dead-end roads going nowhere?"

"Sure—feels like I'm on one right now. Don't suppose you'd reconsider?"

"I don't suppose I would, no."

"Mind if I ask why?"

"I'm not interested in replays. Even less in no-win situations."

Wil put a hand on an upright, looked out across the infield where a ball was making its way around the horn. "Reason I ask is that Jenelle said you'd been a good cop once. That in addition to being friends, you'd been the one to—"

"Mister, you've said your piece and I've listened. Now I got a game to work." He began rolling the wheelchair toward where the red team had started to huddle up.

"You care if I stick around and watch?"

"Your time to waste." Leather-palmed bike gloves slapping the metal rims of the chair.

"Wait a minute," Wil called after him. "Who am I rooting for?"

Tate stopped, looked back to see if the question was on the level, decided it was. "Well?" he said to the players.

"*Braves!*" they yelled. Kid voices—old as baseball.

Wil took a seat on the green-painted bleacher, nodded to the Saturday-morning faithful: parents, siblings, some white-haired men and women. Red took the field first, their pitcher all business and absurdly inaccurate: two runs, no hits, six walks. Blue's turn produced similar results.

As it progressed, Wil realized he'd forgotten the fun of watching a game at this level. For a time Tate's Braves threatened to run away with it, six runs in the third inning alone. But gradually the other team chipped away and by the time it ended were down only 14–12 and threatening.

Each team gave the other a cheer, then everyone walked off toward Explorers and Caravans, Trans Sports and Tahoes. Car doors slamming and engines turning over—eleven-fifteen and the heat beginning to assert itself.

Wil sat there until he and Bob Tate were the only ones left, neither making a move, Tate still with his back to the bleachers. Sprinklers had begun jetting streams of water over the outfield now, sunlight turning them into bright silver arcs. Shouts of children playing on swings and jungle gyms floated in from across from the ball field.

"She tell you they were only five and three years old?" Out of nowhere.

"Didn't have to," Wil said. "I read about it."

"And here you sit."

He said nothing.

"You ever do this kind of work before? I mean with bodies and such? Actual dead people?"

Cop arrogance: the job plus a natural distrust of anybody working the same turf; every cop Wil had ever known, Mo Epstein included, had it—like a virus in the blood. There were times when it bothered him, but not now.

"Some," he answered.

Tate rolled to face him. "How about one reason I should give you the time of day, let alone anything else."

It was ironic in a way—the guy who couldn't walk hard-assing the one who could. Still, Wil thought, he was finding it hard to dislike Tate, despite his edge.

"I saw him, talked to him. The men who roughed him up never went above his shoulders. Not even a random hit. What's that tell you?"

"Shit happens. That all you've got?"

"I think they were ordered not to. I think he's being set up for some reason. Maybe the same reason as then, maybe not. But if it's happening now, who knows about seventy-eight?"

"*I think*. It's all so easy for your types, isn't it? Evidence—who gives a shit? Rules—screw them, too. Cops don't have that luxury. Cops deal in what's there." Not bitter sounding exactly, just no room for error.

"And usually it's enough, isn't it," Wil said. He stood, conscious of the fragrance of wet, cut grass, the sound of a boy's laughter. "Thanks for your time."

Tate watched him drop down from the stands. "Why didn't he look me up himself?"

"He was that close, he said."

"Yeah, well. Way it goes sometimes."

"Put yourself in his place," Wil said. "The whole thing no longer an abstraction. Then tell me that."

He waited, but Tate said nothing.

"Change your mind, the hotel number's on the card."

"Wait a second," Tate said as Wil was moving off. "You ever in the service? You look about that age."

"Four years, two tours—Coast Guard Market Time. You?"

"Air Force. B-52s. Electronic countermeasures."

Wil nodded. "You kept the SAMs off—I had a friend who did that. Got himself a Purple Heart belly landing off Guam."

Tate's head cocked slightly as if picking up a distant signal, his glasses reflecting back a glint of sun. "Hell, not even May and it's summer already," he said. "You want to get a beer or something?"

Wanting to see how far he could push the struts Tommy had installed, Cole DeVillbis kept his foot into it well up the bank. Only when he felt the race car beginning to lose it did he back off slightly, drop down into a straightaway run that had them all looking up from the pit.

*What a sound,* he thought. *Fucking sex should be that hot.* If only the race were across a hundred miles of salt flat, he'd have it made; fucking nobody'd catch him. Which is why he and Tommy were trying to extract every ounce of power the suspension could deliver, speed on the turns the difference between checkered flag and also-ran. These days everybody had the horses. Suspension and nerve, that was it—no fear, taking it to the limit and beyond.

Qualities Cole had in spades.

Which was why he needed to go deeper in before having to ease up—deeper than anybody else. Not bail out so soon. Stuff he'd tell Tommy. Let Tommy figure it out.

Next turn now, loss of control in exactly the same spot. He was tempted to push it, the track empty save for number 19's practice laps, but there'd be time enough. No sense leaving paint or worse on the wall when it didn't count for anything.

Cole did a last one, then he wheeled it onto the apron, gave it a few gooses for effect, guided the car to his area with Tommy walking alongside. Let the throb twang his tuning fork a little before switching off and sliding out through the welded door's window.

"Well?" Tommy asked.

"Not bad, but you gotta give me more penetration on the bends. Tighten it or something."

"You're already higher up the bank than—"

"Tommy?"

"Yeah?"

"Just do it—okay? Or I'll get somebody who will."

Tommy tossed a wrench he was holding into the rolling tool case. Focused on it. "You got no call to talk that way, Cole."

"That's good to know. Tomorrow time enough?"

"I guess we'll see."

"Knew you had another notch left, Tom. *Hasta luego* now."

He crossed the track, mounted the access steps, stepped into the blue-seated bleachers where a few diehards and relatives sat watching the practice. A couple of them pointed to him, his red-and-white coveralls with the racing logos on it, the *DeVillbis Racing* cap he tipped in their direction bringing smiles and giggles.

A car—number 48—roared past, screamed into the turn—fairly high up, he noted. Made him want to go back and boot Tommy Arroyo is the ass. Light a fire under him.

"Cole . . ."

The voice came from several rows up and to the right.

Cole swung his brown-tinted Serengeti Drivers that way, wondering what the fuck. He took the stairs slowly, one at a time. "I'm in a hurry. What is it?"

Chris Alvarez smiled: Hawaiian shirt, dark shades, and a field-worker's hat against the sun's late-morning push. "Time we had another talk," he said.

"Let's define that. Music or stock-car racing?"

Crash made the universal gesture—fingertips rubbed lightly together. This time Cole checked to see who might be watching before turning back to him.

"You crazy doing this here? What's the matter with you?"

"A little raise, for Christ's sake. I'm worth it."

Like the burnout wasn't asking anymore, he was demanding. "And I look like the fucking bank to you . . ."

Alvarez did a palms-up—*if the shoe fits.* "Cost of living," he said. "Probably heard of it, an entrepreneur like yourself."

"Maybe you should watch your mouth and where you shoot it off. Let alone what you put in your damn veins."

"Hey, come on—it's business, is all I meant. And you're a hard man to pin down."

"The answer is no. Hell no. That plain enough?"

"At least think it over?"

"In your dreams, Crash."

There was a moment when he expected a challenge, a little spark in the man's eyes, but then it went out. Alvarez managed a smile, the loser's shrug.

"Sure, Cole," he said. "No need to get huffy. You know me—always the team player."

Cole was about to answer when number 48 stormed the west turn on what sounded like two tires, and the smoking squeal as it ricocheted off the wall and spun down the ramp came close to making him hard.


Wil watched the waitress set down their sandwiches, Tate's beer, his own lemon-flavored club soda. *Phyllis*, her name tag said: khaki shorts, ponytail, white tee with the bar and grill's logo on it.

"There you go, Bob," she said.

"Thanks to you, Phyl."

She grinned at him, caught Wil's eye briefly, said, "Get out of here." Still grinning as she walked away, as though knowing they were appreciating her exit.

Wil and Tate were at a round concrete table outside, cottonwoods throwing shade over the patio deck, Wil still thinking about the ease with which Bob Tate was able to swing out of his car, unfold the wheelchair—lightweight aircraft metals, he'd explained on the way in—and go about his business. Upper torso reminding him of an inverted wedge.

Tate removed his *Braves* cap and put it on the seat beside him, pale scalp showing through close-cropped hair. He started on his sandwich.

Wil did the same, suddenly aware of how hungry he was. "How long you been coaching?" he asked.

"Let's see . . . I got shot two months after Doc's trouble—it was about a year after that." Between bites. "Abbie was ready to finish the job if I didn't get on with something."

"How'd it happen?"

"Couple of druggies fighting over the last Pepsi or whatever. Daytime call, nothing special—I barely can make 'em out through the screen. One minute I'm knocking, next the guy's whipping around with this .22 magnum he's threatening the old lady with. Never saw it coming.

"So I'm lying there as they're puttin' this little Mexican in the car, thinking I'd made it through Vietnam but not Bakersfield. Actually struck me as funny."

He washed down a bite with beer, wiped his mouth on his napkin.

"Bye-bye Sheriff's Department. Bye-bye a lot of things. Guy was out in three years."

"Tough row," Wil said.

"I got through it. What about you? You make it through over there?"

The trees shifted in a breath of air. Spangles of light moved across the tabletop, lit their drinks briefly, and danced away.

Wil spun his bottle. "Three clean rounds when my boat got hit. I was lucky. A friend pulled me out."

"How'd you get pulled into Doc's orbit?"

Wil told him.

"I know Xavier Acosta," Tate said after he'd gotten

to that part. "He was the investigating detective first time around. Got him his bars."

"I'm not following you."

"Donnie's plea did that. Always felt that was kind of convenient for old Zavvy. Let him know it, too." He swiped at a fly buzzing around his food. "Probably just my cynical nature."

"What about Doc?"

"My old pal. Great kid, fun to be with, give you his right arm if you needed it. Wherein lay the problem. Hell of a talent, but a deer in the headlights when it came to reality."

"Not anymore."

Tate took a swig of beer.

Wil said, "You think he did it?"

"Arlene and the kids? Not the Donnie I used to know—not under normal circumstances. But two things: Donnie'd passed up normal long before, and I never figured I'd get shot by a baby-faced dipshit with a .22." He shifted in the wheelchair. "You ever know somebody who was his own worst enemy? Basically good, but tuned to a different frequency than everybody else?"

Wil nodded.

"I saw him about a month before it happened. Donnie was scared, I could tell."

"Scared of what?"

Tate set his sunglasses down carefully. "Of losing it. Not being good enough to keep it going. Always having to do better to live down his old man." He ran a hand over his brush cut. "Which explained all the excesses— at least to me."

"Jenelle said he and Arlene were having problems."

A nod. "She'd told relatives she was thinking of leaving him and taking the girls. DA's office was all over that one."

"That why Doc changed his plea?"

He shrugged, finished his beer. "For obvious reasons, we weren't in touch. Always thought it was a shame, though, his backing down that way."

Wil felt a little rush. "Why is that?"

Tate fumbled in his pants and laid down some bills. Caught by the sudden break-off, Wil countered with a credit card, said he'd expense it, and got hard blue eyes leveled at him.

"Don't take it wrong, but I'm nobody's expense. I'll let you know when you owe me for something."

"You'll give me the chance?"

"My place isn't far from here," Tate added, reaching for a toothpick. "Always figured total immersion was the only true way to get religion."

They were there in a few minutes, an older home in a neighborhood of newer and upgraded ones, Tate's shaded by an enormous sycamore. He paused to introduce Wil to his wife, a thin woman in a flowered shirt, brownish hair cut short. Her face tightened when he told her Wil's interest before leading him out back.

The office was in a converted guest house next to the pitched-roof single garage. From the outside, Wil expected clutter but encountered sparse, clean, well ordered: flat working spaces on top of white file cabinets, PC and monitor, tilt-top drafting table. Numerous baseball trophies and framed team photos.

Tate unlocked a cabinet, slid out a drawer, found and drew out a manila envelope. He rolled his chair over to the drafting table, snapped on a hinged lamp, and spread out a handful of eight-by-ten photos.

"The guy who took these was a friend," he said. "Knew I had an interest, so he made me a set. Have a look."

Wil did, felt his skin crawl.

The exterior of the house was recognizable from his

visit with DeVillbis, the inside shots like nothing he'd seen. They were near impossible to look at, the black puddles and small broken forms, the room in high-contrast black-and-white. Normally mundane items like drink glasses, coloring books and crayons, and a spread-out game board tipped the scene over into surreal.

The photos were cropped without the usual white border, making them feel like windows into which you could fall if you stared long enough. Even harder was contemplating that someone had actually been responsible for what they revealed.

"Been years since I looked at these," Tate said quietly. "Now I remember why."

Wil just shook his head.

"So much for your baptism," Tate said.

"No shit."

"Had to see what you're made of."

"Well?"

"Not yet and not nearly." Tate collected the outdoor shots and the close-ups, put them back in the folder. He rearranged the room shots to fill the spaces and sequence properly.

"Take your time with these. I want to know what you see."

Trying to get past the subject matter and with a magnifier Tate set out, Wil began to case them in earnest, search-pattern methodical. As he did, Tate wheeled himself to a door that angled across a corner of the room and let himself in. Minutes later he emerged to the sound of water rushing and sat silent for another ten. Hawk-on-a-fencepost scrutiny that began to get under Wil's skin.

Then it struck him: sort of an ill-defined something, more a possibility within the confines of captured space and time. Like the unexplained shapes found in ghost-hunter photographs.

Less what was there than what wasn't.

He raised up to Tate regarding him.

"Probably nothing."

Tate spread his palms.

"There's no other damage," Wil said. "At least not that I can see from these. Not even a broken lamp."

Tate's eyes looked hot enough to trip alarms. "And you'd expect that, wouldn't you, a guy so fried he can barely stand? Who passes out that hard? How's a guy like that—even a crack shot with a pump gun like he was—put no round where it shouldn't have been."

"It never came up?"

"It came up. I brought it up."

"And?"

"Close range, that was the rationale. Everybody buying in because it fit when you jammed it in the hole."

"Except you."

Tate nodded.

"Any theories?"

"Like what—who else might have done it? No."

"What about the drugs? Anything there?"

"To my knowledge, Donnie never used that shit. Booze was his thing, Blackjack straight up. People around him, maybe, but not him."

"What about them?"

Shrug. "The usual crowd of hangers on. Good mincemeat material."

"Chance it might be a fallout from the music business?"

"You suggesting a mob hit?"

"Just throwing it out," Wil said. "Doc was making a lot of money, right?"

"Yeah, but no connection like that ever came up. Such as it was looked into."

"Maybe that's—"

"Look, Donnie'd burned his share of bridges by then.

Not the least of them with law enforcement." His jaw muscles worked as though chewing on the thought. "Besides, a month later I had a bullet in my spine and my own shit to deal with. Literally. Try listening to anger-management counseling with a bag in your lap while your wife develops a fondness for the late show."

Wil stared at the photos.

"Didn't mean to go off like that," Tate said. "Just all of it coming back."

"Forget it."

He took a breath. "I keep thinking of the parallels. Not just the way I got nailed, but a dozen others I could name. Things just happen the way they do—trying to look at it that way." Leaning forward in the chair. "But a mother and two little kids just standing there while a blind drunk cuts loose on 'em?"

Wil kept scanning. "Hard to see from here."

"Welcome to the nightmare."

The hotel he'd managed to get into was laid out around a pool and garden area that featured boulders and a running stream, his downstairs room fronting a small individual patio with the pool beyond.

Just out of the shower, Wil heard the announcement that sheriff's investigators were confident divers had found the murder weapon in the Whitney case. Middle of the canal, as though hurled there. Happening also— the female anchor intoned—to be the exact model of expensive shotgun used in another grisly murder nineteen years earlier.

*Swell.*

Which brought another thought and a call: Tate's wife, Abbie, telling him Bob was unavailable right now, her abruptness and tone saying it better. Thanking her, Wil left his phone and room number even though he'd left it before. He was dressed and making some entries in his notebook, about to call Jenelle and report in, ask if she had dinner plans, when the phone rang.

"Sticks with you, don't it?" Bob Tate said when Wil picked up.

"The last thing I want to be is a problem for you."

"She'll be fine. Just had a snootful of it is all. What's on your mind?"

"Forgot to ask you about this guy Quillan," he said, explaining Acosta's remark.

There was a pause. Then, "I guess you don't know. 'Course not—why would you?"

Wil could see grade-school-age kids playing in the pool, part of a soccer contingent he'd seen checking in. "Know what . . . ?" he asked Tate.

"Card the DA hasn't played yet. That spot where Doc used to have a cheekbone? Well, that was Quillan's work. Would have stomped Doc to jelly if I hadn't stopped it."

"How's that possible?"

"Jay Quillan was my partner that day—real piece of work. Didn't last but another sixty days with the department. Got tossed for beating a drunk who puked on him half to death with a baton."

"Doc knew Quillan stomped him?"

"I sent him a note in jail," Tate answered. "Figured I owed him that much. Never heard back, though."

"You think he knew that was Quillan at the truck stop?"

"If he didn't, I'd be surprised. Quillan's picture made the paper, and Doc always had a thing for faces."

Wil said nothing, wondering how he'd overlooked it. Probably because his focus had been so concentrated.

"Still thinking the DA isn't licking his chops here?"

# FIFTEEN

By seven Sunday morning, Wil was up and doing laps in the hotel pool. Saturday night instead of dinner he'd settled for a phone call updating Jenelle; hearing from her about how Acosta and his people had gone through her place for most of the day and had impounded the Ford. Fatigue in her voice the deciding factor in spending what was left of the evening with supermarket deli and a list of things he wanted to ask Doc Whitney directly.

Stroke, breathe, stroke, breathe . . . water bracingly cool, sun yet to warm the pool's surface, early strollers taking coffee back to their rooms. Turn, stroke, breathe . . . *Who's behind a possible frame, let alone why?* . . . stroke, breathe, stroke . . . *What really happened at the Stockdale house?—no bullshit, no macho deflections* . . . stroke, breathe . . . *Who knew you might be driving around when Kroft and Quillan got hit?* . . . breathe, stroke . . . *What does your old man's turning up in an oil waste pond have to do with any of this? With Lute DeVillbis?*

Seventy laps—pushing it the last five until he emerged from the pool, winded but renewed. Especially after a veggie omelette and a buckwheat stack over the Sunday paper, an article on the Kern County Museum setting a thought in motion regarding his last question. Having learned from experience that those who usually volunteered at such places were often walking databases when it came to local history.

He called Kari and got her answering machine, left a message where he could be reached, adding that he missed her and hoped things were improved on the home front, that he'd try again tonight.

Then he drove to the museum.

Florence Alstott was who he wanted, a staffer told him, due at her post in the gift shop in a half hour. Which he used to bend time, the museum itself a dappled mini-town complete with period pieces—structures moved from their original locations and restored—blink your eyes and you're back a hundred years. An idea with increasing merit the more he saw of things.

Florence was much like the museum: pleasantly low-key and similar in age. Pleased by his interest in the concept, she was talkative and happy to answer what she could about an event she recalled. The bones in the sump, Don Lee Whitney's father. That singer who was in trouble again.

She looked at his card. "He's your client?"

"Indirectly."

"That mean you believe he didn't do it, or are you more like a lawyer?"

"Yes and no."

She thought about that. "Know who you really ought to speak to? Leora Graybill. She's the one who pressured the state into cleaning out that thing in the first place."

Wil asked if she knew where he could find her, wrote down the information as Florence was delving into her address book.

"NOW OR NEVER—that's her group. Been giving the oil and chemical people fits for more years than they'd care to remember. Not to mention the bureaucrats. You never heard of it?"

"Can't say I have."

She smiled knowingly. "Think I'd batten down, if I were you. Nobody's quite like Leora."

Wil found it despite her directions, the house seemingly a metaphor for Florence Alstott's description of the woman. Last residence in a block gone commercial: twenties-style yellow clapboard with white scrollwork, gabled entrance and bay window, wraparound porch. White Cecil Brunners enveloped one side. There was even a bench swing in the giant locust tree.

"You the one about Gib Whitney?"

He shaded his eyes, made her out in a wicker chair behind the porch screen. "Yes, ma'am. Name's Hardesty." Through the doors of a free-standing garage, he could see the rear end of an old Studebaker half-ton and a red Beetle convertible. NOW OR NEVER sign à la Neighborhood Watch.

"Florence said you were coming. Through the door and bear right if I haven't scared you off yet. And don't be calling me ma'am."

Her voice had a smoker's huskiness, not to mention surprising carry. Turning the knob, he entered to dated but orderly, saw the opening to the sunporch and went for it, heard a low growl and "Easy, Matt."

She looked about five-zero—gray hair in a loose braid down her shoulder, face strong-featured and deeply lined from the sun. She wore denim overalls over a pink henley, white walkers, round-faced watch on a leathery wrist. Eagle eyes appraised him. From the floor at her feet, a black-and-white-and-caramel Australian shepherd homed in as well.

"That's Matt. He's okay if you are." She accepted his card, scanned and pocketed it, nodded to a glass jar beside the cigarillo she had going. "You like sun tea?"

"Sure."

"That's why it's there."

He poured some into the Dixie cup she'd set out.

"Just to let you know, I usually bite a person's head off before they get this far."

"Probably explains the pile of skulls I saw out there on the sidewalk."

"Some people get fooled by my size is what I meant."

He sipped the tea. "Not too many in the oil business, from what Florence said."

"She talks too much. Always has. Even in kindergarten."

Wil tried to picture it and came up empty as the dog left red alert and settled back down.

"So what's your interest in Gib?"

As he explained—Doc's current beef possibly dating back to 1978, maybe even before that if there'd been anything to Lute DeVillbis's theory about why Doc came back at all, the discovery in the sump—her eyes never left his face.

"Lute DeVillbis, huh?"

"You know him?"

"Spend eighty years in a place, you more or less learn who lives in it." She dragged off the cigarillo, blew the smoke upward like a trucker at a breakfast counter, crushed it slowly in the ashtray. "Always wondered why the DA made that deal if their case against Donnie was so strong. But hell, what do I know?" Creaking back in the wicker chair. "Not still working for DeVillbis, are you?"

"No."

"Matt'd be seeing you out the drive by now if you'd said yes." She eyed him closely. "Which leads us to what it is you want from me."

"History," Wil said, trying to match her directness.

"Background. Anything you can think of to help me get at the truth." He explained about Bob Tate's photos, the crime scene as Tate had detailed it.

"You're sure it's the truth you're looking for?"

"Interesting question."

"And not a bad one to ask yourself." Leora Graybill reached down to trail a hand through Matt's fur. "See, I know Bob Tate and I've heard all that at one time or another. And Donnie didn't exactly help himself pleading guilty to manslaughter."

"Meaning he might have done it."

"Down, boy—even *he* said that, if I understand the plea. And aren't you here about Gib Whitney?"

"True."

She stood, barely taller than he was sitting down, Matt on his feet before she was. "Well," she said, "are you coming?"

The Beetle convertible found a last rut, then slid to a stop off what was hardly more than a Jeep trail, Wil pausing to get his breath, Leora already opening the door for Matt, who sprinted off and began to leave his mark on the live oaks.

The air smelled of warm dry grass.

"You always drive like that?"

She loosened the visor she'd put on for the drive, *NOW OR NEVER* stitched on the bill. "Like what?" Little grin creeping in around her set expression.

*Rommel crossing North Africa . . . Schwarzkopf rolling through Iraq.* "Never mind," he said.

"Good to see you're not the nervous type."

She zipped a bottle of water into a fanny pack and strapped it on, started hiking northeast, Wil falling in step beside her. Here and there an isolated walking beam dipped methodically, compared to the forest of them they'd driven through on the way in, a good twenty minutes off the blacktop. About nine or ten miles, the way Leora had driven it. Even the dog had looked cowed.

"He'll find us," she said, assuming Wil was looking off in the direction Matt had taken. "He's walking point. You know the term?"

"Well enough."

"I had a nephew find it out the hard way. Eighteen years old. You ask me, some people have a lot to answer for."

"No argument here."

Without the wind in their faces, the sun had a push. Leora's pace belied her stature, the hiking boots she'd changed into making staccato crunches on the dry ground. "Watch out for rattlesnakes," she said at one point.

"Happy thought."

"Look at it this way, they're even less thrilled."

They walked awhile without speaking. Wil shaded his eyes, took in land rolling away toward the Sierra in the distance, thunderheads rising up out of the haze. "Interesting country," he said to draw her out.

"Used to be before the oil wells—inland sea at one time, the whole valley. Good fossil area." A crow flew over them, cawing; Leora looked up. "He's headed where we are, about three-quarters of a mile."

Fifteen minutes later he spotted it: a bluff draped with wild grapevine above a fair amount of water surrounded by tules and cattails, sun-cracked mud, blue wildflowers shaded by sapling cottonwoods and sycamores sprouting up from graying taller ones. As they approached with Matt, crows and smaller birds took flight. Half a dozen buzzards grudgingly abandoned a splay of bones and hide.

"God," Leora said. "It's actually come back." She walked around, examining the site wonderingly as Wil wiped at perspiration. "This used to be the worst-looking black mess you ever saw: vernal pool to oil waste pond in a generation. Dead things in all directions—tires, junk, you name it."

"Gib Whitney."

"Yes. And him."

"How well did you know him?"

"Gib knew lots of people."

Wil said nothing. Cocked an eye at her.

"Oh no you don't, I was older than he was. Plus he was married. Hard not to feel sorry for that poor woman."

"What was he like?"

"Where you think Donnie got his looks?" She paused. "Nice kid, by the way—at least I always liked him. Wrote him a couple of times while he was in prison."

"No, I mean—"

"Gib, I know." She looked out over the pond. "Kind of sad under all the looks and charm—this small-time hustler always looking for the big score. Ironic that he wound up here, hot after oil as he was, him and Lute DeVillbis. Always was a cut above that one. You want a challenge, find the justice in that."

"Were you here when they found him?"

She nodded, pulled a burr off Matt. "You believe them drilling in a place like this? I'd come out here all the time before it got turned into the black hole of Calcutta. I used to go skinny-dipping."

"Remote enough, that's for sure."

Her eyes flashed. "You ever heard of Kesterson Reservoir? Birds without eyes? The cancer clusters around McFarland and Earlimart? Nothing's remote anymore. Even if we could wash out the poisons, where do we put them? San Francisco Bay?" She gazed out beyond the pond. "The apocalypse is here and it's us."

"Maybe not," Wil said. "Look at what you've accomplished."

She snorted. "I've lived too long, seen too much that's gone. That's the tragedy—forgetting you ever had it."

"Would you know a man named Rye Rossert?"

"Fecal matter. Don't get me started."

Wil waited for what he knew would come, counting till it did, a full three seconds.

"Like a thief in the night—turn your back and it's his if he wants it. God knows the keys he holds in this county. You ever see that movie *Duel,* with Dennis Weaver? Well, that's Rossert only with a bulldozer. You never see him, just know he's the one running up your backside." She lowered her visor against the sun. "Ask him about La Altura sometime—starter condos he put up for families who could barely speak English, then leased the mineral rights to a company he also owned. Imagine what an oil well in the yard does for property values."

"Know anything about him and DeVillbis?"

"DeVillbis is baby shit compared to this guy. Hell, he owns DeVillbis. Hall of records—look it up sometime."

"You sure of that?"

She rubbed a spot between her eyebrows, looked as if a storm were brewing behind it. "Money and politics. I may be the local wacko, but I like to know who I'm battling. Including those we-know-best enviro elephants and the government . . . which means about everybody at one time or another. Guess when you got a conscience, you're stuck with it." She bent and picked up a stick, held it out for the dog to tote back.

"Let's go, Matty. We're done here."

It was five by the time he'd showered the hike off and was dressing, dialing Jenelle's number.

"I got your messages," he said when she answered. "Six o'clock, right?"

"Shall I make sandwiches again?"

"No, thanks. I had something on the way back."

"Back from where?"

"Nowhere—literally. I'll tell you later."

He hung up, opened crackers and cheese—not wanting to make imposing a regular thing. He was out the door when the phone rang. Already cutting it close, debating whether it was Jenelle calling back with something important, he picked up.

"Only about the eighth time I've tried," he heard Chris Alvarez say.

"You ever hear of leaving a message?"

"Not for this," Alvarez said. "Can you come by the trailer?"

"Not now, I can't. Later, possibly."

"Look, my gig ends at one—plus another half hour to chill. You be there?"

"Depends on the topic."

There was a pause. "Stuff you'll be interested in—guaranteed. Plain enough?"

"No," Wil said. "But what else am I doing at one in the morning."

"One-thirty."

The phone went dead in his hand.

Jenelle was waiting when he pulled up: white slacks and aqua top, hair swept up with a clip made of hammered silver—details he caught himself appreciating but feeling vaguely guilty about. Compensating for it with a mental jot to order Kari flowers. On the way, he ran through his meeting with Leora Graybill, their trip to the pond, and got a frown in return.

"Not to tell you your business," she said, "but wouldn't it be more helpful to focus on the present?"

"Yes, no, and maybe. Sometimes you start where you start."

"Meaning?"

"Find a loose strand, you pull on it. At least I do. It's a little like unweaving—watching what happens to the pattern."

She pursed her lips. "You detect a pattern here?"

"Not yet I don't."

"I see."

"Glad somebody does."

The rest passed in silence. Then they were in the Pretrial Facility lot, walking inside, waiting, finally settling in a different visiting room, women and kids leaning in toward hard-looking men with vacant faces and short hair squared off at the neck.

Doc Whitney looked only a little better this time—less haggard, still tense in his issue browns. "How's it going?" Wil asked into the receiver when Jenelle had finished.

"I been in worse places. You gettin' anywhere?"

"Back to the future."

"Want to say it in English?"

Wil briefed him regarding his meetings with Tate and Leora Graybill, Doc stopping him with pointed questions about Tate's photos, how the man was, his circumstances. Finally breaking off to mention he wasn't sure if his arraignment tomorrow was going to be handled by video or in person. Just that he was told to be ready for either. Pausing a moment as if working up to something.

"What was it like out there?" he asked. "At that sump."

As Wil told him, Doc seemed to focus inward, revealing little of what he was thinking. Asking when he'd finished if Jenelle would give him and Wil a second.

"It's no big deal, Jen. Thanks."

Wil watched the heavy door ease shut behind her, her

profile through the glass as she waited—arms folded across her chest, eyes locked in a stare. Turning back, he almost missed the penciled note Doc was holding tight to his chest, glancing at the men on either side as Wil read it:

> *Don't tell Jen or ANYONE. Eme has a whack out. Word is I'll never make it to prelim. Can't let them know I know or I'm dead now. NO TIME!*

The eyes lasering into Wil's virtually etching it into the glass: FULL BORE. I'M ASKING . . .

Suddenly Doc winked, rose as if it were the last thing on his mind, crumpled the note, and was gone.

# SIXTEEN

*Eme: Mexican Mafia—the letter M in Spanish pronunciation.*

*Street-gang connections and prison muscle.*

*But a hit on a gringo country singer just possibly going upriver for the final time? Why...? It made no sense.*

Wil curbed thoughts that had whirled since dropping Jenelle off hours ago. Doc's admonishment aside, he'd left several calls for Xavier Acosta, finally leaving the hotel for Cheri's. Pulling in two blocks up on a cross street off the drag, he checked his watch: one-forty—cool outside as he locked the pickup and strolled toward the club.

Dance songs still came from inside—juke music.

He poked his head through the door in case Crash Alvarez had been delayed, saw virtually no one but the bartender and a bored-looking waitress, Sunday night obviously not Friday or Saturday. Taking the alley around back, he caught lights on in Alvarez's trailer—none in the others—and walked toward it, scanning the shadows for odd shapes or movement: old habit, paranoia just one of the perks.

But he saw nothing.

He tried the screen, knocked again, heard the stereo

turned down inside, an artist he didn't recognize. Then: "Aaaaaaay—look who's here. Mr. TayVay himself. Come on *DOWN*."

Wil stepped inside past Sid Vicious on alert, Alvarez shirtless and looking as though keeping his head on his neck was a balancing act. He plopped down in the frayed easy chair, gestured to a half-empty bottle.

"No thanks," Wil said.

"Oh yeah, I forgot. Our hero doesn't drink."

Wil tried to spot some white in Crash Alvarez's eyes and gave up, the man looking as if he were peering from the bottom of a chlorinated swimming pool. Across from him, guitar riffs came from a beat-up cabinet that hadn't been open last time he was there, Wil doing a fast calculation and coming up with maybe 15K worth of high-end components.

"Nothing but the finest, right?" Alvarez snickered. "How 'bout a little something between your toes or up your nose?"

"How about giving the junkie shtick a rest and telling me what's on your mind."

"Why, our favorite doctor, of course. Heard you were back and working for him."

"Something like that."

"Tate made that big an impression, huh?"

Out-on-a-limb time, Wil figuring nothing to lose under the circumstances: "It was you fingered him for Cole, wasn't it? Up there at the cabin."

"Now, what makes you say that?" His off-kilter smirk resembling a loopy fun-house face.

"Permanent rent control."

The smirk vanished.

"Lucky guess," Wil said. "Cole buy the beer, too?"

Alvarez reached for the bottle but knocked it over, righting it quickly before much spilled. After a swig, the smirk was back in place. "Hey, life goes on—expenses go up. Cole's a crack shot. He never meant to hurt him."

"No kidding."

"He told me that. You think I'm some kind of Judas?"

"Cole say why?"

"He wanted to scare Doc off or something—how the hell should I know?" Alvarez blinked, wiped his mouth with the back of his hand; something else leaking through the broken smile. "How's he doin,' by the way?"

"Well as can be expected with a hit out on him." Another gamble—seeing Alvarez as compromised but not murderous.

"What hit? That's bullshit."

Wil just looked at him.

*"That all you're gonna say?"*

"You know something, Crash, now's the time. Later won't cut it."

"I know nothing about the killings on the levee. Period."

"But you know something about seventy-eight, don't you? What happened out at Doc's place."

"No."

"And they're related, aren't they?"

"How would I know?"

*"Aren't they?"*

*"I don't know."*

"Yeah, you do."

"Get off me," Alvarez said. "You have any idea what it's like trying to find work with *that* on your résumé? Might as well have done it myself."

"So why am I here, Chris? Money?"

*Bingo in the look, the bloodshot eyes; hesitation in the body language, the man going suddenly inward.* He saw Alvarez feeling the thing turning on him, cold feet after a hot flood of dope and who knew what else to fire his courage. *Keep going.*

"What do you have on Cole?"

"Nothing."

"Then why is he picking up your tab?"

"The hell is this? I asked *you* here, remember?"

He let it go. "How much money are we talking?"

The musician heaved a sigh Wil could smell from the couch, ran a hand over his sweating face. "Twenty thou and a ticket to New Zealand."

"Why there?"

"Because it's a long way from here. The hell do you care?"

Wil ran thoughts, settled on one. "A written statement—Lieutenant Xavier Acosta, Kern County Sheriff's. After you lay it out for me now."

"You think I'm insane?"

"Why sweat it? Nothing I can do without the paper."

Alvarez finished the beer, went and got another from the fridge, held it against his face. "There was a party at Doc's that day. Same crowd, the usual blowout. But this one was different. It was over by four."

"I miss something new here? Please tell me if—"

"Doc ran us off. He was getting weird off some shit. He didn't usually do dope and the stuff hit him hard."

"How do you mean weird?"

"Fed up—Jesus and the moneychangers. Like that. Saying his dead grandfather was watching us from out in the cotton."

"How did the others react?"

Alvarez shrugged. "Hey . . . on to the next gig. Larry had another party lined up, as I remember."

"Larry Fordyce."

He nodded, Wil thinking none of this would be news to the cops. Or anybody else, probably. "So what are you selling here?"

"I look like a loan officer? Cash and the ticket—in hand."

"Tomorrow, if my client agrees. And not without a sample."

Alvarez slumped back, began working the label off his bottle. "You have any idea how much dope Doc bought for that crowd? Try six figures going on seven. I know because I ran it."

"Who for?"

"Nice try."

"Where does Doc's old man figure in it?"

"Fuck if I know."

Wil eyed him, saw tapped—read vulnerable—and decided to push it. "No deal, Crash. You want to talk relevance, you know where I am."

"BFD. Look, I was *there* when a certain phone call came in from Southfork—right around six o'clock, if that means anything to you. Somebody needing a good cleanup service . . ."

*Six P.M., 8/27/78—approximate time of death, according to the reports.* Wil flashed on shotgun blasts, being on the receiving end. "Two little girls, Crash. You knew these people."

"I've done my grieving, thank you."

"Not enough to keep Doc off the rockpile for nineteen years."

"Fuck off. You think that didn't occur to me? With my history, that would have been me in there. Cold turkey—if I'd survived *that* long." He finished the beer in a gulp. "Even so, I was going to do it and take my chances when Doc changed his plea. What was the point after that?"

"But now you're ready to turn your source?"

"Could be . . ."

"How's Cole connected?"

A shrug, Alvarez smiling serenely now—bait plug cast and taken. "Tomorrow morning," he said, rolling the label into a ball and pitching it toward a grocery bag in the corner. "Cash and the friendly skies. *Bye . . . bye, baby-baby, bye-bye.*"

He was still singing to himself and chuckling as Wil let himself out past Sid's tracking eyes.

Wil punched it out onto Edison, his mind in overdrive.

*What really happened out there? What phone call? To where and to whom?* Laundering service—that tidbit fitting nicely with Bob Tate's photos and analysis—not one round where it shouldn't have been: the rhinoceros in the corner. And Doc—Jesus and the moneychangers— the wrath of God finally running off the pagans. And as he did, picturing old Clell Whitney, grandfather and boyhood hero, standing mute and gnarled in the cotton fields. Watching him with hollowed-out eyes . . .

Moving on, who was Alvarez selling out? Cole? If so, why, in light of what Crash had going with him, something obviously behind that. And what of Lute DeVillbis and Rye Rossert? No mention of them, no possible tie-in except money—things always coming back to that . . .

Larry Fordyce? Wil made a note to try and locate Doc's old manager—with luck, a chip in the mosaic. No pattern yet, Jenelle. Still, with Alvarez about to turn on somebody, they were miles ahead of where they'd been.

Maybe things were looking up.

Just then Wil did—snapping to headlights keeping pace in the rearview, about a block behind. Making them as those that had swung in when he'd left the cross street.

Paranoia? Not this time.

He cursed himself for not paying closer attention; couple of detour turns brought the lights up closer. Not crowding, just *there* . . . invisible had it not been for the lack of other cars.

He cut up to 24th—well out of his way—then headed west at an even speed. Under the freeway then up onto it without signaling, the lights still there, maintaining the distance. Southbound now, a stream of big-rigs whizzing by impassively, their drafts rocking the far lighter pickup.

Hold or fold: Wil eased off at California, figuring the message would be clear. *I know you're there. I don't give a shit.*

He was a block from his hotel, blinker on for the turn, the headlights holding, when they suddenly cut out. Wil was vaguely conscious of a dark shape peeling left, then he was in the hotel parking lot, crouched behind the fender, sweaty-palming the .380 off his ankle. Half expecting them to come careening around the corner to finish it.

*Nothing. Deep breaths, let it go. Purposeful walk to the unit that housed his room. Everything as he'd left it.*

*Blinking light on the phone.*

Wil punched in the message number: two from Xavier Acosta returning *his* calls, plus a brief one from Kari. Thinking she might appreciate some good news despite the hour, he dialed Jenelle, pacing until she picked up, obviously from sleep.

"Alvarez knows something he's ready to sell," Wil said after filling her in on the meet. "Something about what happened out at Doc's." He told her the terms.

"My God, that's a lot of money. You think it's worth it?"

"I'd advise two cashier's checks for ten. I think he might settle for one if we had the ticket in hand."

"No," she said firmly. "If there's something to this, I don't want to risk losing it when it's so close. I know a travel agent I can reach before the arraignment and somebody at the bank afterward. Will that be soon enough?"

"For Crash? Don't worry about it—we'll probably be the ones to rouse him."

After confirming when he'd pick her up in the morning, Wil wound down with the country music channel, just after three-thirty when he finally did turn in. Lying there, still hearing a song about leaving Bakersfield, eyes fixed on the ceiling despite his fatigue and the early day ahead. Weighing what was at stake—for him and for . . . *Shit!*

He bolted out of bed, threw on clothes, and hit the S-10 running. Over hotel speed bumps and out onto California in a screech of rubber.

*Blind as a damn bat!*

Luckily the traffic lights were more or less in sync, those he didn't run: record time through town and out Edison Highway.

This time he pulled up in front of Cheri's. Just behind the three patrol units with flashing light bars, static-y detached voices coming from the radios inside. Around back then, where half a dozen bleary trailer people— lights on in all the units now—observed from outside the crime tape, chatted or smoked in silence.

Xavier Acosta was deep in conversation with two uniformed deputies and a plainclothes standing outside Crash Alvarez's trailer. Wil waited until the lieutenant noticed him and walked over, coaxing the last out of a tired cigar.

"I call, you come—that it?"

"What happened?"

"Funny thing, I was hoping you'd tell me."

Wil looked at him. "You really think I'd be here if I knew?"

"I don't believe in coincidence, remember?"

"I was here earlier. I left. I came back."

"Which saves us the trouble of picking you up," Acosta said. "See, we already know you were here, the bartender made you. Question is why."

"I was followed after I left—two-thirty, around there. I didn't put it together soon enough."

"Guess not." He flicked ash off the dead stogie, slipped it into his windbreaker. "Stay behind me and don't touch anything." Leading Wil across the leaves and dirt to the screen door, propped open now with one of the folding chairs.

"That's far enough. Coroner'll be here in about thirty seconds."

Wil looked inside, saw Chris Alvarez still in the easy chair, white face angled to one side. Spoon, syringe and rubber tubing, a razor-bladed box knife lying beside the deep cuts in both wrists. Twin puddles soaking the cheap throw rug.

"Trailerette got ticked at the loud music and called it in. Guess bowser there wasn't much help."

Wil heard a snicker from one of the deputies.

"I'm waiting," Acosta said.

"He wanted to talk."

"That's nice. What about?"

Briefly Wil told him. "Cash and a ticket to New Zealand. That sound to you like a man planning to kill himself?"

"Mr. Alvarez was not unknown to us, drug-wise. Kind of an unstable sort."

Wil said nothing.

"Moot point, anyway. The coroner gets to decide." Acosta checked out the cold cigar stub, put it back in his pocket. "Sure love to find out what he was selling, though. Maybe we should get more formal with this at our place."

"I figure you as smarter than to waste your time."

"Yeah? Why'd you call me?"

*Got him his bars. Always felt that was kind of convenient for old Zavvy: Bob Tate.* Second thoughts—no taking it back once it was out: Tell Acosta about Doc and the note, hoping he'd take it seriously and protect him? Or let it lie, hoping Doc was jail-savvy enough to stay alive on his own?

Flip a coin, you lose . . .

Wil shrugged—*no big deal.* "Just wondering if you knew how long from arraignment till pretrial hearing."

Acosta just stared at him.

"Heat's really getting on my nerves," he added, literally feeling the visual pat-down.

"Usually a deuce, but the DA's talking about speeding it up," Acosta said finally. "Now get out of here before I change my mind. And keep driving, while you're at it."

Wil had turned away when a bulb lit. "Last hurrah," he said as Acosta was striding toward one of the deputies. "Any idea what Alvarez had going on the stereo?"

Acosta looked over his shoulder, spoke briefly with the deputy. *"Alias Doc Whitney,"* he came back. "Ain't that a hoot? Real going-out music . . ."


The occupants of the darkened Firebird watched the coroner's van roll up, two technicians and a man in a short-sleeved shirt get out, speak with the sheriff's deputies outside Cheri's, then head down the alley and disappear around back. So doing, they edged past a tall man with blond hair who got into the white pickup he'd arrived in, spun a U on the deserted street, and roared up Edison.

"Follow him?"

The man riding shotgun shook his head. "We know where he's going. Besides, he's no threat."

"You don't think Alvarez dropped the dime?"

The shotgun rider thought a moment. "Nah. Like he said, he'd have had the money on him."

"So why the frown? It's over. One more *tóxico* checkin' out."

"The way that damned dog's eyes kept looking at me.

Like it was alive or something." A beat went by while they took in the activity up the street. "Who'd want something like that around anyhow?"

The driver shook his head. "Fuck if I know. Got some weirdo shit out there."

"Tell me about it." Raul Garza glanced at his watch. "Damn, check the time. Old lady's going to be pissed if I don't take care of business tomorrow."

"Business . . ."

"Dancing. Tomorrow's our anniversary." He flipped open the cell phone and pressed the button for a preprogrammed number as the driver started the car and eased away from the curb, gentle on the gas to keep the big engine quiet. "I hate dancing."

"No shit," the driver came back. "The endless fucking macarena."

# SEVENTEEN

Seven-thirty Monday morning—two hours' sleep, maybe—Wil pulled up in front of Jenelle's.

He was about to give a toot when she opened the door, pulled it shut behind her: indigo skirt and cream-colored top, the silver squash blossom over it, drapy summerweight lavender thing over that. He reached over and opened the door for her, dark hair briefly catching the morning sun and raising his spirits a notch. Long way to go to make much of a difference.

"I was able to catch my friend," she said as they drove out the gate. "She'll have the ticket by noon. I should be able to transfer twenty from savings, if I've calculated correctly."

Wil saw a café and pulled into the lot. Inside, amid the bustle, hopeful aromas, coffee poured as soon as they sat down—big sips after tempering it with milk, wanting its heat as much as the boost, anything to burn through the fog—he told her.

"Dead?" she said incredulously. "I don't believe it." Searching his face for the put-on.

"I'm sorry."

Distant for a moment, she said, "This can't be happening, none of it. Why would Chris kill himself?"

"He didn't. Somebody did it for him." And to her

look, "Same people who followed me back to the hotel, made sure I didn't change my mind for some reason and go back."

"Are you sure?"

"He was too happy when I left—fat city coming up." He saw confused, questioning. "It had to be to silence him. They even put *Alias* on after they did it—nice little object lesson for anybody paying attention."

"Like you."

"Which means whatever's going on now has its roots in Stockdale. And somebody's getting very nervous."

"Poor Chris . . . What do we do now?"

He checked the time. "You want anything to eat?"

"No."

"Me either." Tossing off his coffee, putting down a five. "And we should get going if we want in."

It was about what he'd anticipated. Media vans parked outside the waffle-windowed Justice Building, reporters and support people clogging the entrances. Armed deputies stationed or walking the crowd, communicating via shirt-mounted radio. Extra scrutiny given everyone going through the metal detectors up to the second floor.

Stern-looking bailiffs eyeballing the courtroom.

After he and Jenelle had secured seats, Wil used the washroom to splash water on his face and down some aspirin. On the way back, he connected with the parole officer's voice mail after looking him up in the White Pages—please call him re Don Lee Whitney—then looked out onto the parking lot where someone in coat and tie was talking earnestly into a bank of microphones as videographers ground off footage and strobes popped.

At that moment a white bus pulled into the lot and Doc was "hustled" inside as the crowd grew in size, latecomers and people from other offices rushing for their look as well. Walking back inside the courtroom,

Wil eased in beside Jenelle, who was staring at the bronze seal behind the judge's bench. At nine straight up, the judge—a black woman with sharp eyes—entered through the side door, the taller of the bailiffs instructing everyone to rise. She sat, shuffled through a sheaf of papers, and looked up.

"Nice to see so many citizens taking an interest," she said dryly. "If arraignments are new to you, as is my guess, watch and learn."

As though responding to her cue, the wall-mounted monitors facing the courtroom came to life and a miscreant at the Pretrial Facility thirty miles away responded to a signal from a deputy by stepping to the podium and facing the camera/monitor there.

"Raimundo Ramirez—that's you?" Half glasses checking the folder at her end. "Mr. Ramirez, the charge against you is arson. Do you understand the charge? You are waiving representation, is that correct? How do you plead? Enter as no contest, sentencing to take place May nineteenth." She turned a page. "Next case, Hector Briones . . ."

On it went, a dozen pro forma arraignments inside of thirty minutes, the court reporter tapping away below the bench. The tall bailiff approached to confer, then nodded toward the back of the room. Seconds later Doc Whitney, in leg and waist shackles connected to a chain and what had to be the clothes he was arrested in, was escorted to a table and chairs on the other side of the barrier.

Wil felt Jenelle's hand slip inside his.

"Quiet in court," the tall bailiff said as the man Wil had seen expounding to the press entered with an assistant and sat down, the judge nodding to them.

"Mr. Whitney, is your attorney present?"

Doc leaned forward as if speaking into a microphone.

"Your Honor, this one's on your tab as well as your conscience."

Her gavel silenced the laughter; even the two from the district attorney's office fought to hide smiles. But it wasn't played for laughs; Doc's gaze held the judge's.

"Don't press your luck, Mr. Whitney."

"What luck is that, Judge?"

"That's enough—bailiff will control the defendant."

A heavyset deputy edged closer; Doc took no notice.

"In the absence of counsel and in light of the seriousness of the charge, Mr. Whitney, court will appoint one. In the matter of the charge, murder in the first degree in the deaths of Farley Kroft and John Jay Quillan, how do you plead?"

Doc's eyes found Jenelle briefly. "Not guilty," he said. "No bargains, no bullshit."

"So entered. Bail is denied. Pretrial hearing is set for"—she checked her calendar—"next Monday at ten A.M."

There was another murmur at that, the one-week acceleration of the process, as the heavyset bailiff led Doc Whitney out and Coat and Tie looked pleased. At that point the video monitors darkened, the tall bailiff instructed all to rise while the judge left by the side door and the spectators began to scramble for the exit.

Rye Rossert turned off the television set in his office. *"Phase One,"* he vamped. *"In which Doris gets her oats."*

Lute DeVillbis broke from his thoughts and looked up. "What's that?"

"John Lennon, joking around on a Beatles album. Come on, you're not that old."

"How come I feel that old?"

"Shit—get some exercise, will you? Go a few rounds

with R.G. He'll even tie one hand behind his back to make it fair. Won't you, Raul?"

"*Sí, patrón.*"

"There, you see?" Rossert said, grinning at Garza thumbing his nose and doing a series of light jabs off the balls of his feet. "Anything for you, Lutie."

"Never stood a chance, did he? Not against you."

"I don't remember asking him to show up around here. What are you saying, Lute, that you'd rather it be us?"

"Never was about me or Cole, was it?"

"*Well, would you? . . .*"

DeVillbis said nothing.

"Hey, Lute, you know the difference between a channel cat and a lawyer? One's a scum-sucking bottom feeder and the other's a fish. Funny, huh?"

"You always know how to bring it down to your level, don't you?"

"Aw, shucks . . ."

"How'd you get like this? No, I mean it, Rye—what turned you into you? I'd love to know."

"Practice, practice, practice." Rossert picked up the bottle of Chivas that DeVillbis had been nursing since they started watching the coverage of Doc Whitney's arraignment. "And Luther? On second thought, chug the whole damn thing."

While Jenelle made them something to eat, Wil listened to a recorded message that under no circumstances would Nelson Gemello be at liberty to discuss Doc Whitney's parole—Wil thinking, *Why am I not surprised?* He then got hot on Larry Fordyce: calls to editors of the country-music magazines on the coffee table. Broadening it to include Nashville recording studios, talent agents, old friends from back there on her Christmas-card list—the Internet if all else failed. Which made him think of the flowers he hadn't sent Kari, the message she'd left that he hadn't returned.

After what must have been the forty-eighth call, each singleton rippling into another several—the name vaguely familiar, call so-and-so who might know—Wil was about ready to close the door on Crash Alvarez's comment about Larry having another party lined up. Still thinking if part of Larry's job was lining up parties, maybe he'd remember who it was that Crash had been talking about giving up—Mr. Drugs.

*You have any idea how much dope Doc bought a year for that crowd? Try six figures going on seven—I know because I ran it . . .*

Baby steps when seven-leaguers were needed; prime longshot material in place of trying to think with a brain that ached for sleep. Which triggered a thought: probably more Jenelle's remark about being surprised if Larry Fordyce were alive than this Chinese fire drill.

Then a voice he'd been holding for came on, someone named Milt in Memphis sounding about half in the bag: "Ol' Bullethead? Hell, yeah. Split for L.A. last I heard, figured there was more money in rap artists. All them gold chains. You find him, ask him if he remembers that night at Bowl-o-Rama, the ladies' room. Heidi the human Hoover. You got that?" He cracked up, then hung up.

More calls, sandwiched around Jenelle's dash to her branch library for copies of L.A. directory pages: talent agencies with progressive-sounding names, bingo after what felt like a dozen, a cool voice explaining that Mr. Fordyce was out supervising a recording session and couldn't be reached. Wil came on like Nashville vice, urgent that he contact Larry Fordyce immediately.

"He ever mention anyone named Heidi?"

"Not that I—"

"Sorry, I didn't catch your name."

"Sherrice."

"Well, Sherrice, I can't be specific, what he did to her, but I'm asking for your help. This is not a nice man."

"Tell me something I don't know."

Wil jotted the address, thanking her Southern-gentleman style, requesting she not notify Mr. Fordyce of their conversation, assuring Sherrice that *he* wouldn't. Hoping she wouldn't change her mind after he'd hung up.

"Found him," he said to Jenelle handing him a tea and the No-Doz he'd asked for. "Now, if he'll just stay put till I get there. You going out to see Doc?"

She nodded.

He blew on the tea, swallowed two No-Doz with it, wrote Kari's number down on a piece of paper. "Tell him to call collect if he has access to a pay phone. Generally they do." He checked his watch—half-past noon. "Nine o'clock should do it."

"I'll tell him. Are you coming back tonight?"

"Tomorrow, mid-morning," he told her, noting a flicker of interest behind *I see.* He smiled at her, trying to be encouraging after the morning she'd had—Alvarez, then the full weight of the system, the odds against Doc, on display.

"Hang in. We're a long way from done."

She touched his cheek, brought his eyes into hers. Her fingers were cool where they lingered—about the point he stopped noticing anything.

"Thank you," she said. "No matter what happens."

"I have a better idea." Throaty from the tea. "Wish me luck."

Ninety-four in L.A., some kind of new record for this day in April, the weatherman was saying. Wil clicked off the update, found a station playing rap songs and made it through three before punching it off.

*Larry, Larry. I hope the money's good.*

*I hope you're there.*

He took the west side of the valley, the I-5 side hope-less at any time of year—jogging east at the last moment to the Hollywood, over Cahuenga Pass and onto Highland, smog shrouding the buildings of downtown, sky the color of spoiled milk unless you looked straight up. At two-forty, Highland was thick with cars.

Pre– or post–rush hour, take your pick.

Following a bumper sticker that read BUSINESS IS GREAT, PEOPLE ARE TERRIFIC, LIFE IS WONDERFUL and Sherrice's directions, he turned at DeLongpre, zigged to a cross street, then another, and found it: a blocky raw concrete two-story with a barred fence and card-activated gate. Behind it were a Mercedes, a Jag, two Explorers, a gold-detailed Yukon, and an older un-washed Prelude.

Wil found a space on the street and went in the front entrance.

Inside were slick surfaces, shades of gray and char-coal, high-tech materials, rap emitting from ceiling speakers. And Huey Newton revisited: a shirtless black man whose muscles looked like carved ebony glaring from the wall behind which two stunning black women sat, one talking heatedly on the phone.

"Delivery's around back," the other one said, glancing at Wil before returning to her paperwork.

"Looking for Mr. Fordyce. Sherrice from the agency said I'd find him here."

She looked up again. "May I—"

"Office matter, just take a sec." He started down a hall lined with offices, heard *"Sir . . ."* as her own phone began buzzing.

Up backless stairs, down a corridor paneled with heavy acoustic tile and more glary posters; seeing a

promising-looking door, he swung it open and caught
BASS. Heads swung his way: engineer behind a huge
sound panel, rapper behind thick glass, backups in their
own booth, heavyset man on the black leather couch—
all listening to playback, the lone white face in the room
a slight guy about sixty in tight-fitting black jeans, maize
tank under something gray and unstructured. Very tan,
shaved head, white beard looking chalked on, no mustache. Sunglasses dangled from cords down his back,
gold chain along the tank's contour.

Gradually the bass planed off; the engineer stopped
tape, looked up expectantly.

"Larry Fordyce," Wil said before anybody could rag
on the take. "You old son of a gun." His best shit-eating
grin.

The white guy glanced at the others. "I know you?"

"Damn straight—my wife Heidi, anyhow." He gave
Fordyce a guy-thing stage wink—*that* Heidi. "Said you
was gonna get her a recording contract, remember?
Heidi Beane the Country Queen?" Winging it totally
now, figuring Larry wouldn't recall and Milt would ap-
prove.

"Took us a while to find you, but we did. She's out
in the station wagon now—all the way from Memphis."
He winked at the man on the couch. "Ol' Lar's a legend
back there."

"*Shit*," Larry said under his breath.

The man left the couch, black leather sighing with
release. "*Country, L.T.*? That what he saying?"

"Through and through," Wil drawled as Larry paled
under his tan. "Best in the business."

By now the talent was looking in from the booth. "Yo
out there. Gonna gimme some feedback or what?"

Larry snapped to where he was and pressed the mike
button, gave the kid a thumbs-up. "Platinum, babe. You
the man."

Wil smiled at the producer, then at Larry; eased toward the door. "I'll tell Heidi to come on up, meet your friends. You gotta see her hair now." He held his hands apart. "It's twice as big."

"Look, L.T.—"

"L.T.—I like that," Wil said.

"I never seen this guy, Bone. Swear to God."

"*Country?*" As though Larry had just taken a dump on the rug.

"Gimme a minute to straighten it out, okay? Won't take a sec."

Wil let himself be pulled from the room, Larry looking prime for a stroke as the heavy door shut behind them. *"Who the fuck ARE you?"*

Wil smiled. "Your call, L.T. Freddy Krueger loose in your career or the man who's buying you lunch."

"You're crazy, you know that?"

"Don't sweat it, L.T. They can't take a joke, fuck 'em." Wil paused to let the waiter set down their pastas, Larry already having made a serious dent in a bottle of Valpolicella. This time of day the Italian restaurant was uncrowded; just the same, Larry had insisted they take a table out back, far corner of the patio, faint sounds of Melrose floating in through the overhanging ficus.

"Easy for you to say." Larry drained his glass, poured himself more, which emptied the fifth. Catching the waiter's eye, he signaled for another. "You have any idea how hard it is breaking in at my age? Not to mention the obvious."

"Good thing you're good."

"Hey, you think I wanna be doin' this shit forever? Why you think I come out here?"

Wil sampled his lunch: baby clams and mussels in olive oil, fresh tomato and basil; good stuff—well under twenty-eight dollars. He watched Larry power down his twenty-four-dollar lasagne. Damn near fifty-two bucks' worth of pasta . . .

"So, how's it going?"

"Fine till you showed up. The fuck you want to know about Doc Whitney so bad for anyhow?"

Wil realized Fordyce probably hadn't heard Doc had been released from prison, let alone the new murder charges against him. Briefly, he explained.

"Jesus," Larry said, washing it down with the red. "What a drag."

"What was it like being his manager?"

"Sorry, babe. I never look over my shoulder."

"And we'd gotten off to such a promising start. Send it back," Wil said to the waiter advancing with the wine.

*"All right, all right . . ."*

He gestured for the waiter to proceed, waited while Larry pinched the cork, swirled, sniffed, gulped.

"I just noticed. You ain't drinkin'."

"Already had my share. What about Doc?"

"Strange bird, but I liked him, the three years I repped him. Put him on the map, that's all."

"How'd you two hook up?" Wil thinking he'd already been around Fordyce too long, the man creeping into his speech.

"Met him at a concert and took him under my wing. Kid never did understand the business. Naive? . . . You have no idea. Always thinking it came down to the music."

"And what does it come down to?"

"Fuck, look around you," Larry said. "It's all packaging—attitude. Like you got. Trust me, that shit sells. You ever do any male modeling?"

Wil just looked at him.

"You want to, call me, okay?" Catching the look. "Right—Doc. Even then, the industry was going soft-core." He shook his head. "But not our boy. It was like he had this death wish or something."

"Tell me about that."

Larry took a moment to shovel in a huge bite. "What happens when you can't change, go with the flow. Look at me for instance: Know where I got the idea for what I am now? Makeovers on *Sally*. Point is," he said, swallowing, "when your label demands one thing and you do another, guess what? And don't think I didn't warn him. Did he listen? Hell no—just kept on going down his own road . . . Blackheart Highway."

"Say that again?"

"*Blackheart Highway*, his fourth album, the one he was working on. The one never got made. Way too country for the playlist. Fork-in-the-road time: Doc going one way, them going another. Creative types—gimme a break."

*Blackheart* . . . "Bottom line, Larry."

He drank, poured, drank. "They canceled his contract. Plus they put the word out on him—T-R-O-U-B-L-E. Nothing I could do at that point *except* bail out." He shrugged. "Easy come, easy go. Kid took it hard, though. No shit, considering."

"Anything you want to add to that?"

"Boom, boom, boom—end of story. Mind if I try one of your clams?"

Wil watched as Larry took one and chewed it, a strange look crossing his face before spitting it out. "He ever mention his father?"

"Hell, what do you think Blackheart was about? The kid was obsessed with him. Not to mention tryin' to measure up to his gramp, this old Okie who might have cleared five thou in a good year."

"What was Arlene like?"

"Come again?"

Wil shook his head.

"Hey, just makin' a little joke. Hot," he said. "And I ain't talking about the weather."

"You're a truly sensitive guy, Lar."

"I'da watched that one if she was mine. Seemed like she was always having sitters in for the little girls, then hittin' the honky-tonks. Big on appearances, though."

"In what way?"

"That house, for example—you see the size of it? That was her. Just kept spending like there was no to-morrow. Didn't surprise me Doc snapped, let alone drank. Know what I'm sayin'?"

"Yeah. What about the drugs?"

"Doc didn't do 'em, no matter what you read. Not till the end, anyway."

"I meant the parties. Did you get the dope or—"

"*Whoa a friggin' minute.*" Fordyce shoved back his chair. "I'm a businessman. Which means the game I'm in is the game I play. You talk trash to me, I'm outta here."

"Save it for the new pals, Lar. Chris Alvarez told me what he ran and you spread around. Now he's dead. And if you're worried about me, nobody *but* me gives a shit this late in the game. So you finish it."

He eased back in. "Crash is dead?"

Wil nodded.

"Damn. I always liked him."

"Who did he run the drugs for?"

"You don't honestly expect—"

"Lar, I've only begun to be an asshole. I've got fan clubs."

"It's been twenty fucking years . . ."

"*Try.*"

Fordyce hit the Val again, burped, closed his eyes. For a second Wil thought he'd drifted off, but then he opened them.

"Mexican kid. Nice little guy. And where that came from, I'll never know."

"He have a name?"

"Figured you was gonna ask; gimme a . . . Sammy, that was it. Sammy Mejia. Never suspect him by looking at him. Probably why they used him."

"They . . ."

He wiped his long forehead: "Don't ask, because I don't know. Only talked with him when he was waiting for Crash, and even that was rare. But I got the impression he was in business with somebody. A relative or something."

Wil had a thought, threw it out on the table: "The name Garza mean anything here? Raul Garza?"

"Nope."

"Two more: Rye Rossert? Lute DeVillbis?"

"No and no. You gonna order dessert?"

"Calories, Lar—the tank." Wil got out a business card, wrote the hotel number down. "You remember anything else, call me collect. Or leave a message and I'll call you." He dropped it down the man's top.

"Oh, yeah, right. I can't wait."

Wil slid his chair and stood up to bring the waiter a credit card, hoping the plastic wouldn't bounce. Then to get the hell out of there.

"It's been real L.T.," he said, retreating. "Don't think it hasn't."

# EIGHTEEN

Wil made Kari's just before seven, pulling up short when he saw the Corvette parked outside her bungalow. Playing it cautious, he circled the block and angled in across the street, slightly down from the Vette. Turned the radio on low and waited.

It was early enough so the drapes were open, dark enough for lights on inside. Enough to see Kari and her ex-husband, Scott: gestures, pacing, silent yelling—a theater of the absurd that reminded Wil of the arguments his mother and father used to have over money after they thought he'd gone to bed. Compounded by his mother's drinking, the beefs finally got so bad he'd crank up the volume on his tinny record player—Buddy Holly, Del Shannon, and the Everly Brothers to say *PLEASE*. Generally that did it, everybody upset then. Nobody speaking to anybody for at least a morning, the only sound the tinking of spoons in their cold cereal bowls.

He took a breath, almost tasted the Cheerios, and let it pass. Then Scott, a studmuffin type reminiscent of Cole DeVillbis, burst out the front door and burned rubber down the block. *Take THAT, bitch.* Wil was tempted to go to her then, but instead drove to the market and bought several bouquets of cut flowers, had the girl tie them into one, gave it three more songs before he knocked.

"Hi." Forcing a smile when she saw who it was.

"I saw him leave. Great timing, huh?"

"I'll take it." Wiping her eyes. "God, it's good to see you."

"Same here," Wil said. "Sorry I didn't call."

She put the flowers in a vase, set it on a table. "He's seeing a lawyer about taking Brian permanently. Moving to Northern California."

"Can he do it?"

"Who knows with the law the way it is? A lot depends on Brian, who he chooses. You want a drink or something?"

He sank into the nubby rocker-recliner, rubbed his eyes as she went to get it. "Some days just keep coming, don't they," he said toward the kitchen.

There was a shatter of glass, and he went to find her bent over brown shards and foam. He put an arm around her, turned her into him, let her blow it out on his polo shirt. "Things even up, is what I meant."

"The son of a bitch just knows what buttons to push."

"I know." He sat her down in the living room, went back and opened a Bud for her, another Hires for himself.

"Fuck it," she said finally. "How's the Whitney thing going?"

He waggled a hand in the air, went through an abridged version for her: Alvarez, the arraignment, Fordyce, Doc himself.

"And I thought I had problems."

"Nobody's minimizing them, Kari."

She tilted the Bud. "Thing is, Brian's using them to make me dance. He'll change his mind if . . ."

Something in her look: folding her hands around the bottle, staring at it. "What?" he asked finally.

"I don't see you anymore."

"All this and blackmail, too."

She nodded. Light from the overhead swam in her eyes.

"He's fifteen, Kari. What happens when he's seventeen and decides he wants something else?"

"I only know I have to fight for him. I'm just so sorry."

"Let it go," Wil said. "Nobody has a blueprint."

"It would only be for a while, and he's having a tough time, too—these are hard years for any kid. Maybe if I say it often enough I won't want to kill him."

"You want me to talk with Scott?"

"No," she said. "He's as manipulating as Brian. Forty going on twelve."

"What about Brian?"

"Later, maybe. Right now he needs some time, the little shit."

Wil leaned back in the recliner, closed his eyes, and tried to summon the energy to be angry, depressed, anything—tell her he knew the feeling. But nothing came.

"Wil, wake up . . . *please.*"

He opened to dim light that hurt anyway, lids filled with grit, that confused spaciness. "What is it?"

"Phone," Kari said. "I think it's your guy. Said you left a message for him to call here."

*Nine o'clock—the time he'd requested Jenelle pass along.* He scrambled up, blinking and stiff. "Doc?"

"Some circus this morning."

"Should have seen the rest of the day."

"Well, I'm here—along with six other guys waiting for the phone. We got three minutes."

"You heard about Alvarez?"

"Jen told me. Fucking bummer. She also said you told her it was no suicide. What's with that?"

Wil beat back a yawn. "He was going to sell me information about the drugs—who he ran them for."

"I don't believe it."

"Trust me for once."

"Crash *did* drugs, he didn't run them."

"Guess again. And Larry Fordyce thought it might have been a smallish Mexican kid he remembered seeing with him." He fumbled for his notebook. "Sammy Mejia. Sound familiar?"

"Wait a minute," Doc said. "You saw Fordyce?"

"Yes, and don't ask. What about Mejia?"

"Not familiar—and you're dead wrong about Crash."

Wil took a breath. "Hear me, Doc. Crash fingered you to Cole DeVillbis. It was Cole who took the shots at us, trying to scare you off from something. You want to plug in here?" Voices in the background, hollow metallic sounds.

"All right, I'm listening. But the natives are getting restless."

"Who took care of the dope expenses?"

"Larry—said it was all part of the deal, that he'd bury it somewhere. Petty cash or something."

"Six figures going on seven . . ."

"Cost of doing business—after a while you don't even notice. We had a ton coming in and Larry handled it all. Smart, huh? Ever wished you could have another crack at it, knowing what you know now?"

"Never. Did you know J. J. Quillan?"

"No. But Tate told me what I owed him."

Wil could picture him touching the spot where Quillan nearly kicked his face in. "What about *Blackheart Highway*?"

"Who told you about that—Jen? No, had to be Fordyce."

"No bullshit this time, Doc, no con. How much did your coming back have to do with your father?"

"You don't let up, do you?"

"Want to run me around some more?"

Pause, the metallic sounds and voices—a sadness, finally, in his: "You have any idea the number of times I wished him dead for not being there? Me? I mean, look where I ended up. Might as well have been both of us in that—"

The background voices suddenly escalated; there were sounds of a scuffle, receiver striking metal, a horn going off, and then, *"Shit, man, get a medic in here . . ."*

# NINETEEN

Blur: Wil's autopilot drive back, Jenelle staring into space, night becoming day. Morning headlines, follow-up to the countless radio and television interviews with county personnel: Acosta, the sheriff, the district attorney—just about anyone who'd comment on Don Lee Whitney's taking a homemade blade in the throat. Dead before help could get to him, the catalyst a supposed racial insult, nobody in the population saying *nada* beyond that. No suspect, the incident taking place in a previously undiscovered seam in the video cameras.

### DEATH OF AN OUTLAW
*Jail Justice: Doc Whitney Dies Alone*

The smuggled-out photo was sure to make somebody a pile: prison towel across the body's upper torso, dark pool spreading out from it on the concrete, deputies faced away and conferring in the hard room. Death in coarse-screen black-and-white.

Wil wondered what all of them were going to do now. Maybe Larry Fordyce had it nailed: on to the next one without so much as a backward glance. Some ride you gave 'em, Donnie, he thought. Rest in peace.

No peace for HIM though, only replay, eyes taped

open to a blocky handwritten note: *Don't tell Jen or ANYONE: Eme has a whack out . . . Eme has a whack out . . . Eme has a . . .* That close to telling Acosta about it that night—finally deciding against.

Like an artery he couldn't reach to stop the bleeding.

Jenelle finally had caved in, taken something and gone to bed, telling him no need to stick around, with any luck she'd be out until tomorrow. So he'd left, parked the truck downtown and simply wandered, knowing sooner or later he'd have to tell her. Heat and his own fatigue shading his attempts to sort through it all.

DeVillbis, Cole, Rossert—answers in there somewhere. Acosta, Tate, Fordyce, Sammy Mejia—assuming he was alive, let alone still around. Supporting cast? So use them, he thought. Do something.

But a wave was building, he could feel it: clear and boiling in the hot light. Paddling out to catch it, riding it all the way down its fragrant amber tube, his funk dropping off like the condensation on a bar glass. One shot at a time at first, then doubles with beer chasers. Hueys lined up over a red zone; the cavalry arriving to turn the tide not a moment too soon.

*That* feeling.

He realized he'd come to a gradual halt in front of black plate glass under a cocktail sign. Dark version of himself looking back at him. *Welcome home, son. Knew you couldn't leave like that. Stone cold? Not even a good-bye?*

"Damn," a voice said. "Looks like you got the dragons worse than mine, if that's possible."

Wil turned, saw a man who reminded him of Cedrick, but older: sixties stoop, face like a peeled red grapefruit. Overdressed for how warm it was.

"It can't be that bad."

"Bad enough."

Pulling on an earlobe, the man said, "Sorry to hear it.

Well, age before beauty. You coming in?"

Wil fumbled in a pocket and handed him the first bill that came out, a five. "Not today," he said. "But slay one for me while you're at it."

"Saint George, at your service." He winked, pushed in the double door, pausing a moment to look back, cigarette-laced bar breath dissipating around him. Then he was gone, the door flapping shut.

Sweating and alone on the sidewalk, Wil heard the words, *You don't let up, do you?* and himself coming back with, "Hang around awhile, Doc. I'm asking."

Wil called Bob Tate's number and got Abbie Tate on the line: no warmth, no sign of recognition, just that Bob was down at physical therapy, back around three.

"Therapy?" Wil asked. Conversation after requesting she tell Bob he'd called and wanted to see him.

"Pool therapy—it helps with his atrophy. Anything else?"

"I guess he heard about Doc Whitney."

"Who hasn't? You're coming by, then."

"If that's all right."

"With Bob or with me?"

Wil chose his words. "Mrs. Tate, have I done something to wind up on your list? Because I sure get that impression."

She released a breath. "He was okay before you got him all fired up. Now he's a time bomb. A man who almost made me a widow doing his damn *job*." Another breath. "See, I was there when they told him he'd never walk again. So I guess that means you qualify, Mr. Hardesty."

"I'm sorry if I—" *Click, buzz.*

Wil cradled the pay phone's receiver, checked his watch: almost one—two hours till Tate. He backtracked, drove to the Beale Memorial Library, and parked. Near

the entrance he passed a ten-by-sixty-foot strip of diverted river enclosed by graceful black bars—quiet dark
water on its concrete-channeled, subterranean way to
somewhere. As if someone had wanted to prove it still
existed.

For a moment he just watched, feeling as if he were
observing an animal in a zoo exhibit. *There—see? Don't
worry, though. Got him right where we want him . . .*

Back at it: second floor, the room behind the reference
desk; Wil scrolled through *Bakersfield Californian* microfilm after checking dates from his notebook and requesting corresponding reels from the librarian.
Confirming information on August 27, 1978, that he'd
gotten from the *L.A. Times* database: nothing new to
speak of except a shot that included J. J. Quillan with
Tate they'd omitted in the *Times* but run here. Both
standing and in uniform. Surreal in light of the legacy.

*Full bore,* he thought. *IOU, in spades.*

One hour down: Wil scrolled into December 1993,
caught the articles about Gib Whitney's bones being
pulled from the oil waste pond. Bullet hole in the skull,
the match on Gib from his dental records; having first
been reported missing June 1964, by his wife, Nedra
Whitney. Wil got the '64 microfilm, the record keeping
spottier here, less systematic, so it took him awhile to
find it.

### LOCAL OILMAN MISSING
*Gilbert Whitney Disappearance*

Less an article than a sidebar accompanying an essay
on oil-extraction technologies. Gib not coming home after nearly a week's absence, according to Nedra, who,
along with local attorney Luther DeVillbis, reported him
missing. Gib last seen turning east onto China Grade the
morning of June 17. . . .

## NO CLUES IN WHITNEY MYSTERY
*Sheriff's Department Requests Public's Help*

But none had materialized, and the investigation—or at least further coverage of it—disappeared from the paper after that. Wil rethreaded the 1993 film, dug deeper, and saw that site cleanup and subsequent discovery of Gib's remains were credited to the persistent efforts of NOW OR NEVER and its founder, Leora T. Graybill, gadfly to Kern County's oil industry. Etc., etc. . . . So far, corroborative.

Wil scanned his notes again and caught October 14, 1978, the day Bob Tate was shot. Checking to see he still had time before Tate was due home, he requested the microfilm for October 15 and ran across

## ONE WOUNDED IN DOMESTIC DISPUTE

Local section again, twenty lines plus the head: responding to a disturbance call, Sergeant Robert M. Tate, 29, blah, blah, blah . . . pretty much the way he'd described it. Except that the call was initiated by Yolanda Elena Hurtado, 18, girlfriend of the gunman—

Wil stopped, read it again—Samuel José Mejia, 17, who surrendered without further incident to sheriff's deputy J. J. Quillan . . . Samuel José Mejia. *Nice little guy. Never suspect him by looking at him. Probably why they used him:* Larry Fordyce's take on the kid working drugs with Chris Alvarez. Sammy Mejia.

Wil scrolled ahead to the sentencing: local-gang-member Mejia pleading no contest, a factor that, along with his age and assertion that he thought it was a rival gang's attempt on his life, had led to a six-year fall. Medium security.

Out in three years, Tate had said.

To where? To what?

Thinking nice-little-guy Sammy would be thirty-seven if he'd made it this far, Wil searched for more, found nothing else, and returned the microfilm reels to the librarian. With the hours inside, the tinted glass and fluorescent lighting—maybe the sun having burned off some haze—things seemed brighter when he emerged. Passing the sixty-foot river, he swore it had a shine that wasn't there before.

Bob Tate was in his office, bent over a spread of eight-by-ten prints, one in black-and-white. Hearing Wil's tap on the doorjamb, he raised up from the magnifier he was looking through.

"Important business here," he said, gesturing to the Little League team photos. "Never have picked one they're all happy with, but you do what you can."

"He and I were on the phone," Wil said. "Talking about his father."

But it was as if Tate hadn't heard. "Pool didn't help. Thought I'd look at these, see if that might work. Finally gave up and got this one out."

Wil looked through the glass, saw 1959, *Northside Drillbits.* Freckled boys in a black-and-white world. One's arm on the other's shoulder.

"Nine years old," Tate said. "Donnie Lee."

Wil said nothing.

"Me, him, all of it. What the hell happened?"

"I don't know, but I'm going to find out," Wil said. "Thought you might want to be in on it."

"Kind of late to shut the barn door."

"You don't believe that."

"How do you know what I believe? And while you're at it, go fuck yourself. Haven't you done enough?"

"Yeah," Wil said. "Too much operator and not enough friend."

Tate just looked at him.

"Sound familiar? There's more."

"I think you'd better leave."

Figuring his best chance with Tate lay in things left unsaid, Wil told him about Doc's note, his own decision to let it ride with Acosta.

Tate wheeled the chair away, stared a moment at the wall. "I don't buy it," he said. "Today's paper listed Alvarez as a suicide. And why would the *Eme* have a hit out on Doc?"

"That one's high on the list, all right."

"Doc knew what he was doing. And guilt's about as useful as cowflop on a boot."

"Not guilt—payback," Wil said, letting it sink in. "Alvarez didn't kill himself, he had it going—money and a trip out of here. He was doped and bled. And I *need* your help."

"Yeah, right, you need my help."

"Good thing your baseball team isn't hearing this."

Tate ran his hands over the chair's steel rims. He took a couple of breaths. "Ruth and Gehrig, is that it? Well, guess what? . . ."

"We'll do." Wil gestured at the old photo. "Better than this."

"You still on the clock with Jenelle?"

"What do you think?"

Tate's glare turned inward, saw something, came back as a glance. "What do I think? In addition to everything else, I'm wondering why a senior homicide detective rolls on a three A.M. suicide."

"Glad we agree."

"Don't get carried away. And why Doc's father?"

"Doc had a fourth album under way—*Blackheart Highway.* Larry Fordyce mentioned it had to do with Gib. Which didn't jive for me until we talked, the way I thought Doc felt about him. And I think all of this shit's linked, just don't ask me how yet."

"Fordyce—his old manager?"

Wil nodded. "Real sweetheart. Figured I'd see if something he recalled meant anything to you."

At the sound of footsteps, Tate glanced out the open door. "Let's take it for a walk," he said as the steps receded. "Things are a little tense right now."

Thinking *Good luck on the high wire,* Wil followed him around the garage, to the drive, out to the street: handsome houses, flower beds alive with color, big sycamores—lawn sprinklers mitigating the heat that much more.

"Nice neighborhood," Wil said.

"Home for a lot of years. So what's the deal with Fordyce?"

Wil reprised it: Alvarez's reference to the parties, Fordyce amplifying—drugs the linchpin. Tate coming back with, "We looked into it. Just seemed like the usual self-destructive-type-implodes-before-your-eyes. Except that it was Donnie."

"You remember what the stuff was?"

"Peruvian, virtually uncut. The wonder is he got back up at all."

"Fordyce contends Doc never did drugs except for that day."

Tate gave him a look. "He have a bridge he wanted to sell you, too?"

"Hey, if you know something here . . ."

"I don't really. Doc and I weren't that close by then, and he wouldn't have used it around me anyhow. I'd just question anything Fordyce said."

Wil thought a moment. "Did Acosta question it?"

"I'd have to check. But don't underestimate Acosta just because he's an officious prick." Tate waved to a woman gardening across the street.

"How hard would it be?"

"To check?" He looked at Wil to see if he was serious,

decided he was. "I still know people. A reason wouldn't hurt, though."

"For you or for them?"

"Hardesty, I'll say it once. Either we trust each other or we bury it now. With Doc."

"Deal. Fordyce tossed out a name—either Alvarez's supplier or his go-between. Somebody I think you know." Not being able to resist the pause. "Sammy Mejia . . ."

He was two steps beyond the wheelchair when he realized Tate had stopped it dead on the sidewalk.

Raul Garza adjusted the kid's leather headgear, gave it a pat. (Had they been getting smaller since he fought? Younger and harder, for sure—but smaller?) All around him training sounds clattered and banged off the hard surfaces of the basement boxing gym.

"Feet moving and your hands high," he told the kid. "Left, left, left, bob, then combo. Get your weight in the punches."

"*Sí. Pero—*"

Garza slapped a right off the kid's gloves. "English, *stúpido.* Where you think you are—Oaxaca?"

"No, sir."

"That's better." Garza seeing himself at that age. "How you gonna get anywhere you don't know the damn language?"

Paolo shouted to him across the ring, Paolo's fighter bobbing and weaving around his corner, eyes on Garza's boy. "Hey, *Raza.* Don't matter none—dozen years, we takin' it back anyway. Paper said so. Then we see who talks what."

Garza tapped his head. "Too many *en la cabeza,*" he said to his fighter, loud enough for Paolo to hear.

Paolo made as if he were climbing into the ring, Garza egging him on, both hoping it would rub off on the round. Then the fighters went at it again, Garza marveling at the speed and agility of Paolo's boy, something to check out, see if Paolo could be persuaded to part with a piece of his investment.

He became aware of a young man looking at him as if he needed to take a piss. He beckoned him over and listened as the kid spoke a few words in his ear. Nodded as the kid withdrew.

After the round, Garza put an arm around his tired fighter, whispered rote encouragement while directing a pointed finger of acknowledgment at a still-grinning Paolo. But his mind was already off the bout and somewhere else, and he left the gym quickly and drove there.

The house was about a mile beyond East High, where he'd gone to school, gotten into so many fights they'd called him *El Púgil* even then. Frequently suspended, he'd used the days to get strong in the oil fields; school and work—each pollinating the other. Steps on a ladder. What the *Raza* types never understood was you *took* what you wanted—that was this country. You didn't wait for it to be handed to you, everybody lining up into one big golden-chain gang. Nobody but nobody was chaining up Raul Garza.

Nobody alive, anyway.

He parked, walked past a sagging picket fence, down the drive, past boarded-up windows and BEWARE OF DOG signs, and in through the jimmied back door. Inside or not, sounds of the Southern Pacific dragging a line toward town made it feel as if the train were in the next room. Like the walls weren't there. Not much different than the shack where he'd grown up.

"In here, *compa*."

"Jesus God," Raul Garza said, entering. "Where you find these places, anyway? Worst one yet."

"Mr. Big, slumming in the old neighborhood."

Sammy Mejia led the two men with him in a *no-shit*

laugh, the room barely furnished, thick smell of dry rot, slats showing through the broken plaster and the stained rosebud wallpaper. He and Raul bumped fists, then Raul took in the others, stocky mestizos with round faces, one rounder than the other. More cautious sounding in their laughter, he noticed.

Nervous.

Raul felt a small rush at that; nothing he needed to assert anymore, just one of the perks. Like being recognized at a fight, still whispers about his title shot—taking the champ the full fifteen. Figuring every slipped punch was worth about twenty—cash that had brought him to this point, well beyond what a win would have meant.

Still, it festered to know he could have had it, all of Vegas hanging by a thread that last round. Sweating bullets. And Raul Garza looking out through the smoke and lights afterward to let the money boys know it could have been his if he'd chosen to fuck them over.

Sammy's comment brought him back: "Thought you'd want to be here for this, man. Go on," he said to the others. "Tell him."

"Tell me what?"

"It's nothing personal," the taller of the men started in. Trying to force eye contact, even though Garza could smell the fear coming off him in waves. Sour as *pulque* in the heat of the sealed-up crackerbox.

"*Es verdad,*" the other said. "We just want what's rightfully ours."

"So what are you saying here? You've not been treated fairly?"

"That was a very important job. Very risky."

"Felix is smart, he beat the surveillance," the other said. "Nobody's saying nothing about who done it, either. Nobody left to link it to after we're across."

"You do the job you're paid for, you figure it's suddenly worth more, is that it?"

The two men shifted, shrugged. "Business is what we're talking here. Being fair."

"That's right," the moon-faced one chimed in. "We just want what's fair."

The universal buzzword. "And how much more is that?"

"Six large," Sammy interjected.

"*Cojones,* I like that," Raul said admiringly. "Felix know you're asking for more?"

Their looks were his answer. "Didn't think so. And when he gets out and tries to look you up down there—what then?"

"Full share, guaranteed," the taller one said.

"With interest," Moon echoed. "Besides, he knows how it works. Felix is cool."

Raul turned to Sammy Mejia. "Sounds like a man to watch, this Felix. Now, what about this other thing—there a problem here? You don't got the money or something?"

"I got the money."

"So pay 'em." He watched the smiles form, their brief exchange of glances.

"Just wanted to hear you say it."

Sammy Mejia reached into a pocket, pulled out a roll of hundreds, and began to peel them off, the men's attention going immediately to the bills. Like flies to carrion, Raul observed.

"Nice you invited me to meet your friends," he asided to the younger man.

"No big thing. Just thought you might want to keep your hand in."

"That's considerate, you know that? You guys aware of what this man did here? You should pay attention, learn something." He looked at the two standing there—

Greed and Fear. Certainly not taking into account the long run as he'd learned to, Rye Rossert to thank for that.

"Then again," he said, pulling out a blued-steel automatic and putting a round in the taller one's eye before Moon could even look over for his. "Some guys never learn."

Ears ringing, bodies twitching at their feet, the room fogged with haze: *"Jesus Christ,"* Sammy said, his eyes wide. "What are you doin', man? Fuckin' me up. I gotta deal with these people."

*"Comida para las naranjas*—get somebody on it. Besides, who's gonna miss 'em?" Raul said. "And Felix never got within ten yards of Whitney."

"What are you talking about?"

"Just what I said. Felix got aced out. Word got out through Viñegas."

"Fuck me. So who hit Whitney?"

"Vin didn't know the guy." Raul bent over and took an envelope out of the fat one's pocket, scooped up the loose bills from the floor, where a flood of red was threatening to inundate them. He gestured with the liberated hit money. "Somebody we'll be hearing from soon, though. Bet your ass on that."

# TWENTY

Bob Tate knocked back his beer, low sun flaring in the glass before he set it down. At just after five-thirty, they had the outdoor patio to themselves. Somewhat cooler—at least to envision the coming evening still as spring.

Phyllis poked her head out of the bar. "I'm off. You take it easy there, Bob Tate." An edge of concern in her tone.

Tate waved without looking up. *"Take it easy,"* he said to Wil after she'd left. "Nineteen fucking years . . ."

"You still thinking Quillan helped set it up?"

A cloud of sparrows disappeared into a nearby tree and commenced loud chirping, the nightly dance for position. Tate said, "Jay knew I was pushing the crime-scene discrepancies. He hated my guts for reporting him on Doc. Only reason they still had us paired was I'd agreed to take him on as a project. Two days after the guy's booted off, he sets out a shingle and lists Rye Rossert as a client. Big stuff for him."

"You know that for a fact?"

"Jay had a mouth; word got around as I was recovering. And the more I reconstruct, the more he let me walk right into it." He spun the empty bottle in his hands. "Ever get so close to something you can't see it?"

Wil let it go.

"Like the blind guy trying to tell the elephant from feel," Tate continued. "Trouble was I stopped feeling."

Wil was going to bring up Acosta, figured Tate was already at work on it, and said, "Regarding now, Mejia alone won't cut it. We don't know if he's even alive, he's not listed in the book. Plus, all we have is him linked to Alvarez via the dope, and not at all to Rossert. Pretty meager. Not to mention ice-cold."

"What are you, fucking F. Lee Bailey? It's a start."

"As in your sources in the department?"

"You got a better idea?"

Wil toasted him with soda water. "Not since looking you up."

In another half hour they had it worked out. Tate would ease back in via his contacts, see if "local gang member" Sammy Mejia had a record beyond Tate's shooting and where that might lead. Wil would see what he could shake loose on the major whys: Why Doc? Why then? Why now? Backtrack over things that might have meant something without his knowing it, questions he hadn't thought to ask.

It was after seven when they split, Wil heading to his hotel to shower and nibble what was around, check messages, finding none. At eight o'clock, he drove past Jenelle's condo thinking she might be up and wanting to talk. Front porch light on, no one home when he tapped on the door, her parking space empty. He was about to call it a night, when a thought occurred, Redtail's being more or less on his way back.

Pulling into the same lot where Cole's Dooley had been, he saw her pickup and parked beside it; saw *her* once his eyes grew accustomed to the dimness. Corner table, cigarette going in an ashtray, the pack alongside; bar nearly empty preentertainment, nine-thirty listed as show time, a few sports playing pool quietly in the next room. She was working on a whiskey sour, looked up as he sat down.

"I came by. How you doing?"

"Sad but serviceable," she answered. "No, wait— that's *tired* but serviceable, isn't it? Whatever . . . least they returned the Ford."

"How many of those have you had?"

"None of your damn business."

Somebody set the juke going, a male voice wondering why he felt the way he did whenever he got around his girl.

"They don't even have him in that thing, you know that?"

"No." *Not surprising knowing who owns it.*

"I told him," she said without looking up. "Ronnie, I mean. Waited for him to come out of his class and told him. Right there on the campus."

Better to let it play out, so he did.

"I just fucking did it," she went on. "And you want to know what he said to me?"

Four sours at least, Wil guessed, though her speech was relatively free of slur. He shook his head as she took a halfhearted pull on the Marlboro and really got into it.

"Who did I think I'd been fooling all this time? That he didn't own a mirror, didn't have eyes in his head? Then he said Crash told him just before *he* died—that a son ought to know who his old man was, at least, and for me to blow smoke around somebody else. My own flesh and blood . . ."

"How did Crash know?"

"I don't know. Doc must have told him."

Wil waved off the cocktail waitress approaching the table. "I'm sorry, Jenelle."

"He thinks I lied to him. How could he think that?"

"He's hurting, too."

She took a gulp of the sour. "Well, I'm not anymore. Doc's dead and that's it—too much hurt already. And if my son doesn't . . ." Her eyes began to fill.

*Stay out or jump in . . . none of the above?* "Jenelle, I need you to think back. Do you know what Cole DeVillbis might have had against Doc?"

She blinked. "What kind of question is that?"

"Just tracking a thought."

"Well, stop it, it's over—time to play 'Taps' and move on. Something I should have done a long time ago."

Wil said nothing.

"Aren't you supposed to be supportive here? Yes, you're right, Jenelle; cut your losses, Jenelle? That's assuming you know how it feels to lose somebody who's like an extension of yourself."

"Nobody you'd know."

She took a drag, tried to focus. "I'm sorry—that was stupid. They were always rivals in school, Doc and Cole. For everything."

"You?"

"For a time, maybe, but just to see how far Cole could get under Doc's skin. Girls aren't blind."

"That was it?"

"Are you kidding?" she said with force. "Cole De-Villbis over Doc? Give me a break." Starting to lose the phrasing if not quite yet the diction. "Now, you . . . you're a different story. One I haven't quite figured out yet."

"Nothing there to figure."

"Still waters and all that, huh?"

"I think maybe I should call you a cab," Wil said.

"That mean you're not interested?"

"What do you want me to say, Jenelle? You're a beautiful, intelligent woman."

"And? . . ."

He made a gesture signifying check to the waitress, who nodded and began adding up. "And things are complicated right now."

"Bullshit. I've seen you look at me. Speak now or forever hold your peace." It was delivered playfully, but the smile fell short, a sand castle in a gale, and she looked away.

"Well, hell," she said finally. "Guess it's just not my day."

"Come on," Wil said over the music. "Let's get you out of here."

Wil opened his eyes to door closing, engine starting. Easing up from the cat who'd settled in beside him during the night, he went to the window, saw sun coming up and Jenelle's pickup heading out the gate. He checked his watch: just before seven. Using the guest bathroom, he smelled her light citrus scent on his clothes from where she'd asked him to hold her when they'd gotten home—about sixty seconds until the deep regular breathing had sent him looking for a spread to put over her. Not wanting just to leave—something about leaving that way not right.

For her or for him?

Lacing his desert boots, he found the note: *Feel like such a dope this morning. Ugh, make that ten. Can't even say I don't remember—I do.* And out on the kitchen counter: *Early day, that'll teach me. You know where the tea is . . .*

Instead he drove to the café from Doc's arraignment morning. Was it only two days ago? Damn. Three cups of coffee, the *Californian*, and a short stack later, he spun a couple of possibilities around in his mind before going back to Redtail's.

She was on duty, it turned out, this time behind the

bar—one eye on some glasses she was polishing, the other on two wake-up callers nursing their drafts at opposite ends. Over by the rest rooms, a kid in a Redtail's T-shirt mopped the hallway in time to a jukebox ditty about country boys and girls.

"Bridgit . . ." Wil said. Head cocked, smile and a finger pointed her way.

"Some memory," she said, obviously pleased.

"You must be close to owning this place the hours you put in."

"*Right.* You ever find Doc Whitney?"

"Turns out I did."

"Which must mean you're now out of business."

"Wrapping up some loose ends."

"Live by the sword, you die by it," she said. "Can't say we're too broken up around here. You want a coffee or something?"

"Coffeed out, thanks."

She brought a fresh draft down to the guy on the left, who nodded up from his newspaper. Returning to the sink, she ran his empty on the scrubber, rinsed it, set it in a rack. "If that sounded cold, I didn't mean it to. Despite what I said before."

"How'd your mom feel about it?"

"My mom . . ."

"Arlene's aunt—right?"

"You do magic tricks, too?"

He winked at her. "Good note taker."

"Yeah? Remind me to watch what I say around you. And I haven't talked to her about it yet."

"You think she'd mind if I did?"

Bridgit raised a *come on* eyebrow.

Wil countered with a raised hand, Boy Scout style, the thumb in.

She shrugged. "Depends on how you come at it. Still

pretty sensitive with her, that whole thing with Arlene and the kids."

"I can imagine. Hey, you weren't working here twenty years ago, were you?"

She looked at him with maybe thirty-year-old eyes.

"Only kidding," he said. "Anybody you know who might have been?"

She thought about it. "Cole . . ."

"God's gift to women, you mean."

She said nothing—his answer. "Hey, sorry, I didn't mean to presume. Maybe I'm just jealous."

"Don't be. And maybe you better go see my mom before you get us both thrown out of here."


*Lynette Bevins,* the writing on the cocktail napkin read.

Wil parked across the street from the house, a narrow-but-deep white single-story in a modest neighborhood a couple of streets off Chester. Pressed-Victorian eaves, indented porch; single ash tree in the grassy strip between street and sidewalk, early K-car parked in its shade. His knock interrupted a daytime TV show, making him think of Larry Fordyce's makeover inspiration, wondering if it came in a blinding flash or over time.

"Yeah?" Big pink overshirt over madras shorts, sturdy legs and white thongs, tinted red hair in blue rollers. A face that said morning vodka and Kathie Lee.

"Ms. Bevins? Bridgit said you might be willing to talk to me."

She took his card, glanced at it, looked up. "Didn't think you were Publisher's Clearinghouse. Talk about what?"

He explained about Doc, loose ends, Bridgit's remark about Arlene. She was shutting the door on him, when a thought held it up.

"There something in this for me?"

Wil pulled out the two twenties he'd stashed, then the

lining of his pocket—*that's it*. "If you're interested."

Debate flickered and died. "I suppose I can put the money to good use. Long as we don't start speakin' ill of the dead. Is that understood?"

"Yes, ma'am."

"Least you're polite."

She stepped back and Wil entered to floral couch, Colonial maple coffee table strewn with *Redbook*s and *LHJ*s, dark-stained rocker in front of a thirty-two-inch TV with Regis talking to someone who looked like Courtney Love. No evidence of Kathie Lee or who the woman sitting on the third stool was.

"I don't usually do this," Lynette said, landing heavily beside an end-table photo of Princess Diana, an unlit votive candle, and a box of Puffs. "It's just that Arlene being so close and all . . ."

"Bridgit told me—"

"More like a sister to the girl. Her own family sure wasn't able to get anywhere with her."

Wil acted as if he'd forgotten to hand her half the money. "Oh? Why was that?"

"Real sixties type—good-hearted, but a free spirit. And pretty. Which can be a curse, the kind of men that attracts. I know it was with me. And I see it all the time on *Ricki*—"

"Men like Doc Whitney."

"I'd appreciate your not saying his name in this house."

Interesting challenge, Wil thought. "What do you suppose she saw in that guy?"

"Oh, you know—celebrity, excitement. And I guess it was for a while until he got all busy and moody. Withdrawn."

Wil waited.

"Like she wasn't even there sometimes. You know he

had three wives before Arlene—what's that tell you? Girls like Arlene have needs."

"Yes, ma'am." Nodding, he caught sainted-looking portraits on opposing walls: JFK and Elvis regarding each other with mutual admiration.

"Now, don't go gettin' no ideas. Arlene was a wonderful homemaker and mother to those little angels. Always had 'em dressed so sweet and nice. And while the girls played in the yard, she'd pour her heart out to me, poor thing."

Wil made a show of fingering the other twenty. "Anything come readily to mind?"

"Now, what have I been saying? She was lonely."

*Hot. And I ain't talking about the weather.* Wil shook his head—sympathetic. "Who doesn't know that feeling? I'm divorced myself."

She looked at him more closely. "Where are my manners? Would you care for a drink? Real easy to get dehydrated in this weather."

"Thanks anyway."

She excused herself, came back with what looked like a Tom Collins in a tub glass. "I don't usually imbibe this early, but this thing about you-know-who has me so on edge . . ." As she sat, Regis nearly fell off his stool cracking up at something. "I knew that man would be her death the minute she left her old boyfriend for him."

*I'da watched that one if she was mine:* Fordyce again. "From the way you describe her, this boyfriend must have been upset."

She took a long swig, ice rattling as she put the glass down and smiled. Smiling back, Wil handed over the last twenty.

"Devastated's more like it," she went on, losing the bill in the upholstery. "And I should know. Anybody working around him could see the effect it had when she left him to go with that loser."

"Yes, ma'am. I just meant any *real* man would be upset about losing a woman like that to a guy like that."

*Regis* gave way to a soap opera, Lynette Bevins edging the volume up. "They're having the wedding today— Vance and Miranda. You know how long they've been wanting this but couldn't because of her dying mother?"

"Matter of fact, no."

"Five years. Exactly how long Arlene was married— seventy-three to seventy-eight. There'll probably be a hurricane or something." Lynette refreshed her tub glass as the show went to commercial; coming back, she said, "Gonna have to run you out of here in a minute unless you like cryin' and carryin' on."

*Come on, come on, come on . . .* "Hard to think of this guy just giving up on somebody like Arlene."

Tipsy coy: "Now who said any such thing?"

Wil gave her wide eyes—*you sly devil.* "He kept seeing her?"

"Let's just say he was patient."

"Nobody's that patient."

"Wrong. Just look at Vance and Miranda there. Speaking of which, you got thirty seconds."

*Seemed like she was always having sitters in for the little girls, then hittin' the honky-tonks.* Honky-tonks . . . Redtail's and Cheri's . . . pay bars straight across the slot if he was right . . .

*Pull . . .* "No happy ending for Cole and Arlene, was there? Just a real-life unhappy one."

Not taking her eyes off the screen, she said, "Sure got that right. That bastard Doc Whit—"

Suddenly the alcohol shine gave way to shock; fear wiping *that* aside as she twisted toward him getting to his feet. "What the hell are you talking about? I never said nothing about Cole."

"And I should have picked it up sooner. Bridgit's working where her mom used to, isn't she? Tell me Cole isn't paying for this place, too."

# TWENTY-ONE

Rye Rossert whapped the ball back on a low trajectory,—just out of reach of the stunningly handsome brunette chasing after it.

"Set, point, and match, hon. Youth ain't all it's cracked up to be."

She ran over to him, threw up the second-serve ball she still had in her pocket, and carried through with a ferocious whiff—mock-driving it at him.

"Scared you, didn't I?"

"I look scared to you?"

"Dirty old man—taking advantage of a defenseless girl."

"You ain't seen nothin' yet," he gloated.

"I can hardly wait."

Rossert was about to say something suggestive, keep up the banter that brought him such satisfaction, her twenty-eight to his sixty-four, when he saw Raul Garza leaning against the fence.

"Gotta go," he said. "Business before pleasure."

"That's not what you said last night." Peck on the cheek. "And I don't like that man."

"Nobody does. Which is why I do."

"I don't get it."

He patted her bottom with his racquet, eyed the cut

of her purple tennis top, what it barely concealed. "You go inside, order us something nice for lunch. Then we'll see." Knowing the reaction some of his club cronies would have when they saw sweet little Judy in that outfit—green as their salads, angina all around. Giving her heart-shaped rear a last glance, he headed over to where Garza waited.

"Some piece of work you got there, *patrón*."

Rossert feinted a left at him and grinned at the reaction, Garza all coiled muscle on a hair trigger. Smartest thing he'd ever done, taking that one under his wing. Exceeded every expectation so far.

Garza's return smile was pure leer. "Anytime you can't handle it—".

"—will be the day. *Qué pasó?*"

"The hag's at it again." Leaning up against a bench. "Filed suit to stop North Hills."

Rossert shrugged it off. "Long haul, remember? She's bound to die sometime. What is she, ninety?"

"Eighty-something. And we might get somebody worse."

"SEP—someone else's problem. What else?"

"One of the steam units blew out. Scalded a guy."

Rossert thought a moment. "Take care of it, but make it look as if we're still hurting for cash. Ninety days, minimum." He let his eyes drift out across the river and up into the foothills. "We're this close—you know that? Few days, a week . . ."

"Yeah. Maybe."

"What? You getting as little sleep as I am?"

Garza let a moment pass. Birds chirped and flitted in the shade around the courts. "The guy who was supposed to make the whack, he got aced out by somebody else."

"I don't understand," Rossert said. "Aced out by whom?"

"One of the Delano essays, most likely. Whoever it is, they got him in solitary. Nobody can get to him."

"I thought they hadn't said who did it."

"They haven't yet."

"But you should know before long, right?"

Garza nodded thoughtfully. "It's been twenty-four hours. Doesn't figure, them people not putting the touch on the money before now."

"*Those* people," Rossert corrected.

"What I'm saying is, I don't like it."

"Okay, you don't like it. What's the worst it could mean?"

"I don't know, some kind of move on us. Hard to tell at this point."

Rossert took a *Chi Kung* breath, let it out. The power within. "Whatever it is, it's trouble we don't need right now. That's *why* the hit, remember?"

"*Sí, patrón.*"

"You know better than to take that tone."

Garza said nothing, just looked at his hands, the faded little pachuco crosses tattooed on the webs.

"All right. See if you can find out who's behind it."

"You don't think that's maybe what somebody wants us to do?"

Rossert watched a rally on the next court, two women arching lobs at each other's baseline. "What do you want, Raul? You have a better idea, I'm not hearing it."

"One of ours saw Dickhead out with that cop Sammy put down."

"And *they're* making you nervous?" Rossert cracked a smile. "Time for some St. John's wort in your corn-flakes."

"*Qué?*"

"Why do I have this feeling you always know exactly what I'm talking about?"

"*No se.*" Garza stretched, adjusted the drape on his

rayon shirt with the birds-of-paradise on it.

Rossert stood also. "You know what's riding here. Put your people to work and see what develops. Then if there's trouble . . ." He made a finger pistol, cocked it. "Make me proud."

Backing down the boulder and grass path, the plantings in full bloom, pepper trees drooping gracefully beyond, Garza backpedaled, threw a series of slo-mo air jabs.

*"Siempre, patrón,"* he said. "Always."

Wil pulled up behind Tate's specially equipped, eighties-vintage El Camino and killed the S-10. It was too early for Abbie to be home from work, so he went directly to the small office in back, fighting the feeling of relief she wouldn't be there. Not that he didn't know how she felt about Tate wanting to jump back in. That was the problem—he did.

"You ever see the inside of your house?"

Tate looked at him through the open door, then again at his work, a stack of photocopies he was reviewing.

"Nothing personal," Wil added. "It's just that you're always out here."

"That maybe tell you something?"

"Yeah—too much. And it's not too late to let go of this."

"Right. So how'd you do this morning?"

Wil told him—Bridgit, his visit to the house, Lynette Bevins—and when he'd finished, he asked, "You have any idea Arlene was Cole's ex-girlfriend?"

Tate frowned. "No. Abbie and I didn't visit after Darla, and Doc never said anything about it when I'd run into him."

"You remember how old Sara Whitney was?"

"Five. Why?"

"You're sure?"

Tate opened a drawer, thumbed through files, pulled one out. "Twenty-nine May, seventy-three, to twenty-seven August, seventy-eight."

"And Doc married Arlene when?"

He checked again, held up the paper. "Ten March, seventy-three."

A silence settled between them.

"All right, I can count," Tate said. "So what? Women loved Doc. No secret there."

Wil sat down.

"You going to let me in on it or what?" Tate said finally.

"An ongoing relationship with a woman who married somebody else. A daughter five years old. Tell me you're not on the same wavelength here."

"If you're saying Sara was Cole's, that's something we have absolutely no way of proving without—"

"Exhumation, I know that. DNA."

"Never happen," Tate said. "Not in this town, not in this county."

Wil looked at him. "Not with what we have now, maybe. You have a problem with it otherwise?"

"*No.*"

"You sure about that?"

Tate turned away. "I'll let you know. And that's the last it gets brought up, all right?"

"Not all right," Wil said. "If it's true, it establishes a motive."

"For what? Loving somebody even after she's decided on somebody else?"

"Enough to do something about it, is what I'm getting at. Five years to stew and obsess? I'm no analyst, but it seems to me—"

"I'm letting the possibility in, make you happy?" He took a deep breath. "Sorry—the damned medication.

You want to hear about these?" He tapped a knuckle on the photocopies.

Wil moved to them, saw rap sheets, criminal-history Xeroxes, county and city paper with one unifying element: *Samuel José Mejia.*

"Busy boy. Obviously you were just a stop along the way."

"Interesting way to put it," Tate said. "Didn't you mention a Raul Garza?"

"Rossert's attack dog."

"I checked for his name, too, but he has no record—at least not around here. However . . ."

Tate went through the stack, separated out a sheet. Near the bottom, he'd circled an entry in blue ink— arrested with Samuel José Mejia, 22, in 1983: Raul Eladio Garza, 29, cousin of the accused. Released when Mejia backed up his denials of involvement in the cocaine residue found in Sammy's trunk, Sammy pulling two years at Tehachapi, out in eight months. Five years after the three-year stint for shooting Tate.

Wil began pulling threads big time: Crash Alvarez— drummer and drug runner ready to turn his source; Larry Fordyce—expensing big-money buys out of petty cash through a Mexican kid, a nice little guy; Sammy Mejia— never suspect him by looking at him, probably why they used him, Fordyce with the impression Mejia was in business with somebody else, a relative. Raul Garza— cousin . . . the word jumping off the page. Maybe a way to nail it shut if . . .

Wil found the number in his notebook and punched it in; listened as the recorded message informed him that Fordyce's home phone extracted before Wil left the restaurant had been changed. No new listing at this time.

*Way to go, Lar. Right in character.*

Checking his watch, he dialed the business number off Larry's card, hoping at four-twenty Fordyce might

still be within range of the office. He retrieved a crumpled piece of paper from Tate's wastebasket and held it
loosely to the receiver, trying to recall how the big man
at the recording studio had sounded.

A woman answered. "Sherrice? Bone here, looking
for L.T. . . . yeah . . . about like I feel . . . thanks." He
waited, then lost the paper, wadded it up as a familiar
voice came on. "Freddy Krueger, L.T. . . . listen up. Mejia's relative you didn't know the name of, I need you
to think back hard—the guy as a boxer, club fighter,
instructor, anything like that. Ring any bells?"

He waited as Tate regarded him, heard Larry's answer
finally, and nodded *yes,* BIG. Still hearing it after the
man had hung up: *"God, you're a pain in the ass. Might
have been a boxer, so what? Always dancin' around and
throwing punches."* Air-puncher, bag-basher Raul Garza
the link they needed to Rossert. Alvarez, Fordyce, Mejia,
Garza, Rossert: rungs on a ladder. Steps toward finding
out.

Flipping the wad of paper to the man in the wheelchair, he said, "Haven't lost much off your fastball, have
you?"

Tate would delve back into the reports on Arlene and
the girls, plus see if further paper existed on Sammy
Mejia. Wil, convinced from talking to Doc that a loop
existed, would try Gib Whitney's trail again. That stra-
tegized, he phoned Jenelle's house, but she wasn't home,
and he decided not to leave an update. Only that he'd
call later.

"Beautiful woman," Tate said without looking up
from a file.

"You could say that."

"Just did."

Wil checked the time, figured maybe, and drove to
the Hall of Records after asking Tate where it was. Get-

ting there right before it closed—flank speed under the
watchful eye of a woman who'd clearly made plans for
the rest of the day—he searched for ownership of the
house occupied by Lynette Bevins.

And found it.

The property was registered to Marston, DeVillbis,
Truax & Hill, not Cole—mild surprise: mental note to
find out more. One step ahead of the locking doors, he
then drove to the offices of NOW OR NEVER, as indicated
by the sign across the mirrored ex-storefront. Behind it,
three older women looked up as he entered and asked
for Leora Graybill. Exchanging glances with the others,
one inquired who was asking.

Somewhat taken aback, Wil extended a card, explained he'd talked with her before. "She go home already?"

"We don't know where she went, just left," the
woman said. End of conversation. Already back to stuff-
ing envelopes.

He left them and drove to her house, found her sitting
on the screened porch, Matt taking an interest in his
approach until she calmed him with a hand. Pale, Wil
noted as he accepted her gesture toward a wicker chair.
"You okay?" he asked. "The girls at the office were
pretty closemouthed."

"Fine. Losing my tolerance for the heat, it seems."
Then, "Girls—wait'll I hit 'em with that one."

Matt settled at her feet, half-closed eyes still on Wil.

"I wanted to thank you again for your kindness the
other day."

"Didn't do Doc Whitney much good, did it?"

"No, but I'm not sure what would have." Leaving out
his not tipping Acosta to the threat, he explained about
not giving up. About shapes beginning to form in the
fog: Alvarez, Fordyce, Mejia, Garza. Rossert, possibly.

"Don't know any of 'em save for Rossert. Him and

his Cumulus Group." She saw Wil's look. "Holding company he owns. Real multiheaded Hydra—cut one off and two grow in. Most people don't know it exists— all they see are the facades. And I didn't think you looked like the giving-up type."

"Which means something, coming from you."

She lit a cigarillo, brushed flecks off the denim shift she was wearing over a blue shirt with maroon flowers. Matt finally closed his eyes. Around them, the house made creaking sounds as the temperature backed off.

"Just out of curiosity," he said. "Do you have any idea why somebody'd want him out of the way?"

"Donnie?" As if she were buying time to consider her answer. "Seems to me you leave out passion and the random things, motives come down to money, money, or money. Around here that means land, water, or oil." She rubbed her temples. "Shed any light on the subject?"

"Not unless you wanted to pick one."

"Hard sometimes to see where one leaves off and the other begins. Water doesn't sound right, though."

"What about drugs?" He explained a bit about the connections.

"I'm not much of an expert," she said. "We talking about the same kind of money?"

"Drugs and oil? I don't know—are we?"

She tamped ash off the cigarillo. "Last fall, Elk Hills sold for close to four billion. Big area with a lot of wells, but it gives you some idea. And I'd say don't bother with Rossert and drugs because he's smarter and greedier than that." Leaning down to stroke the dog's ears. "But then, people kill each other over nothing these days, and you're thinking that's not true here, right? Somebody just not liking him for what happened?"

"Seems less and less likely."

Another drag, the smoke curling upward around her. "We coming around to Gib again?"

"It's a thought."

"Not much we didn't cover before."

Wil said, "Anything you recall in oil that was going on about the time he disappeared?"

She pondered, seemed to arrive at a conclusion. Last hit on the cigarillo before extinguishing it. "Actually, there was."

Doves sounded in the big locust tree; out on the sidewalk, three kids went by on bikes, Leora's eyes following them until they disappeared.

"Steam," she said, as though suddenly recovering her train of thought. "Can't see much now, but go out there when it's cold. It's like wraiths hovering—and maybe they are."

"Not sure I follow."

"Kern River crude—thicker than molasses and twice as ornery. Up until the early sixties, for every barrel brought up, two stayed in the ground."

"So—steam?"

"The idea of applying heat wasn't new, just hadn't been cost-effective. Then, in the late fifties, some of the big companies began experimenting. First with fire, then hot water, then steam to make the crude freer flowing. Steam won—it was cheap and it worked."

"How much freer?"

"Rumor was, up to ten times the number of barrels. But since the companies didn't release their findings, nobody really knew. Fences went up, KEEP OUT signs, paper bags over the gauges. You can imagine what that did for the interest in leases, let alone property."

"I think so."

"I doubt it. Everybody wanted in. Especially people who smelled money every time a well burped."

"Enter Gib Whitney and Lute DeVillbis."

Leora brought her feet up under her in the chair. Matt

raised his head, regarded her a moment, then settled back down.

"You ever heard of the term 'salting'?" she asked.

"Playing a sucker by making him think something's there that isn't."

"Gib could see a boom was coming. Despite his faults, he was quite the visionary—just so happened he had no money. It was Gib who got Lute into it. Lute had some property his folks left him. Leverage for what Gib had in mind."

Wil leaned forward on his elbows.

"The plan was to pick up this neglected tract with unproductive wells on it. Give everybody a good laugh. Then, when the word about steam got around, rent equipment and run up the fences and signs. Let out that something big was going on. Several drinks around the right people later, start moaning they didn't have the cash to pursue it."

"Gas on a fire."

"Had a marked effect on the bidding, all right. Trouble was, there was no crude down there to loosen up."

"And they knew it."

She nodded. "Thought they knew it. Time proved even that wrong."

"How'd you find all this out?"

"Bits and pieces. Secrets weren't exactly Gib's specialty." She lit another cigarillo, blew the smoke out the screen.

"Anything I should be aware of there?"

"If there is, I'll be sure and let you know."

He was rising to leave when he remembered what else he wanted to ask her. "The truck—what year is it?"

"What truck?"

"In the garage. If it's what I think, my uncle used to own one."

"It's a—what—fifty-three? Just a broken-down old half-ton. Hasn't worked in years."

"Mind if I look? I've always had a thing for Studebakers."

"Not to be rude, but some other time." Putting out the smoke and letting him help her to her feet. "Matty and I always have dinner about now."

By the time she'd finished saying the word "dinner," Matt was up and looking back at her from the porch door, an expectant wag going and a knowing gleam in his eyes.

Leaving Leora's, Wil drove to the bluff where he and Kari had looked out over the oil fields. He pictured Gib and Lute DeVillbis out there, playing with fire, so to speak—or more accurately, steam. Burning the wrong person? Seeing the clean round hole in Gib's skull again. And always the same question: How did all of it tie in to Doc?

Like the crude oil itself: blackly impenetrable, unyielding.

Unless you turned up the heat on it.

*Knowing* Leora knew more and wondering how to get it, he finally drove to Jenelle's, took her to dinner at the place they'd gone after visiting Doc at the Pretrial Facility. But she was as preoccupied as he, and after a bit they gave up all pretense of conversation and just drifted in and out of thought. Comfortable enough, but distant.

By eight-thirty, he was saying good night: heading first to Redtail's, then Cheri's after finding out who was performing where. At this hour on a weeknight, Cheri's was still relatively uncrowded, even though two musicians were setting up, one of them the bass player from the Ronnie Pruett night. With the amplifiers not yet on, their tunings sounded thin and insubstantial, the bass player looking annoyed at Wil's inquiry—jerking his head toward the back, then re-straining to hear his cords over the jukebox and the drinkers starting to increase in volume.

Wil walked down the hall, pushed through swinging louvered doors into a kitchen the size of an afterthought—water dripping in a metal sink half-filled with dishes.

Ronnie Pruett was halfway through a plate of burger and fries. This close and aware of it, the resemblance to Doc was unmistakable. Thick dark hair, the same square-jawed features, but with eyes closer to Jenelle's—that unexpected hazel color, echoed by the yoke in his cream-colored western shirt.

"Don't get up," Wil said.

"Hadn't planned on it," Ronnie answered, and it was as if a younger Doc had spoken the words—that same edge. "I should know you?"

"Saw you play the other night. Didn't realize it at the time, but your style reminded me of somebody else's."

"Look, I'm eating here—if that's cool with you."

"This won't take long, you know who I'm talking about. And if you don't see it as a compliment, I'm wasting my time, even though I'm going to say it anyway."

Ronnie stopped in mid-bite. "Who are you?"

"Somebody who cares about your mother."

"Hey, why not? Everybody does." He reached for a french fry as water continued to drip. "Ah, the strong silent type. Don't tell me—you're fucking her, too."

Wil counted to five with the sound. "Here's the deal," he said. "You shut up and hear me out, I won't drown you in the sink."

"Tough guy."

"At least I'm not acting like I'm fifteen."

"Maybe we should take this outside."

"Which will affect exactly nothing."

No comeback, not even a move toward the burger Ronnie had set down; just a stare into space. At that moment the bass player popped his head in. "You okay in here?"

Wil kept his eyes where they were fixed. "Time to grow up, Ron. Let in what's there."

Ronnie hesitated, took a breath; he looked at Wil, then the bass player. "Yeah, Ray, thanks. First set in ten. 'Kern River Girl.' "

"That's our closer."

"Not tonight, it's not."

With a shrug and a glance at Wil, the bass player withdrew.

"All right," Ronnie said. "You got ten minutes."

"Better idea," Wil said. He reached into his pocket, came out with a quarter and a dime, flashed them, put them in Ronnie's hand. "You have more important things to do than listen to what you already know. She's there now. And if you tell her I was here, I *will* drown you in the sink."

# TWENTY-TWO

They met for a late breakfast, Wil wanting another look at the microfilm documenting the discovery of Gib Whitney's bones four springs ago. Seeing nothing much beyond what he'd seen already. Speculation by sheriff's investigators that the gun was most likely a nine-millimeter or something close, given the state of the skull.

Tate hadn't much more to offer—nothing on Sammy Mejia's whereabouts, addresses from his old arrest records not panning out.

"What about the girlfriend?" Wil asked. "What was her name? . . ."

"Yolanda Elena Hurtado. Dead with two others in a drug deal that went south a month after I got it. Never saw nineteen."

"Kind of unhealthy to be around, this Mejia."

"Tell me about it."

"So—any thoughts on where to find him?"

"How about if I tail Garza? Makes sense that he'd know."

Wil mulled it over his tea, Jenelle to thank for that. "And Mejia knows you," he finally said. "Assuming it might actually go somewhere."

"Garza doesn't."

More thought: Abbie Tate, the memory of Paul Rodriguez, his throat cut by the killer Wil had been hired to find—clear today as yesterday. And never again. "Maybe."

"Hey, nobody looks at cripples," Tate said. "It's my edge. That and the sawed-off I keep in the El Camino."

"I was more concerned about Mejia."

As Tate smiled, the waitress set down their order.

"Seriously," Wil added after she'd left.

"I'm an ex-cop, not an executioner. Even if the opportunity did present itself."

"If you say so."

They ate, and with food, Wil's apprehension began to dispel. He went through his conversation with Leora: Gib's apparent oil scam prior to disappearing; his own theory that maybe Gib had scammed the wrong party or parties. "You have any contacts in the oil business?" he asked Tate.

"Regarding the tract she was talking about?"

Wil nodded. "Drowning-man syndrome—anything looks good when you're going under."

"What about sweating DeVillbis to find out?"

"Better to end up there. No point spooking him before we'd even know what he's talking about."

Tate leaned back from his plate. "Got a guy works for the county who'll remember me, I'll ask him." He jotted down the number of the phone in the El Camino, told Wil to call him there or at home to arrange a meet. Then: "Something needs to be said about yesterday. The way I was."

"Who doesn't have moods?"

"There's a reason things are the way they are right now." He drained the remaining coffee, left his eyes on the mug. "Couple of years ago, Abbie . . . The guy at the county I mentioned . . . Anyway, she . . . terminated it. That's how I found out, from a bed full of blood. Point

I'm trying to make is, we're hanging on in more ways than one."

"Bob, are you sure you want to do this?"

"Knew there must have been a reason why I didn't shoot the son of a bitch right then."

"I'm talking about all of it," Wil said. "What it could cost."

By way of answer, Tate backed away from the table and pointed the chair like a battering ram toward the door, looked to be headed right through it if someone hadn't opened it first. Bracing the big rubber wheels against it as the man stepped around him.

"Hey—either we'll make it or we won't. Right?" Loud enough for the entire café to hear.

Wil spent the next two hours in the county clerk's office next to the Justice Building where Doc Whitney had been arraigned. First floor—Fictitious Business Names.

Cumulus Group: Ryland Travis Rossert, principal— no stunner there. Interesting, however, was the supporting cast, minority partners at 10 percent each: Raul Eladio Garza (and so much for Garza as hired muscle) plus something called Northlight.

He looked up Northlight, found Luther Garland DeVillbis, Ryland Travis Rossert, principals. Which brought to mind Lute's comment about Rye Rossert: *fella I do business with sometimes.*

Right.

Checking to see if there was an application for Marston, DeVillbis, Truax & Hill, he cut to the day's big surprise: Cumulus Group as owner—not DeVillbis or the others, names to pad the masthead, as near as Wil could tell. Cumulus Group. Which meant DeVillbis had only a minor stake in his own law practice, as of . . . Wil scanned the document, saw September 1964. The coincidence of *that* beginning to vortex like the vengeful spirits from *Raiders of the Lost Ark.*

*Owns about half the town.*

No disagreement there, Wil thought—DeVillbis or him—tapping his pencil on his notebook until heads turned in his direction. Which galvanized his call to Leora Graybill's house, and when he got no answer there, the offices of NOW OR NEVER.

"Persistent cuss, aren't you," she said after one of the girls had routed his call. "You looking for a job?"

"It might come to that. How you doing today?"

"Like the water's rising and the raft's got a hole. What's your story?"

"You said Gib and Lute were partners, right?"

Hesitation. "Something like that."

"You remember if they had more than just a gentleman's agreement? A name or something."

"With money involved and Lute a lawyer? What are you getting at?"

"I'm asking if you recall it."

Hesitation II: "I recall. Gib used to think Polaris brought him luck—like the old-time sea captains trying to find their way in the dark. Even adapted the old rhyme to it: *Star light, star bright, first star I see tonight. Wish I may, wish I might, shine on me your good—*"

"*North light,*" Wil finished.

"You asking me or telling me?" she said before ringing off.

Nowhere—no bloody where.

Northlight was Lute and Rye Rossert—no mention of Gib Whitney on the current paperwork. And there went that idea for motive.

Wil left the document, went to a dark-haired clerk and asked her where the older documents were on file, the ones that went back decades—beyond the nine years that were there.

"Nine years happens to be as long as we keep them, sir."

"They're stored elsewhere then—right? Hall of Records?"

"Um. I'm afraid not." She answered the phone, seemed surprised when he was still there after concluding whatever she was doing for the other person on her computer.

"Is there something else you wished?"

"Fuller understanding, Ms. Nuñez." From her name tag. "You're saying I would have no way of finding an original partnership filing from, say, the early 1960s?"

"Not through the county clerk, sir. As I stated, nine years is our cutoff policy. After that, they are shredded."

*Shit.*

Thinking that she'd read his thought because he hadn't even turned to leave when she added, "I suppose if you have some time and the actual date, you could rummage through the corresponding issue of the adjudicated newspaper—"

But by then he was already stepping forward to shake her hand. "Ms. Nuñez, you make a forgetful taxpayer glad you're on duty to remind and serve."

"Sir, I believe that's the police you're talking about."

And still it was a long shot.

Six P.M. already: Bleary from the tiny newsprint, hardly enhanced by thirty-year-old microfilm technology, let alone his own fading vision after four hours at it, Wil leaned back, stretched, rubbed his eyes. Still saw page after page of the classified-section notices for fictitious business names required by law to accompany the actual applications filed with the county clerk.

Finally through with 1964 and halfway into '63, he

decided on a break: coffee-to-go and a long stare at the
snippet of canal outside the library as he drank it. Afterward he called Bob Tate, reaching him not at home,
but on his car phone.

"Where are you?"

"Down the block from where I tailed Garza to, a split
level on the east side," Tate answered. "And I forgot
how fucking monotonous this is—guy hasn't left his
house in two hours."

"Try library science sometime." Going through it for
Tate, what he was looking for: some record of Gib Whitney on the original Northlight paperwork.

"How come?"

"Some things Leora Graybill said about oil and
money."

"Interesting coincidence," Tate came back. "My guy
knew Cumulus and some land they own out in the low
foothills north of the river. Sounds like the property in
question. Something we can check out tomorrow."

Wil was on the verge of asking how it went, but
Tate's tone advised him to leave it. "Any chance your
guy knew if it was up for sale?"

"Two for two. Been in escrow about three weeks
now—some Indonesian group, evidently. Has to be part
detective himself, he told me, the way these oil people
turn loose of information." Rustle of paper. "Want to
take a flier at the price?"

"Surprise me," Wil said, rubbing his eyes again—figuring he was going to go blind at this rate.

"You believe two-seventy?"

"Thousand?"

Tate's laugh was both smug and audible. "Million.
That motive enough for you? Guy thought they could
have gotten even more by opening it up."

Whirling, shifting thoughts centered around money—
trying again to make the pieces fit: Rossert, DeVillbis,

Garza, Gib. And Doc, always Doc. Coming up with the usual maddening jumble.

"You still there?"

"I'm here," Wil said. "You get a line on the escrow company?"

"Not yet. But that name Lynette Bevins got me thinking I might have heard or seen it before, so I went back into the files. Some of the people Acosta's team talked to in seventy-eight . . ."

"I'm sure there's a reason for this pause."

"Guess who Cole said he was with the afternoon and evening of twenty-seven August, seventy-eight? Lynette Bevins, age thirty-two. Cocktail waitress and boss's punch—excuse me: romantic interest, according to her corroborating statement."

"Damn," Wil said. "Rack up one for Sam Spade."

"Make that double damn. Garza's just leaving his house in a dark blue Dodge Ram, license number 2GZX . . . 287. Tate rolling. Over and out."

It took everything Wil had to get back into scrolling through the microfilm, but at least the break and Tate's report helped. As if they'd rolled the rock up as far as the crest, and that might be downslope they were looking at.

But, Lord, it was tedious: public notice . . . public notice . . . public notice . . . public notice. Sixty-three giving way to sixty-two, then sixty-one: December . . . November . . . October . . .

*WHERE ARE YOU?*

September . . . August . . . July . . . June . . .

And then: Sunday, June 18, 1961. *Public Notice: Fictitious Business Name Statement. The following persons are doing business as NORTHLIGHT: Gilbert Lenvil Whitney, Luther Garland DeVillbis. This business is conducted as a general partnership.*

Fine print . . . fine print . . . fine . . .

*This fictitious business name statement expires five years from the date it was filed in the Office of the County Clerk. A new statement must be filed before that time.*

Last lap: Checking his watch, Wil saw he had an hour before closing and went for it, changing reels back to where he'd begun, September 1964. Forty-five minutes later he had it—a new filing for Northlight: November 24, 1964—well shy of the five-year mandate. This one listed Luther Garland DeVillbis and Ryland Travis Rossert as general partners. No mention of Gilbert Lenvil Whitney.

Rossert had replaced him.

How—by putting him in the sump?

Wil asked for help, had the librarian make him a half-dozen hard copies of each of the postings while he put thoughts together like layers of papier-mâché around a form. Giving shape to: Lute and Gib scamming the wrong guy—Wil's notion, but consistent with Gib's disappearance and Rye Rossert's entry—Rossert with the muscle, the capital, and the moxie to reap over two hundred mil on his action (if it could be proven) thirty-four years later. Shape to: Gilbert Lenvil Whitney as a documented player—his share of the sale, by law, passing to his sole heir, Don Lee Whitney (note to double-check the code). Doc: the only one in the equation with no seeming knowledge of it, Wil reasonably sure of that from everything he had seen and heard and *knew.*

Or did he?

Doc had come back for Gib, Arlene, Sara, Megan. He'd come back to find out.

Or had he?

At the least it followed that those conspiring to eliminate Doc—figuring he'd come back as avenging angel, or worse, for his share—were the obvious beneficiaries:

Rye Rossert, Lute DeVillbis, Raul Garza (via his Cumulus 10 percent).

RYE ROSSERT, LUTE DEVILLBIS, RAUL GARZA: Jotting down the names, he tried to see something in them, failed, and blocked out another—COLE DEVILLBIS. Why him? Why the shots at the cabin? As usual, no answers.

Spinning with it, the attempt to separate reality from wishful thinking—steel ball from the tilt-maze game and into the hole—Wil left the library ahead of the usual locking doors and headed for the phone. But when he reached Tate, traffic noise and "Streets of Bakersfield" underlay the ex-cop saying he was calling it a night.

And something else coming through strong: *Don't push it.*

# TWENTY-THREE

Eight A.M. Thursday: Wil and Tate reconnected not far from Wil's hotel, at the state's archival office for oil-field maps, Tate following up his contact at the paper with a look at the section grids and well locations on the Cumulus property, about two hundred and fifty in all. Looking over Tate's shoulder, Wil thought he recognized the dirt road flanking it from his trip in with Leora—something to ask her about later. No sign of the pond—different section, probably.

Finished, they grabbed a take-out breakfast and, at Tate's suggestion, took it to a parkway by the river. Already the day was warm, the sky turning milky, the river, fed by its dammed-up lake, running flat and wide. Willows and cottonwoods lined the banks, along with bushes with trumpetlike yellow flowers. Joggers and in-line skaters plied the pathways around the picnic table where they'd set up.

"Nice spot," Wil said, taking it in.

"Deceiving. It's quicksand out beyond those trees. Had to drag for a kid there once. Never did find him."

Obvious Tate had more on his mind.

"I froze, you know."

"I don't—"

"Last night. Garza went to a couple of places and

everything's fine, I'm there with my tapes and binocs. Then he goes to this little house, spends about a half hour, and comes out with Mejia . . ."

Tate took a breath.

"I recognize him right away—the guy is nothing—twenty years older than nothing. So he makes this innocuous gesture, sticks his hand under his jacket—obviously he's packing. And all of a sudden it's like I'm knocking on that door again, and I can barely see inside the house, the gun's going off, and it's slow motion, the bullet coming at me through the screen, and I can't move, and it's almost there, and I can't fucking breathe anymore." He took another, deeper breath.

"Right out of fucking *nowhere*."

Wil crumpled wax paper, dropped it in the bag.

"You understand what I'm saying? I *froze*. Just like some damned rookie. Sweats, shakes, the works—regular war flashback." He ran a hand across his scalp, brought it back damp, wiped it on his pants. "I didn't even see 'em take off."

Wil said nothing.

"Well?"

"First year after I got nailed, I'd wake up drowning in the Mekong. My answer was to drown it right back. Luckily, Lisa kept us afloat—my wife then."

"And?"

"I got some help. It went away."

"End of story . . ."

"For all intents."

"What I'm trying to say is . . . it comes to crunch I might not be there for you," Tate said. "Might want to give that some thought."

"Already have. We any worse off than we were?"

"Look, I'm trying to be honest here, spare you some grief down the line."

"Maybe," Wil said. "You ever go up in a B-52 with anybody who wasn't scared?"

"Nobody I'd trust."

Wil finished his orange juice, tossed the container in with the McMuffin wrapper. "End of story."

After Tate leveraged his contact for the name of the outfit handling the Cumulus escrow, he left to stake out Mejia's place—remount the pale horse, as he put it.

Not expecting much and finding it, Wil swung by the Hall of Records for a look at the deeds to the property circa 1961, the grant deed revealing only the name of the seller, someone named Kenyon, the trust deed listing the buyer as Northlight, Luther G. DeVillbis, signator. The money guy, Leora had said, oilman Gib staying out of the picture so as not to shy the seller, Wil thinking so far it made sense.

Next he trotted across to Fictitious Business Names— Valmont Land & Title this time. Even without Ms. Nuñez there, Rye Rossert was: principal.

Outside now on a cement bench, Wil rearranged the pieces for another run at the puzzle. Rossert acing out Gib Whitney, more than likely physically, if he'd been the one scammed: easy enough to see it. Retribution also coming in the form of Lute DeVillbis signing over his law business? Ditto: Rossert close to owning the man, if the trail of paper was any indication. Close to a done deal: the old Northlight piece, a king's ransom now— Rossert's own firm handling the escrow. Primed to run interference if for some reason they'd left any stone unturned that would link Gib and subsequently Doc to . . .

*Shit . . .*

Wil used the building's pay phone to call Bob Tate.

"Anything happening you can't break off from?" he asked when Tate came on.

"No—and it all looks better by day."

"How about that Little League park in a half hour."

"Fifteen minutes, if you want. It's Bakersfield, re-member?"

"The kid who sings at Cole's?"

Wil nodded. "*That* Ronnie Pruett."

"And suddenly, from out of left field . . ."

Twelve-thirty on a weekday, the Little League field was deserted, sprinklers working to keep the grass from looking like the foothills. Lunchers opened brown bags at tables beyond the outfield; walkers singly and in pairs stepped out with determination.

Wil shifted on the bench they'd chosen and wiped perspiration from his eyebrows. "What I'm saying is, I'm thinking out loud on all of it. But Ronnie Pruett fits."

"Want to tell me how?"

Wil hesitated. "I'd rather have you trust me."

Tate ran callused palms over the chrome rings of his chair. Without looking at Wil, he said, "Trust me, huh? Where in Nam didn't we hear that?"

*Nice one, Hardesty.* "You ever take a close look at him? Who he looks like if you had to guess?"

"Like I spend my time in honky-tonks."

Wil looked across wet grass at the moving arcs of silver.

"Look," Tate added. "I've got Mejia and Garza up to who knows what. And to be perfectly clear, I'm doing this for Doc, not . . . *aw, no* . . . you saying Ronnie's his kid?"

"Ever hear of a rock and a hard place?"

"God, the fun never stops . . ." He shook his head slowly. "No need asking who . . ."

Wil just looked at him.

Tate took a breath. "All right, keep it going and I'll catch up. You're saying Rossert gets scammed, puts Gib down, keeps Lute because he's—what . . . ?"

"Of greater and immediate value."

"*DeVillbis?*"

"An oil and water lawyer with blood ties to Rye Ros-sert—his own if he doesn't go along. Not to mention a similar value system as we've seen from the scam. What greater incentive? And the dates work."

"Then what?" Tate not looking very convinced.

"Time passes. Everybody gets rich. But it isn't enough."

"The foothill piece . . ."

"Steam works better than even Gib figured it would. Or maybe they drill deeper and score. Oil prices triple, except for the occasional dip, and here comes the big payoff. Two hundred and seventy mil."

Traffic hummed; three Labs belonging to a couple jos-tled up, sniffed around them, lit out again at the man's whistle.

"Why now?"

"Elk Hills," Wil answered. "Leora said one of the big oil companies bought it last fall."

Tate nodded. "Three-point-six-five billion."

"Two plus two: If one of the bigs bets that heavily on domestic oil, there must be something to it—here comes the competition. But I think it's more than that. I think Rossert and company put it up for sale on a fast track because Doc got an early release. Something they didn't anticipate."

"Let alone his coming back," Tate said almost to him-self.

"The link to Gib scared them, the off chance they wouldn't cash out clean. But killing Doc outright might have brought the whole thing under scrutiny."

"So frame him. Quillan. No blows to the head."

Wil nodded. "Doc goes to ground, DeVillbis hires me to flush him out so the frame can work. I do, and bang:

Doc's where Garza's—or more likely Mejia's gang contacts can take him out. Everybody agreeing that what goes around comes around."

The sprinklers shut off. Flies buzzed a cola spill.

"What about Alvarez?"

"Different window, but the same closers. Bottom line is he knew things that could get Stockdale reopened, that's why he called me. My guess is he could see it coming as soon as Doc hit town. Just a day late and a dollar short."

Tate was silent a moment. "Cole, you think?"

"Yes and no. I'm not quite there yet."

*But you'll keep me up to speed:* the cop eyes stealing in to say it. "What about this thing with the sale?"

"Almost home," Wil said. "Grand Cayman or someplace if I'm right that Rossert's cashing out across the board. Burning his bridges."

"With Ronnie directly in line . . ."

"Welcome back around."

"*Damn.*" Tate's wheels had made nervous-energy ruts in the dirt. "You have any idea where he hangs out during the day?"

"Jenelle mentioned music classes. A campus not far from her place."

Tate nodded. "Bakersfield College—the juco. And so much for Mejia."

*Unless that's where Mejia's gone,* Wil thought as they rolled for the parking lot; crossing his fingers *not;* almost there when he low-voiced: "Quick look—guy in the Cutlass pulling out—he look familiar to you?"

"Parkway," Tate came back without hesitation. "Did some laps while we ate. I recognize the shades."

"Any ideas?"

"Motor pool'd be my guess," Tate said. "Somebody's, anyway."

"You thinking Acosta, too?"

"I don't know. Possibly." He opened the El Camino's door, prepared to hoist himself in, looked back. "More like it's time to check the safeties off."

If and when, they agreed—no later than two—Wil heading back to see if there were messages and retrieve his cell phone. From the truck he used it to call Jenelle, caught the relief in her tone when he asked how she was, heard Ronnie had actually called to apologize last night. Blown her away. Which led him to casually extend the conversation, enough to know he'd had it right about Bakersfield College, where Tate had gone to warn the kid.

Not wanting to alarm her unnecessarily, he invited her to have dinner, then hung up and dialed first Redtail's, then Cheri's. Driving there, he kept checking for the Cutlass, but saw nothing of it in the afternoon traffic. Still, he parked up the cross street and took the alley to the bar, where a keep he didn't recognize was on duty.

"Cole in his office?"

"Who wants to know?" Transferring Millers to the cooler, "White Line Fever" pouring out of the juke.

Wil winked. "Friend of his with a surprise. Down the hall?" He started in that direction, eyebrows up, ingenuous smile in place.

"Outside," the keep finally said. "The far-left unit."

Wil hit the back steps, saw Crash Alvarez's trailer already had been converted to storage, cardboard cases showing in the windows, the geraniums trampled down. No signs of life in the other trailers, except for the Airstream on the far left, screen in place over an open door. Cole's unmistakable voice coming from it.

He let himself in just as Cole was ending a phone conversation behind a metal desk. Boot-cut jeans and oval buckle, white snap-button shirt with the sleeves rolled up, gray Stetson on a bank of file cabinets. Clutter and racing memorabilia, Snap-On wall calendar and ash-tray, Corona and Pirelli posters, table fan pointed at the ceiling.

*Think steam. Turning up the heat.*

Surprise flickered when Cole saw him. He creaked back in the metal chair and snorted. "Figured you were about as smart as you looked."

Wil smiled. "Couldn't leave without complimenting your shooting."

No change in expression: "If you're talking about my missing rifle, the sheriff's handling that. I'm also due at the track, so make it brief."

"Fair enough: Lynette Bevins—you and Doc and Sara and Arlene. The worst it can get."

"I've heard enough. Get out of here."

*Roll it. Brass ring or bust.* "She was leaving him, wasn't she? It was all worked out. Arlene slips him the dope, then you show up. Regular Sir Lancelot."

Cole's hand went to the phone. "I'm calling Acosta."

"And miss the rest? Hell, this is your *life*." Staring into the man's eyes until his hand left the receiver.

"Bullshit," Cole said as if suddenly deciding. "I'll handle your ass myself." He was rising from the chair when Wil lifted the front edge of the desk and shoved, Cole and contents landing on the floor in a welter of papers, cold coffee, and cigarette butts.

Cole's eyes went very wide, then to the shotgun braced against the split paneling.

Wil got there first.

"Anybody in town not own a pump?" he asked pleasantly.

"Try this neighborhood and running cash to the bank at night, dumbfuck."

Wil chambered a round. "It's coming apart, Cole. Rossert, Garza, Mejia, your dad—time to save yourself. What happened out there?"

Cole just glared.

"Think of the spin your lawyers'll put on it: good-looking guy, local racing hero. It's all public opinion now. Show a little remorse and you're home free."

"Fuck yourself."

"Try this: You finally beat him at something. There they are, packed up and ready to go. But then you let Arlene in on it—minor detail: it's just Sara and her you're taking along, what's yours. No permanent reminders of Doc for you."

"Are you done?"

Wil had to give it to him—boxed in, backed against a wall, some part of him likely seeing it coming for twenty years. "Not nearly," he went on. "At first she thinks you're kidding. Then it hits home you're serious, and she hits back. Push comes to shove and you're laying down the law—maybe threatening to take Sara *unless* she goes along. Hell, you didn't wait five years for *this*. But Arlene's no pushover. Doc's shotgun's been blowing up beer bottles earlier, and she gets it. Tells you to back off, let go of Sara, it's over. Pointing a fucking gun at *you*!"

Cole wiped his mustache with the back of his hand, a bead of sweat working its way down his temple.

"No?" Wil went on. "Then how about she's changed her mind—she loves Doc after all. He needs her and you're odd man out again."

Still Cole said nothing.

"Big mistake," Wil said. "She's no match, and you rip the shotgun away. Maybe neither of you thinks it's even loaded. Maybe it goes off by accident. But all of a sudden you're standing over her. Over *them*."

"*BullSHIT.*"

"That's the polite version, your lawyer's version, Cole as victim. Mine's a little different: I see Arlene for betraying you, then the girls because you can't leave witnesses, and they're screaming, screaming, and you're finished around here unless . . ."

Cole just stared.

"No? Fill in the blanks."

"And if I don't, you're going to shoot me. That's a laugh."

Wil set down the shotgun. "After it's done, you're just clearheaded enough to call Garza, Mejia, or both—the call Alvarez had on you. And they fix it: lose the dope and your fingerprints, put the gun in Doc's hands, unpack the luggage, get you the hell out of there. Whatever it takes. Only it's just a bit too tidy."

"I'm getting up now."

"All for just a piece of your soul. Like father, like son."

Cole launched himself, flailed a roundhouse right that would have dropped Wil had he not spun with it, and as momentum carried him, Wil drove a left to the kidneys. Cole went to his knees, then for the shotgun, but Wil kicked the legs out from under him and he landed awkwardly, the .380 ankle gun at his ear and the fight gone.

Wil backed off the Colt, got to his feet, jacked five double-aught buck shells out onto the floor.

*"Fuck you,"* Cole said as he did. "Let's see you prove it."

"A confession would help. Might even save your life."

"What are you talking about?"

Wil reholstered the automatic. "You're a loose end. Loose ends get snipped off. My guess is sooner from the way Rossert's going to town."

Cole just looked at him.

"You knew about him cashing out, didn't you? Two hundred and seventy mil for the foothill piece? Rest to follow?"

"That's a crock."

"It sure would worry me."

"That's because you know nothing."

"Check it out. Might even get the escrow company cheap."

Just then the door opened and the barkeep stood there with an aluminum baseball bat. Viewing the mess, Cole on the floor, he said, "Thought I heard a commotion. You want me to plant this guy?"

Wil backed up a step, put his left foot on the overturned desk to expose the ankle holster, rest a hand on the gun butt. For a moment he and the keep eyed each other.

"Real Johnny-on-the-spot, you are," Cole said. Rebuttoning the pearl snaps that had come undone, grabbing the Stetson as he shoved past the man. "Just try not to hurt yourself showing this fuck off the premises. And get somebody to clean the place. I got heats to run."

# TWENTY-FOUR

Wil pulled into the cul-de-sac and parked opposite the well, the horsehead part still rising above the hedge, then dipping below it. He strode up the walk to the 34 East building, pushed through the doors reading ROSSERT IN-VESTMENT PARTNERS on the glass. Same spacious reception area, same auburn-haired secretary with too much makeup. As if she'd never left.

"Well, hello again," she said, eyeing him up and down. "And let me guess . . ."

"It's important I see him," Wil said. "Is he in?"

"Nope."

"How about Garza?"

Shake of her head. "Looks like you're stuck with little old me."

"Any idea where they've gone."

"No, they don't usually tell me that, just that they're going out. Can I do anything for you?"

"You familiar with the name Cumulus?"

"What do you think? RIP is a Cumulus company."

"Owned by Rossert . . ."

"Which you'll have to take up with him."

Wil smiled. "I would if you'd tell me where he went."

The smile was returned with interest. Fifteen love.

"Business or pleasure?" Wil asked.

"Anybody ever say you looked like Alan Jackson?"

Thirty love. "Not in the last ten minutes."

She chewed her RIP ballpoint, cocked her head. "Maybe not. And I'd say horseback riding from the way they were dressed, but Mr. Garza doesn't ride."

Thirty-fifteen. "Dressed how?"

"Oh, blue jeans, boots. Like that."

*Which meant anywhere.* "Dress or shitkicker?"

"The latter, I guess you could say."

Deuce. "Mind if I use your phone?"

"There's one over by the couch. You must have missed it."

"Actually I was hoping for something more private."

Annoyance flashed briefly, then was gone—advantage Hardesty. "If you insist, I suppose you could use the privacy suite we maintain for customers and Mr. Garza."

Wil thanked her, found it, noticed there was no door on the privacy suite and little else beyond a chair, a desk, and a phone. He called Tate's El Camino number, got no answer—away from his car, Wil figured. He tried Jenelle's, got her machine, gave it a moment after he announced who it was in case she was screening calls, then hung up, thinking *nobody there* would make an appropriate epitaph.

Seeing the secretary swivel away to take a call, he scanned the office. From appearances, no one ever used it, and he was about to leave when something caught his eye.

It was a phone number, lightly penciled into yesterday's blotter square, the entire month of April due to be torn off in a few days. Instead of the usual dash, the three digits were separated from the four by a small teardrop. On a whim he dialed it, heard five or six rings, and was about to hang up when a slurred female voice answered.

"Tommy ain't here," she said without preamble and before hanging up. "Try the track."

*Tommy . . . the track . . .*

He dialed again, this time asking for Tommy Arroyo before she could get a word in, heard *"What am I? S'fuckin' secretary?"* before the receiver was banged down.

Tommy Arroyo, Cole's mechanic. Raul Garza, Rye Rossert's mechanic. Heads together that night at Redtail's. Cole again: *I got heats to run.*

Wil was halfway through the door before the secretary had even turned at the sound.

The column of smoke was a good hundred feet in the air when Wil pulled into the big lot, parked, raced up and over the concrete steps. Since it was a practice day, there weren't many people in the stands. The few who were either were jammed at the fence bordering the oval, straining to see, or clustered around the burning hulk at the near turn, fire erupting from it as the crews fought to get close enough to be effective with their chemical extinguishers.

Not having much luck.

Then a fire unit roared across the infield and let fly, steam billowing around the wreck and the helmeted shape still visible in the driver's harness. As the flames subsided, the steam dissipated, Wil could see the car's paint was virtually gone, its tires flat and smoldering. Only the outline of the numbers 1 and 9 remained.

And the blackened figure.

In the confusion, he slipped around a security type, sprinted across the track to the apron. Trying to spot Tommy Arroyo in the silent crowd, he finally saw a face that looked familiar, one of the men Lute DeVillbis had spoken to the day they'd been out to meet Cole.

"Rolled it," the man said when Wil asked him what

happened. "Went in high, hit the wall, and fucking lost it. Never saw anything like that. *Son of a bitch!*" He drew in a breath to steady himself.

"Tommy around anywhere?"

"Arroyo? No—he never showed. Cole finally started without him. Poor Lute, I'm just glad he wasn't here."

"Yeah. Anybody notify him?"

The man pointed to a CHP unit, the officer on his radio. "I gave him the number, asked him to tell Lute to stay away. He doesn't need any part of this."

The flames were gone and the smoke, but the acrid smell remained. As did the crowd, watching a crew in protective gloves attempt to lever the driver's-side door off number 19.

"But no Tommy?"

"You still on that?"

"Sorry, but it's important."

"Fuck Tommy—and fuck you. That's Cole DeVillbis in that car. How about showing some respect?"

As Wil recrossed the track—much to the irritation of the same security guy—climbed the stairs, and started down toward people clustered at the now-cordoned-off entrance, he noticed a breeze had begun taking the smoke toward town, and that a ridge of clouds was building in the Sierra.

When he jerked the S-10 to a stop, most of the other spots were empty except for Lute's. Hoping the silver Mercedes meant the man was still in the building, Wil saw the elevator was in service and took the stairs. As he emerged, the doors were just closing on two Marston DeVillbis receptionists he recognized from the other day. Their eyes widened as they saw him, but they made no move for the buttons.

Wil scanned desks, saw no phones lines lit, no evidence of anyone left on the floor. At the closed double doors to Lute's office, he rapped, listened, eased his way through.

Lute's chair was facing the window looking out over the city and the mountains. Wil could just see the top of his bald head.

"Lute," he called softly. "Wil Hardesty."

No answer, no movement.

Walking to him, he saw a face as empty as the building—empty glass in his hand, near-empty bottle of Makers Mark beside the chair. Wil took the bottle and the glass, poured two fingers, handed the glass back.

Without looking up, Lute drank some, then his eyes drifted out the window again. "Storm's coming, you can feel it," he said finally. "The heat's broken."

Wil nodded, pulled a chair over.

"That smoke." Still without looking directly at Wil. "My son burning to death."

"I'm very sorry."

"Before they even called, I knew. It's funny how that works." Overcast was creeping in on the valley now, sullen looking after all the days of brightness and color. He said, "From the time they're little you're afraid. Then they get big and the fear shrinks down to an ember. But it's there. And you're right to be afraid."

Wil let it alone.

"You have any idea what I'm talking about?"

"Yes. It's worse than you imagine."

But DeVillbis took no note, just nipped a finger off the bourbon. Then he seemed to become aware of who he was talking to.

"What the hell are you doing up here?"

"I came to tell you you're in bed with the devil," Wil answered. "But I guess you already know that."

DeVillbis tossed off the whiskey, gasped, poured more into the glass. "I'm going out to the track. Soon as I finish this."

"It's a zoo," Wil said. "And they'll have him some-where else by now."

"God may be slow, but he's a vindictive son of a bitch. You ever notice that?"

"Not God, Lute."

"What are you talking about?"

He went through it: Tommy's home phone number on Garza's day-before calendar pad; Tommy a no-show at the heats where he would surely have been. Wil wasn't sure if Lute caught the meaning, so he added, "If Tommy Arroyo's not in the river already, he will be."

DeVillbis shook his head slowly. "Why Cole?"

"Because Arlene and the kids was a frame-up from day one. Nothing you don't know."

"How dare you?"

But it was soft and unfocused, and Wil rolled: "Cole's alibi was a woman named Lynette Bevins, who's been living rent-free for the last twenty years in a house you own. Similar to the arrangement with Alvarez. Only thing was, Crash went fishing for more. I doubt if Ly-nette knows anything near what Cole did or she'd be dead, too." Wil made a mental note to swing by there—fair warning. "But then maybe a man in your position has to hang on and not rock the boat or drown in Ros-sert's wash."

DeVillbis slumped back in the chair. "We were almost free of him," he said to the window. "After what hap-pened at that . . . god-awful slaughterhouse . . . he owned us. Right down to the bars."

"And Doc?"

DeVillbis jerked his head around. "What was I sup-posed to do, give Cole up—give my son up? Whatever he was or wasn't, Cole's flesh and blood. You have any idea what that means?"

"That you can rationalize anything?"

"It means you save what's yours and put the rest down."

"Live and let die."

"If it comes to that, yes. Something I thought you understood when I hired you."

"Then tell me—how was Gib's crime worse than yours?"

DeVillbis sighed heavily. "Gib was poor. I had some property I inherited and a law degree. Rye liked that, saw the potential. So I lived. Even so, he did this." He held up the artificial hand. "Said it'd remind me if I ever got tempted to cross him again. Actually joked about it . . . bullet in the head or a handshake with a chain saw."

"Were you there when Rossert shot him?"

He shook his head. "I had a wife and kid by then. You want to tell me what you'd have done different?"

"Tough call—especially when the oil was down there after all. Rossert must have gotten a real chuckle over that one. And you must know he's cashing out."

DeVillbis shrugged. "So what? I don't own any of it anymore."

"Right now is about what you know—Cole and now you."

"My son is dead. And you want me to give a shit?"

Wil went over to the desk, found a pocket tape recorder and a legal pad in a drawer, came back and set them in DeVillbis's lap with a ballpoint from the desktop. "End it," he said.

"The truth, is that it? Justice undenied."

"Doc had a son they know about, if you don't. How far does it go?"

"You're dreaming, and I'm not up to it—never have been or it wouldn't have come to this. And guys with Rossert's money don't end up in jail."

"With your testimony, they do."

DeVillbis stared at the recorder and pad.

"His secretary said he and Garza left in boots and jeans—where'd they go?"

Still staring. "The kid have a name?"

"Ronnie. And whether you value your life at this point or any of it, he and Garza killed Cole. That how you want to leave it?"

DeVillbis poured the last of the whiskey, met Wil's eyes. He got up slowly and walked to the window, where he stood looking out at the horizon. "If I tell you where I think they've gone, will you get the fuck away from me?"

Wil called Tate again from the outer office after having Lute lock his doors. This time he got through, but there was static on the line.

"Wind always charges up the ions or something," Tate said. "Can you hear me?"

"Well enough. I'm at Marston DeVillbis with Lute. Cole's dead."

"I know. We've had the radio on."

"We . . ."

"Jenelle. I'm at her place. She's upstairs."

For the first time today, Wil felt relief. "Ronnie there, too?"

"That's why I'm here. She hasn't heard from him— neither has the school. Roommate said he never came home from Redtail's that night. You have any idea how that makes me feel?"

"Yeah, I do."

"And? . . ."

"And nothing—you hearing that? I'm on my way."

"Some glutton for punishment," Tate concluded.

Emerging from the building, Wil felt the wind he was talking about—cool with a hint of dampness. Clouds had edged in on the foothills now, dark gray and looking like extensions of the granite ramparts east of them.

Only the western sky showing blue patches.

He swung by Lynette Bevins's house, found it virtually a shell. At least everything was gone from the living and dining rooms. JFK and Elvis all that remained. A white-haired man walking toward his car with the help of a cane saw Wil peering in the window and hailed him.

"You're looking for the woman next door, she left about an hour ago."

"Thanks. Any idea where she went?"

"Nope. From how fast they jammed her stuff into that U-Haul, her and her daughter, that was the idea."

"Relatives she might be moving in with?"

"Think she had a niece in Tucson, but don't quote me."

"What about friends who might know?"

The neighbor paused at the sidewalk. "Mister, nobody around here knew her. But then I always got the impression that was the idea, too."

Four o'clock: Wil thanked him again and left, recalling Bridgit's remark about Cole: *Hon, you don't know the half.* Wishing her luck as he pulled into Jenelle's complex, Tate's El Camino parked outside her condo.

After Tate had let him in, Wil briefed him where it stood with DeVillbis—that for the most part, they'd called it. "Depends now on whether he's steamed enough to lay it out for the DA. Nothing I'd count on." Then, to Jenelle coming down the stairs: "How you doing?"

"We haven't been able to find Ronnie," she said. "Do you know where he is?"

"No."

"Can we stop dancing here, please?" Tate said.

"Bob explained to you why we're concerned?"

Jenelle nodded. "We had no idea about any oil money—you have to believe that."

"Any idea how they knew about Ronnie?"

She glanced away. "Cole was here a few days ago to sympathize about Doc. Unusual, I thought, but I tried to be polite. Some of the things he asked led me to believe he knew." Her look turning stricken. "Plus, I let some things slip. I suppose from telling Ronnie about it."

"The man wasn't dumb, Jen. He could easily have guessed from seeing Ronnie play." He touched her arm. "You said yourself he already knew."

There was an awkward pause.

"Here and now," Tate said. "All we've got—right?" Then: "DeVillbis tell you where Rossert and Garza went?"

"A possibility. One of Rossert's facades leased Alvarez's cabin from him a while ago."

"Why, I wonder?"

"Not a big stretch to see Crash needing drug money."

"I mean," she said, "what could Rossert do with it, a place that out of the way?"

"R and R?"

Jenelle folded her arms over her chest, but she didn't sit down. "Those guys recreating?"

"What I was thinking." Tate glancing at Wil.

"This is absurd," Jenelle said. "If you think they might be using it as a killing ground, I want to know. This is my *son* we're talking about." No waver in her tone.

"It doesn't necessarily mean that," Wil said.

Tate regarded the fireplace. "No—if Garza and Mejia are involved, drugs become a factor."

She turned to Wil. "Would you mind telling me what we're waiting for?"

"If we go up there to hunt for him and he's not there, we'll have wasted—"

"Time better spent, I think he's trying to say."

"Listen to me," she came back. "We've called everywhere. Bob's even driven by Rossert's estate. If we have a better option, I want to hear it."

"I say go," Tate said. "We can take the El Camino— you can drive mine, but I can't drive yours. Any problem?"

Wil shook his head.

Jenelle said, "I'll get my rain jacket."

"Bad idea," Tate said.

"He's right. Too dangerous, no room, and you're needed here in case Ronnie calls." Thinking she looked pretty incredible for all she'd been through. "That make sense?"

# TWENTY-FIVE

Bob Tate horsed the El Camino until finally he had to slow at the entrance to the canyon. Still, traffic was light, and he was able to hold it around fifty, curves notwithstanding.

"Maybe getting us there should be the priority," Jenelle said casually, Wil noting the tautness in her face.

Tate backed off as they came up on a maintenance truck; for a tense mile, he hugged its tail, surging past at a short-lived wide spot. Luckily, the few oncomers had their lights on—blowing past with wipers going, the road ahead looking black and slick from the first drops beginning to hit the windshield.

Thunder rumbled in the high mountains, occasional flashes coming from where they were headed. Hawks veered and dove like kamikazes. Sensing the wind in the El Camino's handling, Wil cracked the wing, put a hand out. The air felt cool, but hardly cold, and smelled of damp rock.

For some reason the river looked higher than last time, the rapids gray green in the lowering light. Even the willows standing in it looked different now—glossy and shifting. The roar, however, was a constant.

They began to leave the river, Tate picking up speed as the road straightened a bit. But then it began to snake and switch back, and he swore at their pace.

"Any thought to how you want to play this?" he finally asked.

Jenelle looked at Wil.

"Not yet. Size it up from the ridge, then—"

"Don't you *dare* hold anything back because of me," she said with a fury that surprised him. "You have any idea how I'd feel if something went unsaid that could have saved him?"

Neither man spoke.

*"Well—do you?"*

"It's not that," Wil answered for both. "Everything depends on how it lies." He spent a moment describing the scene from memory.

"Shouldn't we call the sheriff?"

Wil thought of Acosta, saw Tate probably thinking the same thing. "When we see there's a need."

"Besides," Tate said. "What's he got that we haven't?" Tapping his sawed-off twelve-gauge between the seats.

That lapsed them into silence, Wil concentrating on recognizing landmarks as the highway crossed and recrossed the river, slate gray punctuated by white-lace riffles far below. Despite the drops growing fatter and more frequent, the mountains still showed heat wave. Yellow grasses bent in the wind off the hillsides; fire-danger signs were already up; the wildflowers were history. Only the pines and retreating oaks seemed unaffected.

In a bit they found the turn. Twenty minutes of dirt road later, Wil saw the ridge, had Tate pull the El Camino off below where the road widened and dipped down. As they approached the crest, found cover in the fringe manzanita about where Cole had, he was conscious of drips off the cedar trees and the smell of ozone, ragged bands of mist fading the far ridges.

He and Tate raised the field glasses they'd brought along.

*"Well?"*

"Four," Tate said. "Ronnie outside with Mejia and Garza, Rossert inside the cabin."

"Oh, God—you see Ronnie?"

Wil handed Jenelle his glasses and concentrated on the wider view: light showing in a downstairs window, nose of a black Suburban poking out around the far corner. About fifty yards from it, Ronnie and who he took to be Mejia working an already good-sized hole with shovels—landing the dirt on a square of black plastic. Raul Garza mixing what looked to be cement in a construction barrow. Something under an olive tarp.

"Not a bad field of fire," Tate said. "While it lasts."

"Say it," Jenelle said, handing back the glasses as if she'd had enough. "They've got him digging his own grave."

"Doesn't leave us much choice, all right."

*"So . . ."*

"So we move," he added, hoping at least it sounded optimistic. "Preempt while there's still light."

As Wil looked through the glasses again, Garza pulled the tarp off Tommy Arroyo, red soaking the front of the white T-shirt and Levi's he had on. Garza and Mejia then muscled him in the hole and tilted in the load of cement, the hole deep enough so that none of it showed from there.

*"My God,"* Jenelle said. "Do *some*thing."

"Preempt how?" Tate asked.

Wil unholstered the .45 from his shoulder rig, checked the action, returned it, a plan forming as he did the same with the .380 Colt. "How good are you with that sawed-off?"

•    •    •

Twenty minutes and only partway to the clearing, Wil began worrying in earnest about the light. The rain had steadied, adding fire to the group's efforts below and to his left; from what he could gather through breaks, Garza already had dumped another load of cement into the hole and he and Mejia were working on a third.

Brush scraped his windbreaker; pine boughs slapped his face. Here on the periphery the going was steep and slippery, and he'd had to go carefully to avoid dislodging rocks and giving himself away. Thinking if he didn't get there within minutes it wouldn't much matter, he began trading caution for pace.

And making up ground.

From the ridge Jenelle had observed that Ronnie looked in slow motion. As Wil glanced that way now, Ronnie sat propped against a tree examining a pile of pine needles he was building into a cone, while Mejia leaned on his shovel. At word from Garza, Mejia pulled another bag from the Suburban, slit it along the top with a pocketknife, and dumped it into the mix.

Wil was closing but not yet in position when Rye Rossert in jeans, boots, and leather half coat emerged to urinate against the cottonwood. He said something to Garza and Mejia, then strolled over to Ronnie, squatted, and began talking to him, Ronnie taking little notice. Even when Rossert reached into his coat, brought out a syringe, and gave it a couple of taps.

*Damn!*

Wil waved frantically toward Jenelle watching through his binoculars, saw Tate separate from the manzanita and start down the incline. Back to Rossert then: testing the spike by squirting some in the air, Wil bringing the .45 to bear on him, vowing no way *that* was going to happen, despite the distance. He was about to shout it down, take his chances, when Garza suddenly noticed the figure in the wheelchair bearing down on them.

"The *hell* is *that*?" he said.

Rossert saw it and straightened; distracted, he lowered the syringe. "Somebody want to find out? Like *now*?"

Mejia whooped with sudden insight. "Check it out— it's that cop I shot." He shook his head. "The fuck's he doin' here?"

Tate angled the chair to a stop about ten yards off Mejia, hands slipping under his camouflage rain slicker. The scalp under his close-cropped hair looked like hard wet soap.

"Amazing how the body compensates for equipment failure," Rossert finally said. "Sergeant Tate, isn't it?"

Tate just sat there.

"I mean, imagine our surprise. And all that way."

"For nothing." Mejia smirked. "Not looking too spry there, *cuate*. Come to cry about your love life?"

"Shut up," Rossert said. Then to Tate: "I haven't time to care how or why you're here, Sergeant. Or how this may look to you. But life is comprised of turning points, wouldn't you agree? For instance, I think you just turned the corner on any further financial difficulties."

No response.

Rossert smiled. "May we conclude that, Sergeant Tate?"

"You're under arrest," Tate said in a voice Wil barely recognized. "All of you, flat on the ground. *Now.*"

It was so bizarre that even Rossert laughed, Wil using it to further close the distance. Lightning lit a near ridge, and several seconds later thunder boomed. Drip continued from the eaves, though a break in the rain made it seem as if it, too, were holding its breath.

"Then there are those," Rossert said, his smile fading, "who'll fuck up a turn down a one-way street."

"Man's a warrior, cuz, gotta give him that," Mejia said to Garza. "Just not too bright."

But Garza was no longer laughing. Hands in his hooded sweatshirt pocket, he scanned the hill and woods for movement. "I don't like it," he was saying. "Can't be just him."

Mejia ended his smirk, reached behind his back, and came out with a stainless-steel automatic. "Sorry, *estropeado*, the man don't like it." He worked the slide. "Lucky we got plenty of room in there."

Tate fired without aiming and Mejia was blown backward a good ten feet, Wil figuring deer slug for the impact as he swung his .45 toward Garza—who by now had his own piece out and was coming down on Tate.

*"Drop it, Raul."*

Garza's automatic left its intended target, snapped a shot in Wil's direction. Wil fired and missed. Tate triggered a round at Garza, but the man was already running for the house, launching himself at the front window. As Wil's next shot splintered molding, Garza crashed through and into the living room.

*Shit, shit, shit . . .*

Wil heard the Suburban roar to life, dirt roostertail from its oversized all-terrains, three more rounds from the shotgun. Then Jenelle was down the hill and into it, banging the El Camino off the Suburban trying to run down Bob Tate; banging it again—this bizarre demolition derby lasting several seconds, the Suburban finally breaking off contact and storming up the hill.

Shots from the house: dirt flying around both Tate and Jenelle, no good angle on Garza from where Wil held cover. *Back door:* From the corner of the cabin, he hit it flush, the light wood bursting inward as Garza spun firing from the window, milk glass and old camp scenics, stamped tin fixtures and cheap plastic kitchen tile exploding across a shoulder-high arc. But by then Wil was firing off the worn flooring, near-full clip to empty, hot-load rounds that picked Garza up and threw him off the knotty pine, swipes of red where he'd impacted.

Wil rose cautiously to haze and dust, shattered glass and wood, the wet hiss of nicked plumbing. Spotting Garza's automatic, he toed it under a chair and bent to the man, saw that he was dead or almost. Blood pumped from two wounds in Garza's chest, one in his thigh, and from his mouth, which gaped fishlike in an effort to speak.

"Kroft and Quillan," Wil said, angling further to pick up any words that came. "A chance to die clean."

Garza gurgled, oozed over red teeth. "Fuck you," he managed. "Try . . . going . . . fifteen . . . with . . ." Then a final wet rumble.

Wil holstered the .45, put a foot on the sill, landed outside. Jenelle was kneeling by Ronnie, holding tight to him as he stared into his lap. Across from them, Tate had just reached the El Camino's open driver-side door. He jammed in behind the wheel, yanking the chair in behind him.

"Get in," he shouted. Firing up the engine.

Wil did, yelled at Jenelle to take Ronnie inside, they'd be back or send help. As her wide eyes disappeared behind them, he replayed her banging off the Suburban again, laying it all on the line, and he felt his heart jump as though a hand had reached in and touched it.

*Pure unreal . . .*

"What about Garza?"

"Dead," Wil answered him. Ears still ringing, he ejected the spent clip, shoved in the spare. "You all right?"

"Are you kidding? Look at my car." Tate had the El Camino floored and, as they hit the ridge, aired it down to the springs before righting it on the dirt. "You see the fucker try to run me down?"

Wil nodded; pines and saplings flew by; he tried Tate's phone and got nothing. Then they hit the highway and Tate seemed to lose all vestige of caution. For a few miles, Wil figured this was how it was going to end— east of Bakersfield, rolling a thousand feet into the Kern, the rain having started up again. Sean Wilson Hardesty, R.I.P.

Tate brought him out of it. "Three Ks' worth of set- tlement money in tires and suspension," he shouted, hands gripped at ten and four. "Just in case it ever came to that."

"Let's hope it was enough."

Tate slid them through a series of switchbacks, then: "Up ahead. You see what I see?"

Wil peered through the wipers, saw taillights, their shape defining itself the closer they got, Rossert at least unable to get much more out of the bigger, less agile Suburban. Tate blinked his brights, closed in.

Wil tried the phone again with similar results.

"It's the mountains," Tate shouted over the wind whistling through the sprung hood and broken grille, the racetrack whine of engine. "Maybe I can get close enough to bump him."

"You crazy?" Wil shouted back. "We'll bump *off* him."

"Not the way I'll do it."

"Forget it!"

"Close your eyes, then!"

Wil hung on as they took a curve in four-wheel drift, felt Tate gun it on a short patch of straight, brake and floor it again. Mercifully there was no traffic, Wil won- dering at that, how long their luck could hold. He saw Rossert bring the big Chevy too fast into a turn, barely make it out the other side.

They were down close to the river now, Tate bringing them into and out of a tight S, Wil close to screwing his pistol into Tate's ear to make him slow down, when they saw it. Light bars flashing on top of two cop units heading upcanyon. Directly at Rossert.

Directly at them.

As they watched, the one behind swung out into the opposing lane. Then both stopped in a shallow V and began pulsing their headlights, Wil realizing now what explained the lack of traffic.

Rossert's brake lights flashed momentarily as he sized up the odds: Wil and madman Tate behind him, rock wall and river for options, both lanes blocked. Or were they? . . . Wil could almost hear his thoughts:

*Last round—no holds barred, no time-outs.*

*Place your bets . . .*

As Tate closed, Rossert hit it: at least the possibility of freedom beyond a dirt turnout, river side. If the Suburban could just make it around the outer white Crown Victoria.

*"Oh, man . . ."* Awed sounding as Tate slowed to watch the Suburban speed toward the block, at the last minute jerk right in an effort to skirt the cruiser.

But Rossert wasn't experienced enough in that kind of maneuver—or the flashing lights impaired his judgment, or the traction wasn't there, or a cop fired at him, or the Suburban was just too big. At any rate, it clipped the Crown Vic as though T-boned at an intersection. Still, it looked as if it had a chance, steadying now as Rossert fought the slide, the whump-down from two wheels. Then it simply ran out of embankment, did a quarter roll in midair, and disappeared.

As they approached the turnout and the river below it, Wil could see the headlights and the aftermarket fog cutters—underwater floods in a pool—the Suburban down at the bow but still afloat. Then a race of current caught it and slowly the Suburban turned turtle and wedged, the spoke wheels gradually coming up to speed with the flow.

For a moment they watched the partially submerged and spinning waterwheels, the boils of red around the taillights. Then Xavier Acosta was at the side window, tapping with the butt of his pistol for Tate to roll it down.

For a long moment Tate just looked at him. Then he cranked the handle twice. "Hello, Zav," he said. "Lotta years."

"Nice that you're so mobile, Bob. Want to bring your friend and come with me?"

As the Crown Vic awaited the tow truck, Wil, Tate, and Acosta sat inside. By then four more units had rolled up, their light bars splashing color on the blacktop and canyon walls.

In silence they'd watched an emergency team attempt to reach the generator-lit wreck of the Suburban, thus far without success. Two EMTs in rain gear stood beside an ambulance van. Awaiting Rossert's body, Wil assumed. His gaze drifted to the highway where CHiPs in yellow slickers directed a crawl of headlights past the turnout where they'd pushed the disabled cruiser. Rain on the car's roof added to the roar of river.

One by one, the deputies waved to Acosta, then left for other duties, passing at the far end of the turnout the Cutlass Wil and Tate had made in the park. Through the windshield, Wil could see the glow of a cigarette as the driver waited for Acosta to finish.

Acosta left momentarily to answer a call on a radio that worked, then came back. "They're okay," he said. "The kid's in for a rocky spell from the spikes they hit him with, but he's going to make it."

"Jenelle?"

"She's with him at a hospital on the lake. It was closer

and they wanted to keep him overnight." He saw Wil's look. "I'll see they get down the hill. Apparently she found a phone in the cabin because that's how we got routed. Good thing—Deputy Broussard lost you in town."

"Speaking of which . . ."

Acosta ignored Wil, looked at Tate. "Not bad work for an odd couple, Bob. Plus a little bump from me."

"Zav? Get screwed."

"Now . . . there's no need for that."

"Tell Deputy Broussard."

"This a private party or can anybody play?"

Acosta flicked a glance in Wil's direction. "You're here, aren't you? Consider the alternative."

Figuring it would eventually unfold, Wil let it go. Tate kept staring at Acosta.

"Why *are* we here, Zav?"

"Because a debt is a debt, and I square mine."

"That certainly spells it out. No wonder you're a lieutenant."

Acosta's forced smile was illuminated by a flash of passing headlights. "It's been a productive day, don't spoil it. I'm the first to admit you people had much to do with it."

Tate grimaced. *"You people . . ."*

"Figure of speech, Bob. You get the drift."

"Drift, I understand."

Acosta opened a pack of gum, offered it around, put two sticks in his mouth when it was waved off. "I'll start at the beginning. Does Wyoming mean anything to either of you?"

"What's a gimp get these days for striking a law officer?"

But Wil ran it and got a faint click. Wyoming—*click-click*—stronger now: Doc saying, *I'm sure he'd rather I live in Wyoming. I'm sure they all would . . .* Something about the way Acosta said it . . . his look now, little smile of anticipation. Enjoying this.

"The photo," Wil said finally. "Doc's body on the concrete. Prison towel loose across the head and shoulders."

"You're smarter than I thought, I'll give you that."

Tate rubbed a hand over his stubble. "Well, I'm not. And you are seriously pissing me off."

"So you used him, too," Wil said.

"I prefer *elicited,* but I suppose the idea's the same."

"Elicited, my ass," Tate said. "The hit was a setup—that's what you're telling us?"

Acosta just looked at him, the smile broadening slightly.

"I don't fucking believe it."

He cracked a window. "We caught wind of the real contract and were inclined to take it seriously because somebody'd taken out Alvarez. Too close to home, we figured. So we proposed a plan: let Alvarez slide as a suicide, jump the gun on the Whitney hit, let whoever ordered it stew about who pulled it off. Make them think end run. Next step, connect the dots."

"In exchange for what?"

Acosta looked out at the progress being made by the emergency crew; a wet-suited deputy attached to a line had reached the wreck and was communicating something to the ones on shore.

"The dropping of all murder charges—two counts, first degree. A bargain, all things considered."

Tate said, "Especially after it became apparent you had no case, except in the media. Something you probably forgot to tell him."

"Make no mistake, he jumped at it. Especially the part about the ticket out—my reference to Wyoming."

"So the whole thing was a sham," Wil said.

"I wouldn't call it that."

"Sorry—I'm sure you've found a better word. Bearing in mind 'elicited' is off the board."

"Try the job, shamus." Ticking them off on his fingers: "Twenty-seven gangbangers nailed. Contender for most valuable drug cache in U.S. history stockpiled around the cabin. Cole DeVillbis's mechanic in a pit of wet concrete. Two more buried in an orange grove. Not to mention a statement from Luther DeVillbis regarding the criminal activities of the man in the water—deceased, it appears—somebody we've been after for what seems like forever." He paused. "All that versus one man in voluntary isolation for a week."

"So it was oil *and* drugs."

"What's that?"

"Nothing," Wil said. "Did Lute implicate Cole in Arlene, Sara, and Megan?"

"At some length." Acosta cleared his throat, paused. "Evidently she tried backing out of a decision to leave Whitney for Cole and it got out of hand. Mejia and Garza did cleanup. Looks like your suspicions held some water after all, Bob."

"There's a fucking understatement."

"You know what they say about hindsight."

"No, Zav, what do they say?"

"Where is he now?" Wil asked.

"Sorry. Some of the gangs have long tentacles and longer memories."

"The ones who bought the dope from Garza via Rossert and acted as distributors . . ."

Acosta shrugged. "They have to blame somebody. Anyway, it's Whitney's business where he goes. And who he mentions it to."

"What about the cash-out money?"

"Said he'd let us know. By the way, that sound you hear is the lawyers stampeding. Be in the courts for years, that kind of dough."

"You're all heart, Zav, you know that?"

He spit his gum out into the night. "I admit to faults, Bob. Ambition for one—arrogance because it's also useful. Which doesn't make me a bad cop, and it sure as hell doesn't make me a dirty one."

"No need to justify for me."

"Shut up, I'm not finished. You were wrong to think that all those years—plain goddamned wrong. You're not the only one who lost when you took that punk's bullet. For the record, I haven't worked with anybody as good since. And if you don't believe that, then fuck you."

"You, too, Zav. We done here?"

"For now."

Reminding Wil of a couple of porcupines getting out of the car. Wary of one another. Outside, the rain had stopped; above the rim of the canyon, he could see moon behind the clouds breaking up, and the wind felt crisper, as though it had changed direction. Acosta peered down the bank at the emergency crew's progress, the diver at the wreck coming up long enough to shake his head.

"Couple more," Wil said. "Did Lute recall any more about Gib Whitney?"

"Rossert—the guy as much as admitted it to him."

"What about the two on the levee?"

"Garza, on orders from Rossert. Three birds with one stone."

"Put together when you learned about the hit," Tate put in.

Acosta just smiled.

One of the deputies relayed that with the windows smashed out of the Suburban, Rossert most likely was under it or caught in some rocks. They'd keep looking for a while. Probing with the lights.

"There's still some things I'd like to go over with Lute," Wil said. "Any objection?"

"None from me." Acosta backing for the Cutlass. "But DeVillbis signed his statement in blood. Actually, it was a .38 Chiefs Special. Maintenance man found him in his office earlier."

Acosta agreeing he'd see what he could do about the El Camino damage, they left, Tate nursing it along to keep the wind noise down.

"Real boot in the stones, Acosta. You believe all that?"

"Barely."

"No idea the prick had it in him."

"A prick, but our prick," Wil said.

"Sort of what I was thinking."

Several miles passed without conversation, then Tate let out with, "*Damn.* So Doc made it. Not only that, free and clear." Shaking his head and hoarse from something, probably all the yelling. "Need a few minutes to let that in."

Like the light in the tunnel that's not the train, Wil thought. And something else: not telling Acosta didn't matter. *It did not fucking matter . . . not then, not now . . .*

He let a nod speak for him, looked out the window.

Stars showed behind the few remaining clouds. At the canyon's mouth, the highway split off from the dark water headed for the weirs and shunts that would disperse it, Wil also noting how placid and sustaining it looked from there. As though burnished by a sheen of oil.

# TWENTY-SIX

Tate drove him by Jenelle's condo where he'd left the S-10. As Wil opened the door and got out, Tate made no move to drive away. Instead he stuck a hand out through his window.

"Probably see you over here for the depositions."

Wil took it, held, and released. "Acosta's sending me the forms. Said I could mail them if I wanted."

Nod. "Home must be looking good about now."

Wil thought about that—what he had waiting, what he hadn't. "Tell me about it. Chasing my clothes around to put them on."

"You ever entertain guests at that beach pad of yours?"

Wil got the meaning. "You'll work it out with Abbie. I've seen you in action, remember?"

"Maybe I'll bring her along. Do us good to get away."

"Anytime." Wil saw him look down at the ignition keys. "Thanks hardly covers it, Bob. I guess you know that."

Tate ran a hand over his crew cut. Sat there. "Not half bad, were we?"

"Policies change," Wil said. "Maybe there's a way to get back in. Acosta, for one."

Tate shrugged, but Wil could tell he was thinking about it.

"Even something related," he added.

"Like what you do . . ."

"Say again? That wasn't me bullfighting a Suburban."

"You don't have to mention that to Abbie."

"Think she'd believe it, anyway?"

There was the hint of a smile. "That's the trouble. She would."

"Take care of yourself," Wil said. "And tell your cleanup hitter she needs to keep her hands higher."

Tate grinned, nodded, and was gone.

Wil took in scrubbed air, crisp breeze blowing out of the north. He started the pickup and let it idle, let his eyes linger on the empty condo, imaging the interior and who'd made it that way.

Somewhere along the line, Doc had contacted her—of that, he was sure. Before Ronnie, he guessed—Acosta or no, Doc would have levered his way out of isolation and been all over that one. Which meant he hadn't known about it. Which meant she . . .

Hearing *Don't you dare hold anything back because of me,* his smile widened before sliding off. And now, Wyoming? If nothing else, it explained her recent preoccupation. Internalizing. Then he thought about his own situation, about Bob Tate's struggle—the toll just to keep *that* in place—and weighed in with: *It's a wonder any of us make it, period.*

Turning on his headlights, he pedaled down the choke setting, splashed through puddles the rain had left, and drove out the gate.

For the first time since he'd seen the club with Lute, Redtail's was closed and dark, a square of paper tacked to the door. Wil didn't stop to read it, just kept going, tires hissing on the wet pavement.

Hungry like he hadn't been in a while, he stopped at a place he'd noted in passing—porterhouse and baked potato, what he really felt like. Six or eight beers came also to mind, but then, nothing new there. Allowing himself the exchange—venal sin for mortal—he jammed in a disgusting wedge of chocolate cake.

*Take that . . .*

Driving to the hotel afterward, he gave in to a post-dinner, posteverything fade, the anticipation of sleep. No thoughts for a full eight. Thinking then of *her*, beside him in the dark. No . . . candlelight, silver necklace on warm skin. Maybe . . .

Car honk jerked him off the line, left into the hotel parking lot, back around to his spot. Plastic key in the door, open it, use the bathroom, leave the light on to see by. Unsnap and stow the .45, see the bed and fall into it. Shower in the morning . . . for that matter, undress in the morning . . .

Then, something . . .

Whiff of cigarette smoke from the unit's patio.

All but certain he hadn't left the sliding glass open, Wil raised himself off the bed, released the ankle gun, checked for a round in the chamber, heard Acosta saying, *Some of the gangs . . . Long tentacles and longer memories.* He cocked the .380. Just as Doc Whitney stepped out of the shadows and into the glow.

Doc took a last drag on the smoke, flipped it away, stood there, trying to hold on to a smile. "Sorry to startle you," he said. "But I seem to prefer it outside."

"Try 'scared the shit out of.' "

"Tougher than it looks being dead."

Wil reholstered the Colt, turned on a lamp, watched Doc slide back the screen and ease into a chair. Black jeans and jacket over a work shirt, black trucker's cap he pushed back as he stretched one boot out over the other. Most of the weight he'd lost regained and his color back.

"Greyhound must be starting to wonder," Wil said.

"I never was much good at schedules."

"Something you make up for in other areas."

Doc looked at him, trying to figure the subtext. "Acosta said he'd briefed you. I went ahead and used your phone."

Wil rubbed tired eyes. "Why stop there?"

Silence, then: "If it means anything, I think I know how you feel."

"Do you? Bob Tate nearly bought it today while Acosta ran his shuck on everybody. Not to mention Jenelle and your son."

"I didn't know about that. I didn't even know when Acosta planned the hit. He said it'd be more convincing for anyone watching."

"Or listening on the phone."

"Hey—it's not like I had a lot of choice."

"Tell it to them," Wil said, thinking of Denny Van Zant; wondering if Doc might be a convenient target for his own unresolved anger. Not that there wasn't enough to go around. Plenty more where that came from.

"Goddamnit," Doc was saying, "I'm trying to say thanks here. Jen told me how you were through all of it. Ronnie and—"

"Mr. Rough-and-Ready."

"You're full of shit, you know that? You're also about all she's talked about."

"Look, I'm glad you're alive, Doc, I mean that sincerely. And I accept the sentiment. But let's leave it there."

"All right." He brought his boots up flat on the floor, hands to the arms of the chair. "Guess that's about it, then."

"Stay put, we need this," Wil said. "Everybody's

dead. But I guess you know that by now."

"So are my wife and girls, if you want me to feel sorry for somebody. And if *you* want to know something, even though Cole's dead, I don't feel the way I thought I would." He rubbed his neck. "Honest-to-God truth is, I don't know how I feel."

Wil nodded. "When you decide on grateful, throw Tate in there. Big time."

"I plan to."

"Not to mention Acosta."

"The way it worked out, you mean."

"Screw that—on balance, you owe him. And nobody twisted your arm to cop to manslaughter." Wil shook his head. "Forget that. Out of line."

Doc looked at his hands, spoke as though picturing it: "Tell you what: My cell had this mirror—not glass, stainless steel. Anyway, somebody'd punched it or something, which made the distortion even worse. Like you were this gargoyle. And every time I saw myself, I knew I *could* have done it." He looked up. "You have any idea what living with that is like?"

"Straight up, Doc. Why'd you come back here?"

He pulled out a fresh cigarette, lit it, blew smoke toward the screen. "The truck-stop food?"

"Okay . . ."

"Fuck it. You're so good at this, you tell me."

Wil rubbed his eyes to clear his head. "Cole comes up."

Another drag. "Far as showing up at the track, I was trying to rattle him, shake something loose. Didn't matter what, and Cole and I always had this one-up thing going. Besides, he knew everybody. I figured that—"

"You never suspected him?"

"Of something like that? Hell, no. Fuck me over and laugh about it, yeah, but do my family? Somebody I'd known for years?"

Wil nodded. "What about squaring up what happened to your father?"

"Like I told you over the phone: square as it's going to get this side of life."

Wil thought about that, about Fordyce's comments re Doc's old man. "Blackheart Highway . . ."

"Speak of the devil," Doc said. He reached into a shirt pocket, came out with an unlabeled cassette he handed over. "That guy Byrd I was telling you about at Folsom, he scored me the guitar and equipment, the time alone. Helped me get the monkey off. Keep it—Jen has the music notes if I decide to do anything with it, which I doubt. Thought it might shut you up, at least."

"It might, at that," Wil said. "You know, once this whole thing breaks, you'll be surprised how many friends you have."

"Yeah, well, I say no a lot better'n I used to." He grinned slightly, as from a private joke. "Besides, they'll have to find me first. And they won't."

"Too bad. They could use you."

"They'll be fine. They'll always be fine." Rubbing a knuckle along the eyebrow scar. "Hell, even the music."

Wil pocketed the cassette, tapped the pocket to remind himself it was there. "What about Ronnie?"

"Don't stop when you're on a roll." Reaching for the glass ashtray on the table beside him.

"Maybe not to the same degree as family and old man," Wil said. "But he's in there."

"Close enough. Anything left on your list?"

"Only the money."

Doc crushed the butt; his eyes came up looking like emerald aggregate, the gold flecks like sparks. "If you think it was that—that I even knew about it—then you'd better draw that little gun of yours. Because you're going to need it."

"Pass, thanks. Just heard what I needed."

He brought out another cigarette, thought better of it, tossed the pack. "FYI, the money's going to Leora Graybill, what she'll see after the lawyers get finished. I've already set it in motion."

"Sustaining thought," Wil said. "You mind why?"

"Because I like the symmetry, that's why. And the shit's a curse: Ask Lute, ask Rossert, all of them. Fucking money—hell, ask me. And it's for damn sure not going to poison my kid."

Wil was conscious of wind beginning to ruffle the curtains from the patio. "He going with you to Wyoming?"

"Hasn't decided yet. And if you're wondering about Jen, I don't know that either." Looking Wil directly in the eyes now. "I've asked . . . but it might be too late."

Wil held it, long enough to *know* before breaking off. "You still remember how to make peach ice cream?"

"What's that have to do with—" Something like a dawning softening the pools of shadow, short of chasing them outright. "I don't think it's—"

"Quit lining up the angles for once and do it," Wil said. "Now one for me: When you see her, I want you to pass something on."

Hesitation, then: "Depends, Hardesty. I'm a fool to a point." ·

"Tell her . . . I thought she was amazing up there."

A nod. "Anything else?"

Wil leaned back against the pillows, all of it catching up—an overpowering rip gradually pulling him out to sea. He tried to picture Kari Thayer in the surf . . . running toward him . . . but it kept coming back to Jenelle at the cabin . . . Jenelle at dinner . . . Jenelle in court . . . anywhere she was. And something else: what it must have been like picturing Jenelle Lockhart from a jail cell—twenty years of *that*.

"Yeah," he said, letting his eyes close momentarily.

"Tell her I'll be sending her a statement . . ."

And that was it.

Groggy and stiff hours later he tried to recall if Doc had said anything else—for that matter hearing him leave at all. In any event, the wind was now a darkly audible presence outside the slid-shut glass door.

# TWENTY-SEVEN

Next morning the wind was down but acting as if clouds still were left to vacate from a sky bluer than any Wil had seen since arriving. For a while he sipped coffee, watched the patterns changing on the pool's surface. Thought about all of it.

Finally he showered, ate breakfast in the dining room, checked the baseball scores just to be doing something normal. He then packed up and checked out, requesting that he leave his things in the room until one P.M. By that time it was ten o'clock, and he placed two calls, the first to Greyhound for a seat on the early-afternoon bus to Ventura. The next was to NOW OR NEVER, where Helen, the woman he'd talked to before, told him Leora likely wouldn't be in today unless it was to pick up the medication she'd left.

"I'm going by there. Like me to drop it?"

She hesitated. There was a muffled sound as if she were getting input from someone else, then she was back on. "That won't be necessary."

"It's no trouble." Getting this feeling from her tone.

"No, Leora wouldn't like it—she's very private. But thanks anyway."

Wil drove there and found nobody home, Matt gone as well. He tried guessing, then had a sudden thought and, with the cell phone, called the museum gift shop off the card Florence Alstott had given him. In a couple of rings, she answered, and he reintroduced himself, inquired how she was.

"Fine, but we're not open yet. I'm here doing inventory."

He asked if she might know where Leora was, heard, "Umm . . ."

"You know, but you're not supposed to tell . . ."

Silence.

"If we announce our engagement, you'll be the first to know."

"Oh, for pity's sake . . ."

After the call, he debated with himself a moment and lost, walked back down the drive. The double doors to the garage were closed and locked, but one side had a window he was able to maneuver upward over the old latch. Checking for watchers, he let himself in over the sill and dropped down into the space left by the Beetle. Leora kept the garage relatively neat: no cobwebs to speak of, no boxes piled high, no black drips staining the swept concrete floor. Tools were stacked or hung on brackets, garden equipment in one section, coils of hoses, ladders, even an old pair of wooden skis with poles. In one corner, an English-style bicycle with basket and bell; in another, a tub washer with the wringer attached.

Well organized.

It also had that pleasant old-garage smell: aged wood, paint and potting soil, motor oil and rubber, automotive and yard. Dust in warm air. But it was the Studebaker he'd come for: the deflated cracked tires, characteristic gray-green finish, the lack of dents, abundance of now-pitted chrome. He checked the taillight glass for the truck's year designation and saw the numbers five and three.

Leora'd been right.

He opened the driver's door and set to work: glove box, under and around the seats, lastly in the bed. Which was where he found it. It was in the large toolbox bolted in behind the cab—in among the wrenches, hammers, pliers, screwdrivers, chisels, braces and drill bits, crowbars. All gathering the patina that make old tools so prized at garage sales.

It was a Luger. A nine-millimeter Parabellum, German-made and well used, its crosshatch grip worn and cracked around the screw—WWII vintage as near as he could tell. Rust covered the metal parts and made the action hard to work and the magazine reluctant. But eject it did, and holding the gun to the light and inspecting the barrel, he found virtually no bright steel—just corrosion.

Fired empty and never cleaned.

Put back and long forgotten.

Twenty-five minutes later Wil was pulling into the museum parking lot alongside the Beetle. Past the Spanish-style facade of the main building then, waving to Florence inside her shop. Nodding at the finger to her lips not to tell. *She comes to sit and think. Helps take the pressure off, although it's hard to tell sometimes.*

Wil edged around the turnstile to the large Victorian and turned left, his eyes scanning the street for Leora. But it was empty—of people, at least. Sycamore trees threw dappled shade across the restored residences named for their pioneer owners—Metcalf and Weill, Barnes and Pinkney . . . log cabin and adobe, bungalow and farmhouse. Pick your period. Around a turn, the district became 1850s commercial, and that's where he saw her: sitting on the porch of a one-room schoolhouse up from some country stores.

Lost in thought.

Matt growled a warning as he approached; Leora

started, then shushed him so Wil could sit. At first he thought she might be annoyed he'd found her, but she seemed beyond that, her smile genuine.

"Just like stepping back in time," he said.

"Isn't it . . . my father had a feed store like the one down the street. His brother owned a blacksmith shop like the one over there. Fact is, too damn many of these other places look familiar, too."

"One of the perks," he said, smiling. Thinking she hadn't heard him, he glanced over, thought she looked smaller than usual in the sundress she wore under a denim jacket, blue socks this time in the walkers. The sky was porcelain without a blemish, the morning cool and pleasant. A few leaves blowing down the street.

"Don't you love it after the rain?" she said wistfully. "Everything getting a fresh start."

"I came to say good-bye, Leora."

"I thought it might be that. All those people dead . . ."

He nodded. "Turns out it was oil *and* drugs—big business. Rossert supplied them to the gangs through Garza and Mejia. Among other things they had in mind up there was moving the stash. That was Acosta's heat. We just came at it from a different angle."

Slow shake of the head. "How much money does it take some people . . ."

"Who knows? Hard to pass up that kind of return when it's what you live for."

Wil expected her to comment further, but she didn't, just sighed and said, "At least Donnie made it." Then, the other shoe he was waiting for: "It all seems so pointless, doesn't it?"

He bent forward, focused on a leaf bouncing past. "How much time have they given you?"

She looked at him.

"Nobody told me," he said. "Just everybody tiptoeing around it."

"A few months, if I'm lucky—no great loss to the pirates around here." She sighed again. "Hell, I'm just feeling sorry for myself. Probably explains why I didn't take your head off the other day. Nothing else would explain it. Right, Matt?"

Hearing his name, the shepherd looked up.

"Not quite sure what I'm going to do about him, though."

Wil let the dog sniff his hand, petted him. "You have my card, Leora. Promise if you don't find someone, you'll call me. Will you do that?"

"Yes." A few seconds went by. "Something else on your mind?"

Wil said, "I found the Luger."

No explosion, no denial, no indignation, no move to break it off. Relief almost in her tone. "My—you have been busy . . ."

"I threw it in the river."

There was a moment's hesitation. "For . . . ?"

"For just knowing. I spoke to Doc. He's square with Gib. Since you said you'd written him, I figured it must have been about that. Letting him in on what happened."

She checked to see if he was serious. "Are you that perceptive, or am I that transparent?"

"Neither. But it was you, wasn't it?"

She stood up, brushed her lap with an unconscious gesture, and stood facing the sun. "I don't mean to give the impression I'm not concerned about . . . the effect all this might have after . . . I'm not here. So before I say anything—"

"Even if I said anything, who'd believe it?"

"Powerful people seeking to discredit the work through me."

"It's under some quicksand Bob Tate pointed out. Would you like me to show you where?"

Her eyes searched his face. Finally, she said, "No.

And let's walk. I want you to know this place."

They walked. Past the general store and bakery, a cook wagon up on wheels, the blacksmith shop; peering in on occasion since none was open yet. And she talked: Starting in 1960, when she first met Gib Whitney at a barbecue for some oil people he was trying to schmooze and she was there to give grief to. Instead of that, they'd found each other, knew something had passed between them.

"You ever see an old film Kate Hepburn was in with Burt Lancaster?" she asked as they passed a rustic courthouse, headed back toward the church. "*The Rainmaker*?"

"Doesn't sound familiar."

"Well, that was us. Me about ten years older than he was and not much to look at. Never even been with a man before—always taking care of my folks, or the work I'd taken on, or some damn thing."

"Till you met him."

A nod. "Married, a kid, no money to speak of. Just big dreams and a shady reputation."

"Go figure."

She smiled. "My charming con artist. Whatever he was with anybody else, Gib was different around me. I suppose it was because I had all this education my father'd invested in, thinking I was never going to marry. Sometimes we'd just talk all night. Our own little world."

"And nobody knew?"

"I told my mother, but she was senile by then and dying. Nedra was used to him not being around—preferred it, from what I could gather. Still, we were very careful, and the opposite nature of our work threw people off. Nobody'd have believed it."

"So what happened?"

"The wages of sin, of course. This big score with Lute

DeVillbis he couldn't risk compromising, his chance at the big time. Oh, I'd find somebody else—me—fifty years old, with no prospects." She reached into her pocket, came out with a tennis ball she underhanded for Matt. "You have any idea what it's like to have a taste of something, only to have it snatched away?"

Wil said nothing.

"I asked him to meet me out there, where I thought he might come to his senses." She tilted her face to the sun. "Funny how much today feels like that day . . . the breeze and the light . . . my father's pistol he'd brought home from the war . . . to scare Gib or something, threaten to shoot myself, I didn't know what. I just knew I couldn't lose him and live. Then he was talking, but I couldn't hear him, there were no words, and the gun was empty, and he was in that . . . abomination . . . the black closing in over him . . ."

Wil led her to a bench. Matt brought the ball over and settled down with it.

"I told him I was sorry. Just . . . so sorry. Then it was dark, and I knew I couldn't stay out there. So I put the gun in the truck and the truck in the garage. I never took it out again."

"Long time to carry it around."

"It was that or end it. I couldn't go to jail because of my parents. At least this way I could make *some* amends."

"And Doc?"

She took a breath. "I tried telling him in person. But he was young and mad at his father and wanted no part of me. Then that awful thing with Arlene and the kids happened. Finally, I worked up the nerve to write him. Took about four letters, but I did it."

Tears had formed, but she ignored them.

"I never expected he'd thank me. But Gib loved him—he was always trying to make his boy proud. I told Donnie that. He wrote back that even if Gib had lived, they might not have made it to that point." The tears were coming now; a worried Matt nuzzled her hand. After a minute she'd willed them to stop. "It's why I was so glad to hear he hadn't died."

Wil didn't ask if Doc had contacted her about the money, decided that he hadn't yet. Glad she was due some good news for a change.

"How did you know to look for the gun?"

"I didn't," he said. "Not specifically. Just some things that didn't add up. Your reaction when I asked to admire the Studie. Most people go for that, or at least humor the admirer."

"And before that?"

"Things you said about Gib, the way you said them. Then Lute telling me he never actually saw Gib killed, an opportunity Rossert wouldn't have missed to impress on him." He rubbed the spot where the bowie had nicked him. "That's assuming Rossert would have killed Gib. Lute said he was first rate in his field. Why not keep that talent around the same way Rossert did Lute—make even more money? It didn't compute." She was quiet to the point he thought he'd lost her.

"Probably just me. Looking for love in all the wrong places."

"Not to mention revenge and hate."

"Three sides of the same coin."

She stood, took the tennis ball from Matt, who'd sensed they were leaving and was already up. Wiping the ball on her jacket, she put it in her pocket. "Needless to say, good-bye is not my favorite word."

"Maybe I'll surprise you and come visit. Maybe you'll surprise everybody."

She smiled, but it was a tired smile, without distance. "Come on, Matty," she said. "We'll be going home now."

Wil stayed seated on the bench and watched them move through time. Finally, they rounded the corner at the old wooden oil derrick and disappeared . . . and he was left with the shifting leaves, the shadows, and the sunlight.

# TWENTY-EIGHT

Wil checked his watch, saw he'd better bust it if he was going to make his departure. Stopping off at a Circuit City, he ran in and bought a cassette player on sale, then headed to the rental company's office. With the mileage plus expenses, it was no problem getting the clerk to give him a hop back to his hotel. For that amount, they'd probably be sending him birthday cards forever.

Twelve-thirty: an hour to go.

He checked the desk for messages, the clerk handing him several that had arrived since they'd shut off the phone to his room. Pocketing them, he asked if the courtesy van could run him to the bus depot, the clerk looking at him to see he was serious before nodding yes. Setting his luggage in the van, he looked over the notes. Three were from Jenelle asking him to call; these he tore up and pitched. The fourth was from Kari from an hour ago, and from the lobby he caught her still at home.

"Hey, cowboy," she answered.

"Pretty confident I'd call back."

"More nervous, actually. How's it working out over there?"

"Tell you later. I'm just leaving."

There was a pause, then Kari saying, "Do I or don't I remember taking you over in my car."

"Don't worry about it. The bus is lovely this time of year."

"I can be there in two hours."

"That I believe," he said. "Something up with Brian?"

"I called his bluff. He's with his dad and already making noises he wants to come home. Scott's a slob, and the girlfriend resents him. The good life, in other words."

"And?"

"And I think I'm going to make him wait till he *really* appreciates me." Taking a breath before, "Wil, I was a jerk to you. I'm sorry."

"Since when is doing the only thing you can do being a jerk?"

"That mean you want me back?"

*Jenelle at the cabin. Jenelle at dinner. Jenelle anywhere . . .* "I might need a little time."

"Yeah?" she said. "How much time?"

He paused for effect. "How's here to Ventura sound— meet me at the station and we'll talk about it."

*"Boyoboyoboy."*

"God, you spinmeisters."

They hung up then, Wil tossing Kari's message in on the torn pieces of Jenelle's, wondering what he was doing. Which meant it must be the right thing. He was even there in time to find his bus and get a window seat, catch a song on a dozer's boom box that had struck him before—strawberry wine as a metaphor for first love and lost innocence. Regret, taken a step further.

Followed by a report about a couple of horrified youngsters sighting the body of a man, clad only in one boot and jeans, floating facedown through the Beale Library's mini-canal. Rushing outside, the librarians had found nothing, and though crediting active young imaginations with the sighting, did agree the current might be swift enough to transport a body back underground in the time elapsed.

The dozer awoke briefly, flipped it off.

Later, as they rolled by rain-blackened fields and crops splashed with light, the mountains rising haze-free, Technicolor oleanders running alongside his window as they approached the Grapevine, Wil popped in the cassette Doc had given him and pumped it to the headphones. One song—Doc and guitar—shit for acoustics—and plenty:

North of here, there's a highway
Ain't that hard to find, just follow all bright
    taillights
'Cause there's a line, you keep it movin'
You know where it's bound for, gonna take you
    all the way

But there's a price, it ain't no freeway
Those who haven't got the toll had best remember
    how to pray
Halfway there, it turns to one lane
You're looking for the shortcut, but all you see is
    hard rain

Blackheart Highway, looks like the right track
But you go down that road, you ain't never
    comin' back
Running out of gas, up beyond the detour
There's bound be another sign,
You know, the one that you can't find

Knew a man, he took that highway
Years ago he called a bet, he ain't even shown
    up yet
Just a man who got lost, searchin' for a someday

*I know I can head back home, and do it anytime*
   *I say*


By the time he'd listened twice—once for the words,
the hard-won understanding in them—a second round
for the music, charting the progressions or trying to—
the coast was coming into view. Thinking about Doc
and Gib, Doc and Jenelle, about Kari Thayer meeting
him in Ventura, he hooked in and went with it. Even if
he was playing by ear.

He leaned back in the seat, felt the sun's warmth on
his face. *By ear,* he heard himself say, the thought coming round again, this time to a silent laugh, or the echo
of one—reverb on a fifties country recording—and he
saw his own father grinning at him and winking, forbid-
den cigar between his teeth, one arm draped across the
Buick's open window, the other over the steering wheel
as they cut loose down the valley's heart, their radio
outdriving even the wind.

*By ear . . .* Hell, what wasn't?

# RICHARD BARRE

## The National Bestselling Wil Hardesty Series

### ❏ THE INNOCENTS        0-425-16109-9/$6.50

The remains of seven children—innocents—are uncovered by a flash flood. Clues are scarce and time is short. Only Will Hardesty, a private eye with more in common with the case than anyone knows, is willing to dig deep enough to find the cruelest of killers...

### ❏ BEARING SECRETS        0-425-16641-4/$5.99

Hardesty must face more than just his past when the discovery of the seventeen-year-old wreckage of a plane—and its illicit cargo—prompts the suicide of '60s radical Max Pfeiffer. But Pfeiffer's daughter knows it wasn't suicide—and she wants Wil to unearth the truth...

### ❏ THE GHOSTS OF MORNING        0-425-16931-6/$6.50

Friendship and murder collide when Wil Hardesty plunges into his past to discover if his best friend Denny was killed in Vietnam or is somehow still alive. And Wil won't be able to stop until he's sure Denny is alive—or both of them are dead...

**"Exhilarating...History, nostalgia, and gritty human realities hooked me so deeply into the world of Wil Hardesty..."**
**—Nevada Barr**